The Polished Moon

Also by Marsha L Burris

Paradox of Professionalism:
American Nurses in World War II

Miracles All Around Me:
The Unexpected Gifts of My Mother's Alzheimer's

The

Polished Moon

Marsha L Burris

Foxtail Books

Foxtail Books
Charlotte, North Carolina

Printed in the United States of America

ISBN **978-0-9914443-4-2**

1. Marsha Burris 2. Army Nurse Corps 3. Nurses 4. 1940s
5. World War II 6. Second World War Europe 7. North Africa 8. Italy
9. France 10. Romance 11. Army 100th Division 12. 398th Infantry
13. 58th Station Hospital 14. 21st General Hospital 15. Courage
16. American Nurse 17. Diary 18. Chinnis - Light Family
19. Women's History 20. Sons of the Bitche

For

Dot and Jack

Contents

Author's Note

The Polished Moon is a fictional account of a true story. As a Lieutenant in the Army Reserve Nurse Corps, Dorothy Chinnis served her country from April 1942 to November 1945 and recorded her activities and observations in a diary while overseas. She was initially assigned to the 58th Station Hospital in North Africa, which ultimately merged with the 21st General Hospital in Italy before moving on to France.

I met Dot several times through my connection to the Chinnis family. She assisted me with research on *Paradox of Professionalism: American Nurses in World War II*, a book I wrote on the contributions of American nurses during the Second World War. Although I regretted that Dot's story was only a small part of the project, I planned to expand the narrative of her war experiences at a future date. Sadly, Dot passed away before I could begin writing her story, but she had entrusted me with a copy of her wartime diary, and I have used it extensively to share with the reader her service to this country.

Because Dot faithfully set down on paper events from her daily life in North Africa, Italy, and France, I could track where she was at specific times, what duties were assigned to her, how she felt about those duties, what worried her, and what she looked forward to.

Although I remained true to the tone and sentiment of Dot's diary, where her entries were vague, I added historical information and context from my own research, and from various members of Dot's family who generously shared their first-hand knowledge with me. Even with that incredible assistance, it was necessary to fictionalize the missing chunks of Dot's experiences overseas. Although I remained true to the essences of Dot and Jack to the best of my knowledge, in places where it was appropriate, I used creative license to add dialog and to construct scenes.

Dates and locations are accurate, based on Dot's diary, and the cities, postings, and hospitals in which Dot was associated are accurately depicted. The eruption of Mount Vesuvius, her visit with the Pope, an autograph from Douglas Fairbanks, Jr on a 100 Lire note, her flight in a P38 (as well as a stint as a flight nurse on a B-17), *and* a honeymoon in Paris, are all actual events that Dot documented.

Captain Dorothy Parsons, Major Lucille S. Spalding, Colonel Florence Blanchfield, and Colonel Lee D. Cady, are real names of actual people who figured prominently in Dot's diary. I changed the names of the nurses who served with Dot to allow flexibility in ascribing them with individual personalities.

Dot volunteered her services to the Army Nurse Corps to care for the troops who were fighting in the war. Simply that, she told me. She was incapable of bragging about her contributions. Nevertheless, in my eyes, she was a hero. Writing her story, giving her a voice, has been a great privilege.

Map of Europe & North Africa - World War II

Overseas service took First Lieutenant Dorothy Chinnis from Fort Jackson, South Carolina to Camp Kilmer in New Jersey. On the *Santa Rosa* Dot sailed across the Atlantic Ocean through the Strait of Gibraltar between Spain and North Africa to arrive at her first assignment, the hospital in Oran Algeria. From Oran Dot's group moved to Tunisia and then to Naples Italy. After Naples, Dot's outfit was sent to the port of Marseille France, and ultimately on to the Ravenel Hospital in Mirecourt France near the German border.

Part One

DEPLOYMENT

One

Diary Entry ~ April 13, 1943
Got my orders for overseas.

Am I willing to die for my country? Dot asked herself the question as she read the overseas assignment orders in her hands. In a war zone, everyone is in danger. *A little late to question my resolve now,* she admitted under her breath before folding the paper and tucking it into the pocket of her duty uniform.

Dorothy Elizabeth Chinnis was the tenth of eleven children born to Edward Hamilton and Ernestine Chaplin Chinnis of Ravenel, South Carolina. When Japan attacked Pearl Harbor, Dot was twenty-one years old. She'd had her nursing degree for a month and was determined to use her medical skills for the war effort.

Initially, Dot applied to the U.S. Navy Nurse Corps but they required their nurses to weigh at least one hundred and fifteen pounds. Dot was twenty pounds shy of meeting that condition but the Army Reserve Nurse Corps welcomed her talents. She was assigned to the Fort Jackson Army Installation in Columbia, South Carolina, a two-hour drive from her beloved Ravenel. A year after taking the oath of enlistment, Second Lieutenant Dorothy Chinnis received her orders to deploy.

On this April afternoon, Dot stood in a quiet, empty patients' ward at the Fort Jackson Hospital. A spring shower freshened the breeze blowing through the open window, bringing in a delicious scent of Carolina Jasmine. As her mind wandered, Dot gazed at white painted iron beds placed in precise rows along a green wall, a color not pretty enough to be called 'mint'. The beds were available for servicemen injured during training maneuvers or ill from a sundry of complaints. Preparations for these contingencies were Dot's responsibility.

Making up beds was a routine exercise for Dot, allowing her to ponder the unknown road ahead of her. She wouldn't have missed the opportunity to use her nursing skills for the war effort for any price, but she had to wonder, would her story have a happy ending, or would it end in tragedy?

Dot brought herself back to the moment. Her shift for the day was almost over but before clocking out, clean linens had to be on every bed in the ward. She did this with the same poise and grace she brought to the operating room. Confidence in her training was strong, but she was uneasy about her future.

Oh well, she thought as she took a deep breath, *just take it one day at a time.* This is advice she would give anyone in the same situation.

"You look like Ingrid Bergman in Casablanca," Fran said to Dot as she entered the ward. Dot turned her attention to her friend and co-worker, but couldn't conceal her startled look.

"How's that?" she said after a pause.

"Ilsa Lund," Fran continued. "The character in the Casablanca film. The gal Bogie fell in love with in Paris at the start of the war. You're the spitting image." Fran leaned her tall, angular body over the single bed to grab a corner of the sheet from Dot. "Anyway, I'm off-duty in five minutes. I can help speed this along for you, if you'd like."

4

Fran Edwards was from Roanoke, Virginia. She had chosen to complete her medical training at Charleston Medical College, as her mother had done the generation before. Dot and Fran had completed their RN training in the same class and had spent the past year at Fort Jackson enjoying the benefits of an Army Reserve Officer's commission. The relatively good salary was most welcomed after living through the Great Depression.

Fran stretched the cotton sheet tightly across the mattress while Dot anchored the opposite corner. They both folded and tucked the sheet into place so sharply that Band-Aids were kept handy. As it happened, the civilian way of making a bed was the exact opposite from the Army way, so the nurses simply reversed the procedure. Up until this point, this seemed to be the only transition required of the nurses by the Army.

"Did you get your orders? Is that where your mind was?" Fran took a closer look at Dot. A naked light bulb hung from the ceiling and cast shadows against the wall giving their benign task a sinister overtone. The rain outside was building into a thunderstorm. The overhead light blinked a warning.

"I got them. Twenty minutes ago," Dot told her, her melodic Charleston accent rang like an enchanting English handbell. "I'm heading overseas, somewhere in Europe, not the Pacific as we had feared."

Stories of combat nurses captured in the Philippines the year before had made the newspapers. It took little imagination to picture their ultimate fate.

"Don't the orders specify where?" Fran asked.

"No, not the ultimate destination. The orders say Camp Kilmer in New Jersey. A ship leaving from New York Harbor would head to Europe somewhere."

The two friends had both applied for assignments abroad. They understood that wherever the Army wanted you, *that's*

5

where you went. Now Dot was taking the next step forward and Fran continued to wait.

In the conversational lull, refrains from Glenn Miller's trombone wha-wah'd the melody of *Chattanooga Choo Choo* from a radio tucked in a cubbyhole at the central nursing station. Fran tapped her foot in time. Her imposing height made her appear self-confident, fearless even. But that hadn't always been so.

As a fledgling student, away from her Virginia home for the first time, Fran had been timid and insecure. She was naturally drawn to Dot's quiet inner strength on the first day of class when the professor asked a question of Dot for the purpose of tripping her up. Dot answered, not in a boastful or over-confident way, but instead approaching the solution methodically with the calm assurance that any problem could be solved by employing the intellect God gave humans. She didn't need to know all the answers herself, just where to *find* the answers.

Fran introduced herself afterwards and invited Dot to join the new study group forming. Fran realized quickly that Dot was a team player, and she could count on the petite and pretty Dot Chinnis. Dot could count on her, too. That is how they found themselves at Fort Jackson on this particular evening.

"You'll be fine, Dottie. I just wish I was going with you. It's the not-knowing that's so hard to take. But never mind that now. More importantly, have you told your sweetheart about your orders?"

Fran had introduced her brother's friend, Jack, to Dot two days after they arrived at Fort Jackson. She was pleased to see her match-making skills rewarded when the two hit it off.

Second Lieutenant Samuel Jackson Light, Jack to his friends, was also from Roanoke, Virginia. He was an S2 Intelligence Officer with the 398th Infantry Regiment, part of the 100th Division. His outfit was assigned to Fort Jackson, and Fran secretly believed divine intervention was responsible in bringing

6

Dot and Jack together at this place and time, certainly something more at work than Uncle Sam.

"I wanted to tell him right away," Dot replied. "But he's in Charleston with the President so it'll have to wait."

"Oh? What's FDR doing in that neck of the woods?"

"He's making inspection tours of military posts, naval stations, and war factories. It's for troop morale. I don't know why Mr. Roosevelt doesn't pop in here. It would greatly improve *our* morale."

"I don't think anyone is much concerned with our morale," Fran said. "And, I assume no travel funds will be expended on our account." She smiled. "We've got each other when we need our spirits lifted, though. But I have to wonder if travel funds will be spent on me since I haven't been informed what *my* assignment will be. Stateside? Overseas? Who knows?"

"The Army makes choices on our behalf now," Dot replied. "I suppose we're Uncle Sam's for the duration…"

"Duration, plus six months!" Fran interjected and they laughed because that distinction had been drilled into them since day-one.

"I will miss you," Dot assured Fran. "And, I'll miss this place as well. It feels like home. But I'm ready to do what I've been trained for."

Jack returned to Fort Jackson the next night. He found Dot in the Measles Ward. Only the two beds closest to the door were occupied. Dot guided Jack away from them to the far corner of the room.

"I received my orders!" she told him.

"Finally," Jack countered. "I know you've been anxious to hear something. Where to, then?"

7

"I'm to take the train to New Jersey. From there we'll board a ship to parts unknown—Europe, for sure, though. My precise destination is need-to-know. It's clear to me that the Army thinks I have no need to know."

"Looks like you're going to be in it," Jack told Dot. "I won't be far behind. With any luck, my unit will be close enough to yours that we can be together occasionally. There's still talk of sending us to the Pacific...," his words trailed off. He held his officer's cap in his hands and turned it round and round like a steering wheel. He looked down at his feet briefly, then quickly returned his gaze to Dot's face and said, "I love you, Dorothy. I will love you forever."

Dot stepped closer to him, close enough to breathe in the orange and cinnamon tones of Jack's Old Spice aftershave. She put her hand on his arm, but didn't interrupt him.

"Being in the middle of this war is now a reality for us both. We'll get through it. I know we will. But for all the unknowns out there in the world, we have no guarantees for what's ahead of us. I want us to have one constant thing we can count on."

Jack laid the cap on the empty bed behind him. He knelt onto one knee and took Dot's hand in his. "Will you marry me? Will you be my wife? I'll talk to the Chaplain and we can say our vows before you ship out."

Jack's jovial nature and light-hearted soul gave way to his serious side. He waited for Dot's answer.

Dot was flooded with a dozen emotions. She loved Jack, too, and realized at that moment just how deeply that love went into her very soul.

"Yes," she said. "I want to marry you..."

Jack felt a 'but' beginning to attach itself to the end of Dot's sentence.

"I *will* marry you, Jack, but, let's get through this war first. If I marry now I'll be discharged. No married nurses in the Army.

No exceptions. And if I'm discharged, I can't be near you in the war zone. That is, if you get sent our way. *And,* I won't be able to help our wounded soldiers. They're suffering, and I can help. You know how important that is."

A push to recruit more nurses into the military was aggressive. Their skills were indispensable and in short supply on the various frontlines of the war. Working directly with surgical teams saved lives. Bolstering the injured solders' will-to-live after receiving terrible injuries ranked a close second in importance. Dot's destiny was set.

"I know," Jack conceded.

Dot nudged him to stand up again but didn't take her hand away. "Is it possible to consider ourselves officially engaged?" she asked.

Jack's cheerful nature returned at once. "Absolutely. Yes. We'll choose your engagement ring tomorrow, then. And I'll wait to say 'I do' until the Army allows it. But I'll hold you to your promise."

"You won't have to hold me to it. I'll marry you of my own free will. But, let's survive this ordeal for now, and then we'll live happily ever after."

Jack met Dot the following day for lunch. He showed her his First Lieutenant Silver Bar. She pinned them on him. "These are shiny," she said.

"They *were* dull as dirt, so I brasso'ed them to the high shine you see before you." Brasso was the creamy liquid used by servicemen to polish insignias and belt buckles on their dress uniforms.

"I need sunglasses to protect me from the glare," Dot teased. "And a clothes pin for my nose." She jerked her head back and scrunched her nose in surprise.

"That's the ammonia," Jack explained. "The polish is made up almost entirely of ammonia."

"It does linger," Dot said. "We could use that for smelling salts in pinch. I think it would wake the dead."

"Enough of that," Jack laughed. "After lunch, we'll drive into Columbia. I know just the jewelry store at Five Points for us to look for your ring."

Brown's Jewelry Store had been in the family for nearly a century. A bay window and a glass door made up the storefront that faced the busy street. Light poured in and bathed the gold and silver objects in sunshine.

A pretty saleswoman, wearing a floral dress, stood behind the counter. She welcomed the couple with a smile because customers in uniform were especially welcomed. The original Mr. Brown's son had been in Company E of the 105th Engineers in France during the first World War and that son was in the back room at the moment, making delicate repairs to a much-loved brooch.

"Hello," she greeting them. "I'm Libby. What can I help you with today?" she asked.

"We're looking at engagement rings," Jack smiled broadly.

Libby walked them to the case that held women's rings. Dot looked over the inventory once, then twice. After her third inspection, she was drawn to a simple yellow gold solitaire ring and pointed at it. Jack saw Dot's eyes light up.

"Can we look at that one," Jack said to the saleswoman. She handed the ring to Jack.

"Let's try it on, love." Jack held the ring pinched between his thumb and first finger in one hand. He turned to face Dot as she held out her left hand.

"With any luck...," he said and slipped the ring onto her finger. It fit perfectly. "...as I was saying! With any luck it will fit you like a glove." Jack laughed at the instant good luck.

"This is the one," he told the saleswoman.

Libby said, "I'll clean it for you. Back in minute." And disappeared into a back room.

When she returned, Libby had put the ring in a tiny white box and tied a thin blue satin ribbon around it. She handed it to Jack and Jack handed her cash to complete the transaction.

Jack placed his hand under Dot's elbow to lead her to the bay window. Libby redirected her attention elsewhere to give them some privacy.

Jack placed the box in Dot's hand. She pulled at the end of the ribbon until it let go, and removed the top. Jack lifted the ring delicately and went down on his knee as he had done in the Measles Ward the day before.

"Will you make me the happiest man in the world, and be my wife?"

"I would be honored to be your wife," Dot answered.

Jack placed the ring on Dot's finger once again. Dot reflected on the moment. The ring was a symbol of Jack's love for her, a promise that she would do her best in this war so that when it ended, she could dedicate her devotion to him. She leaned over and kissed Jack on his forehead. He stood up, beaming, and kissed her cheek. She blushed, and happy tears welled up in her eyes without warning. Jack cleared his throat to stay his own tears. After a brief moment, they regained their composure and said goodbye to the saleswoman.

The couple stepped out of the shop and onto the sidewalk. A street vendor photographer had set up a temporary open-air portrait studio two doors away. He had placed a stool in front of a robin's-egg blue backdrop and positioned a tripod camera facing the tableau. To mark the occasion, Dot and Jack posed for a keepsake photograph.

Jack stopped in to see Dot the following evening while she was on her supper break. "Last night of duty," he stated the obvious. "Are you packed and ready to go?"

"I'm sleeping until noon tomorrow," she told him. "And then I'll start packing."

Jack produced a box of Russell Stover Chocolates. "For your travels," he told her. "They'll be good for a pick-me-up on your train ride."

"These won't last until then." Dot was sure of that.

"I'll make sure you have a fresh supply before your departure day, then. And I'll keep up the chocolate deliveries as often as I can while you're overseas. It's better currency than green backs."

"I don't know if that will prove true for me. I can save money fairly easily, but I'm likely to gobble these up before morning," Dot laughed. Jack was going to miss that laugh.

"I'm worried, Dorothy." Jack's frown reflected the concern he held for her safety.

"Why in the world are you worried? I'm sure Uncle Sam will keep us nurses safe. What good are we if we're sent home injured, or worse?"

"I'd like to agree with you. It's just that things happen in war that can't be foreseen. If I had my way, my outfit would go overseas now so I can keep an eye on your group."

Dot thought Jack's men needed his concern more than she did, and told him so.

"My men have guns and ammo. It's your safety that worries me. You Florence Nightingales carry only a lantern."

Dot chuckled. "That lantern, a caduceus and a prayer will protect us. I have faith."

"I'll pray for you every day and when this blasted war is over and we're back together, we'll never be apart from each other again," Jack vowed.

Dot liked the sentiment but changed the subject before the tears arrived. "Do you know if you'll be here at Jackson much longer?"

"We'll be here a while yet. We'll need terrain training, but not for another month or so. Before we leave here, I was thinking I might go to Ravenel and see your family."

"Do that! I think it's a great idea. But I'll be jealous."

Jack took Dot's hand and kissed it. "We'll talk only of you, and your ears will burn. Then you'll feel like you're right there with us."

———— ·⊱✿⊰· ————

Farewell socials were thrown for the nurses leaving Fort Jackson. Attendance was encouraged even though the women were frantically preparing for the journey ahead of them. Dot was a serious, dedicated professional first and foremost, but her practical nature gave way to a fun side as well. Besides, *fun* made time pass faster, and Dot was eager to begin the next phase of her life—the sooner the better. Dot was a 'rip the Band-Aid' off kind of woman.

For the send-off dance at the officer's club, Dot dressed with Jack in mind. She wore her red skirt, complemented with a gardenia in her hair. She wanted to look pretty for him. What if it was the last time they were ever together? There were no guarantees in life, even truer in wartime. On her departure day, Jack's duties required him to be out of town. He would be unable to see her off at the train station so Dot wanted this evening to be memorable. Of all the goodbyes she had said to her friends, the hardest was to Jack.

After dancing and drinking toasts to the individuals shipping out, Dot and Jack stepped outside to be alone. They stood facing each other in the garden. The midnight blue evening was illuminated by a full moon. Dot saw Jack's face clearly although shadows were cast by massive tree branches overhead.

"Did you use your Brasso to polish that moon for me tonight? I've never seen it so bright and shiny."

"Oh yes," Jack boasted. "Just for you. And while we're apart, wherever you are, when you see that big ol' full moon, it'll be the same one I'm looking at. And you'll know I'm thinking of you. I'll polish that moon for you every night, Dorothy, until we can look at it together again." That night Dot cried herself to sleep.

———

Dazzling sunshine greeted Dot on her departure day. She regretted Jack couldn't see her off, but maybe leaving would be a little less heartbreaking if he wasn't there. At any rate, fewer handkerchiefs would be needed. The notion was poor salve for her aching heart.

"You look like hell, Dottie Chinnis!" Fran joked when she entered Dot's room to check on her progress. "Didn't you sleep at all?"

"I slept," Dot admitted. "But I cried into my pillow a solid hour before I drifted off."

"Oh, that's tough. You'll miss us here and you'll certainly miss Jack. But think of the *adventure!* Think of the *romance!*"

"I don't know about that," Dot chuckled. "But I know this is an historic moment. I hope I don't forget a thing about it."

"You won't!" Fran said. "I made sure you won't."

Dot looked puzzled. Fran handed her a small black leather-bound book.

"What's this?"

"A diary. A Five-Year Diary. Write it all down, friend. All that you see and do. Just a sentence or two will jog your memory for when you're a grandmother and you want to recall this time.

14

My dad's sister did that when she nursed the fellows at Rouen France in 1918. You do the same!"

"I will. I'll go back and fill it in from the day I got my orders. I just hope I'll be back home before I run out of five years of pages." The idea of being away from home for that length of time was not a happy one so Dot changed the subject. "We've been here at Fort Jackson a year, now. Happy Anniversary!"

"Happy Anniversary to you too. I'm going to miss you. Take good care of yourself." They hugged goodbye. Fran ran the whole way to the hospital so she wouldn't be late for her shift and so the tears would dry before she reported for duty.

At the railway train station in Columbia, Dot saw her luggage loaded into the baggage car. She took one last look around at her native South Carolina and whispered a prayer for everyone touched by this terrible war.

Dot ended her meditative moment, took a deep breath and moved to board the train. She stepped across the yellow caution line painted on the platform, and grabbed the handrail. She carefully avoided the gap, and as she placed a foot on the first step, a movement caught her eye. Walking at a fast clip around the ticket hut was Jack's assistant, Ken Jones. She stepped back down onto the platform to greet him.

"Made it just in time," he told Dot triumphantly. "Jack sent this for you." He handed her a paper bag. Dot peeked inside and saw a box of assorted chocolates. She hugged it to her chest. Then Jones placed a silver dollar in Dot's hand and closed her fingers around it. "Jack says to keep it with you always. It'll bring you good luck."

Dot's tears started anew. She kissed Jones on the cheek without a word. Instead of dabbing at her tears with her handkerchief, she used it to wrap the 1921 Morgan coin inside it.

"Gotta find Charlotte," Jones told Dot. "You gonna be okay?"

15

"Everything's copacetic," she responded. "You and Jack. You take good care of each other. You hear me?"

"Yes, ma'am!" Jones yelled over his shoulder. He had turned to respond to his girlfriend, Charlotte Belle, who was waving to him from the station house door. Charlotte was in Dot's group of nurses heading overseas by way of Edison, New Jersey.

Dot climbed up the two steps and passed through the doorway of the train. She paused a moment to look at the treasure in her hand. Believing that Lady Luck was now firmly on her side, Dot claimed her seat on the Jersey bound train.

Two

Diary Entry ~ April 20, 1943
Departure day.

The train ride would take fifteen hours from Columbia, South Carolina to Edison, New Jersey. The passenger seating arrangement provided for two passengers to face two other passengers. The seat cushions were generous, especially if you were as small as Dot. With windows opened throughout the car, a breeze circulated the air. On a warm travel day, it meant the difference between comfort and irritation.

Kitchen staff at the hospital had packed picnic hampers of fried chicken and buttermilk biscuits for the travelers to eat during their long trip. Susan McGill lugged one of the baskets to the seating area Dot had claimed. She was the same height as Dot and when she attempted to stow the basket on the luggage rack above the seats, she couldn't hoist it high enough to make a connection with the shelf.

"You may want to stand up on the seat," Dot said as she set her handbag aside and stood to assist the maneuver. When the task was done, the two women sat in the window seats facing each other.

"Gillie, right?" Dot said to break the ice.

"Yes," she said as she pushed brown curls away from her face. "Well, Susan McGill, to be proper. With a last name like McGill, I was bound to be dubbed Gillie. It has stuck with me from primary school until now."

"At least it's not a nickname like *ol' blood and guts*," Charlotte Belle joked as she claimed an aisle seat in the foursome. "Off we go, Dottie," she smiled at her friend. Other than Fran, Charlotte was the only soul to call Dot by this name.

Dot and Charlotte had grown close through double dates with their sweethearts, Jack and Ken Jones, who were comrades in arms. Charlotte was a tall, graceful, tennis player with golden blond hair. When she and Dot were together, they were often dubbed Mutt and Jeff, but the two women were comfortable in each others' company and were happy to be traveling together.

"Have you been crying?" Charlotte asked Dot. Without waiting for Dot's reply, she continued. "Don't worry. Saying goodbye to our fellows is hard, but we'll be okay. We're tough."

"Speak for yourself," Dot said.

The last seat went to Elizabeth Campbell. She was two years older than her seat mates, with silky brown hair distinguished by stunning silver highlights at the temples. The women had not roomed together in barracks or worked shifts together, but they knew one another by reputation. Proper introductions were in order now that their mutual journey and ultimate destination was set. Although the nurses had very different personalities, they also had much in common. They were surprised that they were all 'Southern Belles', sharing cultural references and a similar upbringing.

Others from the Fort Jackson hospital took seats across the aisle. Cora Franklin, whose plump round face was always smiling, had the reputation for being a sassy but good-hearted trouble-maker. Jane Travers' brown hair and brown eyes served to make her indistinguishable in a crowd. She had never traveled far from home and looked uneasy on this, her first excursion. Anne Stone was small and delicate, almost translucent. She gave an impression that she was fragile and had recently begun to wear a sullen expression. She didn't invite questions about her changed state-of-mind. Maddy Bedford was the smart, cool, calm, intellectual to whom friends turned for support and advice. Wherever she was, she was 'at home' and comfortable. Any onlooker would think, no matter how exotic the environment, that Maddy was in her natural habitat.

The two groups tried to carry on a conversation across the aisle but the racket inside the passenger car made their attempts in vain. As the train chugged down the track, Gillie opened a brown paper bag with great fanfare. The aroma of homemade chocolate oatmeal cookies escaped as though a valve had been opened.

"Have one of these," she offered, nodding her head toward the others in her compartment demonstrating her loveable and easy nature. Putting others first was a primary trait the nurses on this train shared. Dot knew at that moment her silver dollar from Jack had brought her its first piece of good luck.

"Mmmm... where did you get these?" Elizabeth asked.

"My former roommate thrust them at me as we were saying goodbye on the platform. They might be a little salty, though," Gillie teased. "She was crying more than me."

Gillie passed the cookies across the aisle to her neighbors. "It's good medicine," she told them. "It'll help us leave our woes behind."

"Speaking of medicine," Dot dug into her handbag. "Reminds me that Jack gave me a box of chocolates for the train trip." She handed the box over to Gillie. As she held the box, Dot took one for herself and popped it in her mouth. Then she bent down to scratch her ankle. "Blast it!" she said.

"What's wrong?" Gillie asked her.

"Jack and I went for a stroll through the gardens two nights ago. I got several nasty chigger bites from the path."

"Pine straw path?" Gillie asked.

"Yep."

"Okay, let's see." Gillie patted the upholstered seat beside her urging Dot to prop her foot up for examination. "Good lord," she said. "You are turning into one huge, walking chigger."

"Looks that way," Dot conceded. "I put mentholated ointment on the spots but the effects have worn off, obviously. Now, I'll have to paint fingernail polish on them. I suppose that'll have to wait until we reach New Jersey and I can take these stockings off." She bent down to scratch again. "How lady-like of me." Dot laughed at herself.

"You're going to make your ankles sore. Here, have another cookie to take your mind off of the itching." Gillie stopped a moment. A thought formed in her mind. "And, I think we'll have to nickname you, Chigger."

"Lovely," Dot grinned. "It's not as elegant as *Gillie*, but it *is* better than *ol' blood and guts*."

"Whatever you say, Chigger!" The four women chuckled at the joke.

The travelers settled into their journey. Several women chatted. A few others napped or read their Agatha Christies. Dot attempted to write a letter to Jack between the bumps and thumps of the iron wheels clattering down the track.

"Having any luck?" Gillie asked.

"Too rocky. All I've got on paper so far is chicken scratches. I'll wait until we arrive at Camp Kilmer to finish it." Dot snapped the cap back on her fountain pen and dropped it into her handbag sitting on the floor by her feet. She extracted a book from the bag and nestled herself more comfortably into her seat.

"This can take my mind off things until then." Dot waved Daphne du Maurier's *Rebecca* like a white hankie signaling surrender. And surrender she did, to a nap, only a few minutes later.

She wasn't alone. The train swayed back and forth as it traveled in 4/4 time. The rhythmic rat-a-tat-tat of the wheels sent the passengers into a stupor as if a master hypnotist commanded them, *you are getting sleeeepy*...

Before giving in to the Sandman, Dot's mind had drifted away from her book back to the home she was leaving behind, and to Jack. She had no notion when—*or if*—she would see either again. Exhausted from her near sleepless night, Dot slipped into a sound sleep, oblivious to anyone else around her. Then the train jolted fiercely as it rounded a tight curve jogging her awake.

Gillie spoke first. "We think *this* is rocky. Wait until we get on the high seas."

"I will be glad to have that piece of the trip behind me," Dot said. "Where do you believe we're going?"

"No idea, really. Could be England, I guess. Lots of nurses go there first, before being sent along to wherever they're needed. I have a friend from school who is stationed near Oxford. I suppose it's possible we'll go directly to North Africa, though. That's where the news is coming from at the moment. Desert Fox and all that."

Hours melted into a stew of time. When the train pulled into Stelton Rail Station the passengers were hungry again. The drizzling rain was an irritant as sandwiches were handed out to them on the platform. They ate them while huddled in groups, waiting for instructions, then watched as their luggage was stacked onto wooden carts.

"Wonder if we'll ever see them again," Charlotte joked. "I'd be hard pressed to travel four thousand miles with just the items in my handbag." The nurses reflexively pulled their personal effects closer.

A young Army Lieutenant in a khaki uniform walked up to address them.

"Welcome to New Jersey, ladies," he began. "I hope you had a pleasant trip. If you look over your left shoulder you will see two Army transport trucks. This is the preferred method of moving troops from Point A to Point B. You are currently standing on Point A. We need you to be at Camp Kilmer which is Point B. The transportation is not as plush as your daddy's Oldsmobile back home but you may as well get accustomed to lack of comfort now because those days are over for the duration. Grab your hats ladies, and follow me."

Wooden planks substituted for seats in the bed of the truck. It made for a jarring ride.

"My fillings are popping out of my teeth," Gillie said playfully.

"Could be worse," Dot observed. The other nurses looked at her with raised eyebrows. "We could be walking, and it could be *pouring* rain!"

At Kilmer, another male officer, this one older than the last one, met the women as they stood ankle deep in a quagmire of mud. He called names from a roster and pointed the nurses to a barracks. "When you're inside, find your gear and you'll find your bunk," he told them. His task was complete so he about-faced and left without another word.

Dot walked over to the building. She pushed the double doors open like she was entering a saloon. She hesitated a moment for her eyes to adjust to the contrast from light to dark.

Taking in her surroundings she could have described the interior design with one word invented by the Army especially for this occasion: *Drab*. A flimsy partition divided the room so that the first segment of the barracks held two rows of fifteen beds. Belongings for the nurses had been deposited at the foot of each bed.

Dot found her bunk. "Nice strategy," she observed. "It's smart of the Army to assign beds to us. It prevents us from squabbling over who gets a window or proximity to the latrine."

"Choice is the first casualty of war," Anne Stone mumbled.

"I thought 'truth' was the first casualty," Charlotte butted in.

"Never mind which one is first... what's the second casualty?" Cora wise cracked as she chewed gum aggressively.

"In many cases, your life." Anne turned to the bed designated to her and added nothing further to her cryptic statements.

A quick check verified that everything had been brought over from the train which the nurses took as a good omen. It didn't last. A yelp interrupted the banter.

"Not cats!" Jane Travers groaned. She pointed at two tabbies wandering out of the bathroom. "I'm not sleeping in the same room with animals."

Jane was reluctant to sacrifice all personal comforts as an Army nurse, and she certainly did not intend to sleep with four-legged critters roaming free.

"You might *want* to share digs with cats," Dot offered helpfully. A farm upbringing gave Dot a sensible outlook when it came to rustic conditions. She knew that all God's creatures had a purpose. When Jane looked unconvinced Dot added, "Better than sharing a room with the critters cats like to dine on."

Jane reflected on that for a moment.

"Right," she conceded. "Shall I give them names, then?"

"Give who names?"

23

Lauren Bacall's twin stepped into the barracks. Her officer's uniform enhanced her willowy stature. She attempted to set a stern public face but there was a kind, unmistakable, twinkle lighting her eyes. She introduced herself as Major Whitfield. She welcomed the new group of nurses under her care and gave them a brief history of Camp Kilmer.

"It was named for the poet, Joyce Kilmer, who was an American Private killed in action during the Great War. This is a staging area where troops assemble for processing before movement on to their destination. It's chosen for its proximity to the New York Harbor which is our east coast point of embarkation for the European Theater of Operations." Major Whitfield barely took time to inhale as she continued.

"You'll be here with me for about a week before we ship out. There will be twenty-nine of us traveling together, including me. In that time you will see a dentist, and a doctor for your physical exams. You'll get typhus shots and other vaccines. Your blood will be typed, then imprinted on your dog tags. I will make sure you buy and organize the clothing and gear you need whether it's on the official Army issue list or not. Countless legal documents will need to be signed, including a Last Will and Testament." Whitfield finally took a breath.

"During your stay here take advantage of the activities provided for your benefit. There are various sports venues if you want to participate. There is a movie theater as well as music and dancing. Find time to catch one of the USO shows. If you get bored, you have no one to blame but yourself. As you prepare for your trip overseas, I will instruct you on what's important to have and what is not. Anything in the 'not' category, you will send back home." The Major waited for the information to sink in.

"You will be missing out on the pleasure of comprehensive formal military training," she smiled. "A formal four-week training course for Army nurses is in the works but it will not be implemented for several more months. It's regrettable, actually, because the program would prepare you better for your overseas ordeal."

A few of the nurses, the ones without poker faces, looked puzzled. They wondered how it was possible for military training to help them care for sick or wounded soldiers.

"Military customs and courtesies," Major Whitfield answered the unasked questions. "Military protocol runs this man's Army, and we work best in an environment we understand. Hardship conditions overseas will be a challenge when you're looking for a sanitary means of taking care of various personal needs like going to the latrine, washing your hair, etcetera. And, military training increases the survival rate when under enemy attack." Major Whitfield watched the women's faces as reality sank in.

"Your group will join the 58th Station Hospital. We won't be extremely close to the frontlines but we may find ourselves in primitive, and perhaps dangerous living conditions at times, nonetheless. We will discuss this topic more fully before we leave Camp Kilmer. Until then, we'll have an abbreviated form of physical training. Questions?"

Charlotte raised her hand. Major Whitfield nodded for her to speak.

"You say we'll be in a Station Hospital, are there different kinds of hospitals closer to the frontlines?"

"Excellent question," the Major acknowledged. "What is your name?"

"Charlotte Belle, ma'am," she answered.

"Well, Lieutenant Belle, let me lay out the Army's chain of medical evacuation. Mobile Field Hospitals and Evacuation Hospitals are transitory. That means they follow combat troops closely and are typically set up in tents so they can move at short notice. They are near battlefields so they can quickly perform triage on the wounded. Emergency surgery is done there before soldiers are sent on to more permanent facilities. That's where Station and General Hospitals come in to play."

All attention became focused on Whitfield's words.

"A Station Hospital is typically thirty to fifty miles from the frontlines. General Hospitals a little further back than that, up to a hundred miles from the war front. They are more permanent, have more equipment, and they advance more slowly. These last two types of facilities are usually set up in existing hospitals or abandoned schools or factories. They should have running water and electricity. Remember, I said *should*. That may not be true in every location we find ourselves in." She laughed but her audience did not yet understand the humor behind her statement.

"You may think you'll be safe at the Station Hospital," Whitfield continued, "and you should be, but this is war. The enemy bombs where it likes, when it likes. Geneva Convention Treaties be damned. That's the reality."

The group took in what Major Whitfield was saying to them, as much as possible. Their service could be dangerous to them personally, possibly fatal, and the realization was sobering.

"Each of you, as you know, has the relative rank of Second Lieutenant. That rank earns you $88 and some change for your monthly pay while you're in the states. It'll be a little more when you're overseas. Your relative rank carries no actual military status since you are technically Reservists, not regular Army. And, as I've said, as Reservists, you will not receive official military training. Uncle Sam has faith that your civilian nursing training will be sufficient to see you through your war time ordeal. So do I. You have been sworn in as an officer of the United States Army but you will always be a nurse and a lady first. That's who you are. Your name, rank, and serial number are second to that status. Understood?"

They understood. No one spoke. The silence was not awkward. It served to punctuate the importance of the Code of

26

Ethics for the nursing profession. Each trained nurse takes the Nightingale Pledge. They observe the social contract avowing that the patient comes first. They recognize that their focus in the medical profession is on care. The physician's focus is on cure. These women were instilled with the philosophy that character is vital. Good character, they had been told, is who you are when no one is watching. It means doing the right thing just because it is right regardless of the consequences. This view unified them. It's how they understood the distinction that Whitfield was making—nurses are *nurses* first. The Army comes second. Army Brass might be forgiven for misunderstanding the difference.

Major Whitfield brushed a strand of hair away from her face. The movement brought the group back to the present. "Your official uniform will be the white duty uniform that you are familiar with," she said. "That could change depending on your destination and the weather conditions there. I will add this personal recommendation, go to the PX and buy yourself khaki pants and jackets. When you are overseas, you will be pleased to have the choice of using rugged, comfortable clothing in the various situations you will find yourselves in."

Another brief pause. "OK, I will dismiss you for now. Settle yourselves in, then at 1800 hours—six o'clock civilian time— someone will collect you and show you to the chow hall. The PX is open until 2100 hours. Have a look around there before checking out the Officers Club, where you can have a drink and make friends. Friends will get you through the war."

A shopping spree at the PX was the bright spot of Dot's day even though only sensible items were on her shopping list. The most important purchase turned out to be her new G.I. shoes. They were lace-up Oxfords with a lower heel than her duty shoes and had the added benefit of improving the comfort of long distance walks.

27

Dot's new Oxfords passed their first test the following morning during a mandatory three mile hike.

"We were told there would be no official Army training," Charlotte complained.

"They want to get us into shape," someone replied.

"What shape are they hoping for? I don't want to be shaped like my Uncle Eddie." Cora was winded. The nurses snickered.

"I suppose we need training so we can walk up and down staircases in the hospital the Army-way," Gillie offered.

Dot disagreed with a smile. "It's probably so we can get from Point A to Point B, or to the next transport truck without holding up the schedule."

"Stamina and endurance," Elizabeth chimed in.

"At least we're marching in style with these gorgeous new olive drab tin bonnets," Gillie said. "They're suitable for Easter, aren't they?" Gillie looked over at Anne Stone who was walking a few feet away from the group. She had not joined in the conversation and Gillie wanted to include her.

Anne turned to look at Gillie. "I guess so," she said somberly.

They dragged themselves back to the barracks after the hike and agreed that they had experienced a forced march. After some good-natured grumbling, they admitted that at least they had worked up an appetite for whatever was on offer for dinner.

"I will clean my plate tonight," Charlotte admitted.

"I think that's the idea," said Dot.

———

Early the next morning, Major Whitfield gathered the 58th nurses into a corner of a lecture hall to give the deploying nurses more information. The metal folding chairs had been grouped in a semi-circle for the powwow.

"When you get back to your barracks, empty your suitcases," she told them. "Suitcases will not follow you to your destination and footlockers are too bulky to be used. They will be sent back to your hometown by railroad express. Cable your family to pick up your things. All the gear you're taking with you will need to go into your Barracks Bag, or B-bag. You might refer to them as your Big-Bag."

Whitfield picked up a heavy duty canvas duffel bag she had brought with her for demonstration. It was the official olive drab color with a top-load design, two attached shoulder straps that make it wearable as huge backpack, and a carrying handle sewn into the side. If Dot stood inside one, it would come up to her armpits. But when you were packing items you believed indispensable for several years of overseas deployment, it ceased to look large at all.

Jane Travers raised her hand. "I will need two of the B-bags, ma'am. I've already pared down my things. I know what's left won't fit in one of those."

"Regulations, I'm afraid. It's the best we can do. So make your gear fit. End of discussion."

Travers looked irritated but schemed to take the matter over Major Whitfield's head.

"There is a stack of these back in the barracks. The B-bag will hold the main portion of the things you're taking overseas with you. While you're in transit, the B-bag will be stowed in the hold of the ship. It will not be available to you until you reach your final destination. Pack the bulk of your gear in there. Keep back everyday items and two changes of clothes. You'll need that with you topside. Those things will go in your A-bag." She held up a cotton carry-all with a drawstring top that resembled a laundry bag. Same color as the duffel. "You will also be issued a Musette bag."

"What's a *myoo-sette* bag?" Charlotte asked.

29

"Hold on, I've got one here." Whitfield retrieved a tan colored canvas bag fifteen inches wide and ten inches tall.

"It's based on the World War I British Officers' Musette bag. The name is French which roughly translates to haversack, or day pack. G.I.s are issued one of these. Although small and lightweight, they're versatile. The straps configure for use as a back pack or a shoulder bag."

"What goes in there?" Elizabeth asked. "I assume our papers and other personal items will be in our handbags."

"The bag, as you can see," Whitfield opened the bag so the nurses could see a cross-section of its interior "has a divider in the middle that contains two smaller pockets. Put small items here like extra cigarettes, a sewing kit, a pair of socks, a scarf or extra handkerchief, tissues for latrine use. In the rear section, place your towel there and it will double as a cushion for your back if you wear the bag as a backpack. This front section is larger, see, about the width of my palm. Bulkier items can go here like your poncho and K-rations. There's an exterior pocket at the back with a snap closure where a blouse and underwear can be slipped in. The small pouch on the side, also with a snap closure, will hold the extra shoulder strap. Don't put your mess kit in the Musette bag. Carry it separately, even though you won't need it until you line up for a meal, or it becomes necessary to heat your rations in the field. Leave your canteens out free as well."

Charlotte cleared her throat. She had another question. Whitfield nodded to her.

"Is the mess kit to be used instead of plates and silverware?"

Major Whitfield explained that the stainless steel kit, comprised of two oval-shaped pans that fit together edge to edge like a clam-shell (not stacked inside each other), would be used as their individual place setting. One side was used for a plate and the other, when fitted with a handle, might be used as a small frying pan. The space created when the two sides were together held a spoon, fork, and knife.

"You can use the frying pan to warm your rations if you're in the field. Your canteen nests inside a metal cup that you can use for beverages, but also to boil water when that's necessary," Whitfield explained, then continued to clarify the uses of the bags.

"So, in the A-bag, you'll have your change of clothes. Use the Musette bag for other important personal items that won't fit into your handbag. These three bags, as well as your mess kit and canteen will travel with you personally on your voyage. The B-bag will be stored in the hold of the ship. As I said, you will not have access to that. Don't bother to ask. The answer will be no. This is a fact. And to be clear," the Major continued, "if your gear will not fit into one of these bags, it won't go with you. Whatever does not fit, you will mail back home. This is to save precious cargo space. You may take only essential items. The Army considers framed photos of sweethearts and other decorative objects to be excess baggage. If you choose to include beloved mementos or treasured tokens in your possessions, I do NOT want to know."

The Major handed out a sheet of paper to each nurse. "This is a list of clothing items you will need to purchase, at your own expense I'm afraid, before leaving Camp Kilmer. The Army has issued to you the gear it determined to be essential to you, including your official dress uniform. Everything issued to you will be the absolute latest and most up-to-date equipment the Army has. You will be issued skirts, jackets, caps, gloves, shoes, the insignias to be worn on your uniform, and an overcoat. You will also be issued six blue cotton work dresses and six white cotton ones along with your white nursing caps for when you're on duty at the hospital. You have your bedrolls. You have your helmets, and gas masks too. Keep them with you always. Here, on board the ship, and abroad. Always means always."

Whitfield tapped a finger on the sheet of paper and said, "This is a list of additional items to have with you overseas. Buy these items and you will thank me later. For example," she read from the list, "buy two pairs of dark blue slacks, one of wool, one of a washable fabric. Buy two dark blue slipover sweaters to have on the ship. Buy a pair of coveralls and another pair of durable shoes. They will make physically demanding work less problematic. It's why soldiers don't fight a war in skirts and heels." The women smiled in agreement as the truth of that statement dawned on them.

Elizabeth asked, "If we're to work in hospitals, why do we need to be prepared for harsh conditions?"

"You will be in a hospital environment, but the conditions will likely be much more primitive than what you're accustomed to at home. The first nursing units that entered the North African campaign were ill-clothed for their assignment. In fact they waded ashore in their skirted uniforms while being fired upon. It's easier to duck for cover in slacks, or so I'm told. You will be ordered to clean and scrub facilities that are acquired for hospital use and, whether or not you have running water or electricity, it will be easier for you to do your heavy labor in coveralls rather than your nursing uniform. When you encounter cold weather, you'll be happy to have your legs covered. I don't need to remind you that when you climb aboard two-ton trucks for transportation, you can scale tailgates, scramble across cargo, and move and stretch in relative modesty if you're wearing slacks. Make it your personal responsibility to be prepared for these contingencies regardless of Uncle Sam's oversight."

The women were convinced. Before another day passed, they made more visits to the PX and found creative ways to repack their B-bags.

Official activities filled the nurses' days too. They attended a crash course on censorship policies that instructed them on how to prevent transmission of vital information in their personal correspondence. Nothing was to be written in letters that would be valuable to the enemy. Never include location or destination, number of individuals in the group, or what was observed from your vantage point within messages. It was stressed to never write home in a language other than English. If your parents in New York City are better able to communicate in Italian, write to them in English anyway, or otherwise the censorship officer may not know what's being said and become needlessly suspicious. Don't complain or voice displeasure with your situation. It reflected morale, or lack of it, and was considered an aid to the enemy. In short, don't whine.

Nurses of the 58th Station Hospital had come together as a unit. And, as a unit, they went to the processing office to sign their official papers.

"I've never filled out so much paperwork," Dot told Gillie as they sat at a small wooden table. She directed portions of her pay to be sent home and bequeathed her worldly possessions to her mother.

"This seems final," Gillie admitted. She had just done the same, making her mother her sole beneficiary as well. Before departure, each nurse would complete a safety arrival card addressed to her nearest relative. This card would be released after the port received notice of a safe landing.

Dot, along with most everyone in her group, went to church services on Sunday to receive blessings and good wishes for a safe return. Jane stayed behind sulking because Army regulations on the number of bags allowed per person irritated her. The others would not squander a last chance to ask for God's protection. They would set sail in only two days.

Last minute errands were fitted into those two days. More items were mailed home as other items moved up in priority. The women spent hours packing, unpacking, re-packing and then packing again. This was no mere nervous time-waster. Soldiers take time to prepare and ready themselves for battle. To be self-sufficient meant they would not be a burden to others. As Dot went through this ritual, something clicked. She felt taller. She felt strong and competent. A sense of self confidence filled her. She observed the same phenomenon in the other nurses. They knew they had yet to be tested by fire. But they also knew they would pass the test when it was time. These incredible women had chosen a life of service to their fellow humans. They would adapt when necessary to succeed at the job set before them.

Bed rolls and B-bags were carried away at nine o'clock on Monday night. On Tuesday, before the nurses left for the harbor, a Red Cross representative came to see them to hand out official R.C. Ditty Bags. The bags were made of a lightweight olive drab cotton and closed at the top with a drawstring. Every individual who shipped out overseas received one.

"It feels a little like Christmas," Elizabeth said. She rummaged through the items in the bag to see what Santa had brought.

Dot twirled the bag in her hands. "It looks just like our other luggage," she said.

Charlotte look puzzled.

"Someone might mistake us for Rockefeller's, traveling the world with our matching set of bags," Dot clarified. "I wish I had three or four more of these things to organize the small bits I've stuffed inside my B-bag."

"I already have most of these things," Jane complained. She headed to the waste basket to toss the unwanted items.

34

"I'll take that off your hands," Cora said.

"Don't be greedy," Jane said back.

"Well, if you're tossing it into the trash anyway, I'd like to have it. There may be someone on the ship who needs it and we can share. Soap, toothpaste, an extra toothbrush or comb might make a difference to someone. Aspirins, a sewing kit, writing paper, pencils—we can swap these things for items we might have forgotten."

Dot looked at the chewing gum, hard candy, deck of cards, and cigarettes in her bag. "Even though I don't smoke or chew gum," she looked at Cora, "I know my ration of Camels is a valuable bargaining chip when trading for scarce items."

The matter was settled. The extra Red Cross items were redistributed.

By nightfall, the nurses stood for final roll call. Blackout conditions were being observed. All windows were shuttered or covered with heavy dark curtains and no exterior lights were on. In that bleak atmosphere, they marched to the train station. No transport truck ride for them this time.

"At least we've been thoroughly trained for *marching*," Gillie commented.

"Ready or not," Dot countered, "here we come."

<hr />

The train ride from Camp Kilmer to Jersey City took less than an hour. No one said a word. Each woman sat silently with her own thoughts.

At Jersey City, the nurses boarded a ferry boat to New York Harbor. At four o'clock on Wednesday morning, the dock was already a beehive of activity. The nurses were exhausted but were met by more Red Cross volunteers who gave them doughnuts and coffee. The much appreciated pick-me-up worked wonders getting the group through the ordeal of being processed to board the ship. Dot and the other nurses were instructed to march across the gangway at last. They stood on the deck grasping the hand railing of the *Santa Rosa*. Dressed in full uniform and carrying helmets, gas masks, canteens, and personal bags, the women took in the sights of their homeland.

Three

Diary Entry ~ April 27, 1943
Last look at the Statue of Liberty for quite some time.

Forty-one degrees is cold when ocean winds come in from the north. The steel structure of the ship absorbed the chilly temps and redistributed them into the human bodies through the soles of their shoes and through gloved hands holding tightly to the metal railings. The travelers steadied themselves as the ship rocked against bow lines and stern lines.

"I'm taking bets on where we wind up," Cora looked at Dot standing by her side and then at the other women. "Who wants in? We'll call it our destination pool. Your choice. England or North Africa?"

"How much?" Dot asked.

"Two bits gets you in the game."

"I'm not much for games of chance," Dot admitted. "But I'll play. Put me down for North Africa, since you didn't list the Bahama Islands." She dug in her handbag for a quarter and handed it to Cora. Cora moved down the railing to tempt others to join in.

Assignments for accommodations were called out and the nurses made a beeline to their cabins to stow their personal gear. Dot and her three roommates were lucky. Their room was above

37

the water line, which meant that if they were torpedoed, they stood a chance of not being the first to drown.

"I suppose Charlotte and Elizabeth will be along shortly," Dot said to Gillie as they took in the room arrangement. Two sets of bunk beds with a narrow aisle between them overwhelmed the small space. They were both pleased that only one woman was allocated per bed. Enlisted men enjoyed no such luxury and had to sleep in turns. While walking the complicated route to their room, Dot had seen men tucked into every available nook and cranny of the vessel. Although cramped, this cabin had en suite amenities. A sink, no larger than a helmet, sat attached to the wall near a slender door. A toilet and a tiny shower stall were tucked behind the door. All the modern conveniences of home, but in miniature.

Dot claimed a lower bunk, ensuring it would be hers for the duration of the voyage by using the tried and true method of placing her personal articles on the pillow. She rationalized that the taller women would naturally desire the higher bunks. She quickly changed into the slacks and sweater Major Whitfield had insisted should be the shipboard unofficial uniform. She tucked her official uniform back into her A-bag and stowed it under the bed.

Gillie had claimed the other lower bunk but she used the buttocks-firmly-rooted-on-the-mattress method to establish her proprietary rights. She sat as still as a statue, hoping to defy the ill effects from the rocking motion of the ship. So far she was unimpressed with the results.

Charlotte and Elizabeth entered the room shortly afterwards and claimed the top bunks without comment. Dot and Gillie caught each others' eye and secretly made an *I can't believe it worked shrug*. The four women had settled in when the call for breakfast blasted through the loud speaker. Dot, Charlotte, and Elizabeth made for the door but Gillie showed no inclination to leave the room.

"Aren't you going to have breakfast?" Dot asked her.

"Oh, Chigger. I don't want to have food on my stomach that will be rejected later." Gillie was queasy. She imagined disgracing herself when the ship set sail and wanted to avoid that indignity.

"Eat something now," Dot encouraged her gently. "We're still in the dock. No telling when we'll actually set out, and you might waste away to nothing before that happens."

The other two agreed with Dot's logic but saw that the persuasion would take a while. They promised to meet in the dining room later, and departed.

"After we set sail," Dot continued, "you may not want food again for a while. But the nutrients will linger longer than your sausage and eggs and it'll help keep up your strength."

"And if we're torpedoed?" She crossed her arms across her stomach as if to keep everything where it belonged.

Dot didn't have her sea legs so when the ship rocked unexpectedly, she grabbed the bed post. She was determined to face the high seas on her own terms and believed food would enhance her resolve. "The odds are against an enemy attack while we're still in New York Harbor but if it happens, we'll go down with a full stomach. That'll show those Jerries." Gillie gave in.

After breakfast, Gillie and Dot were fortified. They walked around the ship to familiarize themselves with its layout. In daylight, the plain gray paint didn't look quite as dreary as it had in the pre-dawn darkness.

Dot looked back over her shoulder at the length of the *Santa Rosa*. It was longer than a football field, and the sheer size made her feel safe.

"Major Whitfield will be able to get some good marching time out of us," Charlotte said as she came up to Dot and Gillie from the opposite direction.

"I hope she doesn't start today," Gillie replied. "I'd feel better if I could ease into this cruise."

"Funny you call it a 'cruise'," Charlotte laughed. "I was just talking to a swabbie. According to him this old bucket of bolts used to be an American ocean liner before it was requisitioned to move Army personnel. There are tell-tale signs of elegance still evident. Larger cabins, for instance. Lounges with arm chairs we can use for meetings. That huge dining facility should make our travels tolerable."

In spite of its monotonous color and its no-frills fittings for war work, the *Santa Rosa* had indeed retained her elegant pre-war figure. Before the women completed their self-guided tour, an announcement over the loud speakers gave details on when and where the first of many boat drills would take place. The nurses of the 58th arrived on the appointed deck promptly as ordered.

"This is no luxury cruise," the Navy Officer barked at the gathering with a no-nonsense, business-only Brooklyn accent. "I'm Lieutenant Duckworth," he told them, "and I'm going to save your life. If you are on this ship, you are an important component in the Allied Forces. As such, your safety is vital so you can fulfill your duty to God and Country. I will do all in my power to *assure* your safety." No pause for comments.

"We will be crossing the Atlantic Ocean which is large and deep. We will travel within a convoy. The convoy will boost the odds of our safety more than if we traveled alone. Enemy submarines do like to torpedo ships sailing alone. Okay, none of us wants to find ourselves on the bottom of that large and deep ocean but that won't stop Herr Hitler's U-boats from trying. I'm here to tell you that if those bastards—*excuse my French*—if they *do* hit us, we can survive the ordeal. I know, because I have." Duckworth was serious.

"The lifeboat drill is designed to help you do just that," he continued, "but to follow the instructions you must first know

40

what they are. Therefore this drill, and every drill, is mandatory. No excuses."

He handed out a life preserver to each person in his group. He demonstrated how to put it on and how to secure it properly. The rubberized and air-inflated *Mae West* was an improvement over the bulky cork n' canvas vest of the previous generation. He rattled off more instructions on the proper response to ordinary emergencies and then they witnessed examples of the emergency alarm (seven short tones and one long).

"No chance we'll sleep through that," Elizabeth muttered to herself. "It's loud enough to wake the dead."

Muster stations were pointed out. Each nurse memorized her designated location and the number identification of her lifeboat.

"When you're not in your cabin, you must have these items with you at all times," he held up the five fingers on his right hand then retracted one for each article. "Life vest. Shoes. Helmet. Clothing that does *not* include nightgowns or pajamas. And a full canteen of water. Now say it with me."

Everyone held up five fingers and counted down the items in the same order.

Lieutenant Duckworth looked at the women with a dead-serious face. He told them, "If you run up to grab a bite for breakfast you must have these items. If you get up from your bunk at midnight to go visit your best friend Sue down the hall, you must have these items." He knew from experience that his trainees would want to test him on this. He saw the wheels turning as they calculated the value of following this rule in every instance.

"No room for discussion then," Cora said under her breath.

"I'm inclined to want to obey," Elizabeth confessed.

"I see you look dubious," Duckworth conceded. "You aren't the first. I know what's going through your head. I do. But listen

41

to this scenario… you run down to Sue's cabin. You have a good chin wag. The ship is broadsided by a torpedo. The ship begins to list. You're barefoot, in a flimsy nightgown, no vest, no helmet. Maybe you have your smokes, but so what? You have to find a way to get back to your cabin *in-the-dark* to prepare yourself to evacuate. All the other passengers are prepared but *you* must run against the crowd and your actions hold up your comrades. By the time you get to your cabin, and make yourself ready to abandon ship, the ship has shifted again and you cannot make it out to the deck. Maybe someone stayed behind to help you out, but then you both go down to a watery grave."

This example put a new spin on what was expected of the passengers. The nurses became serious, thoughtful.

"You nurses, you've been trained to put others first. Good. Great. But in this case, put yourself first. Make yourself ready *first*, and then no one has to come along and put their life on the line to get you out of a fix. Take responsibility for your own safety foremost, *then* help someone else or you risk the possibility of wasting more lives than your own."

"Damn. He's got a point!" Charlotte nodded her head in agreement.

Duckworth ended with, "Pay attention. Follow instructions. Practice the instructions. Doing so will be the difference between life and death. It's your *duty* to live, to serve the United States of America. We'll have other chats, but for now, you are dismissed."

Reality of the danger the nurses were in dawned on Dot, and not Dot alone, if the pensive mood was any indication. After the drill she and her three roommates went back to their cabin to regroup. The room was neat as a pin. Beds were made and personal effects were stowed out of sight. Dot lay down on top of the covers. She rested for half an hour and when she felt the walls closing in on her in the small space, she went out to the Hurricane Deck for some air.

The Hurricane Deck was covered to protect it from inclement weather but the sides were open to the sea breeze which was warmer now. The deck was high enough for Dot to see the sights around her. Looking out across the water, she saw the Statue of Liberty, proudly standing watch over the harbor as waves lapped at the edge Liberty Island. Dot grasped the now sun-warmed railing to steady herself. *How long*, she wondered, *until I see you again, Lady Liberty?* The real, but unasked question was, of course, *WILL I see you again?*

Dot was beginning to understand the risks she faced as an actor in this war. But she knew those risks were far outweighed by the contributions she could make. No uncertainty on that count.

Wednesday turned out to be a long and unexciting day with no hint of the ship undocking. Other than the lifeboat drill and exploring the various areas of the ship that were open to the passengers, there was little else to do. Gillie was glad she took Dot's advice to eat but anxiety from the waiting meant the meals still didn't settle kindly. Dot and Gillie returned to their quarters soon after dinner for the evening.

At 4:20 on Thursday morning, the *Santa Rosa* finally left shore. Dot had been fast asleep but woke up instantly when the ship moved away from the dock. The movement made her sit upright in her bunk. She contemplated going topside but decided to try for more sleep instead. Before sleep returned, the ship had sailed to open waters where it rocked side-to-side as it reeled bow-to-stern, somehow in one motion. That's a lot of gyroscopic movement for the inner ear to process. The inner ear capitulated its responsibilities to deal with motion by handing it off to the stomach to handle.

Dot made the metal waste can her new best friend as she hugged it tight to her chest. Gillie woke up in response to the ship's movement too and scurried to find her own new best friend.

"Fresh air," Dot prescribed after they regained their composure. She uttered nothing further as she gathered the five-required-items they had been instructed to have with them at all times. The metal trash can made six. Gillie mirrored Dot's moves. They dressed and walked quickly to the nearest exterior deck.

A brief shower had rinsed the New York grime off the steel skin of the ship. The sun soon rose like a glowing apricot and it took some chill away from the sea breeze. Charlotte and Elizabeth, and other passengers, joined Dot and Gillie topside where they huddled by the starboard railing. They compared notes on whose stomach was most like a spinning top and decided that none of them was willing to eat breakfast. Instead, they bided their time until scheduled activities began.

"Look at that," Charlotte swept her arm in an arc indicating the other ships traveling along beside their own. "We're an armada."

"Safety in numbers," Elizabeth said.

"Or a giant banner advertising our position to the U-boats," Jane Travers said.

"Don't be a profit-of-doom," Charlotte teased her. "It's unlucky."

A great convoy of battleships and destroyers flanked the *Santa Rosa* as they initiated their zigzag route across the Atlantic in an attempt to sneak past U-boats out to stop them.

The first planned activity was another lifeboat drill at 9:30 a.m. The nurses were also required to get their typhus vaccine boosters before the day was out. Many of them headed to the

44

infirmary before the appointed hour so they could cross that task off the list. Typhus fever spreads through contact with lice, and lice are prevalent wherever there are crowds such as schools, hospitals, and Army troops traveling to the battlefront on a ship. Head lice jump from head to head and choose to nestle themselves contentedly in the hair. Body lice aren't as picky. They will burrow into any body part they find. A warm human is their singular requirement. Regular washing of clothes in hot water will kill the lice. Ironing clothes with a hot iron kills the eggs. But no one can stand to wash their hair with water hot enough to kill head lice. Anybody can pick up lice, no matter how fussy a person is about his or her cleanliness. Lice jump on hosts that are handy. While they bite and suck blood for their food, they also inject saliva into the wound. Typhus bacteria in the saliva is what causes the disease which manifests itself through severe muscle aches, headaches, and skin rashes. It can be fatal. None of the nurses skipped the inoculation.

The PX was opened for business for a couple of hours. A few nurses diverted their attention from their nausea by having a look around. When humans go into survival mode, they default to prehistoric hunt-and-gather behaviors. Women and men both scavenged for items they anticipated needing. Olive drab tee shirts (otherwise known as 'OD green' tees), clothes washing detergent, and extra cotton socks topped the list. Fellow travelers passed along tips according to their own experiences, or experiences they had heard from others. *Be prepared*—it was a Scout motto for a reason and the nurses took being prepared seriously.

Dot filled her day with activities as best she could. She didn't feel like reading but she was learning the Army way of filling the time, which was standing on deck exchanging stories with her pals. She was aware of being within sight of land most of the day as the ship ran parallel to the eastern coastline of the U.S. It gave

45

her a focal point, some grounding, before they headed into the unknown. Standing in the sunlight for most of the day, however, meant she and the other fair skinned nurses were sunburned. The irritation from that helped divert attention away from their seasickness.

⁕

By the fourth day at sea, two happy things happened. The ship had entered calm waters and most of the passengers had adapted to ship life enough to walk around without carrying their best-friends with them.

"I'm actually enjoying breakfast this morning," Elizabeth announced to the table. There was widespread agreement.

"I'm glad this is no longer the most dreaded activity that I avoid at all costs," Gillie added.

"I'm going to church services tomorrow," Dot said.

"That's a complete change of topic," Charlotte responded.

"It just jumped in my head," Dot defended herself. "If I don't say it now who knows when I'll remember to bring it up. The service will be held here in the dining hall after breakfast. Anybody else want to go?"

Most of the nurses met for church the next day. Dot joined other volunteers to sing in the mixed choir. Major Whitfield had told them that participating in activities helped pass the time. The added bonus of making new friends improved the lethargy and boredom that otherwise clawed at them.

A generous Sunday dinner followed the service. The nurses sat together with their coffee after the meal discussing the Chaplain's sermon. During a break in the conversation, gunfire pierced the Sunday reverence. The women jumped as if someone had shouted 'boo' at them but Anne Stone clapped her hands to her ears and squealed.

46

"What is it Annie?" Maddy asked her. Anne just shook her head from side to side.

"Stay here, everyone. I'll go see what's going on." Maddy pushed herself away from the table. The others tried to calm Anne as she sobbed.

Maddy reported back to the group. "It's a gun drill for the men off the rear deck."

"Why would they do this today?" Dot asked.

"Why not? Charlotte replied.

"It's seems strange to me. Where I grew up, guns were not fired on Sundays."

"Me too, but we have to remind ourselves that the enemy will have no respect for Sundays so we may as well get accustomed to the sounds now."

"I can't take the sound of guns," Anne said as she left the table. Maddy followed her to their room.

"Guns will be giving fire wherever we wind up, Annie. That's the nature of war. You're going to have to find a way to pull yourself together or you'll be little help to our efforts abroad."

Anne sat still, staring at a spot on the floor, willing herself to be somewhere else.

"Annie, did you hear what I said?" Maddy was firm, she had been taught to reign in her feelings and let cool reason prevail. Anne's display of emotion was puzzling to her.

"I heard," Anne replied. She found a handkerchief to dab her eyes with. "It's just that…" Her words trailed off into silence.

"It's just what?" Maddy nudged.

"Nothing." Anne sat up straighter. "Loud noises startle me, that's all. I'll keep a check on that in the future."

Maddy gave Anne time to say more if that was what she wanted, when she didn't Maddy stretched out on her bunk. She was resigned to her failure. "But if you want to talk more, I'll be happy to listen. Or talk to the Major, if you like."

After seven days on the ship, Dot noted in her diary: ...*just more of the same.* She couldn't have predicted the turmoil that would follow her Small Pox shots and the Atabrine doses. Atabrine was a synthetic substitute for quinine. It was used to suppress the effects of malaria but the reactions to these vaccines were noteworthy as Dot wrote on Thursday, May 6: *Sick as I ever want to be from Atabrine. Ready for the monotony of previous days to return.*

Stomach cramps, diarrhea, fever, headache, nausea and vomiting sent Dot to bed where she could endure the entire tedious list of side effects with a tiny scrap of comfort. She wasn't alone. Others experienced similar reactions to the drugs. The symptoms Dot suffered dampened her spirits even more than the endless rise and fall of the ship ploughing through swollen waves.

As if the physical challenge were not enough to deal with, Dot was also homesick, and lonely for Jack. Far from her loved ones, especially her sweetheart, Dot had a good old fashioned cry in the middle of the night when the others were asleep. After she got that out of her system, she felt better. For a while. Then came the explosion.

Dot sat straight up from her sick bed and looked at the bedside clock. It indicated the time was one o'clock a.m.

"What's that?" she asked Gillie.

"I do *not* know but I will go find out. Stay here." Gillie dressed quickly in the dark and grabbed her five-required-items before leaving the cabin.

While waiting for news, Dot, Charlotte, and Elizabeth heard a woman screaming close by. They discussed what the next step should be. Had a torpedo hit them? Was someone injured?

Should they prepare to abandon ship? No evacuation alarm had sounded but the women jumped up and dressed anyway.

"If we go down with the ship, no one at home will know where we are," Charlotte said as she pulled a sweater over her head. "None of us on the ship know where we're going."

"Surely the Captain knows," Elizabeth made a convincing argument.

"Why can't they tell us the destination? Who are we going to tell? And how would we tell them since we're isolated on this ship in the middle of nowhere?" Charlotte insisted.

"Maybe the Brass thinks that if we're torpedoed and captured by the enemy, we'll blab to them where we're heading." Elizabeth's logical outlook was not reassuring.

"It's too late to prepare a message in a bottle," Dot shot back. The other women laughed. "We wouldn't have helpful details for a rescue party anyway." She raised her voice to be heard over the screaming from across the hall.

Dot's attention returned to the present predicament. Must they abandon ship? Would they fall into the hands of the Germans?

Gillie burst through the door breathless. She had to run up two flights of stairs before she found someone with a suitable explanation for the explosion, and then back down the stairs again.

"Depth charges," she spat.

Oh.

Gillie explained. "When ships drop explosives into the water, it's for one reason."

No one breathed as they waited for the reason. "The Captain says enemy submarines are near us. And a threat."

Oh.

"We're in danger," Charlotte stated. "This is not a drill. We should do something."

49

"Charlotte, you see danger everywhere," Elizabeth said in a deadpan voice.

"Uh… only when danger *is* everywhere," Charlotte deadpanned back.

"You're right," Elizabeth laughed. "It is. And now with the enemy patrolling us, we can no longer pretend we're on a tropical cruise to paradise, can we?"

"Nope. This is a war zone," Dot whispered. "Let's prepare as if it's a drill. If we get the alarm, we're ready. If we don't, all the better. But I'm concerned about the screaming we heard. Someone's in trouble, let's find out what that's about."

Chaos had seized the cabin across the hall. When Anne Stone heard the explosion, she lost all pretense of self-control. Cora and Jane jumped down from their upper bunks. Joined by Maddy, they knelt down beside Anne's bed to see what was wrong.

"Pull yourself together, Annie," Maddy demanded but the others offered words of support to Anne in hopes of getting an explanation for the outburst. As Anne screamed, she clawed at her face. No one could calm her hysterical outburst.

"I'll fetch the Major," Jane offered, and left.

"Put your clothes on first," Maddy said. "Take the five things with you."

"You can't be serious…" Jane didn't get the entire sentence out before Maddy's glare convinced her that the command was not a suggestion. She collected her things and left.

Major Whitfield preceded Jane through the cabin door, fully dressed. She told the others to join the women in the cabin across the hallway while she had a chat with Anne.

Whitfield turned a trash can upside down and placed it at the head of Anne's bed. She sat down on it.

"You've got to tell me what this is about," Whitfield said. "We're heading to a war zone where there will be more explosions, more gunfire, and we need you one-hundred-percent with us or we need to send you back home. We can't do that right now since we're in the middle of the Atlantic Ocean. So let's face what's going on with you. Let's see if we can deal with it and resolve it. Now take a deep breath."

Anne did as she was told. It helped. "I'll be fine," she told the Major. "The loud noise just caught me off guard…"

"It caught every one of us off guard but you are alone in being panic-stricken because of it."

"I can't talk about it."

"You must talk about it. It won't get better if you keep ignoring whatever is bothering you. I'm assuming there's an incident that happened since you signed up for overseas duty or you wouldn't have put yourself in this predicament. Tell me when the incident happened."

"A few days before I got my letter to report to Kilmer."

"Were you at Fort Jackson at the time?"

"No. I had gone home on a 48-hour pass to see my fiancé. He lives near my family's farm and he was to join his unit the following week."

"What happened when you saw your fiancé?"

"He didn't want to ship out. He didn't want to go. He'd signed up because his brother did but he's not a warrior, he's a musician."

"I can see why you'd worry for him and his safety, but why does hearing a gunshot set you off?"

Anne shivered like she had a chill. She stared off into space, seeing something happen in her mind. Then she continued. "He'd come to visit. He was going to stay for the night. My father made up a bed for him in the hay loft." Anne narrated the story in a flat tone.

51

"After dinner, we talked a while on the porch. He said he couldn't do this thing, couldn't face going to war. He tried to get me to run away with him. "Let's marry," he pleaded. "Let's make a life together somewhere where nobody knows us.""

We argued. He said goodnight and I believed things would look brighter for us both the next day. He went to the barn. I decided to take another chance on a reconciliation before turning in for the night so I walked down to the barn. When I got close, I heard his handgun go off." Anne buried her face in her hands and sobbed. "It was so loud. I opened the door and there he lay. I ran to him. I tried to stop the blood pouring out of his… ." She didn't finish the sentence. "But he was already gone. There was nothing…" Anne sobbed.

"Did you tell anyone about this?"

"Of course, the police were notified. I gave them a statement. But I haven't spoken to anyone else. What's the point?" She looked at Major Whitfield. "I know how stupid that sounds. I know that I'm screaming like a banshee when I hear a loud sound."

"It's the guilt, Anne."

"What do you mean?"

"With suicides, survivors are filled with guilt. We ask ourselves, did I cause this, could I have *stopped* this? When you hear the sound of firearms and explosions, it's the guilt that you're reminded of. Your fiancé was determined to find a way out of deploying with his unit. He was in a desperate state of mind. Given the circumstances, there was nothing you could do."

"I don't know…"

"Trust me, because I do know. The question now is, *can* you find a way to deal with this? Can you carry on with your own mission? Or do we get you a return ticket back to the states?"

"Can I think about it? I'd like to do my part, but I know I'm a burden in my current state."

"Let's work on it together then."

The passengers arrived at breakfast extra early the following morning to get the scoop on the dead-of-night activity. Their curiosity was not satisfied but it was useful to toss the subject around. Discussing their fears was helpful, the same process that would help Anne as she agreed to discuss her experience with Major Whitfield.

The second Sunday aboard the ship was Mother's Day. Prayers of thanks for their survival so far were said by believers and non-believers alike. No other close calls had awakened the passengers and crew, and Dot began feeling strong and fit and hungry. She opened a can of K-rations, as much for curiosity's sake as for the meal, and found an unsavory collection of food. She laid the contents of the can out on her bunk: graham crackers, canned ham, a chocolate bar, powdered coffee, chewing gum, and four Chesterfield cigarettes. More currency there, at least. Dot saved most of the items for later use, snacking only on the graham crackers for the moment. She understood why battlefield infantrymen became seriously tired of the meals after eating this fare day after day.

Midday on May 10, the travelers spied a speck of land on the portside of the ship. Sheer white limestone cliffs rising grandly out of the Mediterranean Sea came into focus. Dot was standing with a group of friends on the Hurricane Deck.

"Rock of Gibraltar," she said in awe gazing at the sight. "So, it's to be North Africa." No need for an official written memo stating their final destination, the passengers knew exactly where they would disembark. Dot looked forward to her portion of the *Destination Pool* of winnings that Cora had collected at the beginning of the trip.

Dot didn't need to use her imagination to know what was taking place in North Africa. American newspapers had reported on the campaign waged by American and British forces known as Operation Torch since early November 1942, a short seven months earlier. The British had been battling the Germans there much longer than the U.S., struggling for control of the Suez Canal. Whoever controlled the Canal had a passage to the Middle East and access to the Arabian oil fields. Its invaluable oil reserves were needed to fuel the war machine.

At four o'clock in the afternoon on May 11, the *Santa Rosa* docked in the harbor near Oran, Algeria. Passengers made a mad dash to get supper before disembarkation which would take place at 6:00 p.m. The nurses had learned to eat when food was available.

From the boat, the town looks perfect, Dot wrote in her diary. She added an addendum: *Of course, any land looks perfect to us weary travelers right now.*

Twenty-nine days had passed since Dot received her overseas orders. Half of that time was spent at sea. Dot was grateful that she and her shipmates had arrived safely but she would never again look forward to a nice afternoon on the water.

Part Two

NORTH AFRICA

Four

Diary Entry ~ May 11, 1943
Docked 4pm. Mad rush to get supper and get off the boat.

The *Santa Rosa* docked in the afternoon. The nurses had eaten an early supper, grabbed their gear, and gathered on the deck to get a look at the town. It was dry land, and it looked perfect.

Lieutenant Duckworth stood on deck shouted, "Disembark with all your personal belongings. Go directly to the wharf without delay. Wait there for further orders."

Dot criss-crossed the straps of her bags across her shoulders. "I'm not sorry *that* ocean cruise is over," she remarked. Her words carried over the wind to the ears of her traveling companions. They nodded in agreement.

Gillie mumbled something unintelligible in response. As she joined the line making its way down the gangway, she declared more loudly, "I had no idea a human could be seasick for two weeks and live to tell about it." The statement was seconded and carried unanimously as they abandoned, without regret, their floating home.

The women of the 58th Station Hospital had learned the Army way to hurry-up-and-wait. To fill their time, they exchanged news with the line handlers assigned to tie up the *Santa Rosa*.

"The Jerries are on the verge of surrendering North Africa." This was the first news they were told.

"We just got here," Elizabeth said playfully. "And now the war is over?"

"Can we take credit for the victory?" Charlotte joked.

"Yeah," a wiry, tanned, shoreman shot back good naturedly. "Thank God the enemy turned tail and ran as soon as they saw you dames arrive."

The victory was important to the Allies for a couple of reasons. North Africa's coastline was strategically located for American and British forces to enter Europe from the south. Liberating North Africa made its coastline accessible as a jumping off point for troop movements into Sicily which sat like a stepping stone in the Mediterranean Sea between North Africa and Italy. The Allies would hop from Sicily to Italy, and then move north into France where it would reclaim those countries from Nazi occupation. Bases of operation that remained on African soil would continue a supply line of materiel to the fighting men as well as medical services for the wounded.

Before more news could be swapped, a woman with an air of confidence walked up to meet the new arrivals gathered on the pier. She introduced herself as Captain Dorothy Parsons, Chief Nurse of the Hospital in Oran.

Dorothy Parsons was originally from the small seaport of Portsmouth, New Hampshire. She had joined the Army Nurse Corps in December 1940, during the early days of its expansion.

Parsons was one of the first nurses to wade ashore at Oran after being transferred from Camp Shelby, Mississippi. She was slim and stood five foot, six inches tall. A multitude of hairpins tamed her thick dark hair under the officer's cap. Gold wire-rimmed glasses sat low on her nose. Her friendly, spontaneous smile was welcoming. Clutched in both hands was a sheaf of papers—one for each of the newcomers now in her care.

Major Whitfield stepped forward to greet Parsons and to present her group of nurses. Whitfield would assume administrative duties at the hospital while Parsons would continue in her position as supervisor of the nursing staff and daily operations.

After the courtesies had been preformed, Parsons addressed the group. She simply cleared her throat to attract their attention. Kindness reflected in her eyes, accompanied by a glint of mischievous playfulness.

"Welcome to Africa, ladies," she said conspiratorially, as if they shared a secret. "I'll know each of you by suppertime and I will address you by your last names even though you are officers, and as officers, others must address you as Lieutenant. Officially. But to keep things simple among just us, you may call me Miss Parsons, and you may continue to address one another as you have been doing." She raised her eyebrows slightly as if to ask, *are there any questions?*

She continued. "Soon, you will realize that we are *family* here." She looked at Whitfield who nodded in agreement.

"In fact, we will remain family for the rest of our lives. Take good care of yourselves and of each other. Do this and you will have no problems taking care of the boys who come to our hospital." Parsons waited a moment for this to sink in.

"Okay, first things first. When our transport arrives, the men will load your B-bags for you, but keep your kit bags with you, they're your responsibility. The journey will be relatively short, but uncomfortable. We'll be riding in the back of what we would call back home, *cattle trucks.*"

Giggles erupted at the mention of cattle trucks. Parsons didn't mind the interruption. "You've already had the pleasure of being transported in this type of conveyance, I take it."

At this moment, no matter what lay ahead, the most important thing to the nurses standing before Captain Parsons was that they were off the rocking ship and on solid ground. Riding in a bumpy transport truck on dry land was nothing compared to the wave-tossed trip they'd just completed. That's why they giggled.

"No doubt you've heard that victory is won here. Formal treaties will be signed tomorrow. However, don't believe for a moment that the fighting is over. It's not." Miss Parsons surveyed her team. "This will remain a dangerous place for a while yet, and we'll continue to see plenty of action in this area."

Anne Stone raised her hand to ask a question. No one had heard a peep out of her since her breakdown on the ship and there was an intense interest in what she might ask.

"Will we be moving out with the troops after the treaties are signed?"

This seemed like a sensible question. The group was curious for the answer.

"Forward medical units—Field hospitals and Evacs—will move with the troops. More permanent hospitals like ours will lag behind to render medical assistance for casualties brought to us. We'll treat the patients and return them to the front, or we'll stabilize them so they can be sent home." A sea of bobbing heads nodded their comprehension, but Parsons sensed that some of the women had expected to be closer to the fighting.

"There's no glamour at the frontlines," Parsons explained. "Sure, there's plenty of glory. But do not be displeased. Your talents are required here for now and there will be plenty of glory to go around before we're done. Plenty of excitement too, you'll find."

Parsons' competent delivery of the facts put the nurses at ease. She would earn their complete trust in the days ahead and maintain their esteem from this day forward. The women who stood before her were already a well-disciplined Corps because of their civilian nurse training. Although they had left the security of home only a short while before arriving in enemy territory they had seen and read the wartime propaganda, the good and the bad, and accepted that they would serve without care for their own safety for the duration of the war.

Muffled rumbles grew louder. Clouds of dust came into sight. The vehicles pulled to a stop, parking in formation. Miss Parsons shouted over the din of noise, "That's for us."

Dot and Gillie and the others gathered their belongings, tossed them into the bed of the truck then followed after. They plunked their rear ends onto what shortly became the hardest wooden benches they would have the pleasure of gracing with their behinds. They would look back upon this slight hardship as nothing more than a mere inconvenience in days, weeks, months, and years to come.

The truck crawled along at twenty-five miles an hour, taking the better part of an hour to reach the hospital located fourteen miles away.

"Wonder what our facilities will be like...," Jane's jarred speech was barely heard above the diesel engine grinding the large transport truck down the dirt road.

"If Mother could see me now...," Maddy said, apropos of nothing.

"My mama had no idea what I was getting myself into, and I'm not going to tell her now," Cora said.

Elizabeth leaned in closer to Cora so she could be heard. "When you write to her, what will you tell her? I mean, really, can she punish you somehow if she's unhappy with your situation?"

Cora sat quietly as she pondered her answer.

"Mine doesn't know I'm here by my own choice," Dot joined in. "She thinks the Army ordered me to go to Europe. I didn't want to worry her."

"She may be a little worried now that you're in a war zone," Cora offered helpfully.

"True. But my brother Prentiss was at Pearl Harbor." Dot saw the concern. "No," she added quickly. "He's okay. In fact, the way the family found out that he survived is a funny story."

"How can *that* be funny?" Charlotte asked. "A relief, surely, but…"

"My younger sister, Margie, was in a movie theater with our older sister and her husband on Pearl Harbor day. The management stopped the movie to announce that Pearl Harbor had been bombed, so they left right away to go be with Mama, to tell her the news. It took a week to get news from Prentiss, whether he was okay, or not. Western Union called Mama on the telephone to read her the message."

"Oh lord, what did it say?" Maddy asked.

"As you know, cablegrams charge per word, so my brother packed the most amount of news he could in one four-letter word: S A F E."

"I bet that was the nicest four-letter word your mother had ever heard," Charlotte said.

"Mama told Margie she wanted to see it in person, see the actual cablegram. So, the next day Margie called the telegraph office and they sent a copy to her at her workplace. I think Mama will hold on to that thing until the day she dies."

"Your poor mother, she must have been terrified to get the telephone call from the telegraph office," Anne added.

"I think she was just relieved. It would have given her a heart attack to see a cable delivered in person. No one wants to see the delivery boy, or any military personnel for that matter, come knock on your door. But in our case, prayers were answered. Anyway, I didn't want to cause my poor Mama more worry, so I forgot to mention that, in fact, I *volunteered* for this duty."

"My mother and father knew I had a choice." Jane said. She typically didn't share personal information on so the others listened with interest.

"I told them I had a choice and I was choosing to go overseas. Mom was on my side and said for me to go and do what I had to do, that my nursing skills are important. Dad, on the other hand, didn't bother to come to the train station to see me off. He said my place was at home, taking care of the men folk."

"Well, here you are," Charlotte winked. "Taking care of the men folk, all right."

"Yes, here I am. And, I better live through this or I'll never hear the end of it!"

Laughter, a melody in its own key, rang through the truck.

"I hope they feed us right away," Charlotte changed the subject. "I know we just had a meal, but I could eat the leather off my left boot and call it a rib-eye steak."

Dot chimed in, "Don't forget our training, and the instructions concerning eating food. No local food and no water unless it's been boiled and chlorinated."

"Right. And no mingling with the locals," Elizabeth added.

"Their-ways-are-not-our-ways," they howled in unison, spoofing instructions that were drilled into them at Camp Kilmer.

The truck pulled into a field where rows of tents had been set up. This was where Dot and the other RNs would now call home. Their job would be to fill in where needed and relieve staff who had been working without relief since the Americans joined the fight. A welcome committee of nurses, tanned from the African sun, met the new arrivals.

"Glad you're here!" they told them.

"There's more to do here than we can handle even with the war winding down," one experienced old-timer said.

"You are much needed and welcomed," others added.

Miss Parsons handed 3x5 cards to each of the new nurses. On it was printed the woman's name, a letter that corresponded with her particular tent, and a number that corresponded to the cot she was to adopt as her own. Dot looked at her card then glanced up to catch Gillie's eye.

"Cee-One," Dot mouthed silently.

"Cee-Two," Gillie responded in kind. The gods were working to make these two friends tentmates during their stay in Oran.

"After you stow your gear, meet at the chow hall at 18:15 hours." Miss Parsons pointed over her right shoulder to a building that resembled the cinderblock football field house at Dot's high school. It sat a hundred feet down a gravel path leading away from the tents. "And bring your mess kits," she said. Before Parsons turned to walk away, she motioned to Whitfield to follow her.

With just a few minutes before nightfall Dot and Gillie hurried ahead of the crowd to their tent to get themselves settled. Their large bags had been delivered and were stacked outside the entrance. The women located theirs and hauled them inside.

The dark green tent smelled waxy from the water repellant coating. The dirt floor gave it the aroma of a root cellar. Dot walked in first. A narrow walkway ran the length of the tent with four wood and canvas cots on either side of it.

"There'll be eight of us in the tent," Dot informed Gillie who followed behind her. Their assigned cots were the two farthest ones from the tent opening. Elizabeth and Charlotte came in next. They dropped their bags beside Dot and Gillie. Maddy and Anne would occupy the next two on either side of the aisle. Cora and Jane claimed the last two cots nearest the tent flaps.

The trained, disciplined nurses tucked their toiletries into the small pine bedside tables located by each cot. The tent interior was growing dark as the sun set so Dot laid her flashlight on top of her pillow. It would be handy when she returned. The other nurses followed suit. They had learned from experience on board the transport ship that this tiny bit of manufactured illumination was essential after lights out.

"Our tent needs a name," Elizabeth suggested. Several possibilities were tossed out for consideration.

"Let's keep it simple," Charlotte said. "What's Army jargon for the letter 'C'?"

"Charlie!" Gillie chimed in.

"Charlie Tent," Elizabeth put forward. "All in favor?" The ayes carried.

"Where to next?" Dot asked. "In search of bathroom facilities?"

The women followed a path from Charlie Tent into a wooded area and located the latrine.

"No standing in line, then. That's great news," Elizabeth deadpanned.

Dot was puzzled. She stuck her head through the door and saw a wide open room with twelve holes yawning at her. "So this is to be a group activity," she said. "Even *privy* houses at home offer *privacy*." She pronounced it with a short-i as the Brits do.

Maddy was not happy with the communal set-up but boarding school had taught her how to survive in a group living arrangement. Anne and Jane, on the other hand, were horrified.

Gillie continued to explore. Near the latrine, she discovered open air showers. She turned the faucet handle and a trickle of water made a tiny splash on the wooden mat.

"We'll string up rope and attach blankets around this area for some scrap of privacy," Maddy said. No one doubted her ability to make that happen.

When preliminary explorations were completed, the nurses walked over to the chow hall where they were greeted with the disappointing sight of C-Rations for their welcoming menu.

"Sorry, Miss. I mean, Lieutenant." A G.I. on kitchen duty stood at the food counter handing out tin cans of stew to the diners. "Our grocery list hasn't been fulfilled so this is the best we can do today. Better luck tomorrow."

Rows of simple plank-built tables took up most of the floor space of the dining area. The nurses took their rations and looked around for seats to accommodate their numbers. Places had been set aside for them across the room and Major Whitfield was sitting there already. A rickety old chalkboard leaned against the wall. Miss Parsons walked over to it while motioning for her nurses to be seated. The group sat down and faced her as instructed.

Dot popped the key off the bottom of the olive colored can. Using the slot at the end of the key, she grasped the loose tail-end of the metal strip. Twisting the key around and around, the razor thin band that circumnavigated the can came away freely. She pulled the top off and peered inside at the meat and vegetable stew, estimating the calorie-protein content contained within. She was overjoyed that she wouldn't grow out of her uniform from overeating.

After assuring that everyone had something to eat, Miss Parsons picked up a stubby piece of chalk. In a few moments she had sketched a basic diagram of the camp on the green surface.

Pointing to the men's barracks and the armory Parsons said, "These areas are off-limits to nurses." She peered over her eyeglasses again at several of the women who didn't seem to be paying attention. This, the group now realized, was her way of saying *I mean business.*

"And these areas," she pointed to one small corner of the camp layout, "are designated for nurses only. Yes, this includes your open air shower and latrine."

Cora leaned over conspiratorially to Charlotte and whispered in her ear, "I feel as if I'm back in Baptist Sunday School class. Why don't they just truss us up in chastity belts and dispense with all these rules?"

Charlotte giggled, but then thought the chastity belt idea might be a good one. They were here to do a job. It wouldn't do to have their attention distracted from their duties by men in uniforms.

Miss Parsons cocked her head and made eye contact with Cora. With eye contact alone, she was able to communicate, *I got your number!* Then she smiled, replaced the chalk on the rack, and switched off her official demeanor.

"Look, you're tired from your incredibly long journey so I'll dismiss you for tonight. Go get some sleep." To Parsons, her nurses came first. To the nurses, the patients came first. This system always worked.

"We'll reconvene here at oh-eight-hundred tomorrow," Miss Parsons said. "You'll wear your seersucker rap-arounds as your UoD."

Blank faces.

"Uniform of the Day," she explained as understanding dawned on the women's faces.

Benches scraped on the concrete floor as the nurses got to their feet and filed out.

In North Africa, the days were hot and the nights were cold and nestling into their blankets meant sleep came quickly to the exhausted women. Many of their dreams that night took place against a still-pitching ocean voyage.

The morning sunshine brought with it a general cheerfulness. Waking up on terra ferma was an extravagance the team hadn't experienced for two weeks. They looked forward to eating a breakfast that was not likely to reintroduce itself later in an unflattering way. They were happy to be at their destination and ready to get to work.

Five

Diary Entry ~ May 15, 1943
My birthday. Sick from Atebrine.

First order for the first day—get dressed and head to the chow hall for breakfast. A shipment of food had arrived in the Oran port overnight and the nurses enjoyed real bacon and eggs.

Adapting to camp life included learning the ropes of how the Army hospital was run. Before assignments were handed out, however, the nurses were ordered to have their latest round of inoculations. The intent of vaccines was to keep the women healthy so they could care for the patients. And it worked. Except for Dot. She was still not able to tolerate the Atabrine and felt the ill effects instantly. She returned to her cot without waiting for permission.

"Chinnis!" The chief nurse poked her head into Dot's tent. Dot sat straight up in her cot.

"Yes, Miss Parsons." Dot's voice was barely audible.

"Gillie tells me you're sick. Atabrine?"

"Yes," Dot replied. "My body can't adjust to the vile stuff."

Fighting off malaria was important in this region but the side effects Dot experienced from the medication weakened her and was going to cost her time away from her bedside duties. She had no energy to continue a lengthy discussion. Miss Parsons saw the difficulty and reclaimed the conversation.

"The good news is…," the Captain continued, "it's your birthday and you have lived to see twenty-three years on this planet. Congratulations."

Dot wasn't so sure she agreed with the Chief Nurse's optimistic assessment.

"Many happy returns of the day. Now, the bad news is that we've no cake to celebrate on your behalf. The kitchen is woefully inadequate for such things, so apologies there." Dot cringed at the mere mention of food.

"Not a problem, Miss Parsons. I can't eat a thing."

"I can see that. Take a sick day, Chinnis. I'll get the Doc to come by to check on you. Then get yourself squared away. We need you."

Gillie, peeked in the tent as Captain Parsons left. She tossed a gift onto Dot's lap wrapped gaily in the funny papers she had saved back from a discarded Sunday newspaper in the chow hall. "Happy Birthday, Chigger." Gillie sang.

Dot tore the paper away. A paperback edition of *Jamaica Inn* by Daphne du Maurier revealed itself. She smiled and hugged it to her chest. "I can't wait to start this."

"I know you like du Maurier's books. Dibs on reading it as soon as you're done," Gillie said.

Three more tentmates stopped in during breaks in their schedules to present gifts to the birthday girl. Dot's gifts—a fresh bar of Lifebuoy soap, a box of stationery printed with purple violets, and a pack of hairpins—were 'gold' to her. She was pleased and appreciated the thoughtfulness shown to her by her new family.

"Thank you all," she told them, then fell back onto her pillow.

"I see you're still feeling punk," Charlotte said to Dot. "I had hoped you were getting better."

"No better. Miss Parsons is sending the Doc to see me. Maybe he'll have something to help," Dot said. "But I know he won't have anything in his little black bag for the basic *blahs*."

"We've had no mail either." Elizabeth understood where the blahs came from. "But we just arrived. Maybe tomorrow."

"You both know that mail comes in fits and starts here," Maddy said hoping to sound encouraging. "It'll take a while to catch up with us. We'll just have to endure until it does."

The nurses enjoyed their afternoon respite with Dot but they all had other things to do so they left her to rest until the doctor could see her. When he did, he agreed that she should skip the Atabrine doses and eat some solid food.

"I'm not exaggerating when I say I'm afraid I'm going to die from this drug," Dot told the doctor.

"I understand, but let's not let that happen. Food and rest are vital. Tell yourself you *will* live through this, and you will," he told her. "Basically, outlive the symptoms and you'll be back to your old self soon. You can go on duty in a day or two, or call me back in if you don't feel better. We'll go from there."

Dot thought the bromide: 'outlive the symptoms' was the fundamental cure for everything because *not* outliving the symptoms meant death. Since she was unable to come up with a better plan, Dot chose to follow the doctor's orders.

Letters arrived the next day, and as Dot had outlived her symptoms so far, she was able to savor them along with a hot meal and a small improvment in energy.

Morale was instantly improved for those who had a good mail call. After a few days, with a renewed interest in her surroundings, Dot agreed to join Elizabeth and Lucky Pierre to pick poppies in a nearby field.

Lucky Pierre was the Supply Officer for the hospital and its support units. On his uniform was the two silver bars of a Captain. No one seemed to know Lucky Pierre's offical name, but since he was a third generation resident of New Orleans, it was believed to be Peter, followed by an unpronounceable French surname. The lucky-part of the name had been earned, not because of his dashing good looks that beguiled the ladies— he was not much taller than Dot, with a portly build, and hair that had evacuated his head in favor of his eyebrows—but because he had a good-humored, generous personality (which he claimed he inherited from his paternal grandmother). Because Lucky Pierre was smart and personable, anyone who met him felt an immediate kindship.

Dot had met Lucky Pierre on the night of their arrival in Oran when she went in search of a hot cup of coffee. She asked a man loitering outside the chow hall if he could help her.

"Chow is closed for now but I'll find something to suit you." He walked her over to the small building next door. He rustled up packets of Nescafé instant coffee, a tea kettle, an actual china cup, and a can of sterno fuel fitted in a folding camp stove for her to take back to her tent.

"Compliments of Lucky Pierre," he said. "This will set you up for a cozy, relaxing coffee break, day or night." His smile was sincere. Dot saw in his manner that there were no strings attached and it made her want to trade something in return.

"If you ever need a band-aid or your temperature taken, you come see me when I'm on duty. I'm Dot Chinnis."

"I'll do that. And when you're settled, I'll take you to pick poppies. Bring your girlfriends. We'll make it a 'field' trip."

Dot laughed at the play on words and agreed to the outing. When Dot was stronger, she and Elizabeth set a time with Lucky Pierre to do just that.

The three of them hopped a ride in a Jeep that was heading their way. Their driver, Jock, gave them a tour-guide narrative along the way as they passed a few abandoned homes that were only meager huts, really.

"Look over there," Elizabeth pointed at a tree growing close to one of the shacks.

A scrawny old camel was nibbling unhurriedly from the Date Palm tree. He watched them passively as they drove past, not allowing the passersby to disturb his fruit snack.

"That's old Ali Baba," Lucky Pierre said helpfully. "He's too old to use for work so he's been let loose to fend for himself. We often see him on this route."

Elizabeth asked Jock for a quick stop so she could take a photo of the legendary Ali Baba with her Brownie box camera. "I want to memorialize this moment. I've never met a camel before."

Jock made a U-turn. He pulled to a stop in the middle of the road. Elizabeth jumped out to take the photo.

"Go on over there and pet the poor boy. I'll take your photograph with him," Jock offered.

"The picture of him standing alone is just fine. Really!" Elizabeth said. "Besides, I heard they spit, and I don't want to spend the rest of the day with dromeadary sputum on me."

"Good call," Jock grinned at her. He restarted the Jeep and drove his passengers to the poppy field. "I'll finish my job in an hour, so meet me back at this point if you want a ride back to the hospital."

The sun was hot, but a light breeze washed over the poppy flowers making waves of red. "How in the world did you find this place?" Elizabeth asked Lucky Pierre.

"One of my supply contacts told me about it. He says the poppies are used by a drug cartel, but I think it's abandoned. I haven't seen a soul here for ages and it's so beautiful I wanted to share it. It's likely you'll never find yourself in a poppy field again."

"The one poppy field I've ever seen was in the Wizard of Oz movie," Elizabeth said as she picked a bloom, reflexively bringing it to her nose for a sniff. "I hope we don't fall asleep."

"Ha. We may sleep better here than on our rickety cots," Lucky Pierre said. "My ol' Pa who was in the last war… "

"Oh, wait," Elizabeth butted in. "In France?" She hoped to solve the mystery of Lucky Pierre's nom de guerre.

"Actually, yes. He *was* in the trenches of France. Anyway, my ol' Pa said to me before I left the states, 'Boy, see and do everything you can while you're over there. Not just war-related experiences, but tourist ones too. Let those moments get stuck in your brain, not the gore of war.'"

Dot smiled. She had lost her own father when she was seven years old and loved hearing Dad stories. "I like your ol' Pa," she said. "Smart man."

On Sunday the nurses of Charlie Tent attended church services held in the chow hall. Mail call came after lunch and Dot's spirits were improved even more by the four letters she held tightly in her hand. She found a wooden crate sitting in the shade. She plopped down on it to read her correspondence.

She started with the letter from her sister, Margie. Margie wished Dot a happy birthday and hoped the letter and package arrived in time. She told Dot that Jack had come to Charleston for a visit with the Chinnis family one weekend and they went to Folly Beach for a picnic. Dot was pleased that Jack fit in, but felt a pang of jealousy that it was not possible for Jack to have a picnic with her. She read the next two letters. One was from Fran Edwards, her friend from nursing school and Fort Jackson hospital (she had received her deployment letter and would send more information when possible). The other letter was from one of her favorite professors who wished her well in her wartime duties. Dot was delighted to get news from home, but she was most excited about the letter she saved to read last. From Jack.

Jack described his visit to Charleston and how accepted he felt within the family. Dot reined in her envy—all was well at home, and soon enough Jack would be in battle. And, as she would learn, *that's* no picnic at the beach.

Duty shifts had begun for the 58th nurses. To improve survival rates for casualties, nurses in the war zone provided various highly skilled levels of care and treatment. They cleaned wounds, changed dressings, administered blood transfusions, assisted in surgery, and maintained post-surgical care. All of these skills included within the scope of the nurse's professional practice were vital life-or-death services.

Perhaps just as important as giving medical aid, was a nurse's ability and willingness to feed the spirit of the wounded man under her care. Doing that could encourage a seriously injured man to have the will to live. To gasp, or to look at him with pity, was a death sentence. In order to deliver the first outcome successfully nurses needed to take their minds off the gritty reality of war when they were off duty. Cora made an overture in that department.

"Who's going with me to the movie tent tonight?" she asked her tentmates.

Watching the feature films sent from Hollywood to military outposts filled leisure time for Army personnel. Off-duty recreation kindled cheerfulness and a better frame of mind to share with their patients. The Palm Beach Story, a madcap comedy starring Claudette Colbert, Joel McCrea, Mary Astor, and Rudy Vallee had just been announced as the film of the month.

"No point asking what else is playing because there's just one movie *and* we're all going to see it sooner or later."

"Are you not going as someone's date?" Maddy asked. "I'm surprised we will have the pleasure of your company with so many men around."

"I've sworn off men at the moment." Exaggerated gasps filled the tent.

"Count me in," Dot said. "What time is it playing?" She laid a blouse down beside her on the bed that she had mended in the dim light.

"They show it at ten, two and four, plus a show at 8 p.m. so we'll all have a chance to catch it no matter our schedules."

"Oh! Dr Pepper time," Charlotte joked. "With a bonus show tagged on the end."

"Wise-cracker! Who else is in?" Cora asked.

The women coordinated show times with their duty shifts. Dot and Charlotte agreed to go with Cora that night. Popcorn was available for the attendees, and the Red Cross had dropped off crates of Coca Colas as well. The nurses found chairs together in one of the five rows set up and watched the beginning of the ten-minute Movietone news reel that preceded the film. It was from September the previous year so the audience talked through Lowell Thomas' narration. The Palm Beach Story was finally queued up and the room quieted. For an hour and a half, the attendees were immersed in a carefree, zany story.

Dot was on duty the following morning. After breakfast, she hurried to the small office off the ward where she looked at the charts of the men in her care. Doctors' orders were neatly handwritten by the nurse who handed the file off to her replacement during the shift change. For each patient, Dot checked temperatures, medication doses, food requirements, and whether bandages needed to be changed. Breakfast for the patients was important, and enlisted men—EMs—trained as orderlies, helped with that. If a patient was able to walk, he was assisted to the dining hall. If more help was needed, an EM sat by the bedside of the wounded man to feed him. Several of the patients were mobile enough to pitch in which freed nurses to see to more complex medical procedures.

The folder on top of the stack belonged to Private First Class Anthony Roberts. Dot walked over to his bedside.

"Morning, Private," Dot addressed him with a smile. She tilted her head to make eye contact more obvious. He had one leg outside the covers, wrapped in yards of white gauze. His scrunched facial expression told Dot it was time for more pain killers. "Where are you from?" she said as she prepared a syringe of morphine. "Where's home for you?"

"Stanly County, ma'am. North Carolina. Born and raised."

"It's always a pleasure to meet a fellow southerner. I'm from down Charleston-way myself. Let's take a look at your injuries."

Dot bent over the bed. She unwrapped bandages that covered a deep gash in Roberts' right calf. The wound was jagged, muscle damage was a possibility but the tissue around the torn flesh was pink and had no odor. As she applied antiseptic and rewrapped the leg with fresh gauze she said, "This is looking good." The optimism in her tone caught the attention of the Private as he winced in pain at having his leg moved around.

"I know it's still sore," Dot said. "But you're on the mend. Besides a dashing scar to impress the ladies, you'll make a full recovery. In a couple of days we'll get you up on your feet, maybe with crutches at first, and then you can walk yourself to the chow line."

"I was afraid I was going to lose it. The leg. When I got hit by the shrapnel, I looked down at the bloody mess and I thought it was a goner. I was afraid I was going to leave a piece of me behind. If what you say is true, it feels like a miracle."

"Maybe it is," Dot said. She hoped there were plenty of miracles to go around but she saw that a few of the men in the hospital ward didn't feel as lucky as Private Roberts.

"Will I get back to my unit soon?"

"I don't have the power to make those kinds of decisions, Private. My only job is to be right here, right now, and make sure you're taken good care of. But if I was a betting woman, I'd put money on that outcome."

"I can go for that. And, right-here, right-now is not so bad for me after all. These other poor boys, though…." His voice trailed off as he cleared his throat. Like most warriors, Roberts had a sentimental side.

"These other poor boys," Dot broke in as she tucked the bed sheets tightly around her patient, "are not for you to worry about. Not yet. You worry about you. Get yourself healed, then when you're up on your feet, you can help them with their food and their toilet needs and give them an encouraging word. That's it. Okay?"

"Ma'am, yes ma'am!" Roberts beamed at her.

With an economy of words, Lieutenant Dorothy Chinnis took away a sizeable chunk of survivor's guilt that was weighing Roberts down. Dot's next patient was sleeping deeply. He had been given a sedative to relax him. A thoracic wound, once again from shrapnel, was going to have a different outcome for this soldier.

Dot's circle of friends grew from the sisterhood of nurses, to Lucky Pierre the Supply Officer, and most recently to include

Terrio, the Mess Sergeant. Getting to know the guy responsible for providing meals to the camp was not her motivation, she just liked his big heart. He occupied a small villa near the hospital and occasionally provided home-cooked meals for his friends.

Like Lucky Pierre, Terrio knew the lay of the land and made himself at home. When deliveries didn't materialize in their war zone location, he scavenged local sources for food. Although Germany had surrendered North African territory, their position was still very much in a war zone, as were the sea lanes leading to its harbors. An artful Mess Sergeant will find food sources when it's necessary to feed the troops, relying on whatever is handy and available. When prepared carefully, local food need not cause the gastro distress that is likely otherwise. Terrio relied on C-rations only if it was absolutely necessary.

Dot and her friends were invited to dinner on Thursday night at Terrio's villa. He had fixed a stew comprised of unidentifiable stringy meat and a few vegetables bought earlier at the public market. As Dot chewed the first bite, she had a difficult time keeping the food down.

"If I didn't know better, I'd say this is old Ali Baba," she joked.

"That old camel out by the road to town?" someone else asked for clarification. All eyes moved to Terrio for confirmation. He tried to look innocent of the charge, but failed.

"Come to think of it, I haven't seen him around in a while," someone else mentioned.

"Camel meat is a staple food of desert nomad tribes. It has been for centuries," Terrio said in his defense. "I had to make do. It *is* protein, and if you were raised to eat wild game then, it's…"

"…lumpy," Dot completed his sentence. "I *was* raised on wild game, but I'm going to have to decline tonight's fare." She was gentle but firm in her decision. "Instead, may I have a peanut butter sandwich, or anything that doesn't have a first name?"

Terrio was accommodating and after the meal, he conjured up iced lemonade for his guests, made of real lemons. Its fresh tangy flavor was refreshing as well as healthy. If Terrio couldn't convince his friends to eat camel stew, he would at least see to it that they didn't get scurvy.

"I've also got pineapple juice," he told them. "I can send a quart home with you, if you'd like." The nurses of Charlie Tent agreed that was a grand idea. Terrio sent bread with them, to go with the can of spam he gave them as well.

"Great for making midnight snacks," he assured them. "The men in the chow line tomorrow will get a crack at the camel stew that you didn't eat tonight. This will tide you over for now."

"You're too good to us!" Dot told him.

Dot's appetite returned in spite of the camel stew episode. As she was able to eat more food, her strength returned, as did her optimistic outlook on life in general. One evening she and Gillie decided to walk to Fleurus, a small village close to the hospital.

"Are you sure you're up to this?" Gillie asked. She was concerned that Dot hadn't fully recuperated.

"I'm fine," Dot said. "Lucky Pierre said it's only a brief fifteen minute walk."

As they approached the village they saw small shops with apartments built above them for the families who ran them. Effort had been taken to present a friendly, inviting atmosphere for the Allies occupying the area, but evidence of recent battles left scars. The region had been fought for and changed hands several times over the last thousand years, from the Moors to the Spanish, and most recently to the French.

Dot and Gillie noticed that the white-washed buildings maintained a Spanish flavor. The face of one shop had crumbled to rubble, though. And craters in the roadway meant that vehicles, both motorized and animal-powered, careened sharply to avoid the holes like they were inside a pinball machine.

"We'll be lucky to survive the day!" Gillie teased.

Dot pointed to a side path. "Let's follow that. Hopefully, we'll find a café."

When they found a little tea shop, they sat at a table beneath an awning. They ordered mint tea and shared a delicious pistachio pastry.

"What do you think of our tentmates, Chigger? I know we got to know them a little on the ship, but now that we're sleeping together in one big room, I've noticed a few interesting things."

"Do tell," Dot encouraged her.

"For starters, Cora seems extra chummy with the enlisted men. That's hands off for us since we're officers. I hope she isn't being silly there."

"That's on her if she is. She's been through the same training we have and she should understand how the birds and the bees work." Dot was thoughtful for a moment. "I'm fond of her though, she's always cheerful."

Gillie agreed then went on. "Anne and Jane seem to suck the joy out of the atmosphere, though. I don't see the benefit of complaining about the food or the bunks or anything else since there's nothing to be done about any of it."

"They're good at their jobs, though," Dot said. "And we can't all be as delightful as you are." She winked at Gillie playfully.

"That's for sure! I wasn't sure I'd take to Maddy because she's posh and seems so independent and aloof, but she adds class to our group. She's our Momma Duck. Elizabeth is practical. Give her a problem and she'll chew on it until she has a solution. Same with Charlotte. I guess we've got a pretty good group."

"I'd trust them with my life," Dot said

On Friday evening Dot, Charlotte, Maddy, and Anne went with Lucky Pierre to Café Monies. He was showing them a variety of suitable places to visit outside the hospital base. This café was located at the *Mediterranean Base Section Headquarters,* or M.B.S., as it was more generally known. The M.B.S. was organized into a small town with amenities available to G.I.s stationed there. Every effort was made to create an environment where the Americans could relax and feel comfortable.

The group sat down at a table for their meal, but before anyone had a chance to initiate a conversation sirens screamed warnings of impending danger. The women looked at Lucky Pierre.

"Air raid," he said.

The manager of the establishment stepped into the dining room and made a hasty public announcement. "Ladies and gentleman, we have word that enemy aircraft, probably Italians heading back to their air bases at home, are making a bead directly for our location. Please put on your helmets and follow me to the bomb shelter behind this building." He pointed out the direction.

Dot and her dinner companions looked around the table, unable to utter a word, eyes as wide as saucers. A sharp intake of breath substituted for meaningful action. Since the Axis forces had surrendered, the nurses anticipated seeing no combat themselves. They wondered if this was a bad dream.

Dot broke the silence in a calm, matter of fact way. "Let's do as the man says." She stood up and placed the tin bonnet on her head with one hand while grabbing her handbag with the other. She led the way out of the restaurant. Lucky Pierre brought up the rear, making sure no one was left behind. The women crouched in a dugout near the concrete wall, shored up by stacks of sand-filled gunny sacks, just as the drone of aircraft deafened them.

"Don't they know when to give up?" Charlotte shook her head in disbelief.

"They've been ordered home," shouted the manager over the cacophony of sound. "They can't go home with unused shells. They can fly further and quicker if they lighten their load. Don't worry, it'll be over soon and if your name's not on the bomb, you're safe as…," his sentence was cut off as he dove to safety.

Red balls of flames erupted a hundred yards east of the café. That portion of the street had been battered before and was abandoned. The onlookers felt heat radiate from the explosion but had covered their ears too late to block the concussive reverberation. Anti-aircraft guns fired off rounds in the background but did not hit their mark. The guns' presence did alert the pilots, though, that flying this route was not a walk in the park. Navigators radioed the next wave of aircraft to avoid the region.

Back in their tents, the women talked into the night about their experience. The conversations had one theme. *What if…*

"It's no good thinking that way," Elizabeth shook her head. "We're here to do a job. If we wonder what ghoulish things will happen each time we walk around this corner, or that corner, we'll second guess every moment and never get the job done."

"I agree," Dot added. "As the restaurant manager said, our name is either on the bomb or not. It's in God's hands. We just have to get on with our duty."

Charlotte countered, "That may be so but there's no need to be cavalier or to take unnecessary chances. Why tempt fate? We should continue to wear our helmets and duck when there's flack."

Dot thought they had already been rather cavalier by volunteering for overseas duty. Regardless of her bold outlook, Dot wrote in her diary that night: *My first air raid. Scared, not much!*

But the nurses had had their first test by fire, and although it was frightening, they knew they could feel fear and still function.

Their terrifying experience did not deter the nurses from visiting other points of interest in their exotic neighborhood. After end of duty one afternoon, Dot and four other nurses hitched a ride into the city of Oran to have a look around. The Red Cross pamphlet illustrated the fascinating history of Oran and the North African region. Elizabeth read from it:

Oran is a city of a quarter million residents. Its location above the Gulf of Oran in the Mediterranean Sea means that Fort Santa Cruz, one of three forts connected by tunnels, was able to secure the strategic military area built by the Spaniards in 1577.

From this hilltop, an observer is afforded a 360° panoramic view. The Chapel of the Blessed Virgin sits snugly against the slope of the hill just below the fort and is adorned with beautiful Christian iconography. The museum, also nearby, holds collections of Moorish artwork including relief panels and inlays.

The nurses marveled at the sights. They reflected on the long, complex history of Oran and how they, themselves, were now becoming part of that history. While sight-seeing, they stopped at a Red Cross post. Whereas many of the posts operated out of mobile trucks or from tents, this more permanent one occupied a small storefront sandwiched in a row of shops on the main street. The nurses enjoyed a traditional American hotdog supper and washed their supper down with a tepid bottle of Coca Cola.

Six

Diary Entry ~ May 23, 1943
We got a floor in our tent!

A hectic schedule at the hospital eventually gave way to some spare time for Dot and Charlotte. They returned to Charlie Tent to relax, but before Dot could lie down on her cot to read her newest paperback, she had to sweep away a pile of sand that had blown in and settled on her bed covers.

Charlotte commented from across the aisle. "Our accumulated sand dunes are as impressive as any in the Sahara," she said.

"Hyperbole much?" Dot laughed.

"You know it's not far from the truth. It gets into everything—clothes, hair, even the toothpaste."

Dot, satisfied with her efforts to clear the worst of the sand away, tossed herself onto the cot and propped her head on her pillow. There was a danger she would drift off before many pages were read.

Charlotte hovered over an article about the U.S. Women's Air Corps in the month-old McCall's magazine. Out of the corner of her eye, she caught a movement of something that startled her. At first Charlotte wasn't sure what she was looking at, thinking it was some kind of vermin creeping into the tent. Then she spied a small brown arm sliding underneath the canvas of the tent-side, reaching toward the head of Dot's bed. Charlotte sat up and leaned forward to get a better view.

"Dottie," Charlotte whispered. "Dottie," she said again a little louder. "Look to your right, on the ground near the tent's edge."

Dot did as told. Her eyes popped open and she yelped when she saw the little hand reaching under her bed helping himself to something out of her B-bag. Dot grasped his little wrist and pulled the boy into the tent.

It was hard to tell for sure, but the boy looked to be about eight years old. He was skin and bones, no more. His brown face showed surprise at being caught but he was not frightened. Dot thought a little shame should have been reflected in his expression. After all, he was indeed attempting to steal things that didn't belong to him.

"What are you doing?" She demanded.

"Please, miss. I mean no harm. I was looking for something I lost."

"You didn't lose anything under my bed. Let's you and me have a chat with the base commander."

Charlotte followed along in case Dot needed assistance, which she didn't. Before they made it to the commander's office, Dot saw Miss Parsons walking toward them with a quizzical look on her face about what she was seeing. She was curious about what brought this threesome together.

"He was taking items from our tent," Dot stated firmly but without rancor.

Miss Parsons shook her head. "Malik, you promised me there would be no more stealing. Now you will be forbidden to come on base for one week. Do you understand?"

"Yes, miss."

Parsons motioned for an enlisted man to escort the boy off the grounds.

"Local residents have very little," Parsons explained. "They own next to nothing, in fact. We do what we can to help, but pilfering anything not nailed down is a way for them to barter for food. We're tougher on the adults when we catch them at it, so they send in the children because they know we have a soft spot for them."

"It's an odd culture," Charlotte observed.

"Yes," Miss Parsons agreed, "but it's their culture and we try to find a way to mitigate it when it affects us. Move your gear away from the edge of the tent. They rarely step foot inside, they just reach in from the outside."

"It gave us a fright," Charlotte confessed.

———————

Charlie Tent was notified the next day to vacate the premises between 0730 and 1400 hours. Miss Parsons told them that they would be first in line to have a wood-plank floor installed. When the occupants returned and inspected the job, they saw that the canvas sides of the tents had been nailed firmly to the floorboards.

Charlotte believed the floor would help minimize the sand that blew in. "We'll find some rugs, that'll help too," she said.

"I'm so happy about our new floor, I want to celebrate." Cora weighed in on their good fortune. "Let's share our stroke of luck with a party." The Charlie Tent gals threw an impromptu drop-in that night.

New acquaintances stopped by to offer congratulations. Visitors contributed goodies they had received from home—hard candies, cookies, and boiled peanuts. Fudge, made fresh over the Bunsen burner in the patient wards that day, was passed around as the party continued into the evening.

Everyone chatted and got to know each other, sharing news and gossip from home. Nurses assigned to early morning duty ran everyone off at ten o'clock so they could get some sleep.

———————

Over a month had passed since Dot felt Jack holding her tenderly in his arms under the full South Carolina moon. To Dot, it felt like a lifetime ago—a dream almost. She replayed the moment of their goodbye in her mind to make sure that Jack was real, not a figment of her imagination. Her love for him had not faded in any way, but time and distance made her question if she had conjured him up out of thin air. She looked at her engagement ring, that was real. She turned the lucky silver dollar over and over in her hand, that was real, too. The common connection to loved ones at home came through letters. The most tangible bond Dot felt with Jack was when she looked at the moon each night. The two of them were worlds apart but they gazed at the same moon. It was their secret.

In her reverie, Dot wondered why Jack's unit had not deployed. Since his regiment was attached to the Seventh Army, chances were good that they would follow a route similar to Dot's 58th Hospital group. She'd gotten no word of his travel plans, though, and she couldn't have known that Jack's unit was part of the intense training maneuvers in the mountains of Tennessee in preparation for the push through the Vosges Mountains of France into Germany.

Winning the war in Europe required an invasion from the south as well as a landing force on the west coast of France. U.S. troops already on European soil would move to the Italian peninsula, north into France, and then ever closer to Berlin. By the time all that took place, fresh battalions would be needed to relieve those exhausted men at the front. It looked like that would be Jack's unit. She didn't know how much training would be required, nor the amount of time necessary for planning and practicing the mission because Jack's letters included little more than a generalized account of his day and his undying love for Dot. It was all she needed to know.

While writing her own letters to Jack, Dot failed to mention the air raid or any other hardship she tolerated. She would not have mentioned the event even if she had been unafraid of the censors. She wondered what he failed to mention to her.

When off duty, the nurses of the 58th organized picnics and swimming parties at their favorite destination, a Mediterranean beach called Arzew. This slice of paradise was a forty-five minute Jeep-ride from Oran. JoJo Rankin and Timothy Fairweather were drivers with the motor pool and could always be counted on for a lift if they were not otherwise engaged in official Army business.

Arzew Beach was a gorgeous setting for relaxing and daydreaming. Dot sat on her towel looking out over the blue sea. The weather and the view were perfect. Anne had detached herself from Cora who was flirting with several young G.I.s and walked over to Dot.

"May I join you?" she asked. She shaded her eyes from the afternoon sun with her hand. It resembled a salute. Arzew Bay was protected by a crescent shaped peninsula. Sitting in that curve put the sun in the west as it began its descent.

"Certainly," Dot told her. "But I warn you, I won't be as fun as that group." She pointed at Cora and her crowd splashing in waist high water. Cora's squeals carried a distance.

"This suits me better anyway. Although I can't believe I want to surround myself with *more* sand." Anne laid her towel out beside Dot as she laughed at her little joke. It was a sweet, pleasing sound.

"Are you settling in okay?" Dot asked. Her tone was tempered with concern.

"Pretty well. I talk to Major Whitfield twice a week. We discuss the trauma of losing my fiancé. I'm starting to feel more sensible."

Dot had heard the story of the fiancé's suicide but had not heard Anne speak of it herself. She hoped bringing the event out into the light of day was healthy. She decided to be as outspoken.

"There's been talk, of course, I'm sorry to say," Dot said. "How he took his own life."

"Yes. A tragedy for everyone who knew him. Not just me. But I was there, you see. And the Major is helping me realize that although I couldn't help him, I shouldn't let that failure get in the way of being helpful to the boys here."

"That's a fine way to look at it. Would you mind if I added my own point of view to what you just said?" Dot got an affirmative nod. "The way I see it, you may have *failed* to stop your fiancé from dying at the moment but his death is not your *failure*. I hope you see my distinction, because if he was determined to put an end to things he would have found a way. There's no real way to know for sure, of course. But I assure you that no one blames his death on you."

"I appreciate your candor. I'll consider adjusting my point of view, but it still feels awfully fresh."

"I can't imagine. But as Lucky Pierre suggested the other day, we should see and do fantastic and wonderful things while we're here to let those moments get stuck in our brains, not the horrible stuff."

"I agree with that. But don't you miss your fiancé? Being away from him?" Anne changed the subject.

"Every moment of every day. I feel like a love sick adolescent. But that's just the cards we're dealt. We have to make do. And one way of doing that is to have fun with friends. You're doing that. I am too. Shall we pat ourselves on the back?"

"I see your point but here we sit, on the beach, while Cora is over there kicking up her heels with the boys."

Dot smiled. "And now I see *your* point. But would splashing around with googly-eyed men be 'fun' for us? I'm enjoying myself just where I am, thank you very much." She bumped shoulders with Anne. Anne smiled as she understood what Dot was getting at. Finding solace in her own way, and in her own time was another step toward healing.

Back at camp, Dot was resting on her cot, trying to repair from the heat of the afternoon, when Gillie returned.

"Hey, Chigger," she said. "I was talking to some folks just now. They say there's a Bob Hope USO show this Saturday night. Are you free? Want to go?"

All the off-duty nurses went to the show together. The stage had been erected on the side of a scrubby hill near the hospital. Enlisted men and ambulatory patients made their way to the venue where chairs had been set in rows. A number of the enlisted men brought an extra chair with them to the show, just in case it was needed. Good thing, as the crowd grew larger.

At last, the Master of Ceremony asked for a round of applause as Bob Hope stepped out onto the shaded stage. He walked up to the microphone, dressed in khakis looking the world as if this was the happiest moment of his life. The star of stage and film introduced Tony Romano and Dorothy Lamour who joined him on the stage. The applause grew louder. Whistles, catcalls, and shouting rose above that. He thanked the crowd before starting the joke routine. He rapid fired them into the mic, holding the audience's attention by avoiding a lull in the performance.

"Took a while to fly in to this place," he told them. "I had plenty of time to read a novel on the flight. But I'm a slow reader.

On the way back, I'll read the second page." He didn't break for the roars of laughter to fade.

"We hit a little turbulence in the plane. The pilot turned around and asked me, 'are you nervous?' I said yes, it's only my third time up. He said, 'you got me beat, it's just my first.' I said, are you prepared with parachutes for us all? He said, 'don't be silly, the ones with parachutes jumped an hour ago.'"

"And speaking of rough, as we flew over the Atlantic, the **automatic pilot** bailed out..., I've never seen anything like it."

Worries were forgotten for whole moments at a time. Laughter felt good in the belly. It eased the wistful longing for home. Attention sharpened when Dorothy Lamour joined Bob Hope on the stage.

"These boys are having a rugged time down here, I tell ya," Hope told her. "But I wish I was one of them."

"I don't know if you could do it," she shot back. "See, fighting is hard. When you fight, you have to forget all about fear...,"

"THAT'S FOR ME!" Hope interjected.
"You have to forget all about comfort...,"
"THAT'S FOR ME!" He said even louder.
"You have to forget all about women...,"
*"THAT'S FOR **THEM**!"* He ceded.

More howls from the audience. Hope left Dorothy Lamour standing alone near the microphone. He receded into the background as Tony Romano walked forward with his guitar to accompany her as she sang,

I'll be seeing you in all the old familiar places
That this heart of mine embraces, all day through...

In a daydream, Dot saw Jack standing in the garden outside the officer's club at Fort Jackson, dressed in his uniform, saying his goodbyes to her under the full moon. She looked up into the sky over Oran. Another full moon. Bright and shiny. Polished by Jack, just for her.

In that small café, the park across the way
The children's carousel, the chestnut tree, the wishing well

I'll be seeing you in every lovely summer's day
In everything that's light and gay, I'll always think of you that way

I'll find you in the morning sun and when the night is new
I'll be looking at the moon, but I'll be seeing you!

Maybe Jack was looking at the moon too. Right now. But seven o'clock at night here meant it was one o'clock in the afternoon at home. *Maybe not*, she sighed. She would make herself stay up until midnight when the moon would be on the rise in Jack's world. Dot looked around her. The crowd was mesmerized. Dorothy Lamour continued her song.

I'll find you in the morning sun and when the night is new
I'll be looking at the moon, but I'll be seeing you!

Every eye was on the beautiful singer, and tears filled every one of those eyes. Dot was not alone. Each soul in the crowd longed for home, for loved ones far away. When would this horrible war be over?

The song ended, but the sniffing and throat-clearing continued for a while longer. Slowly, the audience began to applaud. The applause grew in volume, accompanied by shouting and hooting at the performance.

Then a G.I.—just one—noticed the nurses sitting together off to the side of the main audience. He stood up and shouted, "Hey, look fellows. Those are our nurses over there." He clapped, slow, deliberate. Word spread through the audience that nurses were present. The show stopped while the men stood up. Shouts of *Hurrah for our nurses!* and *Our nurses are the best!* reached the ears of the women who were caught off guard by the applause meant for them. The wide grins on the young fighters' faces showed how much they appreciated the contributions of the fairer sex and they wanted to show them.

Bob Hope, back on center stage, joined in the swell of appreciation for the women. He stepped nearer the microphone and said, "What a privilege to be here with you! You crawl through the mud and you fight the insects and the weather, in addition to the enemy. You work through days like they are hours. And, yes, *thank you* to our nurses who are here patching up our heroes as they sacrifice blood and limbs and lives." Not a peep from the audience now.

"Everybody back home misses you." He didn't shout it. There was no need to. The audience was silent.

"They have but one thought in mind..., to get you boys back home. They're working hard for you at home. They're making your shoes, your uniforms, your Jeeps, your guns, your ammunition, your tanks. They're doing without gasoline themselves and growing their own food so that the majority of food production goes to you boys here on the frontlines."

These words hit the boys in their gut.

"Thank you all!" Bob Hope told them in closing. "God Bless!"

A church service was held on that same hillside the next day with most of the same people in attendance. Terrio instructed his cooks to make Sunday dinner special. Gravy and potatoes filled the gaps between fried chicken pieces like mortar between bricks. As always, food was craftily stretched beyond expectations.

Miss Parsons and Major Whitfield brought their trays over to the table where Dot's group had gathered.

"A couple of items of interest," Parsons told them matter-of-factly. "Great news about the new floor in your tent." *Always lead with the good news.* "But…"

"There's always a 'but'," Elizabeth interrupted before she could stop herself.

"But, the Army doesn't feel a new floor is important enough to let the four of you stay behind." She had the women's attention.

"Chinnis, Belle, Bedford, and McGill, you'll be assigned temporary duty at the 180th Station Hospital at the Sainte Barbe-du-Tlélat Airfield near Oued Tlelat."

Dot, Charlotte, Maddy, and Gillie looked confused. The Arab words had rolled off Parsons' tongue but landed in their ears like gobbledy gook. Parsons knew by their expressions that a further explanation was needed.

"It's a place twenty five miles southeast of here. Sainte Barbe, we call it for short. Much easier to remember."

"Why are we being moved so soon after our arrival?" Maddy asked. Dot, Charlotte, and Gillie leaned in with keen interest.

"Since you've just arrived, and since there are a lot of you at the moment, we'll spread you around a little. It's called Detached Service. *D-S* in Army lingo. It means you're on loan. It's temporary. The staff there needs R & R. You're not changing your affiliation with the unit, you're still part of the 58th, but you will be substitutes, filling in where needed."

Whitfield picked up from there. "As you prepare to travel, take your personal things with you. Leave behind the extra things you've accumulated for your residence for the next inhabitants of

Charlie Tent because when you're done at Sainte Barbe's, you may not come back here."

"It's barely been three weeks," Gillie remarked. "We're not even settled in."

"Three weeks is a long time in our circumstances," Parsons assured her. "And orders are orders. Prepare to leave at a moment's notice but you should know that it could be a day or a week before you transport out. Look, every sacrifice you make will be hard, some harder than others, but it's worth it. Your contributions are essential, wherever they are needed." The women knew this, but it was always nice to hear.

The last day of the month arrived and Dot's group had not left for Sainte Barbe. As any American worker knows, the last day of the month is Pay Day!! There was no reason to announce the paymaster's visit by loud speaker since the knowledge of his arrival preceded him. He carried enough cash to cover the pay for all the individuals stationed with the 58th. He was protected by an armed guard who stood nearby as the paymaster sat at his desk just inside the chow hall. Enlisted men and officers invested a few minutes of their spare time to stand in line so they could sign for their pay. Dot received combat pay of $131.40 for the month. The amount had been happily increased because of her current overseas status. She cabled most of it home.

The cash that Dot kept back for herself for incidentals was satisfying but meant nothing compared to the V-mail she received from Jack at mail call.

V-mail was a letter-sending process the United States Government implemented for wartime correspondence between soldiers stationed abroad and civilians at home. Bulky letters posted internationally from the U.S. were expensive to transport. To reduce costs, the military developed the V-mail postal system.

The sender, in this case Jack, took his letter to the post office where it would be forwarded to a military postal station. After the censors read it, it was copied to microfilm. Upon its arrival overseas, the letter was printed back to paper near its destination before being delivered. Dot did not care about the tomfoolery that went into V-mail. The only thing that mattered was, *he still loves me*. The letter made her feel ten-feet tall. Dot would do her duty no matter what but with Jack's love, she was ready to face the hardships sent her way.

Dot was over the moon for days and her joy carried her through her first sand storm. There was little warning before the winds blew into the area with hurricane force and whipped the sharp crystalline particles into a frenzy. The sand stung like needles. It was embedded into animate and inanimate objects alike. Sand caused severe damage to the lungs and eyes and a multitude of new medical complaints presented themselves.

"I now know what Lawrence of Arabia went through," Gillie joked to Dot.

When the storm passed, and after the eyewash had been passed around, the women were rewarded for their perseverance when a general announcement was broadcast that a shipment of chocolate ice cream had just arrived.

Seven

Diary Entry ~ June 1, 1943
A true dust storm today.

"Finish packing, girls. We'll be heading out after lunch." Maddy took it upon herself to organize the group going to the 180th Station Hospital at Sainte Barbe.

"At least we were here long enough to get our pay packets," Gillie said. "I wish the Army got our transportation organized as efficiently." She was losing the battle against stuffing 9000 cubic inches of clothing and gear into an 8000-cubic inch duffle bag.

"How did you wind up with more clothes than when we shipped out of New York harbor?" Maddy asked. Her bags were arranged neatly by the tent flap. She walked over to her cot, sat down, and lit a cigarette as if she was having a relaxing Mediterranean holiday.

"I wish I knew. It just grew somehow."

After Charlotte was packed, Maddy turned to Gillie. "Here's a tip," she said. "Roll up the small things and stuff them into your shoes and boots. Put those items at the bottom of the B-bag. Then put heavy clothing on top of that. Roll your other clothes into tight little sausages then stuff, stuff, stuff. You know the rest—toiletries, make-up, and so on, go into your handbag, A-bag and Musette bag."

"I'm sure I can make my clothes and toiletries fit, but I have books and boxes of cookies from home. I can't carry all of that by hand along with the helmet, the canteen, and..."

"No," said Maddy cutting her off. "You can't. But we can chip in and help you eat those cookies to make more room in your bag. You can bequeath those books to the gals we leave behind."

"Come to think of it," Charlotte butted in, "I may have a little extra room, for things like cookies anyway." She winked at Gillie

After Dot, Gillie, Charlotte, and Maddy were packed, they walked over to the chow hall for their lunch. Conversation was light. Miss Parsons stopped by the table. She had one last thing to say to them.

"You'll not be very far away. I'll come visit you in a couple of days and we'll stay in touch. You're not being pushed totally out of the nest so no worries there. Jump in and do your job. The nurses you're relieving are weary and need a rest. You're still fresh and you'll be fine. You have each other and you'll make new friends."

The transport truck was filled with the four nurses as well as several G.I.s who were going to Sainte Barbe's to fill open jobs there. Singing broke out right away.

Oh, give me land, lots of land under starry skies above
  - don't fence me in
Let me ride through the wide open country that I love
  - don't fence me in

The nurses were efficient and competent, and they quickly settled into their new four-cot tent home. Although they were the new kids on the block, they were no longer novices. After they were squared away, they dubbed their canvas home 'Charlie Tent

Two'. Shortened to *Charlie Two*, the tent yielded to the women's care and attention.

"This is like our own cozy cottage," Charlotte commented. She, Dot, Maddy, and Gillie reveled in the extravagance of electric lights and pillows.

"The latrine has flush toilets," Maddy told them after she had taken a peek.

When the women took their first hike up the hill to the chow hall, they saw actual *chairs* positioned at the tables. Sitting on chairs with backs erased any lingering nostalgia for the picnic benches at the previous dining facility.

"We should write back to the others and tell them we got an upgrade," Gillie teased.

"I bet that'll go over well," Dot said. "At least they wouldn't have to spend any more time feeling sorry for us."

A radio sat on the end of the counter, tuned to station playing country western swing. Gillie caught a faintly familiar phrase of music and cocked her head to hear it better.

"What's that?" Dot asked. The guitar riff was metallic, each note sustained before gliding into the next tone.

"If I'm not mistaken, that's Bob Dunn on his steel guitar. He plays with the Milton Brown boys."

Dot wasn't familiar with the genre, or the musicians. She listened a little longer, then said, "Steel guitar? I don't know how he does it, but he makes that thing whine. I can't say I'm a fan."

"I know. It's an acquired taste, and there's nothing whinier than a steel guitar, but my grandpa and his brothers play music that's very similar. Sounds like home to me."

After dinner Dot and Gillie roamed around the new neighborhood and discovered a recreation hall nearby.

"Look, Gillie! A ping pong table." Paddles and a ball sat on the table top invitingly. "Let's play."

"Why not," Gillie said. "We'll count this as our P.T." Dot and Gillie snickered at using ping pong instead of calisthenics for keeping the nurses Army-ready.

"We must be in heaven," Dot remarked. She was sad to leave her friends in Oran but the upgrades in their living situation, including all mod-cons, meant she was able to feel sympathy for the nurses they left behind.

Dot's group received its duty roster. Six wards were dedicated to wounded American G.I.s. Local residents and POWs had separate wards. With sleeves rolled to her elbows, Dot assisted in surgery and took charge of post-op treatments for the patients on her wards. Her shift started at two o'clock in the afternoon. At 8 p.m. she handed her notes to Gillie who was pulling the graveyard shift. She nodded as she looked over them, but wondered why Dot looked exhausted. She didn't see any mentions of unusual actions taken on behalf of the patients.

"What's up, Chigger? Why so tired?"

"I worked harder than ever today," Dot confessed. "Two out of the six wards have dysentery."

Gillie wrinkled her nose in anticipation of what she would face while on duty. *Oh*, was her response.

When dysentery hits a hospital ward of fully-grown, bed-ridden men, it's catastrophic. Intense interaction with each patient is compulsory, cleaning up his clothing and bedding is not optional. Re-hydration with fluids, either by mouth or intravenously, makes the difference between life and death. No warrior wants to leave this world under those inglorious conditions.

Gillie looked at the list of men and their doses of Paregoric. She glanced at the symptoms associated with each patient. Diarrhea, of course, but also fever and vomiting.

"The good news is…," Dot smiled while Gillie waited for the good news. "…the good news is that it will run its course in about ten days."

"Or we could start their de-mob orders now and move them back to the states tonight," Gillie countered.

Dot laughed for the first time in hours. "I like how you think!"

On the following morning Dot had time to write letters to Jack and to her loved ones at home catching them up with her current state of affairs, careful to not violate censorship restrictions. Miss Parsons arrived at the base before Dot reported to work to give the women their African Campaign Pins.

Dot, Gillie, Maddy, and Charlotte completed their assignment with the 180th in nine days. Packing went more smoothly this time and the goodbyes were easier as well as they handed the wards back to permanent staff. Their orders returned them to the Oran area where they were assigned to the 12th General Hospital. The 12th was a one-thousand-bed semi-permanent facility. It occupied several of the villas in the seaside resort town of Aïn El Turk. Complicated restorative surgery was performed routinely here. After post-op rehabilitation, sometimes taking several months, many of the soldiers were returned to active duty and the others were transported home. Infectious diseases were managed at the 12th as well as cases of combat fatigue which could be eased with rest.

The nurses didn't mind the move at all, not that they had a say in their placement, but the base sat right on the shore of the Mediterranean with a gorgeous view. The camp commander's villa was a converted winery and he made the facility available to his people at the 12th. He insured that the food provided was good, meaning it didn't come from an Army-issued tin can or a geriatric camel. Again, the tents had wooden plank floors covered with scavenged scraps of carpet. When free, the nurses swam in the warm 70-degree Mediterranean Sea.

Saturdays in a war zone are just another day. On duty or off, weekends held no more special sentiment for the young folks than other days of the week. Getting mail, however, was worth shouting about. Dot received a letter from her eldest sister, Ruby, which mentioned Dot's letter postmarked May 11, announcing a safe landing. *No destination given.* The complete letter exchange took a month. Two weeks either way. Now Dot had a hint of how long it would take for news from home to reach her.

Before Dot received more mail at her current post, she and her group were ordered to move again. They had been in Aïn El Turk for only five days. They were not told why they were being moved so soon, and they didn't ask. They were mere pawns being moved around the North African chessboard, but they suspected that they were being shifted in anticipation of rumored plans to invade Sicily. They had no direct knowledge of Operation Husky, or that it would take place in a month, but it didn't take a military genius to see that the ultimate path to Germany tracked next through Italy.

With North Africa cleared of Axis belligerents, the medical services scrambled to organize themselves into orderly levels or groups called echelons in response to the casualties created in the battles raging forward of them. The First World War Army hospitals had been stationary for the most part, treating Doughboys and Tommys straight off the battlefields that were also typically static. This generation's warfare was mobile. The challenge to meet the needs of the troops required various and differing echelons to adequately care for them. Triage on the battlefield rendered emergency first aid treatment on site. Those with serious injuries were moved on to clearing or evacuation stations. Men with injuries even more severe were transported to the station and general hospitals where surgeries and other complex procedures saved lives. That's what Dot's group was trained for. In North Africa the logical placement of hospital facilities meant a general migration east to the Bizerte-Tunis area. Medical services would be built up there to respond to casualties resulting from the invasion of Sicily and Italy from the Fifth Army. Time would tell when Dot's group would follow the fighting north into Europe.

"Time for us to pack up the ol' kit bag again, girls," Miss Parsons told the group at the Sunday afternoon meeting. "All of us are going, including Major Whitfield. Pack everything. We'll remain in North Africa, but we won't be coming back to this area again. The trip will take three or four days by train so collect fruit and bread to have handy. Top off your canteens with water, too. There should be rations on board, but we shouldn't trust that there will be adequate food for us all. The accommodations will be rather primitive, or so I'm told."

Miss Parson's assessment was right on the nose. The journey would ultimately take five grueling days.

The nurses prepared for their move all day Monday, buying necessary items at the market in Aïn El Turk and making their farewells to those they were leaving behind. They spent the whole next day waiting with their bags packed. Wednesday was much like Tuesday but they left for the train station in Oran at eight o'clock that night. Boarding the French train, Dot, Gillie, Charlotte, and Elizabeth looked for a passenger compartment to share.

"Here's one," Charlotte shouted at the others over the deafening noise. "Looks like the last empty one." It had two small bench seats that faced each other. Accommodating the four adults was a challenge.

"We'd have more room in a sardine can," Charlotte joked.

"It'd be tight wherever we sat, so let's make the best of it," Elizabeth said. "We want to stay together so this is the penance."

As they settled in, Dot noticed something that appeared to be an optical illusion—tiny black dots jumping and gyrating on the floor boards. Upon closer inspection, she saw that it was in reality a host of fleas doing calisthenics. Or were they trying to escape a hot frying pan?

"Looks like standing room only for humans and critters alike on this train," she said nodding toward the action.

"Oh no! What should we do?" Gillie asked.

"Get a dish of water," Dot instructed. "I'll find some soap to add to it. They'll jump in, and likely not jump out again."

The women worked together. They set the trap hoping to reduce the number of bites they would be scratching by morning. As the train started rattling down the track, they brought out food for their evening meal.

"Not exactly a dining car atmosphere, is it? I'd kill for a glass of wine," Gillie said.

Charlotte answered with, "The sleeping car will be just as finely appointed, I'm sure."

"I know you're being facetious," Gillie replied. "But I'm exhausted and I don't expect much shut-eye on our journey."

"I'm exhausted too. Two days of doing nothing more than *waiting* has worn me out! I can't believe *nothing* is so tiring." Dot kidded back.

"It's still easier than dealing with dysentery in the wards," Gillie added. Heads nodded in agreement.

"I'm not sure I can sleep sitting up," said Elizabeth.

"I can fit in the hat rack," Dot said looking up to the expanse of shelving jutting over the large window. "I'll need help up and down though."

"I'll join you," Gillie volunteered.

They tucked padding into strategic places, and with some maneuvering, the two women stretched out and settled down for the night. Charlotte and Elizabeth each had a bench to themselves. The rocking movement of the train successfully lulled the four of them to sleep without much assistance from the sandman.

Gillie woke up first. She peered over the railing at her traveling companions below her. They looked like pretzels with folded arms and bent knees. Instead of waking them she lowered herself down to the floor boards like she was doing chin-ups. She queued for the toilet at the end of the car with the early-birds.

The train moved the entire day on Thursday except for a stopover at the airfield near Kouba, two hundred miles east of Oran, and another brief break beyond that. Dot and two other nurses jumped off the train and ran a quarter of a mile to the lead car to refill their canteens with water. The women used some of it to brush their teeth on the railroad track.

The day wore on. The oppressive heat made the passengers sluggish. All the windows were opened, but the cross-draft was just more hot air. To shake the torpor they took turns riding on the steps of the train in the opening between the cars, safety being second to the moving air. A brief respite from the heat came when the train tumbled through tunnels. After a meager supper, Dot and her group reprised their accommodations of the night before.

On Friday morning, Dot was sick with gastroenteritis, *food poisoning*, to the uninitiated. For visitors to this part of the world, the question is not *if* you'll come down with this illness, but *when*. The symptoms are more than discomfort and inconvenience. E.coli bacteria in the food and inadequately treated drinking water can be deadly.

Fortunately, the passenger cars had restrooms and the lines formed with a pecking order of needs, determined solely based on the urgency reflected in each face. No sympathy was offered, but neither were jokes. A nod of the head recognized sufferers with the most urgency and allowed them to move to the head of the line. Simply ignoring to comment on the obvious predicament they found themselves in created a cloak of privacy. Dot endured her symptoms with all the grace she could muster.

After their third night on the train, and with nothing more than tomato juice for breakfast, Dot's stomach cramps worsened. Miss Parsons saw her doubled in pain and decided it was time to take action.

"I'm going to have the train stop at the next town with a hospital. We need to get you stabilized with fluids," she told Dot.

"Please let me stay with the group on the train," Dot begged. Pride had long ago been dropped by the wayside.

"I want to keep you with us, Chinnis, but you're not keeping anything down. You'll get accustomed to the food eventually but you're weak and you need more care than we can give you here in this situation."

"I'm feeling a little better," Dot pleaded. "And if I can tolerate some food and water before the next stop, consider keeping me with the group. I don't want to be separated. I don't want to be on my own. I don't know the language. I...," Tears formed. Dot would rather die with her friends than be sent away into the unknown, alone. "I'll get better care staying with the group. I don't want to be left behind. Not at any cost. Surely I get a say about my fate."

Miss Parsons gave in.

That night, Dot ate bread dipped in the wine that Charlotte and Gillie had bought at the last stop. *I'm relieved,* she wrote in her journal. *Tonight's meal went down well, and stayed down too.*

On Saturday, the train stopped for three hours in a market town large enough for the travelers to scavenge for more food. Dot, Charlotte, and Gillie looked for provisions and found bread to buy, but they hadn't returned to the train by the time it was ready leave. The engineer sent a British officer on his motorcycle to look for them. He located them and fetched them back to the train, one by one, with no more than a few seconds to spare.

When the passengers woke up Sunday, their fourth morning, the train stopped briefly for a church service to be held on the railroad track. Dot offered a silent prayer of thanks. This would be their last day on the train, and she was grateful to be with her friends.

Eight

Diary Entry ~ June 21, 1943
Arrived in Tunis. Rode to camp in ambulances.

After a week of travel, Dot's group finally arrived in the city of Tunis. This area of the North African coast extends toward the island of Sicily, placing the 58th Station Hospital closer to the fighting. The hospital had originally been ordered to Bizerte, another coastal town nearby, but Army orders change. The 58th would move in and call Tunis home for the next seven months.

The old Roman harbor town had been a French protectorate city since 1881, an hour's flight time to Palermo. After routing the Germans from the area, U.S. and British forces established their base of operations here to stage assaults against Sicily and Italy, both targets for the next large Allied invasion. Medical facilities in Tunisia would receive casualties from that battle in less than a month. A concerted effort was needed to get ready.

The nurses knew nothing more than rumors of these war plans but they were absolutely clear about their contributions to the bigger picture. Their immediate focus, however, centered on finding their bunks. Setting up the medical facility would follow soon after that.

Returning to an inviting home environment at the end of shift helped the nurses cope with the erratic nature of war. Dot believed a thread of consistency would be maintained if she and the original Charlie Tent nurses could stay together. She found Miss Parsons and asked for that privilege.

"I don't see why not," Miss Parsons assured Dot. "I'll check with Major Whitfield to see what we can do. Keeping roommates together would lend stability to the transitory nature of our job."

The groups were kept together in assigned tents.

"Should this be Charlie Three tent?" Gillie asked.

"Charlie Three, it is," Cora agreed playfully. They began converting their new accommodations into something livable.

"A pillow for our heads, then food for our bellies," Dot declared an hour later.

Charlotte responded. "The order of importance on this to-do list never changes."

The Charlie Three gals set out in search of the mess tent. They found it, and standing at the doorway was a man bending over a clipboard. He moved his hair to one side of his forehead as he looked up at the women coming his way. His smile was welcoming. The women introduced themselves.

"We were hoping to scrounge up some food," Dot said. "We're starving and we'd eat anything."

"Well, not a camel," Cora piped in.

"You've come to the right place. And as luck would have it, no camels on the menu today. I'm Fouché, by the way. Tony Fouché. I'm in charge of feeding every mouth in your outfit."

Cora introduced herself and the others. "Where are you from and how is it that you've come to provide food for this crowd?"

"I'm originally from a restaurant family in Charlotte, North Carolina," he said as he shook their hands. "I'm Chief Warrant Officer in the Quartermaster Corps and directing Food Services has been my job on this continent since the start of Operation Torch back in November 1942. How about you?"

Charlotte told him they had arrived in Oran a little over a month before the move to Tunis. "You've got an important job," she told him.

"Absolutely! An army moves on its stomach!" Fouché quoted Napoléon Bonaparte's famous comment. "No one fights better than a soldier with a full belly. Probably the same for you nurses as well." He peeked his head inside the tent shouting at someone inside. "We'll have something for you to nibble quick as a tick. It'll hold you until mealtime. Why don't you come inside out of the heat while you wait?" They did.

"These are atrocious accommodations, aren't they?" Fouché indicated the broken chairs and wobbly tables where meals would be eaten by the new residents. "Don't worry, though, we'll have it spit-shined and ready for business in time for breakfast tomorrow." Dot cringed a little at the 'spit' reference in connection to food hygiene but let it go.

"Another request," she dared to impose on him further. "We need drinking water to take back to our tent. Is this the place for that as well?"

"Have you got your canteens?" They indicated that they did. "I'll show you where you can fill them."

With food and water in hand, Dot told Fouché how grateful they were. "You're a lifesaver," she said.

"So I've been told," he grinned at her. "Let me know if you need anything else."

The women liked Fouché at once. His generous good nature was his super power.

———————

Early the next day Fouché organized a trip into Tunis with Dot and Elizabeth and two other nurses. The city had been a German base before the Allies liberated it, and the Germans left behind a garbage dump, the clutter of war. Dot cast her eyes over the mounds of debris strewn across the landscape where massive German airplanes lay in great heaps like long-dead prehistoric creatures. Smashed short-wave radios and discarded typewriters were scattered at the foundations of bombed-out buildings. She saw evidence of hastily-dug gravesites dispersed throughout the area, too.

The nurses had been advised to wear sturdy shoes whenever walking around camp, and through the town as well. Their sensible shoes were indispensable in climbing around the rubble and foraging for useful items. Although Tunis was in shambles, Fouché knew where the women could find some usable furniture for their tent.

While poking around in abandoned buildings, the nurses found a functional dresser and two small tables. Dot saw a little stool and appropriated it as well. Clothes and personal items were currently stowed beneath the cots, unprotected from the elements. The tents did nothing to hinder water flow throughout the living space during the rains, a problem they did not have to contend with in Oran. Here, their belongings didn't just get wet, they were ruined with mold and mildew. Furniture would be useful in getting their things off the dirt and out of the mud. A rescued burlap rug would cover the ground between the bunks to further manage the problem.

Hunting and gathering came to an end when the acrid smell of smoldering trash, and what Dot thought might be the stench of rotting flesh, became more than they could stomach.

On the ride back to camp, Fouché told his new friends about the destruction caused by the previous occupants. Infrastructure, such as the water filtering system and access to clean drinking water, was worthless. Buildings had been made unstable, and the plumbing was unusable. Army Engineers were working to remedy these problems, but progress was held up while waiting for construction materials. Re-building the area would be a slow process as they competed for supplies, facilities, and manpower. For now, the compound would be mostly under canvas. Waiting for water, sewage, and power services to run the hospital would take patience.

———◈———

After their long day, the nurses of Charlie Three returned to the tent to put their new finds to use. Fouché stopped by later in the evening to see the domestic improvements. Close on his heels was Hank Wilson, the Officer in charge of Medical Services Support. He wanted to meet Fouché's friends.

"I saw you had lights on," Hank said. Fouché made the introductions.

Hank Wilson, from Long Island, New York, was career Army. His Captain's duties included site planning and materiel acquisitions for the hospital facility. After his cordial welcome, Hank held up a bottle for all to see. "I brought Scotch. Who wants a shot? Its numbing capacity is something to write home about."

"I'll have some, but I won't write home about it. My folks are Baptists. They think I'm still as pure as the driven snow," Cora said. Her friends snickered.

"Is this official government issue?" Charlotte asked as she made her own tin cup available.

"No, this is a personal stash. Uncle Sam can't take care of *every* necessity," Hank held his cup up in a toast.

"Hear, hear," was the unanimous response.

Charlotte continued with the original topic. "The Army sent us here, why shouldn't it provide for all our needs?"

Fouché answered. "The Army prepares us as it sees fit but while you wait for the Army to see to all your individual needs, you won't have that rug or those tables for your convenience. You'll have K-rations of course, but you won't have a nice bottle of hooch or the chocolate fudge you cook up using your own ingenuity on the medical ward."

"I guess you've got a point," Charlotte conceded. Hank poured out another round.

"It's certainly true," Dot added. "Our little canvas hut is looking cozy. I admit I appreciate it more because of our efforts."

"Precisely. Fend for yourself," Hank continued. "Be self-sufficient. Don't wait for others to *do* it for you. The Army relies on us to be able to take care of ourselves."

"So far, we're doing just that!" Gillie jumped in. "Mother and Father wouldn't believe what I'm capable of now." The affable collection of medical staffers transitioned their conversations to home and the loved ones they miss. They imagined what they might be doing at that moment.

"What time of day is it at home?" Dot asked.

"Depends where in the U.S. you call home," Hank jumped in. "For your family and mine, Chinnis, or anyone else living in the Eastern Time Zone, they're behind us by six hours. So let's see, it's 23:30 here…"

Dot glanced at her bedside clock for a quick military-to-civilian translation. It read 11:30. Eleven-thirty minus six hours…

"Five thirty in the afternoon," Hank nodded at Dot. "Time to clock out of work. Time to be home for supper. Why?"

"Just wondering if the moon had risen there," she answered coyly.

———————

Dot and Charlotte washed each other's hair the following morning using an extra canteen of water that Fouché found for them. Their temporary beauty parlor was al fresco since an enclosed lavatory had not been built for the nurses. The result was heavenly. They paraded down to the mess tent to show off and saw that it was now set up, chairs were repaired and arranged around the tables, making the atmosphere orderly and comfortable. They would eat their meals here, but also meet friends when they had free time, to drink coffee and catch up on news of the day.

Another place to meet was at Fouché's villa. He had converted a nearby house into a combination residence and officer's quarters. The villa was a lovely blend of nouvelle French, ancient Roman, and classical Arabian architectural elements. Full-length mirrors graced the living room walls. Lace curtains hung in the doorway and moved invitingly with the evening breeze. Tall windows opened out to a panoramic view of the Arab Bay. Its exotic beauty helped visitors understand why so many cultures wanted to acquire property here, to have and to own.

Dot and her tentmates were Fouché's first guests. When he nailed down a day and time for their visit, he told them his shower facilities would be available for use as well.

"Seems odd to be invited to dinner *and* a bath," Charlotte said after Fouché's invitation.

"We help each other when we have the opportunity," Elizabeth said. "Like when we pass around our food parcels from home, and when Hank brought his Scotch over to share. I'm personally glad to be acquainted with someone who has indoor running water."

"What *she* said," Cora pointed her finger at Elizabeth.

After they arrived at Fouché's, the women took in the splendor of their view in stages. Miraculously Anne and Jane, who were usually glum at the happiest of times, enjoyed the luxuries of the villa.

"It's too gorgeous for words," Cora gushed. "And supper smells wonderful."

Maddy set two bottles of red wine on the table. "Yes, thank you for inviting us," she said. "We bought wine in Tunis."

"We're going to find out how good the local vineyards are," Cora added.

Fouché contracted with a small Tunisian woman named Mariam to manage his home. She was a diligent employee and hired two of her nephews who met her high standards. Mariam served local wine to Fouché most evenings so he was confident in giving Maddy a thumbs up approval. Mariam was in the dining room during the exchange and bowed politely to the women as she took the wine with her to the kitchen to decant.

When the dinner party had taken their seats, two young boys brought in plates of food. Fouché nodded his consent to begin. Everyone did just that.

"How do you afford three servants?" Jane asked. "It seems extravagant."

"Not at all," Fouché said. "They are happy for the accommodations I provide, and the food. I give them a stipend for their service and they share the money with family members. I contribute to the local economy and they, and their family, get some of their needs met. I have a little family money that I use to supplement my pay which means I can share the 'good life' with my friends. It's an agreeable arrangement all around."

"I approve," Cora raised her glass to Fouché.

After dinner, Fouché told the nurses where to find the bathrooms. "There's warm water, there's soap. But more important than that, there's privacy!"

Each woman took a turn.

"I do feel a little odd showing up for dinner, then having a shower instead of dessert," Maddy said. "Although I admit, it is a delicious treat after quick bird baths out of our helmets."

Elizabeth added, "I'll be awfully glad when we get our own shower installed."

Early the following week an electrician installed electric lights in the tents. Reading, darning, ironing, and letter-writing could be managed after dark with that improvement, and since July was blistering hot, ironing was best done in the evening.

"It's hotter here than any Fourth of July in South Carolina I can remember," Dot observed on Independence Day.

"I bet there will be parades galore back home. Wonder if we'll have one here?" Gillie asked.

"Probably not," Charlotte chimed in. "But I hear fireworks."

Native Arabs exchanged gunfire with the French police which sounded a lot like a Fourth of July celebration. But there was no time for nostalgia. Shots buzzed around camp so Dot and her friends put on their helmets and lay low for the night. The next day would be the official opening for the 58th Station Hospital. They wanted to live to see the day.

Dot was up early for her shift. As she dressed herself in the dark she heard the droning engines of a twin engine P-38 airplane flying toward camp. The Luftwaffe called the American fighter a 'fork-tailed devil'. As it circled closer, its sound was deafening. Dot lifted the tent flap to leave and the plane flew so low that it almost took off the top of the tent. She clapped her hands over her ears and ducked as it passed by overhead. She took a quick glance upwards and clearly saw the rivets holding the plane's wings to the fuselage. It was at that point she remembered to put on her helmet. At breakfast, speculation was on the reason for the plane's buzz.

Dot had to leave the mystery to others to solve as she hurried to check in for her shift. Patients had populated the hospital overnight and she did a quick run-down of each man's reason for admittance. Some of them were ill from exposure to the elements. A few were wounded in battle and evacuated from Sicily. She focused her attention on the ones with fevers but was not able to register proper temperatures for them. The heat of the morning was already a sweltering 120 degrees Fahrenheit which prevented accurate measurements to be taken. The nurses made sure those men had extra hydration and cool compresses to bring the fever down to a reasonable range. When Dot got back to her tent at the end of her shift, she found her bed, her clothes, and her other possessions coated with fine particles of sand. The fierce wind had broken their clothes rack. Clothes were strewn wildly around the tent.

"What a mess," she commented as Gillie came in behind her.

"I guess this is something we must get used to while we're living in a desert," Gillie sighed. She picked up the strewn articles and placed them on the bed of the rightful owner.

Dot picked up her own things then flopped down on her cot, smiling.

"You look too happy for someone who has to re-wash her unmentionables!" Gillie noticed.

"I don't care one whit about the wind and the sand right now." She gripped a mass of letters in her hand and waved them playfully at Gillie.

"Good mail call!" Gillie observed.

"Is it that obvious?"

"How many do you have there?"

"Nineteen."

"Jack?"

"No. My sisters. Ruby, Sadie, and Margie."

"The mail censors have been sitting on those," Gillie said. "I bet you a dollar to a donut that your sisters didn't sit down to write nineteen letters to you at the same time."

"Nothing about this war makes sense to me."

Charlotte walked into the tent waving the letters she had just received.

"You had a good mail call, too." Gillie faked a frown.

"It's funny," Charlotte said, "*not* getting mail sends me down in the dumps, but *getting* mail makes me miss everyone more."

The other nurses agreed. Getting letters was the highlight of the day. But it was also a trigger for homesickness.

"We can't have it both ways, though, can we?" Dot mused. "Since we can't be home, we have to accept that this is the next best thing. Look, after dinner, let's meet back here. We'll catch up on news from home while we make fudge. Chocolate is always good medicine for loneliness."

"I can go for that," Gillie said. "I still have some of the Baker's chocolate and vanilla extract my mother sent last week. No need to heat it up, it's already melted! I'll ask Fouché if he has an extra sauce pan we can borrow. And some sweet condensed milk."

"Great idea," Dot said. "Last time we made a batch, we made it in my helmet. The residue stuck to my hair for a week."

Earlier in the experimental stage of making fudge, they could make only small batches in the two-cup pot in their mess kit. To make a larger amount, they used a helmet placed on a metal frame above a can of Sterno or in the hospital ward perched over a Bunsen burner. With a proper saucepan, they could make a bigger batch.

When the women returned to their tent that evening, they took turns stirring the magical concoction of chocolate and sugar.

"Taste it," Elizabeth pulled out a glop of thickening chocolate that clung to the wooden spoon. Cora and Dot opened their mouths like hungry baby birds.

A roar overhead. An explosion. Loud. Frightening. After a frozen moment, the women dashed to the tent opening to peek outside. Dot was first to see the ball of fire that had plunged to earth. An airplane.

"Is that one of ours?" Dot squinted into the dark sky searching for insignia to mark its allegiance.

Gillie gazed intently at the fireball. "No way to tell from here. We need binoculars."

"That's what it's like every day and every night at the battlefront. That noise must be relentless for them there. We have it quite good here. In comparison, I mean," Cora said.

"I didn't see a parachute," Gillie said. "I suppose with any luck, we'll see him admitted into one of our wards before bedtime. Miss Parsons will know the scoop when we report for duty."

———————

Dot nodded at Miss Parsons the following morning when she checked in for her assignment. "Reporting for duty," she said. "Do you know if the pilot of the plane that was shot down last night was admitted?"

"I'm afraid not. He didn't survive."

"Was he one of ours?"

"No. Thank God."

Dot sighed. She was relieved that no telegram would be delivered to an American home for the fatality but was sorry for whoever knew and loved the airman who was killed. Compassion still ran through the veins of the nurses of the 58th. Dot wondered if her sisters on the frontlines were adopting the fighting men's view that the only good German was a dead German.

Miss Parsons broke into Dot's thoughts. "Chinnis, you will have the officers' ward today. A handful of them are critical cases so put on your kid gloves."

Dot had a soft spot in her heart for the enlisted men. The feelings were mutual. But officers were a different sort of creature altogether. In Dot's experience the EMs were appreciative of the care they received. The mutual regard between nurses and enlisted men took many forms—a kind word, teasing banter, or

119

just a chat about home and loved ones. But many of the career officers had a sense of entitlement that sounded like orders barked to a servant.

The unspoken rule in the Medical Corps stipulated that officers left their rank outside the door. Inside the hospital, the medical personnel knew best. Having to tiptoe around delicate egos was tiresome and time consuming. Dealing with male officers was tricky. They rarely followed doctors' orders or nurses' instructions.

Dot looked over the chart of a combat commander who lay on his cot near the duty desk. He was unconscious, with an IV dripping a pint of blood into his tattered body. As he came to, he reached up and pulled the glass bottle of B-positive blood from the pole beside the bed. Much of the red fluid absorbed into the rough-hewn wooden floor before an orderly mopped it up. Dot moved in quickly to limit the damage he was doing to the site where the IV needle pierced his arm.

"I don't want that going into me."

"You must. You lost a lot of blood. This is the only way you'll recover."

"I don't know whose blood it is."

"No, we often don't know that, but we know it's your blood type. See, here on your dog tag, B+, the same type we're using for your transfusion."

"I don't care about that. I want to know where it came from."

"We get blood delivered often. Sometimes we nurses and enlisted men give blood as needed. It's perfectly good blood."

"I don't want a woman's blood running through me. Or a Jew, or a colored person's blood."

Dot looked at him. She explained that having a certain person's blood running through your veins doesn't turn the patient into that person.

"I don't care what you say. I'm not having blood in me without knowing the source. I'd rather die. You are dismissed."

Dot found the physician on duty and relayed the story to him.

"He'll die without the blood," Doctor Randall said nonchalantly as he looked at Lieutenant General Robert F Bailey's records.

"He says he's prepared to do just that."

"His injuries aren't necessarily fatal. With the blood, he'll recover and be back on the frontlines in a couple of weeks. We can't count him out. *Needs of the Army*, Chinnis. He belongs to Uncle Sam. We will not intentionally lose an Army asset because of stubborn ignorance. Go back and insist on the prescribed course of treatment."

Dot went back to the patient's bedside. He had fallen asleep so she began setting up another bottle of blood. When he woke up, he saw what she was doing. He viciously jerked the needle out of his arm again, tearing the flesh at the point of entry.

"I'll write you up, have you court martialed, and sent home. Give me your name."

"Chinnis, sir. Second Lieutenant Dorothy Chinnis." Dot's face turned beet red. Not from embarrassment but from the fury she was holding in. She gained control of herself and said, "You should know that I cannot be court martialed from actions based on doctor's orders for your care."

"I'll find something," he winced.

Dot mumbled 'yes, sir' as she turned to check on the patient behind her who was growing agitated from pain.

"Insubordination!" he croaked. "You'll be out of here before the end of the week."

Dot swallowed her anger. With great effort she spoke using a tone better directed to a disagreeable five year old child. Quiet and controlled. "Your threat is not the least bit objectionable to me. I can do my work here, or in any hospital in the States. To be home with my family, to be safe, to sleep in a decent bed, to be fed at a table with clean linens—surely you realize that is no punishment."

Dot was infuriated at being spoken to so rudely, but she had been taught to hide her emotions when on duty. What difference did it make to her whether this pompous ass received precious blood that could be used by some other, more deserving man? Nevertheless, she was trained to do no harm.

"You'll obey my direct order or there will be consequences," the Officer grunted at her.

"No, sir. You will *not* stop me from doing *my* job." she continued. "I would never presume to tell you how to command your own men, but as long as I am here I will follow regulations to the letter. And if you intend to discipline me for that, you can't do it if you don't survive and without blood you will not."

"Will not 'what'?"

"Your *only* chance to survive, your *only* chance to live, is to have a transfusion."

"I won't take your word for it. I want to see the doctor in charge." The officer barely got those words out before he passed out. Dot hooked him up to the new bottle of blood and asked for a slight increase in morphine to keep him sedated as he underwent the transfusion successfully.

After walking on eggshells all day in the officers' ward, Dot went back to her tent to unwind. It was so stifling hot she had difficulties breathing.

"Oh, bother!" Dot barked, so out of character that Charlotte stopped reading her book and looked quizzically at her.

Dot shared her experience in the officers' ward. "And to top it off, it's so hot in here I think I may melt."

"Put on your bathing suit, pal."

Seeing Dot's surprised look, Charlotte elaborated on the plan.

"Let's put on our bathing suits and lay on the burlap rug. Then when Cora gets back, we'll ask her to pour water over us."

Cora walked in just as she heard her name. "I'd love to throw water on somebody!" She hooted. "I'll not say who, though."

"You had duty on the officers' ward too?" Dot and Charlotte said at the same time. They had a good snicker, then took turns splashing water over each other. It was some relief, and it added to the good news that proper showers would be installed for use in a day or two. Refreshing cold showers at the end of the day would be appreciated, almost as much as no longer having to wash their hair using helmets as a basin.

At breakfast, Dot heard that one of her officer patients got kicked out of the mess tent during dinner the night before.

"Ha! Serves him right for being a bully," she told Gillie in a conspiratorial whisper.

"Why is that?"

"Oh, don't mind me. I'm just angry with my officer patients right now. They order us around as we tend to them, they're conceited, arrogant, *and* obnoxious. Truly they are smart alecks who assume we're here for them to boss around. We're not here to cater to their every need when there are enlisted men who may have much more serious injuries requiring our attention."

"Better you than me," Gillie told her. "I'm not sure I have enough diplomacy in my soul to deal with them without being insubordinate."

"I'm not sure I do either. But thanks for listening. It's good to get the anger out of my system."

On their next free day, Dot and Gillie walked to town to visit the PX. They bought grapes and peaches, and then Dot's eye caught the sight of Tootsie Rolls! She was happy to see the chocolate candy, and knew from experience that this little slice of deliciousness wouldn't completely melt in hot weather. She bought a bag full to share with the enlisted men in her care at the hospital. If she ever came off-duty at the officers' ward, that is.

When they returned to their tent, the sand storm had been so fierce that one of the canvas walls had fallen down. An irritating wind continued for two days before the rain rolled in, calming down the commotion. But with the rain, came swarms of flies. So again, no sleep. At midnight, Dot lay on her cot, wide awake, imagining a nice big bowl of ice cream when Fouché tapped on the tent frame.

"Come up to the mess tent in an hour if you're still awake. I'm going to tune into the broadcast of the President's Fireside Chat. We've got the radio working. Coffee is fresh. See you there?"

The gals agreed. They dressed and walked through the dark camp to hear President Roosevelt. The War Progress Report included mentions of efforts taking place in North Africa. Knowing they were not forgotten in this far corner of the world boosted morale. It was easy to question whether the day-to-day drudgery they endured was making a difference. President Roosevelt mentioned the Allied successes and explained how the North African campaign figured into the larger picture:

...the ultimate objective is to take Berlin and Tokyo, and end the war. In the meantime Italy is going to pieces. Hitler refused to send sufficient help to save Mussolini. In fact, Italian soldiers were stranded and had no choice but to surrender...

Dot heard clearly what the President was saying over the crackle of the wireless receiver but her mind wandered to the casualties she had seen. How many more would she tend to before the war was over? She pulled herself back to the present moment and caught the last sentence of the transmitted message.

*...we shall not settle for less than **total victory**. That is the determination of every American on the fighting fronts. That must be, and will be, the determination of every American here at home.*

───

"You're in a fine mood, Chigger." Gillie made the comment to Dot as Dot walked to the table with a slight spring in her step. It was the day after FDR's 'chat'. Dot sat down beside Gillie with a lunch tray.

"Did you get a letter from Jack?" Gillie asked.

"No, if that were the case I'd be clicking my heels, not sitting in this mess tent. I'm being moved off the officers' ward, though, and today will be the last of my night duty for a while. I feel like celebrating."

"I don't mind nights so much, but they are hard on body and soul."

When Dot reported to the surgical ward the next day, she was briefed on a case that had suffered a shrapnel wound to the chest. The team anticipated a good outcome for him and Dot's cheerfulness was apparent in her care for him. The nurses acted hopeful, even with cases they knew would be fatal. Although the men saw right through it, they appreciated the effort. On this occasion, the optimism was genuine.

Dot's next case, a soldier with a severe head injury, required special duty. She stayed with him and observed him closely. On the third night, the patient began to move around. Dot leaned over him and called his name.

"Private Stowe," she said near his ear. "Gaston Stowe," can you hear me?

Stowe turned his head to look at Dot.

"Where am I?" he asked.

"You're at the 58ᵗʰ Station Hospital. North Africa."

Stowe tried to sit up.

"Stay still. You've had a head injury so let's take it nice and easy."

Stow relaxed back into his pillow. "It hurts," he said. "My head hurts something awful."

"I'll get you something for that." She motioned to the doctor making rounds in the ward. He nodded his approval of Dot's appeal and filled a syringe with a low dose of morphine. When Stowe relaxed Dot put a glass of water to his lips.

"That's good stuff," he told her.

An orderly brought a tray of soft foods. He set it on the patient's bedside table along with a brief word of encouragement.

"Think you can eat a little?" Dot coaxed. She gave him a few bites. It seemed to settle well.

"I'd kill for a cigarette," Stowe said afterwards.

"No need for that," Dot shot back with mock sternness as she pulled out a pack of Chesterfields she kept handy for this occasion. Stowe told her he had a lighter in his pants pockets. Dot found it and lit the cigarette.

"How'd you wind up with us, Private?"

"We were in battle. Then we got the order to pull out and drive to another location. We were going fast around a curve and the truck turned over. That's the last thing I remember. It's stupid how destiny works. I survive the enemy then almost buy it driving in a two and a half-ton transport."

"Your immediate destiny has more sleeping in store for you. Rest for now, then more food. You'll feel better if you do those things." She hadn't finished her sentence before Private Stowe fell into a deep untroubled sleep.

Dot walked over to the mess tent to get lunch. She sat at a table with Hank and another man she had not met. The stranger was tall, with thick sandy blond hair. Hank introduced them.

"This is Captain Ross, Chinnis. He flies P-38s for the 48th Fighter Group. Ross, this is Second Lieutenant Chinnis. She's one of our nurses and a stand-up gal so if you ever get a boo-boo flying in that tin bird of yours, she'll fix you up."

"Glad to meet you, ma'am," Ross shook Dot's hand. He had a slow, deliberate way of moving. If she had to guess, she would say Ross was a Texan. He seemed to be the type who would keep calm in emergencies. His smile was genuine.

"Her young man is in Intelligence with the 398th Infantry," Hank continued. "Rumor has it that his outfit will join up with Patton's Seventh Army over here one of these days soon, so be good. With his intelligence connections, he has prior knowledge of whatever it is that's on your mind."

Ross took this ribbing with good humor. "I bet you miss him something awful, Lieutenant. What's his name?"

"Please call me Dot. Or Chinnis. I forget to respond when I'm addressed with my officer's title," she smiled back. "And, my fiancé goes by Jack."

They exchanged the usual information which always included what they missed most while they were away from home.

"Tumbleweed," Ross joked.

"Sweet tea," Dot countered.

"Have you ever flown in an airplane, Chinnis?" Ross asked.

"Never. And certainly not in a fork-tailed devil... "

"Oh, so you know your airplanes!"

"I know that one because it's distinctive." Dot grimaced. "One of them just about scalped me as I was going to breakfast the other day. Was that you?"

"No. But I may know who it was. I'll tell him his shenanigans were noted. I'm flying one of our P-38s to Oran tomorrow to pick up a bomber and fly it back here. Go with me. It'll be fun."

Dot took only a moment to contemplate the invitation. "What time?" She was excited. "I've got duty at three tomorrow afternoon."

"Be at the airfield at 0700. I'll have you back way before 1500 hours. Wear slacks and a sweater to keep warm. Bring your helmet and your canteen full of water, too."

Dot shivered slightly. She was excited and frightened at the same time. She couldn't wait to tell the others.

When the women of Charlie Three returned for lights out Dot told them about her plans for the next day. As she answered their questions, Maddy came in.

"It's been a pleasure ladies, but I'm being placed on detached service with a group in Palermo, Sicily," she said. "I must pack up my things."

"You can't leave us. You have a year's lease and you'll lose your deposit if you vacate early," Charlotte said.

"Orders." Maddy looked resigned.

"We need you here. Why do you have to go?" Anne asked. She had become dependent on Maddy's reassuring support of her and felt stronger because of it.

Charlotte added, "We're doing well on the front. All indicators point to our success. Shouldn't we have more staff here than there?"

"More medical staff is required there to take care of the casualties on site. Lives can be saved if we get to them faster.

128

Gals on the frontline need a break. I'm one of the ones tapped to go. I'll be back, they say. But for now, I'm going camping."

———————

Dot was up early enough the next day to get a good breakfast before setting off to the airfield. She followed Captain Ross' instructions as she took her seat and buckled the harnesses.

"Why are we going to Oran?" Dot asked.

"We'll be sending these fighters to England soon. They'll escort bombers going from Dover to Berlin, or somewhere in between. We're gearing up for something big there. I don't know anything official, just talk and speculation."

Flying is exhilarating... Dot would write in her diary later. But at the moment, since she had remembered to bring her camera, she wanted to take photographs of the scene below. As she focused on the specks on the ground, Dot could understand that when bombs were dropped from this height it meant pilots and bombardiers were insulated from the havoc they wreaked below. On the ground, infantrymen often looked an enemy in the eye. In face-to-face confrontations a man takes account of his actions. From this distance, nothing looked real or human, nothing was recognizable. She accepted, reluctantly, that this was the way of war. Then her thoughts returned to the magic and miracle of flight, and she became lost in the experience.

———————

Dot was on night duty again. A British patient asked her to write a letter for him. She lit a lantern on his bedside table—the moon was off-duty. *Where is your Polished Moon tonight Mr. Light?* She asked silently.

Before leaving at close of shift, Dot asked for a bottle of Listerine to take back to her tent. She and Charlotte were giving each other treatments to rid themselves of head lice.

"Disgusting things. Where, oh, where did we get this plague?" Charlotte complained.

"From the men, of course," Dot answered back. "They lie in a foxhole all day long, or visit a brothel, and pick them up. Or worse." They groaned at that.

"Then they come here and lay on these pillows that ten other men have used. We change and launder the linens, but they jump onto our hands, and we scratch our heads… and Bob's your uncle."

"Are you British?"

"No, but I nursed one yesterday. He used the phrase."

"There's no end to our worldly education, is there?" Charlotte laughed.

<hr />

Captain "Click" Aspen's Commanding Officer sent him to the day-clinic run by the 58th when Click's in-grown toenail had been declared a detriment to the war effort. He was usually the life of the party, and if there wasn't a party, he made one happen. More important than that, he was a damned good pilot. The pain from such a small thing like his toenail made him grumpy and no fun to be around, and was causing bigger problems for the squadron since the distress hindered his concentration.

"I'd rather go to the doc for hemorrhoids than for a toenail," he snarled.

"Well, you're becoming such a pain in the ass because of this thing you may as *well* be a hemorrhoid!" the CO barked. "Get it fixed. Today."

Click walked into the ward and asked the orderly to find somebody who could fix his toenail.

"You trying for a medical discharge, buddy? 'Cause you might want to ratchet up your complaint a notch."

"You wise-cracker. I wouldn't be here at all if my CO hadn't ordered it. I follow orders, see?"

"I see you limping like you lost some toes somewhere along the way."

"I got my ten toes, but the way I feel right now, you can have 'em all."

"All right, keep your shirt on. I'll put you on the list. We'll fix you up, but it might be another hour before the docs are out of surgery. Mess tent's that way," the orderly pointed out the window. "And the latrine is back there."

Click went in search of some chow then to the latrine to take care of personal and private business. Too late, he realized there was no toilet paper handy. He waited until a grunt came in and he 'encouraged' him to bring in a fresh supply. *The humiliations just keep piling up*, he thought.

After the surgeon cut the nail plate out of the tissue, Dot bandaged Click's toe and handed him his shoes.

"Don't wear these for two or three days," she warned him. She made up a package of antibiotics, peroxide and something to dull the pain then sent him on his way. He walked out of the clinic in his socks and caught a ride back to the airfield. He felt instant relief from the worst of the pain and was glad to have taken care of the problem, but he still wasn't over the humiliation of being stranded in the latrine. Early the next morning he neglected the no-shoe order, put on his flight boots, flew low over the camp in his B17, and dropped two dozen rolls of toilet paper over the hospital.

"That's the type of bomb I can handle," Dot said out loud to her tentmates as they dressed for duty. They had no idea who in the world had conceived such a plan but they were learning to go with the flow. "Now if he makes another pass and drops Banana Splits, I will love that pilot for all time," Dot laughed.

Nurses usually kept their spirits up easily enough, except when the patients' injuries were too devastating to shrug off. At times, they despaired over the uncertain world that would follow this war. For whoever had a bad day, her chums stepped up and tried to get her mind on something else.

Dot's bad day was a Sunday evening. Visions of injured men were seared into her brain. Changing dressings on torn flesh, protecting what was left of an arm or a leg, having the foul odor of necrotic gangrene linger in the nostrils, and looking into the disfigured face of a young Private whose own mother wouldn't recognize. She couldn't erase the images.

One friend after another stopped by Dot's tent to ask her to dinner in town, or suggest another activity to take her mind off things. In the end, she decided to go for a walk around the camp to get away from the bloody bandages and sunken eyes of the gaunt men who watched her every move. She was unable to avoid thinking about her patients, so she stopped in at the surgical ward to have a friendly word with them.

As her eyes adjusted to the dim light, Dot saw that Purple Hearts were being awarded to two of her patients, as they lay in bed, for injuries received in battle. Over a million of these medals were awarded during the war. Of the two she witnessed, one man had lost a leg and was waiting to be transported home, and the other man had sustained a head injury so severe that he would never be able to hold down a job more complicated than bagging groceries.

That's a little consolation for them, I hope. Dot forced this thought. *Or some consolation for their families.* Tears streamed down her cheeks silently. She knew each man would rather his circumstances be vastly different.

So many of these young men will go home broken in body or mind. Such sacrifice. She couldn't stop her brain. *But they were fighting for America's freedom against the tyranny of fascism.* Dot knew there was

132

nothing more important than winning this war but she had difficulty placing these horrific consequences of war into their proper perspective. She returned to her walk around the camp to reflect and to pray.

After supper, she returned to her tent. Fouché stopped by to cheer her up. He told her that her friend, Captain Ross, the pilot of the P-38, had shot down three more planes.

"He's an Ace now!" Dot was pleased for him. "I need to accept that this is what passes for good news in a war zone."

Morning brought another war zone issue to light. Dot lifted the flap to her tent as she was leaving for breakfast. Directly facing her, after popping up overnight, were three patients' tents.

"Look out here, Charlotte." Dot motioned angrily in the direction of the new tents, literally in their 'front yard'. Inside the tents were patients who were convalescing after injuries or illnesses.

"Who in the world thought *this* was a good idea?" Charlotte ranted. "We have precious little privacy as it is, and we need space where we can be ourselves when not on duty." Like Dot, Charlotte was upset.

"What can be done?" Jane asked as she peeked outside.

"I'll have a chat with Hank," Dot promised. Before suppertime, the tents were moved. A fresh batch of fudge would be made and delivered to Hank before morning.

Nine

Diary Entry ~ September 6, 1943
Jerries dropped 200 paratroopers, so we were told.

September arrived without the cool autumn breezes folks back home were enjoying. Rumors flew through Tunis that a resurgence of German forces was expected in the area. Some, they were told, could drop in by parachute. It made the hospital staff nervous but Miss Parsons kept her nurses on track with her assurances that the 58th was well-guarded against attack.

One afternoon the Charlie Three nurses greeted Click who had just flown in from Palermo. "Look who I've brought to see you," he said to Dot. Maddy had been walking behind him, obscured from Dot's line of sight. When she veered off course to make a beeline for Dot, Dot couldn't believe her eyes. Maddy's manner remained as elegant as ever, but she was thin. Her shoulders looked like a wire coat hanger holding up loose-fitting coveralls. Fatigue was tattooed on her face and her eyelids were poised at half-mast.

"I'm so glad to see you," Dot said to her. To Click she said, "I see your new job is hauling precious cargo. Well done, you!"

Click smiled at Dot and gave her a thumbs up as he headed over to the mess tent for coffee. Dot guided Maddy to Charlie Three.

Dot settled Maddy on her own cot and heated a pot of water for coffee. The other women gathered round to welcome their friend and hear her news.

"How is Palermo," Charlotte asked her gently. "What's it like to be at the front?"

"No time to get bored there," Maddy said. "The casualties are non-stop and the medical staff can be on duty for twenty-four hours at a time, maybe longer if necessary. But when off-duty, you still can't sleep because the shelling is so loud. Nothing blocks out the noise so why not be available for bedside care. The wounds are similar to what we see here but before they're cleaned up. We go through pails and pails of water and loads of soap just washing the dirt and mud off the men so we can get an idea what the injuries are. The medics tell us to do what's absolutely necessary for each case, no more. They tell us to not concentrate on *who* the individual is. But *they* don't do it. And we *can't* do it. So our hearts break for every man who comes our way. No different from the work here except for the immediacy of our responses."

Dot handed Maddy a steaming cup of instant coffee and a block of fudge. She took a sip and a bite before she continued.

"The nurses I'm working with have been on the frontlines for ages. Some of them are a little jumpy. Shell-shocked, I suppose. There are plans to get them to rest camps so they can recuperate and last until the end of the war. Your body does not get accustomed to being in stress for such long periods. Living with the fear of death or anticipating a catastrophic injury takes its toll. It's a race to see how long you can hold out and be useful. The men in combat deal with this every day."

"When we get them here, they're of two minds," Dot added. "They desperately want to return to their unit but feel guilty that they are having a break from fighting. They believe they're letting down their buddies who are back in the foxholes."

135

Back to Maddy. "The soldiers and the medical personnel desperately need a respite from the hunger, the danger, the fear."

Moments of silence passed while each woman reflected on the circumstances of war in her own way.

"What do you need, Maddy? What can we do for you?" Dot asked.

"Sleep," she said. "I need to sleep."

"Okay, but first, eat a little something."

The women pooled the food they had handy. Maddy ate with more appetite than she knew she had. Then her friends tucked her in for a little shut-eye before making themselves scarce for the next four hours.

Dot walked over to the admin tent and cabled money home. This was money she didn't need for herself and she didn't want a large amount of cash lying around in the tent. She walked around the camp, trying to chase away the blues that overwhelmed her. Maddy's account of the battlefront made Dot loathe the state of affairs the world had gotten itself in. But the war *was* necessary. She understood that. Hitler had ignited an inferno of human misery and it must be stopped. But the costs and sacrifices of war, in human lives... .

An air raid alert snapped Dot out of her musings. *Poor Maddy*, she said to herself. *Can't get away from the thunder of war even here.* She headed back to the tent to check on her friend. Maddy was awake but looked more rested as she sat up in bed.

"Should we head for the hills?" Maddy asked. "Or is there an air raid shelter?"

Dot assured her that they were safe for the moment. If the warning became more desperate, someone would let them know. Maddy relaxed and Dot offered her the cheese and crackers collected from Fouché's pantry.

Maddy observed Dot more closely. "You look more lively," she remarked. "I was afraid someone had licked the red off your lollipop before my nap."

"I went for a walk. It helped me get things in perspective after listening to your war stories. It's the loneliness that gets to me, and being homesick…"

"Love-sick, more like." Charlotte had come back to the tent and plopped down on her cot.

Dot gave Charlotte the side eye. She allowed a hint of a grin before continuing. "The *important* thing is that we're doing good work here. I'm glad to be a part of it."

"True," Charlotte agreed. "And it's funny how air raids become just something to contend with. The fear is real, of course. And I can see, I suppose, how dealing with them for extended periods of time would make you batty, but as a nurse, I go into 'fix-it-mode'. The lulls between the crisis situations are my undoing."

"We could send you back in my place," Maddy grinned at her in jest. "If that would make you a happy gal."

At supper that night, rumors continued to travel throughout the mess tent that German paratroopers had dropped into an area north of Tunis. The nurses pitied the ones who might wander into camp. Soldiers attached to the 58th were protective of their nurses. The enemy didn't stand a chance if they wanted to get up to mischief there. More insidious news concerned the nurses, however. Orders to attend a mandatory class on military courtesy. The next day.

Maddy had to return to the front early in the morning. As they said their goodbyes, Maddy assured them she was okay. "Imagine how lucky I am," she said. "At least at the front no one has to take a Military Courtesy Class."

"I know *four* officers by name who would benefit from this class more than any nurse," Dot muttered under her breath. "Come back to us soon, Maddy. We'll keep the light on for you."

<hr/>

On September 8, 1943 General Eisenhower made the official announcement that Italy had surrendered. Everyone knew that fighting wouldn't stop just because papers had been signed by some officials, but it was a victory anyway, and celebrations were planned. The news meant moving again, but moving was a sign of success. Dot walked back to the tent after joining the toast to Hitler's ultimate demise. She found Charlotte sweeping up piles of sand into a makeshift dustpan and tossing it outside the tent flap. A large dune was forming.

"Along with the military classes that Army command has ordered us to take, and the extra duty we're assigned, how are we supposed to find the time to clean up these sand messes?" Charlotte moaned.

"Now we know what it felt like when the Walls of Jericho fell down," Dot told her. "We're living in historical times."

"*Hysterical* times, you mean." Charlotte cackled.

"When you're done with Operation Sand Removal, let's get ready for our next class. Our participation puts Miss Parsons in a good light," Dot said.

"And her success is our success," Charlotte declared. "I keep asking, *why now?* Why does the Army want to make us military ready now?!? After we're in a war zone? We were okay when they dropped us off the troop ship and now we're not?"

Charlotte was spoiling for a fight. Dot did not egg her on but said, "It won't hurt for us to learn the official Army way of things. The new skills will be helpful. Besides, when in Rome…"

"When in Rome," Charlotte broke in, "when in Rome, I will want a bottle of Chianti and a heaping plate of Ravioli!" Together they marched off to the mess tent for their class.

After the class was completed, Miss Parsons made a quick announcement. "All off-duty nurses will report to the training field at 0800 tomorrow. Sorry," she added. "This comes down from those higher than me."

Dot and the other nurses reported to the training field the following morning as ordered. They were instructed to line up and walk through a shed set up with jets of weapon-grade mustard gas. The drill would teach the women to precisely position their gas masks increasing their chances of surviving a gas attack. When Dot took her turn inside the shed, she removed her mask too soon. She ran outside, bent double, and heaved her breakfast onto the ground in an unlady-like manner.

"Again, Chinnis," the Sergeant barked at her. "Keep the mask on until you see the sign from me to remove it." Dot started to protest. "I know you were just sick, but Jerry doesn't give one skinny dog pile of poop that you find your protective equipment inconvenient. Mask on. Back through the shack again. Now!"

"I learned an important thing today," Dot confessed at dinner. "To keep my gas mask on longer than I need to. No short cuts."

"They'll make proper G.I.s out of us yet," Gillie chimed in.

Two hours after training, storm clouds rolled in bringing torrents of rain. It was a hint of the weather to follow. The new policy of making its nursing members more 'Army' extended to new allotments of official G.I. clothing. OD green coveralls were more rugged than the seersucker dresses the nurses wore as their summer uniform. The Army fatigues were not pretty, but they were useful. Wearing them gave the women a heightened sense of the can-do spirit, more than when they wore dresses and stockings. Slacks or coveralls, and sturdy shoes, facilitated doing the physical labor required of them in the hospital more comfortably.

Heavy rains continued, beating against the tent like pellets. Dot recognized the value of her new G.I. raincoat and other sturdy clothing as temperatures dropped. By late September, the 58th had been in Tunis for three months. They saw the seasons change from sweltering summer to rainy autumn. Protective clothing reduced the hardship of nasty weather on the women as they went about their work.

Early Wednesday morning, Dot looked at the pocket calendar on her bedside table and realized it was Ruby's birthday. *Happy Birthday, big sister*, she thought. She dressed in her new G.I. duty uniform and went to work until it was dark again.

A cold gray day greeted her the following morning, as did another hard day at work, then to bed early. There was nothing else Dot wanted to do between shifts besides sleep.

The rain continued. With it came fierce winds that blew and battered the tents for hours at a time. Dot was inside alone, ironing her uniform, as she watched the sides of the tent billow like a giant beast gasping for air. To add to the clamor, airplanes flew over in great swarms, heading to the heat of battle. Dot contemplated her fate if the tent poles gave way and the tent fell on top of her. Then her thoughts redirected to the airplane formation above and she realized that they were heading for the battle over Sicily. Progress for the Allied war plan, but danger for the men and women on the ground there. Dot said a prayer for them.

At work that night, Dot oversaw five medical wards full of men with malaria. Managing the flu-like symptoms and the jaundice meant no pause for a break. One of her patients saw her fatigue and gave her a Milky Way candy bar to cheer her up. Dot accepted it, but with reservation.

"Thanks, but you should keep that for yourself, Private. It'll go down good when that fever breaks."

"I want you to have it, ma'am. A little reward for your good works."

"Just doing my job, soldier. Like you. No gifts required."

"No, ma'am," the soldier told her. "It's much more than a silly ol' gift. Call it a token of appreciation. It's so lonely on the frontlines, you see. We're either too hot or too cold. We're hungry much of the time, and scared too. All of us. Not of death. I'm prepared to die for my country. But I was scared of this, of being wounded, or sick, and not being able to take care of myself. And here you are, like an angel. You take care of me but you don't make me feel like I'm a helpless child. With you I know I'll be patched up and back on the frontline with my buddies soon. We've heard about you nurses, how amazing you are. I want to do something to show you I'm grateful that you're here, for being in it with us. You're in danger too, but you came. The kindness you show us men means the world to us."

Dot's fondness for these infantrymen couldn't be hidden. She bent down and kissed his forehead. Totally unprofessional. Then she swallowed the lump in her throat. "You men are good as gold to us. You make our job worthwhile. So how 'bout we split the candy bar?"

"Deal," he agreed.

Dot was frazzled by the end of her shift but this exchange energized her. Her conversation with the Private would stay with her for the rest of the war. She knew now, more than ever before, how important her decision to postpone her marriage to Jack was. Here, she could make a contribution. For a few of her patients, all she could give them was her undivided attention before their last breath. Others would be patched up and sent on their way. She felt a hint of satisfaction that her work made a difference. It put her own pain of loneliness in perspective.

141

Another patient offered Dot a peanut bar the next night. She suspected the snack had traveled more miles than the bar had nuts but accepted the man's gift with graciousness as well. She admitted that it tasted pretty good.

When Dot returned to her cot that night, she was sure she would sleep like a baby, but the late October temperatures were dropping considerably at night, so she tossed and turned instead, convinced she would turn into a popsicle. The next day was so cold that she wore her thick, woolen G.I. underwear, three pairs of socks inside her boots, and a scarf while on duty. When she mentioned this to the Private who had given her the Milky Way, he told her, "put more blankets *under* you. It'll keep you warmer. Guaranteed."

Dot, Elizabeth, and Cora slept warmer with the new bed cover arrangement and were rested enough to venture into Tunis the next day. They wanted to buy Christmas cards to send to loved ones and needed at least a month's head start for their holiday gifts and cards to reach the States in time. The women stopped in at a photographer's studio to have their pictures taken to commemorate the occasion. They stayed home the next night and listened to a borrowed radio. The Armed Forces Network had begun a series of broadcasts in July airing pre-recorded entertainment shows. The program this night was a segment in a series called "G.I. Journal". It starred Kay Kyser, Fred MacMurray and Mel Blanc. While listening to the broadcast, Dot and her tentmates wrapped and packed boxes of Christmas presents to be sent home.

Dot walked into the mess tent after mail call the next day holding a parcel and a letter. She set the package on the table where Anne was sitting.

"What do you have there?" Anne asked.

"From Ravenel," Dot said. "From my mother. A Christmas gift, I would wager. Funny."

142

"What's funny?"

"Funny, this has traveled five thousand miles to get to me."

"And it's early, too. Good for you. I bet there will be many Christmases in January if other loved ones at home are not as johnny-on-the-spot as your mother," Anne said.

V-mail from Dot's sister mentioned news of Jack making Captain. Dot was happy for him but knew she mustn't let him know she heard news of it somewhere else first. Jack's letter with the same announcement came three days later.

Mail is delivered on holidays in a war zone. And because of that Dot got two more packages on Thanksgiving Day. Brother Ed sent twenty-four walnuts. Jack sent a Pecan Roll and after-dinner mints. She would share the bounty.

Fouché and his team made a perfect holiday dinner with turkey, fresh lettuce, oranges, and a pie. After having their fill, Dot and her friends took a walk around the grounds before going to bed. The wind was icy cold and snuggling under wool blankets, with extra-added blankets under her bottom sheet, made Dot feel almost cozy.

The day after Thanksgiving, Gillie and Dot planned a trip into Tunis for the day. "Go with us," they told Charlotte.

"I'm sick as a dog," she told them. "I got some flu-thing. I'll stay in bed, see if I can beat it." Elizabeth stayed with her.

When Dot and Gillie returned, they noticed Charlotte's empty bed. "Oh, good," Gillie said. "Charlotte feeling better?"

Elizabeth shook her head 'no'. "Just the opposite," she said. "She took a turn for the worse. Miss Parsons insisted she be moved to a hospital bed. They've got IV fluids going for the dehydration. She's had non-stop vomiting and diarrhea since you two left."

Dot walked over to the hospital tent and found Charlotte. She was resting, finally. Dot sat with her until morning. Charlotte was sleeping soundly by then so Dot went back to the tent to freshen up. A wood-burning stove had been installed and Dot appreciated the toasty warmth now that winter was squarely upon them. Before leaving for breakfast, Dot noticed the tent had become warmer than was healthy. She told Cora, "I hate to say this, but we need to open up the tent to let cool air in."

Cora agreed. "Looks like the middle pole might catch fire."

She pinned the tent flaps back. The tent cooled quickly. "Too hot, or too cold," Cora told Dot. "Choose your poison."

After breakfast, Dot and Jane went to mail call. A small package from Jack and two letters were waiting for Dot. A larger parcel had Jane's name on it and she assumed it was a Christmas present and tucked it away. Dot opened Jack's gift without delay, and clasped the dainty gold cross and chain around her neck.

"Shouldn't you wait until Christmas Day?" Jane asked.

Dot was taken aback. This decision wasn't Jane's to make. With a frown she didn't try to hide, Dot said, "Why wait? Who knows if I'll even be alive long enough to see Christmas Day."

Charlotte walked up and heard Dot's comment. "It's not as fatalistic as that, Dottie. See how fast I recovered? It's because I'm such an optimist. And you should be too."

"I stand corrected," Dot said, trying to be a good sport.

Dot joined a group of volunteers practicing carols for the Christmas Eve service. The choral ensemble had strung paper garlands in the patient wards as well as preparing songs for the service. She also volunteered to toast almonds for the patients who would be bedridden during the holidays. For those able to attend the evening celebration, a small Christmas gift was handed out to each. More gifts were taken over to the men confined to their beds. The nurses enjoyed wrapping cigarettes, lighters, boot laces, socks, playing cards, and other gifts for their charges.

When the Christmas Eve program had ended, Dot and others wandered over to an Egg Nog party hosted by the 58th. When they returned to Charlie Three tent, they were greeted with roses and carnations that Dot had bought for decoration. The women drank their rations of Coca Colas then tied red ribbons around the bottles to add to the festive atmosphere.

On Christmas morning Dot slept until late morning before attending a candle light luncheon. Hank dressed up as Jolly ol' Saint Nick and visited each table. Everyone wore a cheerful smile, but in their eyes you could see reflected a longing for home, and the concern for so many friends, family, and acquaintances who were in harm's way.

A lull fell over the camp at dusk. Dot crawled into her bed for warmth and wrote letters home—it made her feel close to them. For the next few days after Christmas, nothing remarkable happened.

Four days after Christmas, the 58th Station Hospital received orders to evacuate their patients and to pack up their gear. Questions abounded, but answers failed to materialize.

The question on everyone's mind was, *will we ring in 1944 in a new country?* After seven months in Tunis, the group was well entrenched but it was time to pare down to basics again and prepare to move.

When all the patients had been transferred, Miss Parsons told her nurses, "All of you will move over to the lab in the Nissen hut near HQ. That will be your temporary home. The tents will be dismantled and packed for travel."

They obeyed.

A chow line was organized again and everyone knew to bring their mess kits. On New Year's Eve Charlotte went with Dot to the PX to get a bottle of champagne. They would see the New Year in with style but the celebration would be in North Africa.

The following day turned out to be a pretty tough day for most of the revelers but not for Dot. She rang in the first day of the year without a headache and was quite pleased with herself.

Wind and rain continued nonstop as the group waited for their orders. They now had no stoves. With no heat, and nothing to cook on, there were no more hot snacks. There was nothing left to do except play the waiting game.

Dot fought the tedium by engaging in the age-old Army ritual of packing and re-packing. After she had completed her second-stage packing the second day of the New Year, she and Charlotte hitched a ride by ambulance to the 33rd hospital. It was located nearby and they wanted to visit the nurses there that they had known at Fort Jackson. There were no stoves there either so they went to visit friends working in the sick tent just to keep warm. They sat around and shared news if they had it. The Russians had crossed over the Polish border on the Eastern Front. That meant German forces were retreating and *that* was a good omen for the Allies.

Thirteen days after the camp had been put on alert, Dot received a letter from her sister Ruby telling her that their brother Prentiss, who had been at Pearl Harbor on the day of the Japanese bombing, would be home on Dec 29th. *He would be there now,* Dot thought, and she was happy for her mother.

Orders to move hadn't come, so another trip to the PX was planned. Dot bought two more pairs of OD green pants and a field jacket.

"The Army wants to make men out of us nurses," she said to Charlotte.

"True. The men *would* rather be comfortable than look pretty." Charlotte remembered Major Whitfield's comment at their orientation at Camp Kilmer: *It's why soldiers don't fight a war in skirts and heels.* "The clothes aren't stylish but they *are* sensible. And warm. Speaking of warm, one of 33rd girl's tents burned up."

"At least they've still got tents," Dot cracked. "Here we sit on a rock in the middle of a deserted post."

"I expect they're eyeing our rock with longing now that they don't have a tent." Dot couldn't poke a hole in Charlotte's logic.

By the middle of January, no one was surprised that they had to spend another dull day waiting. It became harder and harder to look busy. Gillie cooked sausages over a small open fire to share, and Miss Parsons popped corn.

Dot was up early the next morning, but with nothing to do, she spent the day reading. By dark, the order to move out was finally passed along. All personnel would be packed and ready by the following morning. An ice cream supper punctuated the end their time in North Africa.

Before going to bed, Dot experienced one last memorable moment. She and Charlotte had gone to the latrine. Dot was inside her semi-private stall and in the relative quiet of the nearly empty room, Charlotte heard Dot say, "Uh oh."

"That doesn't sound good, Dottie. What's up?"

"I just dropped my dog tags down the latrine..." Dot's voice trailed off.

"How'd you do that!?!"Charlotte laughed at the predicament.

"Don't ask. I'm not going to try to get them, either."

"What are you going to do?"

"I'm going to apply to H.Q. tomorrow before we ship out to have another set made, unless you're volunteering for search and rescue."

"I'll help you fill out the forms."

Part Three

ITALY

Ten

Diary Entry ~ January 19, 1944
On the hospital ship 'Shamrock'

Dot's unit joined their counterparts from the 33rd hospital for transportation to the harbor. There, the hospital ship *Shamrock* waited for them. Their next base of operations would be in Naples, Italy. Estimated travel time shore-to-shore, twenty hours. After finding bunks on board, the nurses searched in vain for life vests. They looked for life boats and for emergency stations, too. As darkness fell, the passengers were dismayed that the ship did not observe blackout rules as the hospital had done in Tunis, and as the *Santa Rosa* had required on their voyage from New York to North Africa. The hospital ship had no guns, nor was there any other obvious means of protection. Catholics and a few Protestants made the Sign of the Cross.

"I feel like a sitting duck." Dot voiced her misgivings about their safety. Gillie nodded in agreement but didn't add anything. She was afraid it would jinx the good luck they needed for a safe crossing. A group of six British nurses and a French ambulance driver shared the starboard deck with Dot and Gillie and overheard Dot's comment.

"How is it that we are 'sitting ducks'?" the Frenchman asked. Dot told him how exacting the crew of the *Santa Rosa* had been about their safety during that trip. In retrospect, the transatlantic experience seemed safer than the shorter one soon to be in progress.

After a light supper, Dot returned to her cabin to sleep. Sleep was uninterrupted by sea-sickness, since the ship never left the harbor during the night. By lunchtime the following day, passengers were able to wave goodbye to the African continent. The ship sailed north past Sicily while the passengers read, played cards, and swapped war stories to while away the hours until supper and bed time. When the sun came up, early risers saw the western Italian coastline in the distance. By lunch someone recognized the Saracen tower of Praiano and pointed it out. Next, they glided past the town of Sorrento jutting into the sea lanes. Dot spied the Isle of Capri on her port side, and for two more hours the *Shamrock* continued northward, ultimately arriving in the Port of Naples. Dot found Miss Parsons to ask when they would disembark.

"No one is going ashore anytime soon," Miss Parsons told her. "There's no docking space. Prepare to spend another night on the ship."

"Why isn't there docking space?" Cora had walked up in time to hear the conversation.

"Soldiers are going ashore from the ships ahead of us. Supplies are being unloaded as well. There's a large operation in the works, and it takes a while for the logistics involved to take their course. We'll have our turn, but not today."

As the sun set, Naples harbor went into blackout. Mount Vesuvius spit glowing red embers skyward as a backdrop to the Italian countryside. The light show mesmerized passengers waiting to go ashore.

"That's phenomenal," Dot said to Jane who had walked up to the railing for a better view.

"It's scary!" Jane answered.

"I doubt the hot cinders will reach us out here," Dot reassured her. "Besides, it's not erupting, it's just 'threatening' to erupt."

"I have a bad feeling about this," Jane continued. "If the Germans don't get us, looks like Mother Nature will."

"But just imagine! We get to witness a once-in-a-lifetime phenomenon. It's more history in the making." Dot wished she could help Jane see the positive side of the predicaments they found themselves in.

"Oh, well that makes me feel *much* safer." Jane actually cracked a smile at Dot's joke. Progress, Dot thought.

The *Shamrock* slid into dock at ten o'clock the following morning. As the nurses came ashore, ambulances arrived to transport them to the medical center. They were glad to be inside enclosed vehicles since the combination of near-freezing temps and the pouring rain chilled them to the bone, no matter how warmly dressed they were.

Their destination was the Mostra Fairgrounds, a short drive outside the town of Naples. Mussolini's government had built exhibit halls on several acres at this location in 1940 to celebrate Italian colonial achievements. Now that the Allies were in control of the area, the facilities were converted to a comprehensive hospital center. Several units would collaborate to provide medical and other support services to the forces tapped for the imminent invasion at Anzio Beach. Operation Shingle would take place within twenty-four hours on the beachhead, a hundred and forty miles north of Naples. It would position them for a march to Rome.

Dot's group was dropped off at a large, multi-story brick building where the women gathered in the lobby. Captain Parsons and Major Whitfield addressed them.

"We have space to spread out here," Parsons told her crew. "You'll find three or four beds in each room but I'm going to assign just two of you per room." She held a sheet of paper above her head. "Pass this around. Your room and roommate assignments are listed here."

Whitfield added, "after you drop your gear, follow me to the chow hall. Bring your mess kits."

Dot located her name on the list, the room number, and her roommate.

"You're with me, Charlotte. Third floor."

They hauled their things up the stair case and opened the door to their room. It looked as if it had been used as a small office. The exterior wall had a set of two large windows. Three beds were pushed against the remaining three walls. The roommates stowed their gear quickly, grabbed their mess kits, and walked back down to the ground floor. The nurses gathered and followed Major Whitfield along a path to another building. They knew a proper dining facility wasn't yet established. Tony Fouché had warned them on the ship that hot cooked meals would take at least another day or two. Dot didn't care what form the meal took, she was starving.

Standing in the chow line, Dot and Charlotte watched dirty, half-starved Italians—young and old—hold out old steel pails, hoping to collect food scraps. On their way out after eating, the women passed another group of local residents peddling fruits, nuts, and cameos hoping to make a sale. Dot felt sorry for them and wondered if there were guidelines in place to help these pitiful residents. By the time she got back to her bunk, she was so tired that the only thing on her mind was a good night's sleep.

Dot woke up to frost on the window panes. She was surprised that she slept warmly through the cold, rainy January night, even without a stove. No wonder that walls and floors were considered remarkable architectural achievements.

After breakfast, duty assignments were handed out. So far, there were no patients but the nurses' quarters needed to be put in order. Dot and Charlotte were assigned latrine detail. There was only one bathroom, on the first floor, but it had running water and privacy for the women.

"Mustn't grumble," Dot mumbled as she mopped the floor until she was exhausted. Charlotte scrubbed Johnnies and wiped down the sinks. A soundtrack of artillery fire exploded in the background. Word of the amphibious assault on Anzio Beach filtered into camp, but these guns were closer than that. From their bedroom window the women observed blazing fires created by explosions.

"How close is that fighting to us?" Charlotte asked. They had washed and pin-curled their hair and were now looking out the window.

"I can't judge distance. But it's within view. That's close in my book," Dot shrugged.

Two days later, when the bitter weather continued, the nurses' thoughts turned to the G.I.s on the frontlines. The cold would only add to their misery.

Several days after arriving in Italy, the hospital was making progress toward being ready to receive casualties. Charlotte was up early and had eaten breakfast when she ran into Dot hurrying across the fairgrounds. Charlotte was bundled up in a sweater, a jacket, and an overcoat to insulate her from the frigid damp morning. She looked like a tick about to pop.

"I barely recognized you," Dot told her. "All I can see is your nose."

"It's me," Charlotte assured her. "Passes are being handed out," she told Dot. The frigid temperature meant Charlotte's words came out in a white cloud. "Let's get one!"

"Passes to where?" Dot was game for nearly anything, but better to be clear from the start as to where Charlotte intended to take her.

"The *Muhlenberg*. You can catch a ferry out to it throughout the day."

SS Muhlenberg was a cargo ship anchored in the bay of Naples. Its most popular feature was the PX. Since a land-based PX had not been set up in Naples, the ship became a shoppers' paradise for necessary personal items.

"Do you think it's safe?"

"Of course. Uncle Sam wouldn't purposely put us in harm's way." Charlotte stopped to hear her own words, frowned, and continued. "Look, we sat out there in that boat like a little rubber ducky, *with lights on,* and nothing happened to us. The ship's Captain wouldn't lure us into a shopping spree if it wasn't safe. Let's get a group together. We can go this afternoon. You in?"

"Count me in. Check with Gillie. She'll want to go if she can manage it."

Dot, Charlotte, and Gillie bought a case of cokes each, light bulbs for their room, several packs of Camels for the G.I.s who would soon be in their care, and semi-sweet baking chocolate for making fudge. An air raid greeted them when they returned to land. They were in the habit of having their helmets with them at all times and put them on for protection.

When she got back to her room, Charlotte set her helmet on the floor by her bed and belly-flopped onto the thin mattress. She looked frazzled. "Jeez, Dottie. How are we supposed to sleep with that racket every blessed night?"

"Sleep with the pillow over your head," Dot suggested.

"Oh, right. Then when I die from suffocation, it'll be impossible for my dead ears to be bothered by the noise."

"That's not like you to be so cynical."

"I know. I'm just tired. Don't pay attention to me," Charlotte yawned.

"We'll go back out to the supply ship tomorrow and look for ear plugs. We'll get several sets, sell them, and make a fortune."

"Deal."

Fouché saw Dot and Charlotte at breakfast the following morning. "Did you hear the news?" he asked them.

"We've only been awake twenty minutes," Charlotte said. "What news?"

"The *Muhlenberg* was bombed during that air raid last night along with a couple of other ships anchored in the bay."

"That can't be," Dot contradicted him. "We were just out there ourselves."

"Even so, a German bomb hit it and seven people were killed. You'll know two of them from Tunis."

"Who?" Dot and Gillie in unison.

"JoJo and Fairweather. Your drivers back in Tunis."

"I remember. They drove us to Arzew, to the beach. Good men," Dot added.

"Rescue team couldn't find Fairweather's body," Fouché hung his head.

"Poor soul," Charlotte whispered.

"There'll be a service tomorrow afternoon at the Chap…,"

Dot and Charlotte cut Fouché off in mid-sentence. "We'll be there," they said.

———

Another air raid roared above the compound overnight making sleep impossible. Since the southern coast of Italy was in range of German bombers, they frequently made passes to remind the Yanks that the war was ongoing, in case they had forgotten. Fighting on the ground continued close by as well.

Dark clouds, the color of a nasty bruise, hung heavy in the sky. When they unleashed the rain they held, the fairgrounds turned into a huge mud hole. Anyone with free time helped lay wooden walkways to facilitate foot travel between the residential areas and the hospital wards. When the original walkways sunk into the muck, new ones were built on top of them. The nurses' barracks was in fair shape but other buildings were bombed out and useless. As sick and wounded men began to trickle in, they were housed in tents until the Army Corps of Engineers could repair or build proper structures for them. Many of the beds in the wards were currently being occupied by staff members who were fighting bronchitis or pneumonia from the horrid wintry weather.

Dot and her pals had dodged being sick with anything more than a head cold, so far, and it made it easier for them to develop a routine. On their next free day, several of the nurses signed up for a tour of Pompeii.

An Army Regional Command bus waited for them early one morning for the tour. The ancient city of Pompeii had been buried, along with its sister city, Herculaneum, after Mount Vesuvius erupted in 79 AD. Tons of ash and pumice covered the region, reaching the height of a six-story office building, and wiped out a civilization. When the forgotten city was discovered over sixteen hundred years later, excavation revealed a snapshot of what the height of the Roman Empire looked like. A moment in time was frozen for following generations to study. It was one of Italy's most popular tourist attractions.

The next most popular attraction was Mount Vesuvius. Since the war, parts of Italy lay in man-made ruins. Other areas, like Pompeii and Vesuvius, were Acts of God. Both were frequented by the Americans. Sightseeing trips in Italy were dangerous for them, however, because of thieves and pickpockets who crowded the train stations and entry points into the site. Americans were warned to watch their money and other valuables since it was common for locals to steal cash for food. The Army protected its nurses as much as possible from this desperate, impoverished population by providing safe transportation to and from the sanctioned tours. Sailors and soldiers were on their own and were obliged to use less reliable forms of public transportation, making them targets for a shake down.

On a Sunday afternoon, the 58th nurses organized a group to see Mount Vesuvius.

"What's the appropriate attire for watching a volcano spew its molten contents?" Charlotte asked Dot.

"I don't know what fashionable trend-setters are wearing this year but I know what I'm wearing. A pair of Long Johns under my coveralls and the comfy saddle oxford shoes my sister sent me."

"Perfect. Mind if we look like the Bobbsey Twins? Except for the saddle shoes, that is. I want to wear boots in case we have to slog through more mud."

Dot and Charlotte joined Gillie and the others at the Red Cross tour office. The bus drove slowly along rough roads for an hour. When it stopped at the drop-off location, they were high above the clouds. It was quiet. Droplets of condensation swirled at their feet giving the area a misty dreamlike feeling. Dot stepped down to the ground from the bus and promptly smelled burnt rubber. She looked first at the tires of the bus as if they were the culprit, then realized it was her own shoes that were overheating.

She hopped from one foot to the other. Her steps got higher and higher until she looked like an Army grunt running in place for PT. The bus driver watched in amusement.

"The soles of my shoes are melting," Dot shouted at him.

"Try to get over to that path," he gestured over Dot's left shoulder. "Walk on that sandy stretch. You'll be all right there."

Dot hopped over to the pathway like a frightened bunny. "Should we be carrying fire extinguishers with us?" she shouted back to the bus driver. He laughed at her. He'd seen this happen on every trip and always had a good chuckle. Maybe he should start warning his passengers before real damage was done.

The tourists walked to a platform that allowed them a better view of the volcano. They pulled out cameras for snapshots of the mountain. There had been no explosions from the mouth at the top yet but rivers of molten lava spilled over the far rim and down the eastern side of the mountain. The women took photos of themselves using the dramatic flowing volcanic magma as backdrop. They took more photographs of the scenery around them when the clouds cleared revealing a stunning birds-eye view of the countryside.

Dot and her traveling companions had no way of knowing that they would not be coming back for another visit. Within two months, Vesuvius would erupt for seven days straight. Those who lived in the vicinity of the volcano were the last to witness the phenomenon. The volcano has not erupted again since 1944.

Another official sightseeing tour was organized for the city of Naples but Dot and the other nurses believed they were familiar enough with the local area for the time being. What they wanted was to get on with the next stage of their journey, seeing to wounded warriors. So they stayed on base to wash clothes, write letters, and mentally prepare themselves for the arrival of injured men.

160

Duty rosters were finally posted a week after the 58th had arrived in Naples. The attacks at Anzio Beach were brutal and soon the wards filled up. Casualties were brought by train and by ship. It was not uncommon for three hundred soldiers to be dropped at their door step at one time. The problem was finding cots for them safe from the elements. It was also a strain on the staff. Dot was given two wards to supervise which included Arab and French patients in addition to the G.I.s. A French General came in early one morning to see two of his men and saluted Dot. Dot looked at him quizzically.

"I'm not sure that I qualify for a salute, sir," Dot told him. "I'm a nurse, as you can see." She had blood stains down the front of her uniform and an armful of soiled dressings she was rushing to dispose of.

He responded, "Mademoiselle, you *are* an officer. Never forget that. It is my honor to acknowledge it."

Dot stood up straight and returned the Frenchman's salute. She couldn't wait to tell Charlotte about the exchange. But when she got back to her room that night, Dot's story would have to wait. She and Charlotte had a distinguished overnight visitor.

Sitting on the spare bed was an attractive dark-haired woman attired in a wool tweed two-piece maternity outfit. Dot stopped abruptly when she spied her. "Oh, hello."

"This is Mrs. Vanderbilt, Dottie." Charlotte introduced the stranger sitting on the spare bed. The last name was, of course, famous. She was noticeably pregnant. Dot entertained several questions at one time.

"How do you do?" Dot's manners automatically kicked in.

"Very well, thank you. I was here on a mission of mercy on behalf of the Red Cross and now I must get home before the little one is born an Italian citizen." She laughed cheerfully.

"You're welcome to whatever comforts of home we can offer you here. Are you waiting on a flight?"

"No, there's a hospital ship bound for the States in two days. I've arranged to be on that."

"It won't be the Queen Mary," Charlotte said. "But they'll take good care of you. That's a fact. We'll put together a travel kit for you before you leave."

During their time with her, the nurses learned that Mrs. Vanderbilt's husband was the son of the Vanderbilt who died a hero in the sinking of the Lusitania. Dot and Charlotte introduced her to their friends who found her gracious. Before she set sail, Dot and Charlotte prepared a box of snacks, paperback books, and several bottles of wine for her journey.

Another guest arrived before the week was out. Once again she was assigned to Dot and Charlotte's room. This woman had been working as a dietician in the dining services department of the 21st General Hospital. She was one month pregnant, and had been able to quickly arrange her marriage to the baby's father before being sent home. Dot and Charlotte listened sympathetically to her story and prepared the same travel supplies for her when her transportation home was organized. Before bed linens were washed and dried and the spare bed remade, another guest showed up.

"The Brass has mistaken our room for the Ritz-Carlton," Charlotte told Dot at lunch.

"How so?"

"We have another lodger."

"Is she traveling on the two-for-one plan too?"

"She's a front-line surgical nurse on her way home for a thyroidectomy. I think she'll be with us for one night, and then catch a flight home in the morning."

162

That night, Dot and Charlotte heard hair-raising battlefront stories from her. But she was not happy to be going back to the states, she would much rather stay in the fight.

By the following night, yet another visitor benefitted from the now-notorious guest room. She was a nurse from the 9th Evac Hospital and was five months pregnant. She was not married but put on a brave face in spite of the challenges ahead of her. Dot and Charlotte made sure the woman was warm and fed. They offered her friendship during her stay and prepared a travel kit for her as well.

On the morning of their temporary roommate's departure, Dot and Charlotte walked over to the dining hall for breakfast. "We shall hang a sign on our bedroom door," Charlotte told Dot. "It will say, SCANDALOUS BOARDERS ONLY. "

"And we'll be the envy of the entire base," Dot agreed.

<hr>

A beautiful layer of snow arrived on the second Saturday of February. It wouldn't be long before the foot traffic trampled the pristine whiteness into muddy sludge, but it was nice while it lasted. After her shift, Dot ate supper then decided to relax back in quarters with a book. An air raid pre-empted that plan when sirens interrupted the evening's activities, announcing the imminent arrival of enemy airplanes. Afterwards, when the camp settled down, an assessment showed no major damage to report, but another air raid surprised the camp just after midnight. Sleep was hard to come by which meant fatigue and irritability for all. Nevertheless, being cold, cranky, and short tempered meant you were alive. And that's a good day. It was a good day for Dot and Charlotte to have a visit from Hank and Fouché, as well.

"We found something you want," Fouché told them.

163

"No way. Not possible. I want my fiancé *and* a steak dinner, and I know you don't have that," Dot said.

"Okay," Hank conceded. "We have something you don't *know* you want."

"I'll bite. What is it?" Charlotte piped up.

"Hang on. We'll have to haul it up the stairs. You can reward us with a glass of that Italian Rosé. I know you have it tucked away for a special occasion. This is such an occasion." Fouché looked like the cat that ate the canary. He wanted to tell the secret so bad he had to pretend-zip his lips.

After a few minutes, Hank and Fouché hauled an ancient oil stove into the room and a can of fuel oil. They set the stove near the windows. They also placed two new wooden stools by the stove for Dot and Charlotte.

"You're absolutely right, boys. This is the best present ever." Charlotte poured out generous portions of Rosé.

"How can we let you know how much we appreciate this?" Dot asked.

"We need to be included the next time you fix a batch of fudge," Hank said.

"That's easy. Consider it done," Charlotte agreed.

"One more thing," Fouché said as he and Hank were leaving. "I wanted to let you know that the exhibit hall on the other side of the dining hall, the one that looks just like this building, has a basement. The Corps of Engineer fellows are bracing the walls and the ceiling with extra timbers and turning it into a bomb shelter. So far, damage has been minimal. We've been inundated with the noise of the flyovers, and hit by some flak, but who knows what the bastards are capable of. What I'm saying is, if it gets bad, get yourselves to the shelter. You'll be safer there than here." The women agreed.

Meanwhile, Dot and Charlotte enjoyed the toasty warmth of their oil stove. Since its installation, stoves were found and set up in the other rooms, too. The downside was they emitted a grimy residue from use. It meant that Dot and Charlotte, and their housemates, had to set up cleaning schedules to keep the soot under control or they would never pass inspection.

Dot and Charlotte went beyond maintenance. They found a few yards of floral fabric to make curtains for their windows. They added a discarded cabinet to their growing inventory of furniture, and cut colorful photos out of magazines to pin neatly on the bare walls.

"Our Ritz-Carlton is becoming a 'home'," Charlotte bragged. Dot agreed.

In one day, Dot processed fifty-six British patients into her ward. They arrived late in the afternoon and in the rush, Dot lost her fountain pen.

"Are you okay, Chinnis? You look annoyed." Miss Parsons had stopped in to see how the new patients were settling in.

"I lost my fountain pen," Dot told her. "It's not a horrible problem, but it's a gift from Jack. I'm sentimental, I suppose."

"Keep faith, I'm sure it'll turn up."

It did turn up. One of Dot's patients found it lying on the floor by his bed and returned it to her. Dot vowed to add him to the fudge-list.

Just after breakfast the following morning, all fifty-six of the British patients were evacuated back to North Africa. This was a new pace that Dot would have to get used to.

Dot was assigned special duty the next day with a British officer who had *mitral stenosis*, a narrowing of the heart valve. This issue was compounded by pneumonia but his prognosis was good with individual attention. Dot was tops at that, but after her shift was over she was so tired she went straight back to her room. She had crackers and peanut butter stashed there and wouldn't have to go back out for supper. The plan was to have a shower, read in bed, and turn in early. Dot had initiated the first step of her plan when Gillie walked into the shower room with a similar plan. She spied Dot, standing in the middle of the floor, towel wrapped around her as water sprayed wildly all around. Dot's eyes were squinched tight as she yelled, *NO! NO! NO!*

"What's going on with you, Chigger?"

"Look at this." Dot held her hand up. A silver handle was in her grasp. "I pulled this off the cold water faucet."

"What did you do that for?" Gillie was doubled over in hysterics.

"I guess I don't know my own strength. I had no idea I could pull the plumbing apart with my bare hands."

"I guess things could be worse," Gillie chided Dot through giggles.

"Really? And how, may I ask, could it be worse?"

"We could have no running water at all!"

"Oh, ha-ha. This is not *running* water. This is *erupting* water, and it puts Vesuvius to shame."

"I'll find Hank or somebody to fix this. Stay where you are."

"Not likely. You go get help. I'll get some clothes."

The next evening Dot was on special duty again. A young Lieutenant had been released from the O.R. after having both of his legs amputated. She cared for him throughout the night. Since he didn't stir because of the anesthesia, it gave her time to think. She reflected back to the hospital in Tunis. The wounded men brought to them there had been triaged and stabilized before reaching their hospital. Here, Dot's crew saw the men shortly after they were carried off the battlefield. She trained her

166

intentions on caring for them, trying to reduce their pain, and comforting them as they worked through their trauma. A radio played quietly nearby. It was a local station broadcasting Italian Opera non-stop. She turned the dial and found music that was modern and recognizable so the men on the ward had something to focus their attention on when they were awake.

Several men were drugged into a comatose state. One sandy-haired youngster sat propped up on one arm looking at the back of his comrade in the bed next to him.

"Hey, Petey," he whispered softly. "It's me, Tank. We're going to make it pal. We're safe now."

Petey's head lay still on the skimpy pillow, but his eyes were opened. Dot was in his line of sight. "The nurse over there," he rasped, "she looks like an angel."

Blood gurgled out of his mouth because of a chest wound too severe to close. Dot walked over to clean him up. As she leaned over him she detected the faint, lingering, orange and cinnamon scent of Jack's Old Spice aftershave. The familiar fragrance caught her off-guard and she forgot to breathe for a moment. Petey coughed. He hadn't noticed Dot's distress.

"I'm afraid we're dead and in heaven," Petey said to Tank with difficulty.

Tank heard the death rattle and knew the score. It was only a matter of time before that destination would be reached for his pal.

"Well, old friend," Tank said a little louder. "If the angels there are as nice as these gals, I won't mind."

"Me neither. See you on the other side." Petey left this world as peaceful as that.

At midnight, three successive air raids hit close to the base. Dot went to the window and looked up into the sky. The moon shone bright as day. It was beautiful. And *yes*, she thought, *it's*

167

polished bright. But it was a beacon, a spotlight, a neon sign pointing an arrow to their location. The explosions were loud and destructive. Extra medical staff was called in to deal with the shrapnel wounds caused by the bombs. The bed beside the man with sandy hair had become available.

⸻

March brought warmer temperatures. The nasty, but necessary, oil stoves were needed less often. Bombings increased. German planes flew over their heads one night just after midnight—their favorite time—but it lasted only a quarter of an hour. The Americans had by this point moved in several 90mm anti-aircraft guns. When they sounded off, it was a successful deterrent to the raids. A sigh of relief had passed through the residents of the camp. Collectively they wondered why the Army hadn't brought the guns in sooner.

Dot and Charlotte had been holding up pretty well under the pressure. Fortunately, the entire 58th group was enduring better than some of the other units. In the morning, one of the nurses from a unit closer to the front was admitted with hysteria.

I don't know why this doesn't happen more, Dot wrote in her diary. *We see and hear so much that is gruesome, frightening and nightmarish.*

Having seen the woman in full panic, Dot was still upset after her shift was over. She went for a walk to calm herself. The fresh air and the physical exercise helped. She was surprised when, that night, she was able to drift off into a peaceful sleep. It didn't last.

The camp was awakened at 1:30 a.m. by another bombing raid. This one was drawn out so long that the nurses dressed themselves and ran over to the new air raid shelter that Fouché had told them about. They got no sleep, but they could sleep

168

when they were dead. The goal was to prevent that event from happening on this night. Instead they talked.

Charlotte turned to Dot and asked, "Do you feel brave, Dottie? We're sitting here cowering in the dark, but we're brave, aren't we? Just being here makes us brave, right?"

"Well, I don't know. Are we particularly brave for merely following the call to be nurses? I mean, I suppose we have inner strength that comes to us in a time like this..., a sense of self-preservation comes to us so that we can do what's necessary to stay alive. We maintain our wits because we know we need to survive. We know we'll be needed once we can get out of the shelter. And we *do* like being needed, don't we?"

"I know I like it. But I'm scared silly. Does that make me a coward?"

"Yesterday I was talking to a little red headed Lieutenant from Texas that was brought in with a fever," Dot said. "The fever broke so we prepared him to rejoin his unit. 'I don't want to go back,' he said. 'I used up my luck and I'm afraid when I go back to fighting I'm going to buy the farm. I'm afraid I'm not going to make it home. I'm afraid this war is going to be the end of me.' He cried. He cried like a kid. And he was a kid, really."

"What did you do?"

"I told him, 'you have to go back to your group. You have to go do what you're supposed to do. You have to hope, and you have to pray. We pray for you too. Every day. Your family and friends pray for you as well. You don't know when your time will come. Only God knows that. So until then, have faith that you'll be okay. The thing that *is* within your control is that you go back to your unit and you do your best for them no matter what comes after. You'll be proud of yourself if you do that. You'll hate yourself for the rest of your days if you don't. That's all you can do because being in the heat of battle *is* frightening, there's no way to get around that."

"That's so true," Charlotte agreed.

"Then that Lieutenant asked me, 'Have you ever thought you were going to die?'"

"What'd you tell him?"

"I told him, 'Yes, but not from combat. I was terrified that I would die from the Atabrine we took for malaria. On my twenty-third birthday, back in Oran, I was so sick that I was convinced I was going to die. When the Doc came to see me, he said: you'll make it. And I *believed* him. And I *did* make it. Clearly, or I wouldn't be here.'" Dot and Charlotte laughed.

"Then I told the him, 'You'll make it. Be confident that you'll live and you'll go home when this is over.'"

"What if he doesn't? You can't possibly know."

"Because from now until he ships home, or gets a one-way ticket to the hereafter, he'll have a better time of it if he has optimism for a good outcome like I did. If he sees gloom and doom as his future he'll be miserable and that misery will spill over to his buddies."

"I like your attitude. But it doesn't answer my question. Are we brave, courageous? I tell you, I'm about to jump out of my skin right now."

"The way I see it, it's not a matter of *feeling* brave. It's the act of *doing* what we can to help out our fellow man, regardless of how we *feel* while we're doing it, that makes us brave. Doing our job, whether we're afraid or not, is what's important in the end."

"Thanks, Dottie. This has helped me a great deal."

———

It took several weeks, but the mail eventually caught up with the 58th Station Hospital. Dot picked up a letter and three packages

170

addressed to her and took them back to her room to open. The letter was from Fran, her former classmate and friend from Fort Jackson who introduced her to Jack. Fran couldn't say exactly where she was heading but she said it was more north than North Africa and that perhaps they would meet up in the middle somewhere. Dot took from that cryptic message that Uncle Sam's plan was to send Fran to England and then on to France from there.

In the packages that Jack sent her were a sterling silver U.S. Army ID bracelet, a bottle of Rendezvous perfume, a sweater, and a leather wallet. Since he was still stateside, he could find items that were not readily available at the battlefront.

The other package was from her sister, Sadie. Sadie had sent her Mademoiselle, Vogue, and Glamour magazines. Her younger sister, Margie, sent her three bottles of Coca Cola which Dot saved back for a celebratory event. If one didn't present itself, Dot would make one up.

Dot and Gillie were free the next day so they organized a trip into Naples. Mount Vesuvius was visible from there, blood red and exploding. In one of the shops, they asked a store clerk if there was cause for concern.

"No, not here. We are safe here."

They wanted to believe him but a significant lava flow was quite visible. When they spotted two MPs standing by the doorway, they asked them the same question.

"You're safe here. We've blocked roads going up higher though. No one is allowed near enough to be in danger. If you were in danger here, we'd evacuate you."

The smoke and fumes were choking the women. As they walked down the sidewalk to a café they were sprayed with cinders. They looked back at the MPs to alert them but by then they had wandered off.

171

"I'm not entirely sure their assessment of our safety is accurate," Dot commented. She brushed soot off her sleeve.

"What was your first clue?" Gillie was not amused either.

On her next shift, Dot had a hundred and fifteen soldiers from the frontlines in her ward. Many times, the hospital had no patients in the morning, and then over a hundred casualties would be brought in by supper time. After the men were categorized, they were sent on to the 21st General Hospital or flown back to North Africa to be readied for travel to the states. The nurses often worked double shifts because of the lack of staff. This routine varied little during the cold winter months.

Eleven

Diary Entry ~ March 29, 1944
One year since I've seen Mama.

Dot caught a small break in her grueling schedule and used a bit of her sparse spare time to relax in her room and catch up on writing letters to family and friends. The letter to Jack, she saved for last. Charlotte joined her in the endeavor and they shared a bowl of popcorn. At midnight, long after they had gone to sleep, an orderly from the hospital tapped on the door.

"Doc wants you in surgery," he told them. "I hate to wake you, but it's an emergency."

"What's wrong?" both women asked in unison.

"I don't know, I was just told to fetch you, both of you." Dot and Charlotte thanked him and dressed quickly.

They walked into the building where the lights were low so the men could sleep. Beyond the rows of beds, a brighter light shone through a door propped open with a metal chair. This was the entrance to the operating room. Doctor William Beauchamp stood over the lifeless body of a young G.I. Dot and Charlotte walked closer to them.

"You asked for us?" Dot broke the silence.

"Yeah, I did. But it's too late."

"Oh, sorry," Charlotte was truly sorry. "We hurried…"

"No, you're fine. I mean it's too late for this poor soul."

"What happened?" Dot asked. She could see the side of the man's head was obliterated. She had no recollection of a head injury being checked into her ward.

"It's Private Donovan. Twenty-one years old. He was brought in after your shift. He had an abdominal wound. He probably would not have survived it but he had a service revolver in his things and he finished Jerry's job."

"You mean he shot himself?" Charlotte's distress registered in her voice.

"He did. I thought we could do something for him. When I got here he was still breathing. That's why I called you in."

The doctor looked bewildered. Dot told him, "I'll find an orderly to see to the body." Beauchamp didn't move. "I'll find coffee for you too, if you'd like."

He brought himself back to the present. "I'd like that. I have to fill out a report on Donovan. It might take a while. I have to figure out what to put on the death certificate."

"It'll be awfully hard on the family to know he took his own life," Charlotte picked up on Beauchamp's dilemma.

Dot said, "Yes, but wouldn't they rather know the truth?"

"The truth," Doctor Beauchamp considered the meaning of the word. "The truth is the enemy shot him and that would have been the cause of death if that damned pistol hadn't been handy. Do we take the small comfort of a 'killed in action' designation from the family?"

"I suppose he was technically KIA. He wouldn't have shot himself if he hadn't been wounded in battle." Dot covered her face with her hands. She wondered how in the world things got so messed up.

174

Beauchamp took a deep breath. "Get me that coffee, Chinnis. The humane thing to do is to put the blame of this man's death at the feet of the enemy."

<hr />

April arrived and brought warmer, dryer, weather with it. Sunshine buoyed morale in spite of the casualties that continued to come into the hospital from the Italian front. Dot's shift was slower than usual. The men in her care were waiting to be evacuated to the States or to North Africa for convalescence. While they waited, they read books, or played poker for cigarettes. Dot felt more like a hall monitor than a healthcare professional. On one of her passes through the ward, she looked out the window and saw Fouché pull up outside the building on a confiscated German motorcycle, complete with side-car.

He saw her through the window. "Come on out here, Chinnis," he shouted. "I know you want a ride." She shook her head in a slow, no.

"Go on, Sis," one of the poker-playing patients encouraged her. "We'll be fine. Have a go at it. Do it for us. It'll be a sight to remember."

Dot declared that a five minute break wouldn't hurt anyone so she went outside to see the machine. It was a BMW R75, which meant nothing to her other than reading it on the side of the gas tank. Without further deliberation, she jumped in the sidecar and nodded to Fouché that she was as ready as ever. He stomped on the starter which sparked the bike to life. He twisted the throttle a couple of times with his right hand to hear the throaty growl of the engine, he released the clutch with his left, and off they flew. The wind in Dot's face took her cares away. Until, that is, they passed Colonel Cady, the chief medical officer for the 21st General Hospital. He did a double-take at the motorcycle passenger in a nurse uniform.

Dot gave him a sharp military salute.

———

Easter Sunrise service, held on a grassy hillside, was enchanting. The welcomed springtime weather was the topic of conversation at the elaborate breakfast provided for the church-goers afterwards. Dot and Gillie pulled out the snapshots of Mount Vesuvius they had taken in late January. They had picked them up the day before and only now had time to look at them.

"It's a joy to see how high up we nurses are on the priority list of Uncle Sam's auxiliary services," Gillie joked. She was referring to the months' long wait for their film to be developed.

"I guess developing our photographs isn't as important to them as it is to us but good things come with patience." Dot was triaging the photos trying to decide which ones would accompany the letter she was writing to Jack that evening. She knew he would find it hard to believe that Dot was one of the last humans to set foot on the volcano before its eruption. She had melted shoe soles as evidence, though, and she couldn't wait to show them to Jack.

Miss Parsons stopped by the breakfast table just as Dot finished sorting the snaps into piles.

"A minute of your time?" Parsons had put her hand on Gillie's shoulder but she was looking at Dot. Gillie made her excuses and left.

"Two things, Chinnis. Your name and Elizabeth Campbell's name were the first two pulled out of the hat for R & R. Very scientific. You'll leave in two days, for Naples. It's a forty-eight hour pass. You'll be at the Turistico Hotel for nurses. You can pamper yourselves a little, and sleep an entire night without air

176

raid sirens blowing out your ear drums." Dot thanked her and was sincerely grateful for a break at last.

"The second thing is that when you get back, you'll do a stint as a flight nurse. You've flown, I believe..." Dot nodded her head in the affirmative, finding no good reason to deny it.

"We will be evacuating casualties from another location to our facility here, and I want steady, confident nurses to assist me. There might be enemy sightings, though."

"There are enemy sightings here, Miss Parsons. I'm honored to be chosen for this duty."

"And I'm glad you've had experience in the air, Chinnis. Experience on a two-wheeled vehicle too, I understand."

"Yes, ma'am," Dot tried to keep a straight face but failed.

Dot and Elizabeth wished their two days of peace and quiet at the nurses' hotel in Naples would never end. With good food, rest, and no responsibilities, their energy was boosted and they were ready for the coming weeks of hard work ahead of them. Before the evacuation flights began, the nurses of the 58th Station Hospital gathered for photographs. Rumors circulated that their unit was going to be absorbed into a larger hospital and the women wanted to capture their original group identity for posterity.

Dot and Sylvia Bryher met for the first time as they rode out to the airfield with Miss Parsons. Sylvia was barely five feet tall, with short dark hair and eyes of emerald green. The Jeep deposited the three of them on the tarmac. Dot took in her surroundings and noticed a tall man walking toward them. A pilot's cap angled over one eyebrow barely hid his thick golden curls.

"I'm your pilot, Captain Robert Lawson. Bob, to my friends," he introduced himself. "And if you fly with me, you're my friend." he said to them. He punctuated the greeting with an engaging smile. "Parsons, Chinnis, Bryher." He pointed to each woman in turn. Correctly.

"All aboard for Bari," Lawson stated, more like a train conductor than a pilot.

"Where's Bari?" Sylvia asked.

"Best way to describe Bari's location is like this," he seemed to be addressing Dot. "Currently, you and I are sittin' on a great big boot." Lawson picked up his foot slapped the toe as he continued, "And that boot is kickin' Sicily out between the Mediterranean Sea and the Tyrrhenian Sea like it's a soccer ball. If the toe of that boot was to make contact, that soccer ball would wind up in Barcelona. And will *they* be surprised! So, here we are," he tapped midway up the boot laces. "Now, on the other side of this boot, here…," he slapped his foot on the heel this time, "… is the Adriatic Sea. There's a place that sits roughly in line with where we are right now, the port city of Bari. In Bari, we have home-grown Americans who have suffered the ill effects of this war, and we're gonna go get 'em and ee-vac'em back here."

Dot, Miss Parsons, and Sylvia fell into Lawson's bright blue eyes and believed they had won the prized job of the century. The flight crew joined the party and hurried everyone along.

The women were fitted into parachutes and directed into the plane which had been modified. Rows of metal and cloth straps that medical litters or stretchers could be affixed to, lined both walls of the plane. The riggings ran four levels high.

"This is temporary," the gunner said as he directed them through the plane. "The usual transport is a C-46 but we couldn't get one requisitioned in time for the operation. This is a B-17…"

"A Flying Fortress," Miss Parsons said in awe.

178

"Yes, ma'am. Something to discuss with the ladies over tea when you get back to…"

Miss Parsons looked at the airman, eye-to-eye, while subtly pointing to her Captain's bars.

"As I was saying, ma'am, this is a B-17, as you probably already know, and," the gunner indicated the benches placed in the nose of the plane, "you get these seats of honor." His smile was genuine.

The Flying Fortress design incorporated a ten-panel clear plexiglass enclosed gondola in the nose of the plane underneath the pilot's cockpit. In battle, the near-360 degree view allowed a mounted machine gun to fire in almost any forward direction. The nurses ducked their heads to enter the fish bowl.

"Best seats in the house," the gunner told them. "Enjoy the view. You'll see nothing but G.I. Joes on your way back, and not a one of 'em will be as pretty as Cap'n Lawson or me. That's a guarantee."

Before the gunner had seated himself, the plane took off from the airfield. Dot was mesmerized by the view. It was like watching the world go by through a huge picture window that surrounded her. The other women were spellbound as well.

"This is a bird's-eye view." A reverent awe tinged Sylvia's statement.

"Why didn't I bring my camera?" Dot wondered out loud.

The plane landed two hours later. Casualty pickup went smoothly. Orderlies belted the patients and their litters into the riggings for safety. Bottles of blood and saline were tacked up on support struts and secured before takeoff. The passengers appreciated the negligible turbulence until an American P-38 buzzed them, all in good fun, on their approach to the home airfield. The B-17 responded with a tilt and a swerve.

"I guess this is how the fly boys show off," Sylvia observed.

"Oh, yes," Dot said. "They will buzz so close to buildings and tents that you will get a crew cut. They've been known to drop toilet paper rolls on top of you if it suits them." Sylvia looked intrigued. "I'll tell you more when we land, when I don't have to yell," Dot shouted at her.

Miss Parsons sent a message to Lawson through the helpful gunner. "Tell him to stop the fancy flight shenanigans or he will personally be cleaning up the vomit in his airplane."

The airplane righted itself immediately and flew without deviation for the next few minutes. Before he landed at the airfield, though, Lawson took the initiative to fly his passengers over Mount Vesuvius, for an historic view of the crater full of molten lava. He also couldn't pass up taking a quick, friendly fly-over of the base before landing, just to display his flair for flying one more time.

The day had been long. Dot ate her supper quickly and insisted on lights out before 10 p.m. She wanted to be up early for her second flight. It was uneventful, but just as exciting as the first day.

Dot had drifted off to sleep after her second day in the air when another massive air raid took place over the fairgrounds. The constant harassment of the German Luftwaffe wreaked havoc with everyone's nerves. The rains had returned, accompanied with gray skies, and that added to everyone's gloomy outlook as well.

"We've got to find a way to improve our mood, Chigger," Gillie said at supper. "We're no good to the soldiers if we're doleful."

"Doleful? I don't even know what that is. But if it means sad, then I agree. But the reality for me is that it's just another day away from Jack, and from home. Sometimes, I just want to stay in quarters and sulk."

"Enough of that! Look, no matter what we're going through, somebody else has got it worse. Life must go on. We've got to find an excuse for a celebration." Gillie was adamant.

"Okay, I concede. This Friday is the Anniversary of the 58th. Let's throw ourselves a birthday party. We'll invite everyone we know, and everyone they know."

The nurses organized the celebration, decorated the chow hall with flowers, and convinced Fouché to requisition gallons of ice cream to accompany the cakes he baked for the crowd.

———

Back on regular duty, Dot was assigned to the isolation ward. She cared for men with smallpox, spinal meningitis, scarlet fever, among other contagious diseases. It was hard duty, but on top of that the Brass decided to initiate a surprise inspection. Her cases were extremely sick but they attempted to lay at attention as the Officers paraded through.

After her shift was over, Dot stayed late to make a batch of fudge for the men on her ward. She made an extra portion to take to Hank. As she walked through the door to his office, she saw that he was listening to the radio.

"Monte Cassino will fall soon," he told Dot.

"They've been working toward that end for a while now."

"When our boys get Cassino, that'll be the breakthrough we need to head to Rome." He looked at the sauce pan that Dot was holding. "Is that what I think it is?"

"As promised."

"I can't take all this good news at one time! But I will sure give it a try."

———

Dot wanted to join in the general optimism running through the base, but at a personal level, she was in a funk. It was her second birthday overseas but she didn't feel like celebrating. She was weary from days and nights of caring for humans, mangled through no fault of their own, compounded with getting little sleep because of the air raids. Dressing for work was a routine, accomplished without thought. Dot's sluggishness made her late leaving the barracks so she skipped breakfast and walked directly to the hospital. Before she finished her rounds, Captain Lawson stopped by the ward to see her before his sortie.

"Little bird told me it was your birthday. And I wanted to bring you something." He placed a small bunch of Talisman roses into Dot's hands.

"Oh my. Where in the world did you find these?"

"We fly boys have our sources," Lawson said. Then he handed Dot another small item folded inside a letter-sized envelope. "This is for you too."

"What's this?" Dot asked. She extracted a tiny silver bell out of the envelope. The bell was no larger than an acorn. She turned it over in her hand to get a better look. A short silver chain was attached to a loop on the top of the bell. An inscriptions on the side read: *Capri 1944.*

"It's a Capri Bell," he told her. "For good luck. Monks living on the Isle of Capri make them. Air Force pilots and other crewmen wear them on their flight jackets. See? I've got one here on my zipper pull. Guaranteed to bring us back to base in one piece."

Dot liked the lucky charm and clipped it to her jacket, but something gnawed at her conscience.

"I can't thank you enough, Bob. This is a surprise, a much appreciated surprise, but I have to be honest with you, I have a fiancé at home. He's due to be here in Europe with his outfit before the year is out, and we're going to be married as soon as the law allows. You're really special, but Jack's the one for me."

"I had heard that piece of information. I hate for you to think I'm gettin' sweet on you, because the truth is I have a girlfriend too. I guess I just wanted to do for you what I would do for her if she was here. Does that even make sense?"

"Well, I'm not sure it does. And I'm not sure your girlfriend would see gifts showered on me as a good thing for her."

"Now you put it that way, I'm pretty sure I don't want her to know I just gave you roses."

"If you don't want her to know, that's an indication that roses for another woman is not a good thing to do."

"Damn. Want me to take them back?"

"I'd like to keep them, but I want us to be clear about our relationship. I'm friends with Fouché, Hank, and the other men here, but we're just *friends*. That's all. No hanky-panky."

Lawson looked relieved. "Whew," he said. "I have to admit I didn't quite know what I was doing here because I do love my girlfriend, but I like you a lot too. I wanted to get you something for your birthday, but I didn't know men and women could be friends, you know, *just* friends, and now I'm…"

"Bob, stop digging. Look, what you did was thoughtful and I'm pleased by the gift. We'll leave it at that, okay?"

Dot sent Lawson on his way and she went back to work. No one else mentioned her birthday. As the day wore on she wondered if everyone else on base had forgotten. Two letters came from Jack but no parcels. Not one person other than Lawson wished her a Happy Birthday. The boost from Lawson's gift began to vanish. Dot went off-duty and walked over to the chow hall for dinner, although she'd rather just crawl back into bed. When she entered the dining area, the crowd broke into song. Dot's face turned red from being the center of attention but she was pleased to be remembered after all. She hesitated before leaving to see if a cake appeared for her. When it didn't, she started back to her room. Gillie met her there with a bar of chocolate and a new paperback book. Charlotte, Elizabeth, Cora, Jane, and Anne came by with gifts for the Birthday Girl, too. They stayed up until midnight talking, pleased to have no air raid for Dot's special day.

A cablegram from Dot's mother came the next day, wishing her a Happy Birthday. War news arrived of U.S. troops' victory at Anzio and Cassino, and Dot allowed an element of optimism to seep into her expectations for a positive outcome.

For the next two weeks Dot met the challenges of her job head on, although once again she felt herself nearing the limits of her good temperament. She was beginning an inner dialog pep talk just as Captain Parsons poked her head through the door.

"Nurses' meeting in an hour, Chinnis. You'll be off-duty by then." She didn't need to say, *be there,* because it was understood. Parsons' words could have sounded like impersonal military orders barked coldly, but the chief nurse's tone and manner always reflected her fond regard for her charges.

The meeting was held in the far corner of the dining hall. A bag of boiled peanuts were passed around as Parsons stood at the head of the long table.

"Okay, everybody listen up. More good news. We're going to begin another rotation of leave starting on Sunday. Chinnis, you're at the head of the list."

Chatter of 'lucky dog' and 'no fair' was good natured.

"You'll take a ferry to the Isle of Capri for a few days. I can send just one of you at a time, so no buddy system on this, I'm afraid. Pack your bags tomorrow, Chinnis. You'll leave Sunday morning from Naples. Red Cross will handle the arrangements. It's my understanding that you will lack for nothing."

"This sounds a little too good to be true. The whole plan seems awfully hasty," Cora said. Her open, trusting nature was long gone.

Miss Parsons was silent a moment, contemplating her response. Then she confided to the group. "The battles that will win us the war will expand and accelerate. We have to be ready for that. Fatigue is a huge enemy to the medical services. We can't afford to let our boys down because we're exhausted and can't bear the sight of more blood. Sometimes the Army actually plans ahead. And, *sometimes* it moves fast. When it does both of those things at the same time, it can be inconvenient, and a little scary." Laughs.

"Each one of you will have a turn," Parsons continued. "I've drawn up a calendar which I'll pass around now, then I'll tack it to my office door for you to refer to later. Any questions?"

Dot's comrades gathered around her to congratulate her on her good fortune. She promised to update them with travel tips on her return from the adventure.

Dot spent Saturday packing and on Sunday, she caught a ride to Naples. The ferry to Capri sailed at 3:30 that afternoon, arriving at the island in time to check-in and change for dinner. At the Quisisana Hotel, dinner was buffet style. The selections were stunning and Dot savored her good luck, along with the good food. She sat at a table with other Americans who were also on leave. One dinner companion shared what he had learned from a tourist pamphlet.

"This hotel is the largest one on the island," he explained.

Dot had noticed its sprawling, vast, size when she approached the entrance from the funicular, the cable car that brought her and the others up the hillside from the harbor. The hotel was painted a bright yellow. Lush, green vines grew on the exterior walls creating an inviting tropical quality.

"The gardens are inspiring and should be enjoyed in leisure, not in haste," the officer recited from memory. "The hotel's name: Hotel Quisisana or *Qui si sana* is Italian for 'here one heals'. I believe it was used as a hospital or nursing home at some point in the last century, I can't remember now," he grimaced with embarrassment.

Dot appreciated the significance of the hotel's name. She needed to heal and repair. She would use this time to do just that, starting with a nutritious and delicious dinner of fresh seafood pasta, and a fruit dessert. Back in her room, Dot took time to appreciate the accommodations. Her room had a gorgeous view. A lemon-scented breeze drifted through open windows and complemented the lavender fragrance of the bed linens. The bathtub had hot and cold running water.

Luxury!! Dot wasn't sure if she said that out loud or not.

Dot slept well. In the morning, she ate a fine breakfast served on festive hand-painted china. She read the pamphlet from the reception desk which offered advice on places to see and things to do while on Capri. Pride of place on the list was a visit to the villa built by Roman Emperor Tiberius. To get there, Dot joined a tour group gathered at the funicular which would take them down to the Marina Grande. From there they walked to the historical site. At the villa, they also attended a talk on the history of Capri.

After an alfresco lunch, Dot and the other tourists split up into taxis that took them to Anacapri, an elevated area of the island. There they paid a visit to Chiesa di San Michele—*Church of the Archangel Michael.* The octagonal shaped church was built in the baroque style in the early 1700s and is home to gorgeous hand-painted ceramic tiles, some of which portray Adam and Eve being kicked out of Paradise.

The next stop was Villa Ciano. It belonged to Mussolini's daughter, Edda Ciano, whose husband had been finance minister to Mussolini. When Galeazzo Ciano realized that the Fascist cause was lost, he voted to reinstate King Victor Emmanuel III to his full constitutional powers. In response, Il Duce had him killed by firing squad. His widow was currently in hiding.

Dinner and dancing at the magnificent Hotel Paradiso ended Dot's first full day on the island. She was up early for another superb breakfast the next morning, and joined three other women on a tour to the Blue Grotto. At the dock, they met a row boat captain who would steer their tiny boat to the grotto.

"Buon giorno, Signorine," he addressed them. "Vieni con me..." Seeing little comprehension on the young women's faces, the captain switched to English.

"Come, come, quickly, presto. We must hurry, Signorine. We must not miss the low tide or our effort is for nothing alla Grotta Azzurra."

They obeyed the orders but not fast enough to please the Signore. He encouraged them with, andiamo, andiamo! Which they had learned meant, *let's go!*

The grotto was a hollowed out cave in the limestone cliffs located on the western side of the north shore of the island. It was dubbed 'blue' grotto because of the particular quality of the sunlight that passes through the seawater in two places—at the entrance and through an opening in the cave under the water. A quirk of physics filters out the reds of the color spectrum, allowing only light from the blue range to enter, giving the grotto its name-sake bright blue luminescence.

When the captain maneuvered his boat into a line of other row boats waiting to enter the grotto, he gave the women more instructions. "The mouth of the cave is poco... errm, small...."

Indeed it was a mere six feet wide by three feet high. If the water had not been at low tide, the entrance would have been below the water line, making entry impossible without scuba gear.

"When it is our turn, we must all lie flat on the bottom of the boat, like this. Si? There is a chain embedded in the rock at the entrance. I will grab it and pull the boat inside. Then you can sit up proper."

The women understood their instructions. They waited for the boatman's word to collapse into a heap. When they were successfully inside the cave, they were surprised by how bright the interior was. They had expected a dark hole but the water held so much light that the effect was magical. The cave itself was the size of an Olympic-sized swimming pool, but as deep as a 50-story office building. They were captivated by the glittering quality of the water.

"Is swimming allowed here?" One of the women asked.

"No, no. No swimming allowed. But when Emperor Tiberius lived here he used this as his own personal bathing pool."

Dot wasn't sure how this could be known. Nonetheless, she nodded in approval, as did the other ladies.

When they returned to shore, a swimming expedition had been organized for the women. After that, the group wandered in and out of island shops where they bought handcrafted ceramic cups and bowls, and handmade leather sandals. No one said no to the amusing donkey ride through the Capri countryside before being deposited back at the hotel in time for dinner.

Dot was determined that her third morning would be more relaxing. After a lazy morning, she dressed for a lovely luncheon at Casa Morgano's. In the afternoon, she joined a group of Americans for a swim in the cobalt blue waters that surround the island. How she wished she could enjoy basking in the warm sunshine with Jack. She missed him and being apart from him tugged at her heartstrings. She turned her gaze to the dark towel she sat upon. A rainbow of colors danced on the fabric. It surprised her. A rainbow? There was no rain in sight. She moved her left hand to touch it and the colors disappeared. She repeated the motion and the same thing happened. Then Dot realized that the rainbow, the symbol of a promise, was being created by the sun refracting through the cut surfaces of her engagement diamond like a prism.

"You're with me, even here," she whispered to Jack, with wistful longing.

That night was Dot's last before heading back to the hospital base. Like many of the American troops who were on Capri for R&R, she went to La Palma for dinner. Irving Berlin performed for them. He sang 'Alexander's Ragtime Band', an oldie but a goodie for these young people. He sang 'What'll I Do' and 'Putin' on the Ritz'. He ended the show with 'White Christmas' even though it was not Christmas. But the song gave voice to the longing for home felt by service men and women across the globe.

Thursday was travel day. Dot set an alarm for 7:30 for one last mouthwatering breakfast before catching the ferry for Naples. She was tired, but it was a different tired than the weariness of watching her patients suffer. This tiredness, she could rest up from.

———————

"I need another vacation day to rest up from the vacation," Dot told Charlotte.

"Afraid it doesn't work that way, old friend," Charlotte teased as she headed out of their room. "You need to get a move on, or you're going to be late!"

Dot reported for duty with only minutes to spare. She was hit immediately with the news that her beloved 58th Station Hospital would cease to exist in five days time.

"Wonder where we'll be sent," she said to Gillie, who was on duty with her. "This is sad news. I hope it doesn't mean we'll be broken up and sent to the four corners of the earth."

"All things change, Chigger," Gillie told her. "And who knows? Maybe this will be a better move for us in the end."

"How do you figure that?"

"If we are transferred to a general hospital, which is bigger, we'll have more opportunities to see a wider range of cases. Those experiences may help us in our civilian lives."

"I like it that you can think that far into the future. I can't even comprehend the possibility of being home again. It feels like we're stuck in a bad movie that's playing over and over."

"That rest vacation made you cynical."

"Not particularly. But it made me know there's more out there than war-torn bodies. But here, war-torn bodies are our reality. Don't listen to me. We'll make the most of the new assignment. We're good at being adaptable."

"We need to talk to Miss Parsons. She'll know," Gillie suggested. "And we can organize more group photographs of the 58th before we disband. We'll look at them when we're old and gray, and gloat about what beauties we were."

"You do think into the future!"

"Reaching the 'future'… it's a goal I aspire to."

"Now, is all I can do. Just right now."

"We're a complementary pair then."

———

190

On June 5, 1944, the 58ᵗʰ Station Hospital was ordered to merge permanently with the 21ˢᵗ General Hospital. No one seemed to know where the 21ˢᵗ was bound for next, but it was confirmed that, for now, they would remain together in the current location. Dot, Charlotte, Gillie, Cora, Anne, and Jane gathered in the dining room to chat about their future over coffee. The wireless played pre-recorded music in the background as they discussed various possibilities of what lay in store for them. It was past midnight before they began to gather their things to return to barracks. Before they left, Fouché hurried into the room. "Have you heard?"

"Heard what?" a chorus responded.

"It's started. The invasion. Our boys are heading to the coast of France from England. When they land, a new phase of the war will start."

"Is it on the radio?" Charlotte headed over to the set to find a newscast of the event.

"It won't be public information yet. I got a coded telegram from a contact in Portsmouth England.

"I guess this is the beginning of the end of the war," Cora said.

Hank walked in and joined the conversation. "I remember in late 1942, Churchill said, ...*this is not the end. It's not even the beginning of the end. But the end of the beginning.* So, I agree with you, Cora. We'll go a step further than Churchill and declare we're at the *beginning of the end.*"

"Do we dare celebrate?" Anne asked meekly.

"No," Fouché was emphatic. "We'll hold off on that for now. For now we pray."

Dot couldn't believe her ears. This seemed like the best sort of news.

Cora said, "Look, if the good ol' U. S. of A. is involved, it'll be a success. Just you wait and see. But I'm sure no one would turn down prayers."

The friends were too excited to go to bed so they saw the sun rise together. Miss Parsons came in for breakfast and saw her nurses. "I wager you've heard the news. We'll monitor progress throughout the day but for now we've got seventy surgical cases to see to that just came in from the Anzio Evac Hospital. I need all of you on duty, STAT."

The nurses worked double shifts until every soldier was stabilized. News of the Normandy invasion animated them with adrenaline. As Dot left the group to head back to barracks she saw Maddy walking toward her, like an apparition.

"Maddy! You're here." Dot didn't know why she stated the obvious but she was surprised to see Maddy and didn't quite know what else to say.

"I was moved to a hospital in Caserta after Sicily," she explained.

"Where's Caserta?"

"Twenty miles north of here, on the highway to Rome. I've got a 24-hour pass and I wanted to see my 'family'. I'm like a homing pigeon. Always finding my way back."

"I'm so glad you're here. We got news too. The 58th has been consumed by the 21st. Now, Miss Homing Pigeon, when you fly home, you'll have to use *them* as your beacon."

"Fair enough. Any other news?"

"Yes. And lots of it. Mostly good. We'll find supper for you and fill you in, then we want to hear what you've been up to as well."

After she had eaten some food, Maddy looked more lively. Her stories were chronicles of bravery and hardship in the face of constant danger. If anyone had the grit to endure these challenges, it was Maddy. But the challenges were taking their toll on her. She was so thin Dot was afraid a breeze would blow her out of reach like a helium balloon.

"You've got it tough," Charlotte sympathized. "We can listen to your stories all night long if that's what you need, but if you need a good night's sleep, come to our room. There's an extra bed there, we'll make sure you get peace and quiet."

Maddy was right to return to the 58th. Her friends looked after her, and twenty-four hours of uninterrupted rest would make a difference. A home-cooked meal would help too. When she woke up, Fouché had made her an epic breakfast. Dot and Gillie sat with her as she ate. Then it was time to find Hank to ask for advice on transport back to Caserta.

"Go see the driver for the Weapons Carrier. Rusty's his name. Tell him I need him to take Maddy up to Caserta. He'll get her there, no problem."

How in the world he was so sure, Dot couldn't imagine. But she told Gillie to stay with Maddy and she went to see Rusty. Rusty was cooperative and told Dot that there was room for her to ride up and back with him if she wanted. She said there would be three of them in all.

"The more the merrier. Leave in an hour?"

On the dusty, rough ride to Maddy's medical installation, she explained how her unit was set in position for the evacuation of the Fifth Army's wounded. They saw primarily men who had seen battle at Monte Cassino and the Liri Valley.

"We see mostly casualties from the Anzio beachhead area," Dot said. "Americans, of course, but a lot of our patients are French."

"If our boys meet up in Rome, like you say, and if the Allies take Normandy, we'll wind up in France, on our way to Berlin." Enthusiasm with a dash of hope had worked its way into Maddy's

193

voice. It seemed to give her strength. No one had anything to add.

After a brief lull, Maddy snapped out of her trance. She looked at Dot. "How's your Jack? Has he deployed? Is he here?"

"He's still stateside," Dot told her. "But he's due to ship out to Europe, not the Pacific. Every letter says, 'We'll be there soon. We're preparing to ship out.' I don't know. If he misses the war altogether, I'll be pleased. But he won't. So I hope they get a move on."

"I bet there's plenty of war to go around for a while." The fatigue had crept back into Maddy's voice. Dot pulled Maddy's head over to her shoulder and let it rest there until they arrived in Caserta.

Twelve

Diary Entry ~ June 12, 1944
Must move bag and baggage to cubbyholes
full of ants and cots with no mattresses.

"What are you reading?"

Dot was dressed for duty and on her way out of the barracks when she came to a dead stop at the main entrance door. A typed note was stapled at eye-level. Dot was reading it when Jane walked up behind her. Dot pointed to the notice. "Look," she said.

ORDER TO VACATE BARRACKS
ALL OCCUPANTS
MUST REMOVE BELONGINGS
BY 1700 HOURS JUNE 13
NO EXCEPTIONS!

"That seems abrupt," Jane complained. "I don't recall Miss Parsons mentioning this…"

"…which means she doesn't know," Dot added. "She likes to keep us informed to minimize surprises. Let's find her and see what she has to say about this."

Dot and Jane knew Miss Parsons would already be in her office. They headed in that direction.

"It's true," Miss Parsons admitted to Dot and Jane. "I received orders five minutes ago. You say there's a notice on your barracks door already? I can't say I'm happy about that. Okay, I'll update the group at lunch. For now, you two get your breakfast and report for duty."

After breakfast, Dot walked over to the hospital ward. It was a ghost town. The men had been moved out. Dot assumed they had been transferred to the 21st General Hospital facility located on the other side of the fairgrounds. She heard a noise in the laboratory area and went to the see what was going on there. Doctor Beauchamp was placing a large black microscope in a velvet-lined case.

"Well, Chinnis, it's the end of the line for us."

Dot looked puzzled.

"They're sending all of you over to the 21st. They're sending me up to Normandy to a field hospital. I came in to pack up the lab gear that belongs to me personally. It'll be useful on the frontlines. They'll have you sorting and packing everything else. The 21st will make out like bandits, having the best nurses in the Army, and the best damned equipment too."

Dot blinked tears away. The reality of losing the identity of the 58th hit her heart. She was afraid the big change meant a breakup of *family*. She fought to keep her composure as she asked Beauchamp, "When do you head out?"

"This afternoon," he said. "They're flying me to Portsmouth England for a couple of days. Then I'm to be delivered in a dinghy, like George Washington crossing the Delaware, to the coast of France to join up with a forward unit."

The image made Dot smile. "The men at the front will be lucky to have you, but you'll be sorely missed by the 58th. The *former* 58th, that is."

"I'll keep in touch with the unit. Now go make me proud." Beauchamp cleared his throat. He picked up his microscope in one hand, a satchel that held his surgical instruments in the other, and made a hasty exit.

Hank passed him in the entranceway. As he surveyed the state of things in the ward he said to Dot, "Packing day, I hear."

"Looks that way. Everything we have is to be sent to the 21st General. We're being absorbed. Would you happen to know where I can get my hands on more boxes?"

"Boxes on the way as we speak, and I'll do better than that. I got three men you can put to work."

Dot thanked him, made a pot of coffee, and waited for her crew to show up. They worked quickly and had only a few items left to deal with when they took a lunch break. Dot was interested to hear what Parsons had found out.

"Pack everything you own tonight," Parsons said. "You'll vacate your current residence first thing in the morning and move into a space closer to the 21st for the time being. Take just your personal items, what you can carry or put in your B-bags. That means no furniture, no draperies, you know the drill."

The women took this news like good sports. They belonged to Uncle Sam and wherever Uncle Sam wanted them, that's where they would go. Yet, when they looked at Miss Parsons giving them their instructions they wondered why she appeared to pity them. They waited for the other shoe to drop.

"Moving to the 21st is good for us," Parsons insisted. "In the long run, at least. But for a while your accommodations will be a step down from what you have now. Please, just keep in mind the nurses on the frontlines and their primitive living conditions."

Parsons dismissed the women and Cora broke the silence. "Well..., that's ominous."

Conversation buoyed the women's spirits as they packed and readied themselves to be moved again, like gypsies. They chatted about their time at Camp Kilmer, and when they came together for their first taste of deployed Army life in Oran and Tunis. They patted themselves on the back for being a happy band of adventurers. The bravado helped ward off homesickness and the prospects of whatever lay ahead of them. On the following morning Dot and the women of the 58th moved bag and baggage into the Hot Sulphur Bath House, a mile and a half from their former barracks.

The design of the bathhouse allowed two women to inhabit a small 8-foot square cubbyhole of a room. Dot was not happy. "I'll share this little closet with you, Charlotte, but I don't see why I must accommodate this colony of ants as well."

Each room had two cots, no mattresses, and a narrow space between the cots. Dot and Charlotte scrounged for a crate to use as a bedside table. Otherwise, their things would have to be stored on the damp concrete floor beneath their cots.

"I hope we get an upgrade before the mold and vermin move in making themselves at home in our clothes," Charlotte said.

The nurses of the *Former* 58th, as they saw themselves, reported for duty the very next morning at 7 a.m. The 21st still had patients and the nurses worked until 5:30 p.m. It was ten and a half hours of confusion since the folks at the 21st didn't know what to do with the extra help. By the end of her shift, Dot was so tired she didn't care what kind of bed she had to sleep in. The next day was a repeat of the one before, including another early bed time.

After two days of work in the new facility, Dot, Charlotte, and Anne walked over to Miss Parsons' office. They had not seen her and wondered if she needed help packing. They found her organizing papers at her desk. Dark circles around her eyes indicated a lack of sleep on her part.

"We stopped in to help move you over to our new home," Charlotte said by way of explaining their drop-in.

Miss Parsons stood up and stretched her back, a way to postpone her news.

"I just received amended orders."

"Where are we off to next?" Charlotte said.

"*We're* not off to anywhere, sadly. I'm off to Anzio to the 105th Station Hospital as their chief nurse. The 21st currently has someone in that position, Major Lucille S. Spalding is her name. The Army will use me here in Italy for a while longer."

"What will we do without you?" Anne was distraught.

"We'll have none of that, Stone. You'll be fine. Besides, this posting may be temporary. The war's moving fast and nothing is forever. You're here to do a job. Just do *that* job," Miss Parsons patted Anne's shoulder, "and all will be well. Keep your focus on your work. You've done that so far. I expect nothing less whether I'm your chief nurse or not."

"Yes, ma'am," Anne responded.

Miss Parsons continued. "Major Whitfield will be transferred from the 58th to the Peninsular Base Section."

Charlotte looked puzzled.

"That's the base of operations for Italy. She'll be valuable there."

Dot and Charlotte said nothing. They were in shock.

"Now, get on with your day," Miss Parsons told them kindly. "We'll see each other before we have to say our goodbyes."

On the way back to their cubbyhole barracks, the women stopped by Supply to put in an order for mattresses, an attempt to improve the creature comforts of their new domicile.

As news of Parsons' reassignment was shared, morale among the old 58th group deteriorated. They knew they'd be okay, but this was an unexpected kick in the gut, and they realized how much they leaned on the strong shoulders, metaphorically, of Captain Dorothy Parsons.

Before the women had time to recover their self-confidence, an official inspection was ordered. If it had been an inspection of the hospital facilities, they would have passed with flying colors, but the inspection of their barracks was uninspiring. The women did their best to spiff up their current residence but with little success. What consequences could the Army possibly levy on them if they failed their inspection? They could think of none worse than their current fate.

———

In late June, war news remained encouraging. That, and the consistently warm and dry weather, improved everyone's outlook. Dot received a newsy letter from Jack. Over a week had passed since the last one and she assumed his unit had been busy preparing for deployment. He mentioned that after their months of preparation in the Tennessee Maneuvers, he had been afraid that the 398th would be relegated to a mere show-regiment. He now had it on good authority, he told her, that they would be in Europe soon. He was ready to join the fight.

Dot was *not* ready for him to join the fight. She was, however, joyful at the prospect of their reunion when he arrived on European soil. She knew that *somehow*, they would make that happen.

The 58th nurses had kept to themselves, not integrating with the 21st crew, so Major Spalding decided that a reception would make the new members of her team feel more welcomed. At the

200

reception, they met Colonel Lee D. Cady, M.D. Commander of the hospital. Each nurse introduced herself in turn.

Dot presented herself and said, "It's nice to meet you, Colonel."

"It's not exactly our first meeting, is it, Lieutenant? I think we met before today."

"No sir, I…" Dot stopped herself as she had a flashback to the day when Fouché gave her a ride in the sidecar of the German motorcycle. She had saluted Colonel Cady, in a rather sassy fashion, on that day. "I stand corrected, sir. Nice to see you *again*."

The outcome of the warm and friendly gathering was successful. The ice was broken between the 21st and the 58th, and the two groups realized they were here for one shared purpose.

While the warm glow of détente was still new, Elizabeth got word that her brother, Tommie, was injured in battle.

"You look like you got bad news," Dot told her.

"I did. You know my brother is here. Fighting up at Anzio."

"Oh…" Dot couldn't hide the worst thought reflected in her face.

"No, not killed. But hurt. Bad. He's lost an eye." Elizabeth hesitated, trying to maintain her composure. "His hand was blown off."

"Where is he?"

"He's at the 17th General Hospital in Naples."

"I've got the day off," Dot said. "Let's go see him."

Dot and Elizabeth found Hank. He organized a ride to Naples for them. Inside the hospital ward, Elizabeth spied her brother in a bed halfway across the darkened room. They walked over to his bedside quietly. Most of the men were sleeping.

"Tommie?" Elizabeth whispered as she knelt down beside his bed.

"Sis?"

"I came as soon as I heard. God. What happened?"

"I don't know. I can't remember. It happened so fast. We were taking fire, then my eye was on fire. Whatever hit me must have knocked me out because when I woke up, I was here. Something took my hand too." He raised his left arm, at the wrist was a stump covered in gauze.

Elizabeth struggled to hide her alarm for her brother's welfare, but his current state shook her deeply. Tommie seemed calm, however, as he looked past Elizabeth to Dot.

"This is Dot Chinnis. I've written to you about her. She wanted to come see you too."

"Very nice to meet you Miss Chinnis," Tommie said.

"Dot, please. We're all friends here. What can we do to help? Is there anything we can get for you?"

"My gear was brought in with me, could you locate my cigarettes?"

"We can do that," Elizabeth assured him. "Are you eating okay? We'll find food for you, if you want."

"They're feeding me pretty good," he said. Then as an afterthought he added, "Some fruit, though. I'd sure appreciate that."

Dot assured him they'd get those things before they left Naples.

"I guess this is your ticket home, little brother," Elizabeth relaxed and placed her hand on his chest as she teased him gently.

"Yeah, you might be right. I need both eyes and both hands to fire my rifle at the enemy. You know, I had Uncle Nub on my mind before you came in. And how he lost his foot during the Great War. If I was a betting man, I bet I'll soon be known as 'Nub Junior'. I guess there are worse names. But I'm damned if I can think of them right now." He laughed at his joke but winced

202

with pain. Dot went off to find the duty officer to order more morphine for Tommie.

"What can I do to help you, Tommie?" Elizabeth asked.

"I'm okay, really. The pain is bad, but I feel so grateful to be alive, Sis. I thought I was a goner. I did. An eye? A hand? I've seen buddies blown into hamburger. *Young guys.* Younger than me, I mean. There, and then *gone.* No future for them. Families will be hurt forever over that. I just wonder if I'll ever get a girl. My good looks and charm might not be enough to woo the ladies."

"That's where you're wrong, brother dear. Find a hook for that missing hand, and an eye patch. Then reply to questions with *Arrrhhh....* . I dare say you'll be the most dashing pirate to ever walk the Poop Deck."

Elizabeth and Dot waited for the morphine to mute Tommie's pain before running over to the PX. They bought him several packs of Lucky Strikes, some figs and pears, and a couple of magazines. He was sound asleep when they returned so they set the things on his bedside table. Elizabeth wrote a brief note:

See you tomorrow,

Sis

Dot and Elizabeth returned to see Tommie the next day after their shift. He remained in physical pain but continued to feel grateful to be alive. The nurses believed the positive attitude would help Tommie heal.

———

On Monday, Dot stayed in barracks. She was upset over Elizabeth's brother, and unhappy with their current residential arrangements. She tried to imagine the living conditions of frontline nurses in comparison to her own, but it didn't help. Mundane chores kept her busy. She did her laundry by hand, and hung her clothes to dry on a line she had strung up between two hooks already embedded in the wall. She organized her gear for greater efficiency, always a work in progress. Although these tasks had their practical purposes, it didn't stop Dot from contemplating Tommie's injuries, or Jack's approaching arrival. She realized that with Jack, as with Tommie, she would not be able to remain objective about her feelings if he was injured. She would love Jack no matter what, but where pain or injury applied to her sweetheart, it was a totally different thing.

Pull yourself together! Dot told herself. *What will happen will happen, so just pray for a good outcome for us all.* Then she realized that there was no good outcome for many of the patriots fighting this war, so she accepted that the situation was bigger than her. There was little she could do beyond her job. The melancholy lessened when she shrugged off the weight of the entire U.S Army.

Dot savored her hours of solitude. It was good to have time to reflect. But too much of it brought a pang of loneliness, so when the others trickled back in, she was grateful for the company. They re-grouped and went to find supper together. That night, after lights out, Dot drifted off to sleep with no trouble. But at midnight she heard a noise that did not sound like nurses going to the latrine. She sat up, pulled a jacket around her shoulders, and found her flashlight. She wakened Charlotte.

"I heard a noise. I'm going to go investigate but I wanted someone to know in case I don't come back." Dot's whisper was conspiratorial.

"Give me two seconds and I'll go with you."

Together the women went to the exterior door of the spa building. They spied a drunken Second Lieutenant, the single gold bar on his jacket sleeve clearly identifying his rank. He was unmistakably inebriated as he broke into the nurses' barracks.

"What are you doing here?" Dot demanded. She hoped her voice was loud enough to wake the others.

"I'm here to pay a visit to the nurses who live here."

"It's the middle of the night," Charlotte challenged him. Then she saw that he was brandishing a pistol. Was he making a threat? "Are you looking for anyone in particular?" She questioned him more explicitly.

Elizabeth had come out of her room and saw the exchange. She snuck out a back door to find an MP. The MP came promptly and hustled the Lieutenant out of the building without any further ordeal.

"What in the world was he up to?" Elizabeth asked.

No one conjured a satisfying scenario. The women decided to request locks be installed on their doors, ASAP.

At the end of July, war news was still good for the Brits and the Yanks. American forces were moving up the boot of Italy and the Soviet army was having military successes in Eastern Europe. President Roosevelt was running for an unprecedented fourth term as President in an attempt to continue the momentum of favorable Allied outcomes. News of an assassination attempt on Hitler reached them, but ten days late. It meant that Hitler's closest officials were divided on his Nazi policies. Another 'plus' in the U.S. success column.

In Dot's personal world, a V-mail from Jack was the highlight of her day. He wrote that he would be arriving soon. No elaboration. She was happy, but full of worry too. A trip planned to Rome helped ease her anxiety. Since the Allies had entered Rome in June, Rome had become a relatively safe place for sightseeing.

To make the Roman holiday feasible, Dot and Gillie negotiated a deal with Rusty. He would request a day's leave and secure access to a Jeep. In return, Dot and Gillie would feed him the best Italian food money could buy. Rusty thought this was a bang up deal for him. He assured them that Rome was only a couple of hours drive. The tourists left after breakfast but the drive took closer to five hours. Rusty fought through cratered roads in a Jeep with no shock absorbers. The Willys Jeep was built to respond to a score of various tasks but neither comfort nor a smooth ride was an objective on that list. The group made time for a good Italian meal, but that left little time to walk around the city before they had to leave.

After they returned to base, Dot went directly to her cubbyhole. She was on duty early the following morning and needed to sleep. When she woke up the next morning she felt like she was catching a head cold, but reported to work anyway. She felt better by the end of the day, well enough at least to go with Rusty to the PX.

"I've got something to ask you, Chinnis. It's important."

"Anything."

He handed her a folded piece of paper. Dot briefly wondered if it was a love note.

"It's my parents' address. Will you write home to them if, you know, if it comes to that?"

"Of course, Rusty. But there won't be a need."

"They're sending me to the front next week. I don't know what this next move will be like. But I know I've been lucky so far. If I get into a sticky situation, I don't mind. I want to do my bit. But for some reason I'm scared of this next move, Chinnis. I know it sounds like I got the jitters. And I guess I do. So anyway, you'll write home for me if it comes to that?"

"I certainly will. Now before you take off, let's try for one more trip to Rome. You get the Jeep and the time off, I'll plan the rest."

"It's a deal," he agreed with a smile.

———

Dot was as good as her word. She wangled a 48-hour pass to Rome for her, Charlotte, Gillie, Anne, and Rusty. They took off at ten o'clock Sunday morning, heading for the Atlantico Hotel, a suggestion she'd gotten from Fouché. When they arrived, much quicker this time, the hotel had no vacancies, so they tried at the Continental where they had better luck. It was early August and hot, but that didn't stop their plans to walk to Vatican City. They saw it as a good sign that Pope Pius XII was present. He said a prayer and a blessing for those in attendance.

Rusty had bought a Cook's Tour Guide from the hotel desk clerk for the tourists to organize their sightseeing of Rome on Monday. They saw the Catacombs, the Coliseum, and several ancient churches. A delicious supper of pasta, bread, and wine topped off the evening. The travelers were up early on Tuesday to return to the hospital, and real life.

By mid-August, Rusty still hadn't been moved to his new unit. Operation Dragoon, the invasion of southern France, had just begun and he believed that would be his destination. He was restless, and ready to jump into battle. Dot didn't feel the same. She was glad he was still with them and told him so one evening at supper.

That night, before dawn, Dot's area was battered by an air raid. Flak hit the camp, causing destruction wherever it struck. The wards filled up, and all personnel were called to duty. Hours later, when the casualties were stabilized, the nurses went to find some chow. Hank met them at the doorway. His face was contorted in anguish.

"What's wrong?" Dot asked him.

"I just got word. A driver was killed in the raid."

"No." She shook her head trying with all her might to prevent what she knew was coming next. "Don't say it, Hank. Don't say his name out loud." She dropped into a nearby chair.

Dot wrote a condolence letter to Rusty's mother in Pennsylvania describing their trip to Rome, and his kind support to all his comrades, male and female, on the base. She had a snapshot of Rusty in Rome, standing in front of his Jeep with his arms crossed on his chest, smiling like a kid. She enclosed it with the letter, licked the stamp, and sent it with a prayer.

Although the war news was hopeful overall, at a personal level it continued to take its toll.

Dot tried to compartmentalize her grief over losing Rusty. She put it in a little imaginary basket and set it aside. But his death weighed heavy on her heart. One of Dot's patients had a leg amputation to his thigh and was in terrible pain. She did all that was humanly possible for him and when he was scheduled for an air-evac to the U.S., Dot got up early, in time to see him off. The base took another air raid at eleven that night. Dot couldn't sleep so she volunteered to spend the night helping Cora with one of her patients who was hemorrhaging. When she signed in for her regular duty the following morning, Dot had five new patients. She stabilized them, and made them comfortable but that night, another air raid rained more flak on the camp before the clock struck midnight.

Sleeping was not in the cards, which was probably a good thing. Gillie spotted one of the patients, who had evidently lost touch with reality, wander into the nurses' barracks. She cursed the red tape that delayed the lock installation for their barracks doors. She shouted for the other women for backup. The soldier was shouting gibberish. He flailed his arms hysterically.

"Run out and find an MP," she told Jane. "He can help us get the man back to the hospital ward. Tell him he doesn't seem to have a firearm and we don't want him hurt."

"We also don't want him coming or going as he pleases," she replied. "I'll be right back."

When that emergency was dealt with, the women calmed themselves and returned to their cubbyholes to sleep. Elizabeth took a detour to the nurses' latrine. She saw another man there. He seemed to be drugged out of his mind and tried to duck and hide when she approached him.

"What are you doing here?" she demanded.

He froze. She shouted for help. The others came running.

This unpredictable behavior unnerved them all. Dot looked up to see if it was full moon. It was. Shining brighter than ever. *You can cut back on the polish for a bit, Jack,* she said to herself. *That big ol' moon is wreaking havoc and NOT in a romantic way.* To the others she suggested they use the buddy system if when going to the latrine during the rest of the night.

Conditions did not improve. The next night's air raid took place just after midnight. The sky was lit up with the 90mm guns blasting the fighter planes overhead. At breakfast, a sleepy Dot had found an old newspaper and was reading an editorial saying that the war would end by October 1, a month away. She was right to be skeptical.

The weather was turning cold and rainy, and it was not yet September. The latest letter from Jack arrived. He'd be leaving the States in a week's time, and on the European side of the Atlantic days after that. Dot doubted Jack's travel itinerary was set in stone. If Army-time was the guideline, she wouldn't hold her breath for his arrival before Christmas. She hoped for sooner, of course, and she prayed for calm weather for his crossing.

Dot reported for duty the following day where she was greeted with new patients flown in from Southern France. After getting the men settled in, Dot went to put on a pot of coffee to share with them. She turned to walk to the laboratory and saw a tall handsome man with dark wavy hair walk through the door, followed by Hank Wilson. Dot assumed the man was a friend who needed a quick patch up of some type—a bandage, perhaps, or aspirins. Hank smiled at her like he was bursting to tell a secret, because he was.

"Chinnis, you got a minute?"

"Of course. What do you need?"

"I want you to meet my newest friend, Brian Aherne."

The name was vaguely familiar but Dot couldn't place it. She searched her brain for someone she met back in North Africa. She came up empty.

"Glad to meet you," she said and stuck her hand out.

"Very glad to meet you too, my dear. Wilson has told me about you. He has the fondest regard for all of you nurses, but you seem to shine above the rest."

Dot cut her eyes over at Hank, making a face. "Well, he'd be wrong about that. I do make him fudge on occasion, though, so that's probably the reason for his favoritism." She returned her attention to her new acquaintance. "Is there anything I can do to help you?" She still wondered if he needed medical assistance.

"No, no, Chinnis," Hank broke in. "Aherne is a movie star. He's married to Joan Fontaine."

Joan Fontaine, Dot had heard of. She had seen her in Hitchcock's film, *Rebecca,* playing the part of the second Mrs de Winter, but she wasn't familiar with Aherne's work.

"You're a long way from home," Dot told him.

"As are you," he replied with a captivating smile. "I'm here to do my bit too. I'm with the USO show. We have a touring production of the play, 'The Barretts of Wimpole Street'."

"A performance?" Dot had heard no news of a USO show at the base but was interested.

"Yes. Katharine Cornell and I are reprising our roles from the Broadway show. Do you know it?"

"Oh yes. The account of Elizabeth Barrett Browning, her father, and her life with the poet Robert Browning."

Aherne's broad smile showed he was pleased Dot knew the story. "Would you like tickets?" he asked her. "You don't need any to get into the show, of course, because we'll have enough performances to accommodate all who want to come see us but they *will* get you front row seats. How many do you want?"

Dot asked for tickets for her original 58th crowd and for Fouché and Hank as well.

"How can I thank you?"

"I would like to sample some of that famous fudge!"

"I'll make a fresh batch tonight."

The tickets were for Monday night. Everyone managed time off, calling it the gala event of the year. The women dressed in their best OD greens. Adding a neck scarf or some jewelry was overlooked by their superior officers, and made a nice touch.

Dot filed in first, followed by Hank, Gillie, Elizabeth, Fouché, Charlotte, Cora, Jane, and Anne. Dot's seat was next to the hospital Lieutenant Commander. She had met him at the

211

meet-and-greet but didn't imagine he would remember her. She made polite small talk until the lights flashed, announcing that the show was beginning.

After the first act, Dot leaned forward and looked to her left to see if her party was content. They were. She looked to her right to see if she recognized the theatergoers further down the row. Two seats away, she saw a face she recognized but did not know personally. She blinked in classic cartoon double-take form, and sat back hastily. The movement didn't go unnoticed by the Lieutenant Commander.

"You're in good company tonight, Lieutenant," he told Dot.

"I might be hallucinating, sir," she laughed, embarrassed.

"He's exactly who you think he is…"

"Douglas Fairbanks, Jr? How in blue blazes?"

"He's a Navy officer. He's been in North Africa, then he was part of Operation Husky in Sicily. He's the one who developed the deceptive unit called 'Beach Jumpers' for the U.S."

Dot looked puzzled.

"They're the boys who parachute into an area away from the official invasion point. 'Beach Jumpers' draw the enemy to that point, making them believe it's the actual invasion. When enemy resources are pulled away from where we actually want to attack, our guys have a better chance of success. He learned it from the Brits. It's dangerous but effective. He participated in *Dragoon*, the southern France assault. I wonder if he's on R&R, taking advantage of our entertainment offerings. Want me to ask?"

"Good Lord, no!" Dot was shocked at the prospect.

"All right. But I'll do this for you." He pulled out his wallet and extracted a 100 Lire note. He passed it to the famous actor with this request. "One of our treasured nurses is a fan of yours." He nodded at Dot. "Would you mind autographing this for her?" Dot's face turned red.

Fairbanks autographed it and handed it back to Dot personally, with a smile. Dot couldn't believe her life.

—————

Hospital staff had been alerted that a move was imminent. Every available person in the 21st was employed to pack the wards in preparation for that. Where to this time was the question on everyone's lips. Dot and Elizabeth paid Tommie another visit. He was getting his color back and needing a little less morphine for pain. They placed bets on who would be moved out first.

On Thursday, September 21, the official alert to move was given, but no departure date. The hospital had only a handful of patients left in their care, and they would be evacuated in the next day or two. Rains settled in again, but that wasn't news. The 21st nurses welcomed staff from the 3rd General Hospital who came to stage with them while they waited for their next assignment.

By the following Tuesday, all hospital equipment was packed in preparation for the move and the electricity was shut down. It wasn't until Friday that the group stood retreat, the ceremony signifying the official end of duty. The next day was pay day. They got paid in French money.

"I guess we're going to France!" Dot stated the obvious as she ate supper from her mess kit. She was in bed by eight o'clock in anticipation of the trip ahead. When she woke up the following morning, Charlotte was standing in the middle of the cubbyhole, completely dressed.

"Are you a guardian angel watching over me?" Dot asked.

"No. Just twiddling my thumbs."

Dot looked at Charlotte like she was crazy. "What do you mean?"

"I was just at the chow hall. Word is, there's no movement for our group today."

213

"But it's four days since we stood retreat."

"I guess hurry-up-and-wait, is the only hurry we'll see," Charlotte scoffed.

"That's actually good news. I can go see Tommie one more time."

"He flew out last night. Elizabeth heard this morning."

Dot was glad he was on his way home. She sighed.

"What's that sigh for, Dottie?"

"Lost another bet. I was sure we'd beat him out of Italy."

———————

A wake up call went out to the camp at 0500 on October 5. Personnel prepared to move out. It had been two weeks since the initial announcement of their movement. The nurses dressed for travel, which meant donning rain gear. Each truck was assigned sixteen nurses. They set out in convoy to Naples Harbor where the hospital ship, *Ernest Hinds,* was anchored. When it set sail at dawn the following morning, Dot looked back at the city. "Eight months, and fifteen days," she muttered.

"What's that?" Charlotte asked.

"We were here eight and a half months. In many ways it feels like a lifetime."

"Yes," Charlotte responded. "It was a life time for some."

Passengers who were willing to wager a bet guessed that the ship would take them to Marseille in two days, spending one night at sea. Anyone adding an extra day to that for good measure would have won the bet. From Friday to Sunday, the boat rocked and rolled across the Mediterranean. Dot's appetite tolerated nothing more exotic than water, fresh apples, and soda crackers.

The *Ernest Hinds* remained idle in the harbor at Marseille on Sunday morning. Dot looked towards shore, then at Elizabeth standing at the guard rail beside her. "I was going to write home about arriving in Marseille, the Côte d'Azur, *the* resort to the rich and famous," Dot said. "But look at this, this is nothing to write home about."

Debris from the Allied landing operation was left behind and the garbage scattered on the beach was repulsive. Scuttled German ships meant a maneuvering of arriving ships that wanted to unload its cargo. When the *Hinds* was finally tied up, the passengers' bags were unloaded, but not the passengers.

Monday rolled around and still, no one disembarked. For the entire day, the nurses sat on the deck, looking at land.

"It's as if we weren't expected," Cora joked.

Finally, after breakfast on Tuesday morning, the order to go ashore was given. It was October 10, ten days past the date the newspaper editorial Dot read back in Italy had said the war would be over. For Dot and her fellow travelers, there would be plenty more war to endure.

Part Four

FRANCE

Thirteen

Diary Entry ~ October 10, 1944
Up at 6, off the boat at 8, convoyed from Marseille to St Zacharie.

Passengers remained on the *Ernest Hinds* for five days before they were allowed to go ashore in Marseille, France. The 21st General Hospital staff were then trucked from the port to Saint-Zacharie, an hour away. The group would stage there and wait for news of their ultimate destination.

Dot, Elizabeth, and Gillie roomed together on the third floor of Hotel Green Mountain. Dot unpacked quickly, wanting to settle in, when orders came for her to report for detached service the next day. She re-packed her gear before tracking down the chief nurse, Major Spalding, for more information.

"Oh, good. You've heard then." Major Lucille S. Spalding had directed the nursing staff at the 21st Hospital since before it left the states. She knew from Captain Parsons that Dorothy Chinnis would handle any assignment professionally. "We need you and Charlotte to join the group going to the 46th General Hospital in Besançon." Spalding pronounced the town's name by slurring its three syllables as if she were a native. It sounded like, *Bee-zahn-sohn.*

"I remember the 46th bunch from Oran. Are you sure it's just DS? I would hate to be separated from what has become my family."

"No need to worry. There's another Station Hospital merging with the 46th but they've not arrived. You'll fill in until they show up. There'll be forty of you nurses and eight physicians hitching a flight up to the hospital."

"Where is it located?"

"Besançon is what the Army calls a *strategically placed citadel city*. To us noncombatants, a hilltop fortress. It's located four hundred miles north of here, near the Swiss border. It's only recently been liberated from the Nazis. There's still hostile territory between here and there so ground travel is too dangerous, but when you get there, you'll be relatively safe. The 442nd Infantry Combat Team is there to watch over the area."

Dot had heard of the 442nd. It was big news when they took Hill-140, a strategic piece of ground in Tuscany that had been defended by massive German forces. With that victory, the Allies pushed closer to Rome.

"Your flight leaves at three o'clock in the morning." Spalding saw that the wicked time of departure surprised Dot. "I know, it's an ungodly hour but the tour guide who made the arrangements doesn't seem to care. While you're in Besançon, the rest of us will leapfrog you on our way to the Ravenel Hospital in Mirecourt. It was a huge psychiatric hospital complex for the entire Vosges area until the Germans took it over. We've booted them out and now we'll occupy it. It's two hours further north of where you'll be. We'll all be together there when you're done at the 46th."

"Ravenel?" Dot wasn't sure she heard correctly.

"Yes, do you know it?"

"No, not at all, but I grew up in a little town in South Carolina, where my mother still lives, and it's named Ravenel. It's interesting that I'm half-way across the world heading to a place called Ravenel."

"I know your neck of the woods, Chinnis. Huguenots settled in that area. Perhaps the French Protestants originally came from this area of France and wanted to remember home by giving your town that name."

"I suppose I've seen weirder things since this odyssey began, so who knows? I'm relieved that I'll be able to reunite with the group."

Dot slept briefly, getting up at midnight to prepare to leave. She and Charlotte joined the group climbing into the back of a supply truck. The predawn morning was cold but the passengers had worn long-johns and boots, and wrapped themselves in winter wool coats. The truck drove westward, back through Marseille, and onward to the air field at Istres. Istres had been a Vichy airfield until the Americans seized it for their own use two months earlier. The 64th Troop Carrier Group used the facility now, running the Douglas C-47 Skytrain troop transports in and out of it. But even with the early start, Dot's group arrived too late for their flight out.

"Hey, I know what we can do," Charlotte snapped. "We can sit around here and *wait*."

"I'm becoming an expert in waiting," Dot replied.

The group killed time at the canteen playing cards, chatting, writing letters. The usual. They slept that night in a nearby stable.

Dot looked at Charlotte. "The tour guide who booked our flight *and* our accommodations should be fired. I'm no longer having fun on this excursion."

Charlotte had no snappy come back. She just shook her head as if to say, *typical.*

Up at 4:30 the next morning, the temp was chilly but the wind was subdued enough for the C-47 to take off for the American airbase in Luxeuil. At Luxeuil, nurses and doctors exited the C-47 and sat idly on make-shift wooden benches on the airfield waiting for ground transport on to Besançon. The airbase was only seven miles from the front and for five hours, the group listened to steady gunfire playing in the background. At last, trucks arrived to haul them the sixty rainy, cold, miles to the 46th General Hospital.

Dot and Charlotte and the other nurses checked in with the chief nurse at the hospital. They were given lodging in what had only recently been German barracks.

Dot wrote in her diary: *Everything messy. Not impressed with filthy conditions left by German soldiers.*

"It's a place to sleep out of the rain and the cold," Charlotte conceded.

"I'm trying my best to be grateful for that much, at least. But I may need you to remind me. Often."

Dot and Charlotte chose beds at the far end of the row. Before finding places to stow their belongings they went in search of food. Sandwiches made with cold, congealed, canned ham was food in 'name' only, and it was welcomed only because sleeping on an empty stomach was the greater evil.

When Dot woke up the following morning, she heard rain pelting against the window like someone spraying a fire hose. *Lovely*, she thought.

She and Charlotte wore boots with their duty uniform, not caring that the utility of fashion choice would turn no man's head at the meal line. Dining was still at mess kit level since a more permanent facility had not been set up for the camp. Still, they had a basic level of comfort. Food, protection from the elements, and a comrade to share the rough with the good.

They reported for duty and observed the frantic pace under which the hospital staff worked. Every nurse had pulled many long shifts, without exception, and they were worn to a frazzle. Dot and the other new nurses' attitudes changed from wishing for better barracks conditions to being glad they were there to help out.

The schedule for the next few days was as follows: Work. Eat. Sleep. Repeat. To change things up, Dot and Charlotte caught a ride into the town of Besançon during a rare chunk of time off.

"Are you looking for anything specific to buy?" Dot asked Charlotte.

"I heard there was little fighting in this area so I hope some merchandise will be on the shelves."

"I don't hold out hope myself. This was a big resistance area. The locals are skeletons. I'm sure the Nazis who were here until very recently took anything of value. It's what they're good at—taking things that don't belong to them." Dot shook her head.

"It won't hurt to go have a look," Charlotte pressed the issue.

"Okay. I guess I'm up for an adventure, whatever happens. What are you looking for? Anything in particular?"

"I'm hoping to find a sweater to fight off this never-ending chill I feel to my bones. Maybe we'll luck up. And if we don't, it'll be fun to explore." Charlotte was more optimistic than Dot.

If Dot and Charlotte had hoped to inject a little amusement into their monotonous schedules, the plan failed. They peered into shop windows looking for items of interest while idle local Frenchmen leered at them. Two men walked up and stood unnervingly close to them. Two others made improper sexual advances.

"Let's get out of here," Charlotte whispered. "There's nothing for us in this town."

They caught sight of a Jeep driver from the hospital and hailed him to stop.

"You gals look as if you've seen a ghost!" He said. He was concerned for them.

"Something like that," Charlotte replied. "You heading back to the hospital?"

"I am if you need me to. I'm Sonny Harper, PFC. 'Harp' for short." Harp pushed his thick glasses up the bridge of his nose with his middle finger and nodded politely.

"I'm Charlotte, this is Dot. We'd love a ride."

"Hop in. I'll have you there in a flash."

"No need to fly on our account," Charlotte assured him. "Safety is higher on our priority list than speed."

"I wish I *could* fly. That was my first choice when signing up but my eyes weren't too good. Instead I got stuck with these BCGs."

"BCGs?" Dot asked.

"Yeah. Birth Control Glasses. These things are so hideously ugly, no girl will look at me twice. These eyeglasses are better than any contraception device because it means there will be no chance of an 'encounter', if you know what I mean. Anyway, I got stuck with these things rather than a pair of wings. Poor me," the Private mugged.

"Don't you worry, Harp. Your fancy eye-wear will be in style one of these days. Just you wait and see." Charlotte was encouraging.

The women were seated and PFC Sonny Harper turned the Jeep around to head to the hospital.

"The Army beat 'style' clean outta me, ma'am. I'm full-on infantry now."

Dot leaned forward from the back seat and yelled over the wind whizzing past her ears. "I'm awfully glad you're an infantryman now, Harp. They're the best of the best."

"Yes," Charlotte added, "I have to say, Frenchmen here lack your chivalry, etiquette, and just plain ol' good manners." Charlotte was spitting the words out as she voiced her disgust.

"You mean you got chatted up by some French guys?"

"Not chatted up at all. It felt like we were slimed, and it caught us by surprise," Charlotte continued.

Dot jumped in. "We're not naïve, we're Army nurses. We deflect good-natured innuendos from our American boys every day. This was a whole different ball of wax."

"I want a shower," Charlotte shivered. "This was not the type of adventure I had in mind."

Harper agreed that the area lacked universal appeal. "It's the austerity the locals have lived with all their lives, even before the Nazis showed up. The Germans shelled them and what little they had, the Germans took that too. To us Yanks, this is just a place to go through on the way to somewhere else."

Dot nodded in agreement. Harper added, "At the best of times, these folks are gruff, rough, and uncouth, so they make do with what they can poach and…"

"…well, the French bastard we encountered today tried to poach our virtue," Charlotte fumed, "and we ain't havin' it!"

"Duly noted, ma'am." Sonny Harper would keep an eye out for the nurses. No harm would come to them, if he had any say in the matter.

———

On duty the next day, Dot directed the transfer of patients from the fourth floor to the ground floor. When she returned to barracks that evening, she found that two more nurses attached

225

to the 46th had moved into the space she and the other DS nurses already occupied, making it a snug fit for all. Charlotte commented on how similar their current residential situation was compared to boot camp at Kilmer.

"One huge difference," Dot said. "We don't have a tabby cat to keep us rat-free." She pointed at a small brown furry body as it flattened itself and ducked under the door leading to the hallway.

"Dottie, to be truthful," Charlotte looked serious. "I don't have a good feeling about being here. The whole place makes me feel out of sorts."

"You think we're in danger?"

"No, not that. But, we're unwelcomed. The folks here aren't awfully friendly to us."

"I wouldn't be concerned," Dot reassured her. "We're short timers. No one wants to make a personal connection when we'll be separated again before long. We've got each other and that'll have to do."

"Well, the food stinks, too," Charlotte made a declaration.

Dot scrunched her nose up like she'd smelled a skunk.

"Not smelly, silly! But we've been spoiled and here we are eating rations morning, noon and night. Our barracks are cold, dirty, inconveniently located..."

"Okay. Stop for just a minute, Missy." Dot placed her hand on Charlotte's shoulder like a school teacher talking to her student. "How in the world did you become such a snob in the time since we've been deployed? You never complained before."

"I don't know. I'm just tired, is all. Love me anyway?"

"Always." Dot hugged Charlotte to reassure her.

Keeping up morale was a struggle and after a few days of making the 46th 'home', Charlotte was still not herself.

"I want to do my best here, Dottie." Charlotte was stretched out on her cot staring at the ceiling when Dot returned to quarters after her shift ended. "But I'm so far down in the dumps, I can't climb my way out with a ladder."

"Conditions here will improve. It takes a while to get things in place. We're not with our group, and we feel the loneliness from that as well. You've just got to hang on."

"My outlook would improve if I ever got mail in this godforsaken hell-hole of a pit."

"Don't hold back. Tell me how you really feel." Dot was unhappy, too, because the mail had not caught up with them. "Let's look at the bright side," she continued. "When we go to bed at night, we're out of the cold and rain. That can't be said for our fighting men, or many of the medical personnel closer to the front."

"We've been DS'ed to Camp Limbo," Charlotte said. "Or better yet, we should call this place Camp Purgatory. When we've paid for our sins, can we move on?"

The location of the 46th made it isolated. War news was not reaching the hospital staff, letters didn't reach them either. Dot and Charlotte loathed to visit the only town close to them. The medical workers struggled with coughs, colds, and flu, but they showed up for duty without protest. Except for Charlotte. She was irritable again and protesting her unlucky lot.

"We've dropped off the face of the earth," she told Dot. "And no one knows to come look for us. There's nothing more exciting to do here than go to work and sleep."

Dot knew it was best to let Charlotte get these grievances out of her system.

"I'm on the verge of getting the heebie-jeebies," Charlotte confessed.

"Is that a technical term?"

"Shell shock," Charlotte said loudly. "Battle fatigue." A little louder.

Dot looked at Charlotte closely to see if she was kidding. She wasn't sure.

"Dottie, I'm serious," Charlotte continued. "If I start screaming hysterically, you have permission to slap me."

"I've always wanted to use that particular medical procedure. Trust me, I'll be happy to use it to calm you down. By the way, we added forty-two French patients to the wards on my shift alone," Dot said. She wanted to see Charlotte's reaction.

"The more the merrier, I always say!" Charlotte was teasing now.

"Oh. Is *that* what you always say?"

"Well, that and a whole lot more, with a nice mix of salty words I've learned, compliments of the Army."

On the following day, Dot pointed out a sheet of paper on the notice board to Charlotte and said, "Look at that!"

Charlotte read the notice. "We've got orders to return to the good ol' 21st. *Tomorrow!*"

Dot laughed. "I'm going to miss using slap-therapy on you. And, you know…, we've actually been here only ten days."

"Ten days! Feels like we've done a thirty-year life sentence here." Charlotte was ecstatic to rejoin the old crew. "At dinner tonight, I shall dance a jig on the table."

"And, I'll take photos," Dot said. "We'll share them with the 21st gals when we meet up with them. Now, let's go pack!"

A brilliant and bright sunrise greeted Besançon the next morning. Dot and Charlotte said a few hasty goodbyes before joining twenty-four others in a convoy of ambulances to the Ravenel Hospital in Mirecourt, France. There they would be back with old friends. The procession of brown panel vans resembled caterpillars crawling across the French countryside. Although France had technically been liberated, fighting continued as Germans attempted to hold their ground near the German border. Dot felt protected in the convoy but the fact that it was necessary was disturbing.

The group stopped once, at the 9th Evacuation Hospital, for a ten minute comfort break. Frontline guns were close, and they roared without pause. Dot hoped the sounds of war wouldn't be as loud at their final destination.

The prodigals paraded into the hospital compound just after lunchtime. Dot and Charlotte shed their feelings of displacement from their time in Besançon and welcomed Mirecourt, part of the Alsace-Lorraine area near Belgium and Germany, as their new home. They hoped it would be their last *home* until the war's end.

The ambulances parked in an area marked HQ to let their passengers out. The travelers received billeting instructions along with directions to their quarters. Dot and Charlotte discovered that the 58th nurses were all living on one floor of the building. What a difference it was, to be back in the fold. In the middle of their jolly reunion in Cora's and Anne's room, Major Spalding knocked on the door and entered.

"Pleased to have you two back with us." She looked at Dot and Charlotte. "You'll like it here. Well, as much as anywhere that's not home. If you've got a minute, I'll bring you up to speed."

"Our minutes are your minutes, Miss Spalding. *Major* Spalding, I mean." Charlotte was wondering why in the world she wanted to make a good impression, but she did.

"Either title is fine. Let's sit down." Spalding had their undivided attention. They gathered round the chief nurse like campers roasting marshmallows around a campfire.

"Quick update on room assignments. They were posted when we first arrived. Charlotte Belle, you will move in with Elizabeth Campbell. Chinnis, you'll move in with McGill. Our new hospital site promises to be finer and larger than the ones we've had before. We'll be in buildings—not tents—and that goes for patients and personnel alike. True, there's no heat in the buildings, but that should be fixed soon. We hope. Our facility will be a cutting-edge facility for our men to receive medical care. We'll have modern operating rooms, full-service dental care, laboratories, and various wards for patient care."

"Our specialties will include, cranio-cerebral cases, spinal cord injuries, and maxio-facial reconstructions."

Miss Spalding continued, "Of course we'll also handle fractures, illnesses, ophthalmic damage, and other urgent care matters. We're setting up a dental department, complete with a prosthesis laboratory, but that's not relevant to us."

Spalding, like Parsons, had an air of confidence and competence that matched her kindness. Her nurses wanted to do their best for her.

"I'm delighted that you can be in one building and on the same floor. Make it a happy place. As soon as we can, we'll get partitions built. Dividing some of the spaces into smaller rooms will give you a little privacy. Something quite scarce in the Army. Am I right?"

Cora shouted an 'amen, sister' from across the room.

"We'll still have rough living conditions for a little while longer, but soon we can transform the rooms into something more civilized. The acres of farmland and woods around us are beautiful. Enjoy that beauty. Mirecourt is charming, and yet the cold and rain and mud up to our ankles—not so much. So, dress accordingly. Forget style. Wear plenty of warm clothing. It will keep you healthy. Whether at work, or going into town, dress in your heavy slacks, your high-top boots, your flannel shirts, and field jackets. I simply will not tolerate seeing any one of you shivering in the cold with blue lips. We've got work to do. Our interests and energies right now must be focused on preparing for casualties. You know the drill. Clean, clean, clean."

"We know that drill well enough," Anne said. She was much recovered from the trauma of her fiancé's death and an asset to the group. "It means we'll be able to provide somewhere nice for our boys after they've been cold and dirty in their foxholes for who knows how long."

"Precisely. Thanks for taking pride in the unacknowledged and under-valued duties we perform. Thus endeth the sermon of the day. Duty rosters are tacked on my office door in the medical building that you can see just there." Major Spalding pointed out the window. A wooden sidewalk had been built up to the entranceway. "The supper line forms at 1800 hours. See you there."

After the chief nurse left, and before Dot and Charlotte could ask questions, Cora brought them up to date.

"Fouché is here," she said, "but there's no supply line in place for the food. We have one chow hall, for everyone. *Everyone*. But there are rumors that eventually we will have an officers dining area. Very posh."

"For now," Cora continued, "we line up outside in long lines with our mess kits and then we sit on boxes inside to eat our

231

meals. After we've eaten, we stand in another long line for the honor of washing our mess kits."

"That doesn't sound too tough." Charlotte was so glad to be back with the group, standing in line was no hardship at all.

"Well," Cora continued. "As I said, there's no proper supply line for food so much of what we're eating right now is of the dehydrated variety. You know, powdered eggs."

"We got fresh potatoes and cabbage the other day," Anne chimed in.

"Oh, and real meat after that," Jane reminded them.

"Wasn't a lumpy old camel, was it?" Dot asked.

"I had forgotten that," Cora roared at the memory. "It seems like an age ago since we were in North Africa. But no, I'm sure it was frozen chicken."

"Chicken!" Charlotte's eyebrows raised in interest. "Boy, oh boy. I'm glad to be back with the gang!"

After unpacking some of their things, Dot and Charlotte followed the others to the chow hall. When they had gotten their food, they scooted wooden boxes into a circle and continued the orientation process.

"The 21st looks tip-top," Charlotte said. "Compared to what we just witnessed back at the 46th."

"You should have seen it when we arrived here," Elizabeth said. "The guys have made great progress in setting up the hospital and the support services."

"As a permanent establishment, we'll be four thousand beds strong." Anne had pride in her voice.

"That's a pretty large operation. What will the duty be like?" Charlotte asked.

"Command is still working that out, but this is how I understand it so far," Anne continued. "Of course, as Spalding told us, we have to clean up the wards. Then we'll be assigned to specific floors. I guess you noticed when you drove in that we have twelve big buildings. Not all of those are hospital wards, but most of them are. You won't believe this, but when the Germans knew we were coming, they poured cement down the drains. All the water pipes are clogged, along with the drains. Just to sabotage the facility, their idea of scorched earth, I guess. It'll take some time to fix, but the engineers have done a great job so far."

Jane pitched in. "Each nurse will be assigned a minimum of forty patients, possibly spread across two separate floors. If we're lucky, we'll get to buddy up and share duties but the patient load will be quite large. Oh! By the way. We heard from Maddy. She's at a field hospital near Épinal but she hopes to be re-attached to us before Christmas."

"No better news I wanted to hear," Dot admitted. "We'll all be together again. Except for our dear Miss Parsons and Major Whitfield. Maybe they'll catch up to us too."

Dot and Charlotte were happy to be reunited with the 21st hospital group. They weren't troubled by a large case-load for the time being, which made settling into a routine a pleasure. Their joy increased when mail delivery caught up with them."

"Hey Chigger," Gillie called from across the walkway. "Letter from Jack? You have a sublime smile on your face."

"Seven letters," she waved them at Gillie. "Three are from his P.O.E."

"Which point-of-entry? Marseille?"

"Yes. They landed October 20. Three days ago. I'm impressed the mail moved so quickly."

"Tell me again which unit he's with."

"He's with the 398th, part of the 100th Division." Dot looked back at the letter and relayed the information to Gillie. "...they

233

came over on the *U.S.S. General William H Gordon*. Oh, look. He says they went through a hurricane somewhere on the Atlantic before making port."

"Oh, God! I would have hated that!" Gillie turned green just remembering their Atlantic crossing.

"He says his outfit will be near here before long and then we'll meet up."

"Dream on, girlfriend. What's the likelihood of that? France is big. Europe even larger." Gillie wasn't trying to be cruel but she didn't want Dot to get her hopes up just to have them dashed if Jack's orders took him in the opposite direction.

"This moment of Pepto-Bismal-Pessimism was brought to you by…," Dot mimicked a radio commercial.

"Brace yourself. Because if you don't get to see Jack while he's on the continent, it'll be awfully disappointing. Don't set yourself up for that."

"You know Jack. If he says he will find a way to see me, then he will. Period. End of discussion." They both laughed.

"Let's make a bet then," Gillie challenged. "If Jack shows up, I'll take your shift for two days. If he doesn't, you take mine."

"You're on, but if he shows up *and* marries me, you'll take on my workload while I'm on my honeymoon."

"Deal! And I get to be your Maid of Honor."

"That's a win in my column on both accounts. Now let's get some chow."

Working extra hours in preparation to receive casualties meant the nurses had little time for personal chores like washing and drying and ironing their clothes. Major Spalding suggested nurses take their laundry to a woman who lived at a farmhouse just outside the hospital base. Dot and the others found Madame

234

Clotilde and struck an agreement with her to wash and iron their duty uniforms. After setting up arrangements satisfactory to both parties, the nurses returned to the base to scrub more wards.

Cora commented, "I'd rather do my own laundry if it meant Madame Clotilde would take over this scrubbing. Anybody with me on that?" A chorus of agreement answered her back.

At the end of shift the next day Dot and Gillie went into the town of Mirecourt to look for wool sweaters and warm gloves. Being so far north meant constant freezing temperatures and the late October icy wind cut through their winter garments. In their hunt, they were not successful.

Gillie had an idea.

"Chigger, the woman who does our laundry, I wonder if she could knit us a couple of sweaters since there are none to be found in the shops."

"No doubt she *could* do that Gillie, but she needs wool yarn and I don't see that anywhere for sale either."

Gillie paused a moment then said, "You know what Mirecourt is famous for, don't you?"

"No. I must have missed that update since I haven't been here as long as you have."

"Making lace, and handcrafting violins," Gillie said matter of fact. "I can't play the violin, but I'm awfully attracted to lace. Look across the street."

"You know lace won't keep us nearly as warm as wool," Dot answered her with a poker face.

"You're right, but they *are* accessories that a woman needs for a date. And if you win the bet, you will be happy to have these items handy to show off when Jack comes."

Dot was persuaded. She and Gillie walked up to the glass doors of the shop and read out loud in unison, *DeMaris Boutique de Dentelle,* painted in gold-tone letters across the double door. On display inside were silk Chantilly laces, embroidered and beaded laces, Guipure lace, and French Tulle netting, among other items of interest *pour les femmes*. If they hadn't been trained to have decorum under stress, they would have squealed like school girls. When they left, they had tissue-wrapped packages containing silk and lace handkerchiefs, face powder, and perfume.

On Saturday, Dot went to mail call. She received more letters from Jack and sat down on the spot to read them. They had worked out a numbering system for their correspondence and it helped Dot establish the order in which the letters had been written. She decided to start with the most recent, and work backwards but the news was too good to carry out the plan. When she read, *I should be at the 21ˢᵗ on Sunday, 29 October...* Dot's heart skipped a beat. That's tomorrow, she realized. She could read no further until she took this in. She would see Jack tomorrow. It had been a year and a half since their goodbyes at Fort Jackson. A million thoughts went through her mind. She rushed back to quarters to share the news.

Dot was on pins and needles all day Sunday. She expected to see Jack at any moment, and the sympathetic looks from Gillie and her other friends were no help as she fretted through the day. To keep busy, she hand-washed some of her personal items and organized her toiletries. She reported for duty at 5 p.m., disappointed and let down.

"Jack never showed," she confessed when she got back to the barracks after her shift. "I don't want to talk about it."

Monday's sleet made pathways slippery. The weather matched Dot's mood but she was not alone in being chilled to the bone. Warmth was just a word, she thought to herself, just a memory. But, countless American troops in the field had little or no protection from the weather in their foxholes. Dot stopped her depressing inner dialog and chose to be content with her circumstances, such as they were.

Tuesday saw no improvement, bringing another freezing day for staff, and no sign of Jack. Dot's will to remain positive was tested further. *Our morale is so low we are walking on it,* Dot scribbled this in her diary, the single entry for the day.

On Wednesday, a letter reached Dot from Jack:

Dorothy,

We're in France now. I've got Jones, Blake, Holmes and Dutko with me. We're marching inland to the staging area but the rain makes the fields a muddy mess up to our knees. We will push toward the French-German border soon. That's as specific as I can be. We are allowed to go into the towns to buy French wine, watery beer, and fruit if they have it.

I've pinned down where you are. Talk to your Communications Officer, he'll know our location and about when we'll be in your area. See you soon!

Jack

Dot looked for Captain Flanner, the CO for the Ravenel Hospital compound. She found him at chow the next night and asked him point blank for an update.

"They're in Épinal today, Chinnis. Twenty miles or so south of here. They'll be here in a day or two."

A day or two, she repeated to herself.

Dot was off-duty the next day. She spent it bouncing around like a pinball looking for things to keep her mind away from various self-concocted scenarios that would prevent Jack's arrival.

Before going to bed, she inspected the night sky for evidence of Jack's moon. The cloud cover was thick. No moon.

"No matter," she said to the darkness. "I'll see the real thing very soon." Dot knew she wasn't the only lonely soul in this war. She turned inward and let her own pain flow. Her pillow absorbed the tears.

Friday, November 3 was cold. No surprise there. Walkways were once again iced over but Dot was determined to keep up a cheery front. While scrubbing and sanitizing a surgical theater, she put her pity party behind her. A few hours later, she regarded the sparkling effect that soapy water had on the grime and laughed that this was her great achievement of the day. Her mother had taught her that cleanliness was next to godliness and she breathed in the results of her efforts.

Someone shouted, "Let's get chow," and the cleaning crew headed over to the chow hall to join the long line.

Standing beyond the line, Dot spied Jack and another officer. She missed a step and faltered. The other man was Ken Jones but he had changed since she knew him at Fort Jackson. He looked less like a kid-brother. The two men were standing together talking. Jack's feet were planted slightly apart and his hands were clasped behind his back. He turned his head away from Jones to survey the group of women approaching. Dot was one of them. They caught each others' eye. Dot questioned the reality of the moment. It had been so long in the making, and she had played this scene over and over in her mind many times. She was afraid she was hallucinating.

"Jack," she whispered and put her hand to her mouth. "My Jack is here," she said a little louder.

Dot's brain tried to register the reality of the moment. She considered pinching herself. "Jack!" she shouted, daring to call his name out loud instead, a test to see if he was real.

Dot's voice reached Jack like a bell ringing through the clamor of voices. A huge smile broke across his lips. Dot peeled away from the lunch line and motioned Jack to follow. He hurried in her direction.

"I thought you'd never get here," Dot said more calmly than she felt, trying to maintain some decorum. What she really wanted to do was to rush into Jack's arms and never leave.

"I wasn't sure about that myself." Jack looked back at Jones. He motioned for him to continue to the chow hall without him.

Dot stopped and looked back at Jones. "Where *are* my manners? Ken, please forgive me. It's great to see you and we'll catch up soon but I bet you want to see Charlotte right away. She'll be in that crowd, heading for lunch. Follow the line and you'll find her."

Just then Dot caught Charlotte's eye as she stood in the chow line. Dot nodded her head in Jones' direction and mimed, "Look!" She was pleased to witness another happy reunion as she guided Jack to a small officers' conference room in a nearby building. They stepped into the unoccupied office.

"I thought you'd never get here," Dot repeated.

"You knew I'd get here! You just hoped I'd get here earlier." Jack smiled as he pulled Dot into his arms. They stood together, a refuge against the war. Dot breathed in Jack's Old Spice and finally decided to trust her senses. This was no dream.

After a while, Dot motioned to the settee and suggested they sit down. "How long can you stay?" she asked.

"I have to head out at 1630 hours. That's 4:30…"

"I know what 1630 hours is, silly. I'm in the Army too."

"So you are. And here you've been in the thick of things for what probably feels like forever. I've been worried about you." Jack held Dot's hand. He wasn't sure if he was dreaming either, to tell the truth. "Your letters meant the world to me, it kept me from going crazy. But nothing compares to the real thing. To this moment. Right now."

Dot soaked in the significance of the moment. Finally she asked Jack, "Did your whole crew come with you to Europe?"

"For the most part. We had two men reassigned, but as you saw, Ken is with me. John Holmes too. Blake will organize reconnaissance and feed me intel on enemy positions behind the lines. And Dutko's my driver. He works magic getting humans to their destination." Jack couldn't take his eyes off Dot's face. If he did, he was afraid she'd disappear.

"So, the moon," he said, changing the subject. "Did it pass inspection? Was it bright and shiny enough to impress you and all the others?"

"*All* the others don't know anything about your contribution to moon maintenance, dear one, and I'd love to keep it that way. But I'll say this, all the full moons I've seen since I've been over here certainly have my seal of approval."

Jack puffed out his chest in pride.

"You are so full of yourself, Captain Light. So tell me, what would you like to do today?"

"I'll tell you exactly what I'd like to do. Now that nurses can marry and maintain their active status, let's get our legal docs in order for our wedding."

Dot clapped a hand to her mouth to stifle a giggle. Jack narrowed his eyes at her, wondering what the joke was. "Why is that funny, my dear?"

"I just won a bet with Gillie. She agreed to take over my duties while I'm on my honeymoon."

The laughter subsided and Jack became serious. "Do you think there will be any problems with your chief nurse?"

"No problems there. When the U.S. Army lifted the ban on nurses being married, I checked out the procedures and was told

240

that we have to be married by French officials. I guess that means a City Clerk or the Mayor?"

With a straight face, Jack said, "Well if Charles de Gaulle himself was here, he could do the job. I talked to my Commanding Officer. He said we have to wait two months from the time we submit the paperwork for the wedding date, which is why I want to get it in the pipeline today."

"Why do we have to wait? We can get blood work done today."

"Men in the forces are getting married over here, to lovely Mademoiselles, even if they already have a wife at home. The Army now investigates to make sure we're not collecting wives in every town we occupy."

"Oh well," Dot sighed. "We've waited this long, what's another couple of months? It'll give us time to plan. For instance, where to have our honeymoon."

"Nothing but Paris for us, Dorothy. We'll have our honeymoon in Paris!"

Dot let that soak in. Her heart skipped a beat.

"I remember when you asked me to marry you in the Measles Ward back at Jackson and I had to say 'no'," she said in a soft voice. "I can't believe we can finally tie the knot!"

Dot and Jack spent three hours together. In that brief time they submitted their intent-to-marry form and laid out a basic plan for the big day. Dot told Jack goodbye, trying to hide her concern for his safety. She would show him no tears, only a smile for him to keep in his memory until they saw each other again. He was heading back to his company's HQ in Épinal which was close in miles but nearer the German border. She knew casualties from the fighting in this area would be brought to the 21st. Nevertheless, Dot walked on air for the next two days.

November of 1944 was cold in northern France, but heat began to circulate in the radiators in their barracks, and there was hot water for showers too. Dot was grateful, and grateful to have seen Jack. She prayed that he'd be kept safe throughout the ordeal ahead of him.

A mix of fighting men from the front, and local citizens who had nowhere else to go for medical care, were admitted to the hospital. At times, there was no heat or water on the wards for them but the nurses dealt with the hardships by applying a healthy dose of practicality and good humor. Dot had heard no news from Jack for a week. She dug deep to find her own good humor, but as everyone told her, 'no news is good news'. She realized she was capable of strangling the next person who said it to her.

"Can't you find something to be happy about, Chigger?" In the barracks, getting ready for bed was the best time for heart-to-heart talks. Gillie was worried about Dot's state of mind which seemed to have deteriorated since Jack's arrival.

"Don't pay attention to me. I'm just a Sad Sack. You know, I wasn't awfully worried for Jack's safety when he was in the U.S. but now that he's here I'm concerned for him constantly. I'm elated that he's nearby and we'll be able to see each other occasionally, but the contrast between that happiness and my current melancholy is what gets me down. Before he arrived I didn't have these huge mood swings. But what can I do?"

"Actually, you did have them then too, if we're honest."

Dot considered this information for a moment then agreed with a sheepish grin.

Gillie said, "Worry won't make him safe, old friend. If it's his fate to survive and marry you, then he will. It's not in your hands though. Just be glad he *is* here and you *do* get to see him when possible. But say something optimistic for goodness sake. You're bringing me down too."

"The snow would be beautiful if we weren't so cold." They both laughed out loud which felt good.

Dot's observation was spot on. The snow was beautiful but the cold was miserable. Local residents working at the hospital presented with complaints of chilblains. This skin irritation was caused by extensive exposure to cold and moisture. The blisters were usually on the feet and toes, but they were also found on the legs and fingers and the ears. It was different from frostbite and trench foot, but the soldiers were surely dealing with all three of these consequences of the natural elements. Friars Balsam, a type of aloe, was found and applied to the affected area, along with applications of iodine. Comprehensive treatment for this problem included advice to keep warm and dry. The nurses organized a drive to collect appropriate clothing for the locals and their families.

Dot found a few moments to daydream about what late autumn would be like back at home. In South Carolina the middle of November would mean pleasantly cool days, wind-swept leaves on front lawns, and the aroma of wood fires drifting through the air.

"Penny for your thoughts!"

"Hank! I knew you were here somewhere but I couldn't track you down." Dot wanted to hug this old friend but settled for a professional grasp of the forearm.

"I heard you were a Johnny-come-lately yourself. But the gang's all here now."

"We're hoping Maddy will rejoin us soon. Miss Parsons and Major Whitfield have been assigned elsewhere and we were told they won't catch up to us. But, yes, most of us are together again, and it's a wonderful thing. What's *not* wonderful is our food," Dot was teasing now. "I need to talk to Fouché. I don't think much of his meals these days if he's the one responsible."

"He's working on it. The food quality will improve soon. Supply lines to Mirecourt have quite a few miles to cover from the port. How about I order up a cargo plane to drop food parcels for us? I'll tell them to rush the order because Dorothy Chinnis is wasting away to a mere will-o'-the-wisp."

"You do that! I'm sure they will get right on it." Dot snickered. "While you're working miracles, move this polar air mass over to Germany."

"I wish I could ol' gal. But here in northern Europe, the weather is stacking up to be the coldest in decades. It's historic."

"So was the eruption of Mount Vesuvius. I can't tell you how glad I am to get to experience yet more record-breaking history."

"Enough of that. Let's get a cup o' Joe while we catch up."

Before Thanksgiving arrived in 1944, incoming casualties went from a drizzle to a downpour but the hospital staff dealt with it like pros. There was little time to rest or eat *or* ponder a personal love life. The bleak French winter dampened spirits, but men on the frontlines endured far worse conditions. The hospital staff had it easy by comparison and they knew it.

Fourteen

By mid-November, most of the casualties brought to Ravenel Hospital were from the 100ᵗʰ Infantry Division. Jack's unit was attached to that large group and since Dot hadn't heard a word from him in over a week, she talked to the G.I.s admitted to her ward, asking them which company they were with. She listened for anything that might relate to Jack's circumstances. A Division includes over 10,000 men, she knew that, but this man's Army was a small world and she hoped for a crumb of news.

Dot learned through the grapevine that the 398ᵗʰ Infantry Regiment was ordered to break the German defensive line at Raon-l'Etape, a village that lay an hour closer to Germany than Mirecourt. It was a crossroads for supplies to the German military and the supply line had to be stopped. Cold and rain and mud were as challenging as confronting enemy forces. American infantrymen took cover in soggy foxholes as they returned artillery fire, advancing slowly, but advancing nonetheless.

Within the 398ᵗʰ, Jack served in the 1ˢᵗ Battalion HQ as the S-2 Intelligence Officer. He made strategic use of information given to him from various sources. His best source was Staff

245

Sergeant JD Blake. Blake commanded a squad who worked behind enemy lines undetected. They were ghosts. When HQ needed to draw up a strategy to drive the Germans out of an occupied area, they called in Blake who penetrated enemy territory, gathered the intel, and delivered it firsthand. Radio communications couldn't be relied on. Processing that intelligence into actionable plans gave the fighting men an advantage in battle.

"He's busy," Gillie knew exactly what Dot was daydreaming about. "He's busy winning us this war. He'll get word to you when he can. He's always found a way up to now."

"...*up to now*," Dot whispered. "So why not *now?*"

"Look!" Gillie redirected the conversation as she motioned to the administrative tent. "Mail call. Let's go see if we got anything today. Christmas is coming up. I bet Christmas gifts are sitting there waiting for us." She raised her eyebrows and smiled to provoke interest.

Three Christmas packages had Dot's name on them. Friends and family had learned from experience that parcels posted from the States take their jolly good time arriving overseas, so they were sent early. No one back home wanted their loved ones to wake up on Christmas morning without wrappings and bows of their own. One of the gifts was marked 'Don't Open until Xmas'. Dot opened the two not marked at all. Her sister Sadie sent a stack of magazines which would be passed around after Dot devoured them. Margie sent her a cotton slip, bars of fragrant soap, and the high-heeled pumps she wanted to wear for her wedding. Puzzle pieces were falling into place for that special day, and Dot's mood improved in response.

Finally, on a Wednesday in the middle of November, Dot received two letters from Jack. He explained that he was bogged down with the current mission but all was well otherwise. No call

246

for concern. Dot jotted one thought in her diary: *I can breathe a little now.*

Days became just a number to cross off the calendar, and they ran together with little variation, until Thanksgiving. The hospital crew appreciated Fouché's effort to make the holiday meal special. He had assembled an able kitchen staff of enlisted men and Italian POWs. They worked overtime thawing, then roasting the forty seven frozen turkeys that had arrived the day before. There were pies for dessert made from a shipment of canned pumpkin and sweet potatoes. The rain refused to let up, of course, and the bitter cold had made itself at home, but the special meal, and two more letters from Jack, made the holiday bearable.

All the nurses went to a 12-hour shift the following day. Because they worked until exhaustion, it was difficult to manufacture the energy for even a shudder as German planes strafed the area.

"That huge Red Cross clearly painted on a round patch of white upon the roofs should be a giveaway that this is a hospital, not a military strong hold," Dot mused to no one in particular.

"It may as well be a bull's eye for the Germans to aim for," Charlotte answered. "They have no compassion for people at all, do they?"

Dot shook her head. "I worry for the human race, sometimes."

Shift work was hard on mind, body, and soul. The harsh and demanding conditions under which the nurses worked challenged them. It took effort for them to survive the cold, and sleep was frequently interrupted by air raids. The accumulation of these conditions produced fatigue, and Dot felt those effects keenly. She was astonished how her energy miraculously returned when Jack made a surprise visit to the 21st.

"How did you get time off?" Dot was delighted to see Jack. She hadn't hoped to see him again anytime soon.

"As an officer, I'm allowed some freedom. I chose to use it here, there's nowhere else I'd rather be. I have to return to HQ by four in the morning though, so it's not a great deal of freedom, as you can see." The couple spent their few hours together having dinner in Mirecourt.

Mirecourt had six thousand inhabitants, give or take, and when the hospital wards were full at the 21st, the total population of the area was doubled. The main street through town was no more than a mile in length and in that mile, despite the austerity of war, Mirecourt's location made it a vital hub of the Vosges. As such, it was able to offer goods and services for most needs. At the top of the list was food, with flavor. Dot and Jack stopped in at the Café de Luce for dinner.

A red checkered tablecloth covered a small round table near the window. A lighted candle burned between them in a glass dish. Their American uniforms prompted a friendly welcome from the waiter who greeted them in broken English. He explained that there were no printed menus, instead he told them the three options available for the evening. Dot and Jack ordered the onion soup with cheese and bread. Coffee and fresh éclairs would follow for their dessert.

"It's nice to sit in a chair for a meal instead of leaning against a tree eating cold rations. The view's much nicer too." Jack watched Dot's face, illuminated by the flickering flame.

"And you're a big ol' romantic goof ball," Dot responded offhand. After she patted her curls into place, she looked at Jack more closely. Since he arrived at the hospital, she had been absorbed in the moment, in being near him and hearing his voice. Now, sitting across from him at the café table she noticed a new badge pinned to his uniform just above his service ribbons. The silver rectangle was filled with blue enamel. Sitting on top of the blue field was a Springfield Musket. The rectangle was attached upon an oak-leaf wreath. She knew what this insignia represented. She knew the prestige of its meaning.

"You've seen some action." Dot's tone was solemn.

"Oh, yes. We've been busy." Jack didn't pick up on the significance of her statement.

"No, I mean you've been in combat. You've been under fire. She pointed directly at his Combat Infantry badge. I know why that's an esteemed award."

"We held our own."

Dot's expression revealed her concern before she could mask it.

"It's why we're here," Jack said. He looked at Dot tenderly. "You know that. It was time my unit got its feet wet. Now, we're in the game."

He gave Dot some time. She closed her eyes. She couldn't wrap Jack up in a blanket and protect him from harm, it would be like a straight jacket. She wouldn't allow him to do that to her either. Neither of them would like the restrictions. She changed the subject.

"Charlotte and Jones are re-united and look happy."

"They do. I don't think they wrote to each other as much as we did," Jack said. "I never got the impression that they were as seriously in love as we are, though."

"I suspect they're heading in that direction," Dot speculated. "Even if they're not as love-sick as we are."

"We were bitten hard by that bug, weren't we?"

"I'm not sure if that is a good thing or bad thing," Dot joked. "Every waking hour, I worry about you. But, I'm going to get that fear into perspective."

Jack looked doubtful but let it go. Dot continued, "Charlotte and Ken decided to play it loosy-goosy and let fate direct the course of their relationship. *If the universe wants us together, it'll happen.*" Dot repeated what Charlotte had told her.

"Should we have played it that way?" Jack seldom doubted himself but now a hint of uncertainty nudged his conscience.

"That might have been easier, now that I think about it." Dot was fighting to hold back a giggle as she saw the shocked look on Jack's face.

"Oh well! You're going to get tired of seeing me now. I'm going to be underfoot often because your friends have made me an honorary member of the 21st General Hospital. As a result, I intend to make a nuisance of myself with frequent visits."

"I'll eat my Wheaties for strength and endurance to meet that challenge. Now, back to Charlotte and Jones."

"Ah, yes," Jack said. "They approached things different from us, but they seem to be a good match." Dot nodded in agreement. She looked down at her plate and sighed. A gesture Jack didn't miss.

"You all right, Dorothy? Are you sad?"

"No, not sad. I just had a fleeting wish that we weren't getting married in the middle of a war. That we were home with our family around us."

"I can understand that. And, of course we can wait if that's your true wish. We can do whatever we want, there's absolutely nothing that is rushing us."

"I want to be your wife, and the sooner the better. It's just that I get down in the dumps when I'm so tired. My head and my heart tell me to seize the day. Besides, we probably wouldn't be having a Paris honeymoon if we weren't already in the country courtesy of the good ol' U.S. of A."

"It'll be a grand day. You'll have McGill by your side, and John Holmes has agreed to be my best man. Who will give you away? Hank? Fouché?"

"I've contemplated that situation a great deal. But how do I ask one over the other? Isn't it a 'crowd' to have two men giving me away? The solution, I decided, was to ask Colonel Cady, the C.O. of the hospital. He's accepted."

"Brilliant. Will Fouché organize our wedding dinner?"

"He insisted. And of course his Italian helpers volunteered to bake our wedding cake. It will be a proper international effort on our behalf. Speaking of international efforts, as you know, we must be officially married at the Mayor's office in a civil service. We have an appointment for ten o'clock on the morning of January 15. You will need to bring 36 Francs to pay the marriage tax."

"You're telling me I need 36 Francs to buy you? I wish I had known earlier. I could have been saving up. As it is…"

"Ha! You're getting a bargain, Mr. Light. Conversion rate for that amount is less than one U.S. dollar."

"That's true! So we start out at the Mayor's office. Where do we go from there?"

"We'll have our wedding service at the Ravenel Hospital Chapel at 3 p.m. Sergeant Douglas has been rehearsing songs he will sing for us, accompanied by the POWs who have formed a chamber orchestra. The reception dinner is at six that night."

"That's a long day." Jack caught Dot's frown. "No, I'm not complaining at all. I'm pleased that we get a whole day just for us. That's a real gift, and I'm grateful."

Dot relaxed when she saw that Jack was pleased. She wanted the day to be perfect.

251

"I've got updates for you too," Jack said. "I've arranged to rent an apartment here in Mirecourt for us. It's located above a butcher shop. Small, just one room, really. It's furnished with a bed, a sofa, and a kitchen table with two chairs. There's a little kitchen area that has a sink with running water and a hotplate. The bathroom is just across the hall, but I think we share that with another tenant. We have windows on three sides since we're on the end of the building—the front one looks out over the town. I was thinking that we'll go there for our wedding night. Dutko can pick us up there the next morning and drive us to Paris in his Jeep. I've discussed the rental terms with Monsieur Éduard. He says we can keep the apartment as long as we want it. I thought it would be nice for us to be able to slip away together, just the two of us, whenever I can get to Mirecourt."

"Perfect. Absolutely perfect. I hadn't allowed myself to dream that we'd be able to set up our own little home while we're still in the middle of this wretched war."

After dessert, Dot and Jack bundled themselves up against the cold night and walked back to the hospital. Carrying their helmets was as natural as breathing, so when the air raid came, they were prepared. They escaped injury but the German fighters strafed the hospital compound, causing damage to one of the storage buildings. Still, there were no fatalities and that was a triumph in itself.

Dot said goodbye to Jack in the lonely pre-dawn morning. At lunchtime, she went to mail call and was rewarded with a parcel from her brother Charles and his wife Ema Nell. They included photographs of their two year old son, Sam, and a Christmas gift for her. Looking at the precious baby gave her hope for the future.

The hospital admitted patients around the clock. The wards were so busy that nurses missed meals and failed to get adequate sleep. They kept crackers handy to snack on, which were poor substitutes for nutritious food, but better than nothing. The long days and poor eating habits took their toll. Dot's body aches, sore throat, and chills were warning signs of flu, but she reported for duty wearing a surgical mask. She would do all in her power to decrease the transfer of germs, but she wouldn't skip a shift and lay that extra burden on another nurse. She was determined to do her part as the men under her care had done. Leaving work late that evening, Dot had missed supper *and* mail call. She stood on the icy wooden stoop leading to the newly-opened officer's dining hall. Underneath a dim single light bulb, Dot was bent almost double, sobbing into her hands.

Watching from a distance, Major Spalding made a decision. Meals would henceforth be brought into the hospital for staff while on duty. Spalding encouraged her charges to make time for three squares a day. The decision paid dividends. Improved nutrition was essential for the rundown nurses.

For Dot, the latest news from home came in a cablegram from her sister Sadie. She and her husband Tommy Sanders announced the arrival of their second daughter, Dorothy Elizabeth. *They named her for me,* Dot recorded in her diary. *It makes me so happy.*

With buoyed spirits, Dot suggested that the nurses on her shift get ingredients from Fouché to make a batch of pulled-taffy for the patients. As they were executing the plan, Crazy Ellis showed up. Staff Sergeant Jim Ellis was everybody's favorite medical supply officer. He had been attached to the 21st from its deployment. Since Ravenel Hospital was so large, he and Hank (from the 58th), worked together to guarantee equipment and supply needs for the hospital were met. Crazy Ellis had a boyish face, red hair and freckles which made him a look-alike of Mickey Rooney's Andy Hardy character.

Crazy Ellis was a wise cracker who never failed to make everyone laugh. He walked into the ward on this day and congratulated himself for showing up in time to do a taste test of the taffy just as it hit the desired consistency, pronouncing it 'perfection itself.' As he meandered through the wards, he spoke to the men, offering encouragement. On his second pass of Dot's ward he spotted an officer he knew. The officer had a bandage around his forehead and a hospital gown wrapped around his upper body. Ellis marched over to him, saluted him, then proceeded to flip him over onto his stomach. The hospital gown opened down the back, revealing his bare buttocks. Ellis patted him on the 'cheek'. "Your face is familiar," he said, "but I can't remember the name." The ward erupted in howls.

———————

A note from the jewelry store in Mirecourt arrived for Dot in mid-December.

"What's that?" Gillie asked as she walked up to Dot.

"The wedding ring I ordered for Jack has arrived."

Gillie smiled, she was pleased. "Wedding plans are shaping up, then. Are you allowing yourself to get excited?"

"Yes, but I won't rest until I say, 'I do'," Dot replied with a hint of levity that Gillie hadn't seen in a while. Dot glanced over at the circular drive as a Jeep drove half-way around and stopped. John Holmes jumped out of the car and ran across the pavement. Dot's heart stopped.

"Don't worry. I'm not bearing bad news," he shouted as he got nearer. "All is well but I have a message to deliver nearby and Jack wanted me to stop in to see you in person. He wanted me to bring you up to date with the news from his end."

Dot and Gillie suggested they walk over to the dining hall for coffee and something to eat.

"How are you getting along, John?" Dot asked as they sat down together at the end of an empty table.

"Better, now that we're here. I had my doubts for a while. It looked like the Brass was going to use us for nothing more than their fund-raising parades. We're pretty, every last one of us boys, but we wanted to get in the fight. We're awfully glad we're finally here at last."

Dot smiled. She always loved John's subtle sense of humor.

"Aren't you frightened of the outcome?" Gillie asked. She was serious. She knew they were in harm's way. She also knew the toll of war.

"We can't think that way. We're focused on one thing, and that's defeating the enemy. Que sera, and all that. What we do on any given day is up to us. The outcome is up to a higher power, a power we don't have the right to question."

"Well, I dare question," Gillie admitted. "But never mind that. What can we send back with you? Coffee, socks? Name it."

Gillie was still talking but Dot was watching Holmes' face closely for a betrayal between his words and his message. There was none. He was at peace with the mission and his part in it.

He answered Gillie, "No. We're squared away for now. But I'll start a list when I get back to my unit and talk to the guys there." Then he relayed the information he had from Jack. "Nothing I'm telling you is top secret. You might not read it in the Stars and Stripes but the local newspapers will be reporting it. And Jack wanted you to hear the facts straight from the horse's mouth, so to speak, rather than trying to figure out the truth."

"Truth about what?" Dot asked. "That sounds ominous."

"Exactly. The newspapers will blow the stories out of proportion. Here's the thing, I just left Jack at the Bitche."

255

Holmes pronounced the word, 'beach'. Dot wondered how Jack's unit had wound up back at the coast. Her facial expression said as much.

"No, not a *beach* like that. B-I-T-C-H-E," he spelled out. "It's a citadel town a little over a hundred miles northeast of here."

Dot nodded her head in understanding and said, "The way you spelled it, I would have pronounced it a little different."

"That is a common mistake," Holmes winked at Dot.

"What's going on in this citadel town? Is it more dangerous than usual?" Gillie asked. Dot was curious, too. If Jack was so close, why didn't he drive down with John Holmes for a visit?

"Probably no more than usual," John said. "But it's important. Extremely important. It sits along the Maginot Line. Are you familiar…"

"…oh yes," Dot butted in. "The concrete fortifications built along France's eastern border. A good idea that didn't measure up to its boastful intentions, since the Germans basically just went around it."

"Yes, and the Jerries took it over for their own use, and they've dug in. *We need them out.* Taking this area back is integral to our overall plans because when we've removed them out of Bitche, the 100th Division can push toward the Rhine River. We cross the Rhine, then we're on our way to Berlin. We hit Berlin and we can stop this madness."

Dot believed deep in her soul that the 100th Division, the *Soldiers of the Century*, as they called themselves, would make that happen.

"Our boys are good, and we *will* take the area."

"I know you will." Dot was sincere.

"But it takes a lot of planning and intel. That's why Jack's not free to make a visit and why I'm here. He wants you to *not* be concerned if he can't write for a while, or visit. Oh, and he sent this to you." Holmes extracted a small box out of the cargo pocket of his fatigue trousers. From the box he took out a dainty silver chain and clasped it to Dot's wrist.

"I'll write him a thank you letter tonight, but please tell him how much I appreciate the gift. I'll send taffy back to him through you. If it never arrives, though, it'll be our little secret."

Holmes threw his head back and laughed out loud. "I can't promise that *all* of it will arrive, but I'll make sure some of it does."

A comfortable pause parked itself between their joking and the serious report from the front. Holmes took a long drink of his coffee then continued his account of the unit's current situation.

"There's a lot going on at Bitche. We're also dealing with spillover activity from the Ardennes Offensive. The Germans have launched a campaign to stop our incursions into Europe since the Normandy invasion. They've stopped the Allies at the large forest there. The newsmen are calling it the Battle of the Bulge, although you won't read much about that in the Stars and Stripes either. The objective of the German Army is to divide us in two to halt our push to the German capital.

"I knew there was a lot of fighting. We get casualties from the 100th but I didn't have a good idea of the strategic importance of it all," Dot said. She was absorbing everything Holmes told her and Gillie. It was good to know the truth of what was happening at the front, but the reality was hard to take.

"We'll win it. No question about it." Holmes mistook Dot's serious expression for doubt of victory. Dot had seen the human carnage necessary for that victory. She grimaced because she realized it could happen to these men she knew personally.

Holmes continued. "The Germans will use up their scarce resources and we'll prevail." Now he looked nervous. Dot wondered if he was trying to convince himself as well as her. "No doubt about that," he said a little louder. "Right now we're slowed down a little but that's all. It's tough on our troops, but Jack, he'll be ok. He's a good soldier. He's got good men. He sends his love and said to tell you, and-I-quote, 'I'll be there for the wedding'. And so will I. No need to worry."

Holmes stood up, put his cap on. Mission accomplished. Dot and Gillie stood up too. Gillie said her goodbyes. Dot accompanied Holmes to the Jeep, walking arm in arm.

"Thanks for stopping by. And thanks for the update. It helps to have an inkling of what you're doing in the heat of battle, what your role is in that battle. I'll wish you safe travels back to the unit and I'll say prayers for you, for you all, until I see you again."

"Those prayers help more than you know. You being here, all of you nurses being here, well, it makes a difference to us that you're here. So thanks for that."

Gillie rushed back before Holmes pulled away. She had a brown paper parcel tied with string. "Your taffy!" She looked at Dot. Her expression said, at least *one* of us remembered. Dot patted her on the back and said, "At least one of us remembered."

The battles that Holmes had described to Dot and Gillie meant more casualties for the hospital in Mirecourt. Stress from assisting in facial reconstructions and amputations, as well as trying to repair mutilated flesh, were piled on top of non-stop worry for loved ones in battle.

The Battle of the Bulge, and the assault on towns along the Maginot Line, caused anguish and suffering for everyone, military and civilian alike. There were no exceptions. Dot was afraid she was close to a nervous breakdown from the fatigue, and from the

258

sights and sounds that played on a loop inside her head. She'd seen the effects of others who had been overwhelmed by the extreme conditions they worked in, although it was rare. But she wasn't alone in this fear. Every nurse was anxious lest she be next. No one wanted to be humiliated in that way. They believed the remedy was to work harder, to keep their attention on others.

Christmas was getting close, and getting ready for the holiday was a welcomed diversion from the bloodshed the nurses witnessed daily. Working out details for the wedding helped too—anything to fool the mind into believing something good was on the other side of this experience. It was healthy to believe that this hellish war wouldn't last forever, although it already felt like eternity.

"What's the difference between forever and eternity?" Dot asked Elizabeth as they shared an evening shift.

"One has no end. The other is mere infinity," she replied.

"Ha-ha," Dot said.

Five days before Christmas, the hospital was assigned additional nurses on detached service. With their help, the original crew was able to go back to an eight-hour duty roster. The relief was welcomed. Jones came by to see Charlotte on Christmas Eve, but Jack couldn't get away. Dot had pulled night duty so she didn't feel especially disappointed. An air raid over Mirecourt ushered in the sacred holy day. Dot witnessed fireworks of a battle playing out close to the hospital.

"Can't the Jerries leave us in peace for this one night?" Dot said to her patient.

"Of course not, ma'am," the young Private said. "They don't wish us well."

"I guess Santa's sleigh will have to find another route into the base."

"Our boys will get him through safe and sound, you can count on it."

Dot was thankful Jack wasn't here to experience the fire fight, but then she questioned what he was dealing with instead that kept him from a visit. When she went off-duty, Dot slept most of Christmas Day. She made no mention of the holiday in her diary, only this: *Feel very lonely.* A feeling shared by all who were away from home.

Jack was able to work out a surprise visit to see Dot the day after Christmas.

"I'm glad you're here but I've got duty from three to eleven tonight," she explained.

"That's fine. I'll relax a little, get something to eat, and park myself in an out of the way place until you're free again."

Jack didn't want to be too far out of the way. He wanted to be in the middle of the activity. He enjoyed being in the clean hospital environment witnessing the good work being done there. He found a section of the hospital near Dot's ward where a dozen nurses busied themselves with patient care. He let them know that he had brought with him a crate of liberated wine from a winery in the Vosges Mountains and left it with Fouché to dispense.

"Keep that up," Fouché had told him, "and they'll name a wing of the hospital after you."

"Look," Jack informed him, "if I wind up here in need of care, I want to make sure they are motivated to save my bacon."

"I hear you. But you know as well as I do those women need no outside motivation. They will always do the right thing."

"I do know that. But being bumped to the head of the line can't be bad."

Jack was joking, of course. He knew, without a doubt, that Uncle Sam's nurses were the best on earth, with or without gifts of wine. He just wanted to do something special for them.

While he waited, Jack bummed a cup of coffee, and claimed a chair that allowed him to survey the action.

In Dot's ward, a Belgian soldier had been admitted with a critical head wound. With constant vigilance, this man would survive, and Dot would see to that. She called to Jurgen, the teenage German POW who had been captured as the Germans fled the area. He was more like an orphan than an enemy combatant and the hospital staff adopted him. He was cheerfully attentive to the needs of the patients, and he was smart enough to realize that his alliance with the Americans meant he had access to food and a warm place to sleep in addition to having some meaningful work to do.

A clear night had descended on the base. The nearly full moon was bright, and once again, it spotlighted the large Red Cross painted on the rooftops. The various crimson 'plus signs' stood in contrast to the carpet of white snow hugging the grounds of the base. As a lone German bomber passed overhead, the pilot disregarded the Red Crosses and dropped his last remaining bomb before heading back to the Colmar-Nord Airfield. His bomb hit the water tower near Dot's building. The explosion rocked the hospital wards and everyone in them. Patients who were able, scuttled out of bed, dropped to the floor, and rolled under the bed for cover. Staff sought doorway frames and stairwells to wait for the worst to pass. Dot ran to the bedside of her Belgian patient to protect him from falling debris.

Jurgen ran up to Dot and gestured to the floor as he pleaded, "Get flat, Miss. On the floor. Lie down." He tried to physically push her to the floor to protect her. "Where is your helmet, Miss? I will get it…"

"Blast it all!" Dot shouted. "I left the blame thing back in the nurses' quarters." Dot was beside herself. She had learned the drill well and was never without her helmet. She wondered how she could be so forgetful.

"Use mine," Jurgen insisted as he placed it on Dot's head.

"Okay," she agreed. "But I'm staying with my patient. You must go to the stairwell. Now! That's an order."

Jurgen obeyed and Dot protected her patient.

When the raid was over, Jack ran over to Dot's ward. A quick visual survey told him that she and her patient were both unharmed, but the large helmet sitting lopsided on Dot's head made Jack ask, "Whose helmet do you have there, Dorothy?"

"Don't ask," she said. "But I'm thanking God for young POWs who are deferential to their elders."

"I'll make sure to commend him when I see him."

"I'm glad you have yours on. Did you see any injuries on your way over here?"

"Nothing catastrophic. But, good grief! I'm considering heading on back to the battlefront..."

Dot was shocked. "No, Jack! Not yet."

Jack rocked up on his toes, then back on his heel, his hands behind his back. This mock-posture and his sly smile were clues that he was having a joke, so Dot stopped protesting. Instead, she asked, "And why are you going back to the front, dear one?"

"It's safer there!"

An hour after the air raid, Hank had information on the airplane responsible for dropping the bomb. "That plane will *not* bomb us again," he boasted.

New Year's Eve arrived. With no one to kiss to ring in 1945, Dot wrote in her diary: *No water in quarters and another black out - a fitting end to this year.*

This was Dot's second New Year's Day away from home. She took a moment to recall where she had been one year before—North Africa. She had moved several parallel degrees of latitude northward since then. Progress, surely.

In recognition of the day, Fouché provided a turkey supper for the base but the meal was followed unceremoniously by the customary and usual black out.

The following week brought Dot two consecutive days off from work. This was rare and she used them to catch up on laundry and sleep, but also to shop for gowns for herself and her Maid of Honor. The dress she had chosen for herself was a light yellow (called *French Lemon*) satin dress with an organza overlay. The dress was adequate but the color made Dot's skin look a bit jaundiced. She was settling, and she knew it, but there was no other option. Dress shops longed for a return to a time when they once again offered an array of fashion choices. That time was not likely to occur while the war continued.

Dot's friends helped pull together wedding trousseau items of clothing, lingerie, cosmetics, and other accouterments needed by a bride on her honeymoon. Elizabeth, Charlotte, Cora, Jane, and Anne were exhausted from their schedules but they came together to help Dot and Gillie prepare for the ceremony. A celebration of love in this time of war was an occasion to be honored. Also, they heard that Fouché's Italian bakers were making Dot and Jack's wedding cake and wanted to be chosen for the taste-test before the big day, Monday, January 15th.

On Monday, one week before the wedding day, Dot placed a call to Jack at HQ in Bitche.

"We're in the middle of it here," Jack shouted into the handset of the field telephone.

"I know. Holmes told me you were working to break the Maginot Line. I won't say more but I understand it's an important mission, Jack. We've got wiggle room on the wedding date if…"

"We're holding our own but we take a pounding every day… progress, but slow…

"Do we need to change the date for the wedding? Jack? Are you there?"

Lag time and the crackle of static on the telephone line made smooth conversation impossible.

"We've got the upper hand here. I'll be with you on Sunday the 14th. We're a 'go' for the 15th. You can depend on it. I'm squared away for that date and the week after for our honeymoon. It's going to be swell, Dorothy. No worries on that."

Dot attempted to carry on with business as usual for the rest of the week but she was restless with anxiety. She worked her ward and went for a routine dental check-up. It was mundane activity, but it passed the time.

Captain Wynne called Dot early one morning at the Ravenel Hospital Admin Office. Someone was dispatched to track down Dot to receive the call. Wynne, an officer Dot had known in Naples was now in Lunéville, France after a hard-won battle there in September of 1944. The situation required an American contingent to re-establish and administer the city. Captain Wynne was called on to do that.

"Is that you, Chinnis?"

Dot had trouble hearing the caller through the telephone handset.

"Wynne, is that you? Where are you?"

"Chinnis! Good to hear your voice. Look, I heard you're getting married. I'm an hour away from you and I want to come to your wedding. Got room for one more?"

Dot was pleased to hear from her old friend. She gave him the details of the wedding plans. Out of the blue, she asked him, "Have you heard from Maddy? I've been trying to track her down. She's vanished."

"She's here. She's in Lunéville working in a town clinic that the Army provides for the locals. She was in ill health from being on the frontlines. She earned herself a little break with this deal. I know she wrote you. Didn't you get her letter?"

"No. I didn't. Bring her with you, Wynne. I want to see you both."

"She's not up for travel, Chinnis. Not just yet. She'll be fine, though, so don't worry. I'll catch you up when I see you!" Dot wished him a safe trip.

Back in quarters, Cora, Elizabeth, and Charlotte came by with a surprise for Dot. "Look what we found!" they shouted in unison. They held up a taffeta floor-length dress the color of robins' eggs.

"It was in the window of the boutique in Mirecourt," Charlotte elaborated. "Just asking to be your wedding dress."

Dot stared at it in awe. "This is the one," she said. The color, the design, and the princess sleeves (especially) won the day.

———

Saturday, was W-Day minus two. The codename for the wedding date had been dubbed by Dot and her friends. It was spent bustling around taking care of last minute details. Sunday morning was W-Day minus one. Dot was up early ironing a blouse she wanted to take to Paris. Since Jack would arrive soon, she wanted to have her chores completed.

Charlotte poked her head into the room and said, "Jack's here. He's at the dining hall. He asked if you'd meet him there."

Dot unplugged the iron and rushed over to greet Jack. He looked troubled.

"What's wrong?" she asked him.

"As far as you and I are concerned, all is fine. But I've got bad news, Dorothy. John Holmes won't be at the wedding."

"We'll wait for him then," Dot insisted. "We can adjust the schedule a day or two until he gets here."

"That's not it. He's not coming at all."

"There's only one reason John would miss this…"

"Yes…," Jack cleared his throat before continuing. Dot looked into his care-worn eyes and waited. "My best man, he's…," Jack took a deep breath. "Damn it, Dorothy, he's been killed." A silence fell between them.

───※───

The wedding rehearsal progressed as planned that night, but there was an undercurrent of sadness that John's death brought to it.

In their room after the rehearsal, Dot and Gillie changed into pajamas and, like teenagers, did swan dives onto their beds. Before twenty seconds had passed, Gillie watched Dot slip into a funk.

"Life goes on, Chigger," Gillie stated lightly. "I'm not being dismissive of John's death. You know I wouldn't do that. But look at it this way. We're all here because there's a war. These fellows who come to our hospital, we see to their injuries. We do our best. Then we leave it in God's hands. We carry on. We go on in *spite* of the sadness and pain we feel for them. It's our obligation to do that, to deal with reality of what is handed us. But right now, you've been handed the opportunity to marry the love of your life. Wrap the happiness you feel in that precious

266

moment around the sadness for the loss of John, but dwell on the *happiness* part. Take it. It's yours. Do not let it be diminished by this blasted war."

Dot's eyes glistened at the speech. "You're right, of course. I needed to hear that. I was afraid that my joy, my happiness, would diminish the ultimate sacrifice John made with his life."

"I don't think that can happen," Gillie assured her.

After a moment of reflection the sadness diminished a little and Dot's expression changed to a different emotion, one that was hard to decode.

"You're pulling a 'face', Chigger. I can't tell if it's good or bad."

"A thought just popped into my head. This is my last day of single life," Dot said as she smiled. "Now, I'm too excited to sleep."

"You may not want to sleep, but by golly, I've got to try."

Dot shut her mouth, but not the inner chatter. Monday morning finally arrived for the bride-to-be. Today, she would become Mrs. Jack light. Let the day begin.

Fifteen

Diary Entry ~ January 15, 1945
MY WEDDING DAY!

"Wake up, Gillie! It's my wedding day." Dot had turned her head on the pillow to face Gillie across the room. Snuggled under the covers, only her pin curls were exposed. Dot watched her breath make clouds in the cold room and tried to provoke Gillie into wakefulness. Gillie's pep talk from the night before had made a world of difference in Dot's outlook.

Eager to make her appearance at the Mayor's office for the civil service, Dot dressed quickly. Ken Jones had agreed to stand in for the late John Holmes as Jack's best man. He and Gillie would accompany the couple into town as witnesses.

Standing at the door of the Mayor's office, Jack whispered in Dot's ear, "This is your last chance to back out. Stepping through this door leads to a lifetime commitment for us."

"I do have cold feet," Dot whispered back, "but *only* because it's thirty degrees out here! So let's do this. I'm anxious to get this 'lifetime commitment' legalized. And for your information, Mr. Light, I consider this the best day of my life." Jack knocked smartly upon the door.

A clerk opened it to the wedding party and welcomed them in out of the cold. He explained that the Mayor would perform the service, the marriage tax would be paid, official papers would be signed, and then the union would be completely legal. Jack jingled the coins in his pants pocket. In his heart he knew exchanging them for Dot's hand in marriage made him the richest man on earth.

After the service was concluded, Gillie and Ken returned to the base to finalize preparations for the three o'clock ceremony in the Chapel. Dot and Jack stopped in at a café to force themselves to eat an early lunch before they were due at the church.

"Isn't it bad luck to see the bride before the marriage?" Jack wondered out loud.

"We *are* married!" Dot teased. "The civil service is the legal part, the church ceremony is our pledge before God. Even if we skipped town right now for a head start to Paris, we are legally married for all the world cares."

"Hmmmm…," Jack wondered if they could bug out early and get a jump on their drive to Paris.

"Of course," Dot picked up on Jack's train of thought, "this *next* part is where everyone went to a lot of trouble for us. This *next* part is what will stick in our memory."

"I'm teasing you, Mrs. Light. Let me settle the bill and we'll head to the base."

———————

Gillie was stretched out on her bed, looking over her to-do list when Dot returned.

"There you are!" Gillie said. "We've got to get you dressed!"

"As I just reminded Jack, technically, I'm a married woman now, and as a married woman, you can't tell me what to do." Dot was sassy.

"Being married will not stop people from telling you what to do, my dear. You best learn that today. Now, first things first. Here's what needs to be done."

Gillie directed the pre-wedding maneuvers like it was Operation Overlord Part Deux. The two friends dressed, applied a modest amount of rouge and lipstick, then checked themselves in the mirror. They gave each other nods of approval, grabbed their bouquets, and headed together to the Chapel.

At the Chapel, Gillie preceded Dot down the aisle. Dot entered on the arm of Colonel Cady as the small orchestra played Wagner's Bridal Chorus for her. The groom beamed at his bride and thanked Providence for the pure good fortune of marrying the love of his life.

The Chaplain stood at the center of the raised platform, arms outstretched, and welcomed the guests. He greeted the couple and issued the Declaration of Intent as Dot and Jack turned toward each other. Jack took Dot's hand and promised to love her through sickness and health, and richer and poorer. Dot promised the same.

"I'll read now from the First Book of John, Chapter Four," the Chaplain said.

> *God is love; and he that dwelleth in love dwelleth in God, and God in him. Herein is our love made perfect, that we may have boldness in the Day of Judgment: because as He is, so are we in this world. There is no fear in love; perfect love casteth out fear.*

"This particular scripture is appropriate for us today," the Chaplain explained, "for Dorothy Elizabeth Chinnis and Samuel Jackson Light, especially. The circumstances we find ourselves in on this day, this war we fight for the righteousness of all mankind, *is* frightful. Love lessens the damage of fear and therefore it is no small miracle that you have found love amidst the ugly backdrop of war. God will bless your love. Of this, you can be sure."

As the Chaplain sat down, he nodded to Sergeant Douglas who was also sitting on the platform. Douglas stood, clasped his hands at his belt buckle, and winked at Dot before queuing the musicians. They played a few measures of the music as an introduction. The tenor sang a perfect pitch performance of *O Perfect Love*. When he sat down, the Chaplain returned to his place facing the bride and groom. They exchanged vows and they exchanged rings. When the Chaplain pronounced them husband and wife, he blessed the newlyweds and invited Jack to kiss his bride.

Jack paused and looked into Dot's blue eyes. A faint smile broke across her lips. He traced her cheek with his fingers and her smile grew. Dot tilted her chin up and Jack leaned down to kiss her lightly. He pulled back a little and met Dot's gaze with a devilish grin. He kissed her again, this time with all the joy and love he felt for her.

———◦⋘⊱⋗◦———

Fouché had planned the reception dinner for Dot and Jack, and he was determined to have plenty of food available for the guests. In time, the couple cut their wedding cake. It was large enough to require a table of its own. Six successively smaller square layers rose into the air like an ancient Aztec temple covered in pristine white snow.

Food and dancing, laughter and merriment. These things provided a breather from the business of war for the wedding party. Fouché also remembered to ask an assistant to bring a camera. One of the snapshots included Colonel Cady, Major Spalding, and the Chaplain with the bride and groom. Everyone

271

looked at the cameraman when prompted, except Jack. He couldn't tear his eyes away from the love of his life.

When the festivities wound down, Gillie wrapped two large pieces of wedding cake in wax paper. She wedged them safely in a box for Dot and Jack to have when they were in Paris.

"Include an extra piece for me, will you?" Dot asked Gillie.

"Okay," she agreed but looked puzzled because it wasn't like Dot to ask for more than her share.

"Tomorrow is Jack's birthday!" Dot told Gillie. "I intend to feed him cake in bed for a birthday surprise before we drive to Paris." Gillie was excited to add to the surprise.

The couple bid farewell to their friends as they ran through a shower of confetti. Ken Jones pulled the Jeep up to the curb and drove them to their Mirecourt apartment.

———

Dot was awake and making coffee on the hot plate early the next morning when Jack sat up in bed, rubbing the sleep out of his eyes. "Something is wrong with our plans, Dorothy," he said. "We should have planned to stay here a day or two just to sleep and rest up."

"We'll rest in Paris, dear one. But first…," Dot presented Jack with a plate filled with cake to accompany his coffee. "Happy Birthday, husband."

Jack beamed. "Dutko will be here with the Jeep to pick us up in twenty minutes. I don't have time to eat all of this by myself. I'll need help!"

"Glad to be of assistance. I'm also glad we'll have this little place, just the two of us. Our first home."

"To our first home," Jack clinked his coffee cup with Dot's in celebration.

PFC Stephen J. Dutko, Jack's driver, was right on time. Jack trusted him with his life, which explained why Jack arranged for the Private to be their chauffeur to and from Paris. Spending a week in the City of Lights was generous incentive for Dutko to agree to the plans, but he would have done it for Jack without the perk.

The two men made sure Dot was snug in the back seat of the open Jeep before they climbed into the front. The Jeep was no shelter against the elements. Near-freezing temperatures cut through their wool coats and sturdy boots. Before they had driven an hour, Dot's lips took on a blue tinge. They were so cold and hungry that they stopped at a café in Neufchâteau. The proprietor seated them near the hearth to thaw out with the warmth of the fire. With food in their bellies, and fingers and toes defrosted, they continued on their journey. After making three more stops, the trio reached Paris in the early afternoon.

Dutko delivered Dot and Jack to the doorsteps of the Hôtel de Paris located on the Avenue de la Grande Armée, an eight minute stroll to the L'Arc de Triomphe. Dutko set their bags on the sidewalk. The doorman motioned a bellboy to the curb.

"You found accommodations at the G.I. hostel near here, right?" Jack double-checked Dutko's plans. "Good. We'll be here one night so I'll send a note to you with the address of our next hotel when I know."

"Yes, sir. That's fine." Dutko's orders were to have fun, but not too much fun. "I'll see you and the Missus in five days."

"Good man. Now, explore the city, Dutko. See the sights. Visit museums. Who knows when you'll be back this way again. You'll be the talk of your hometown with those experiences, maybe even more than your battlefront tales."

Dutko assured Jack he would look into that but he knew he'd rather find a dance club and socialize with the fairer sex.

That seemed infinitely more fun than filling in a cultural void the Army left in his life. Besides, if truth be told, he didn't care about the opinion of the folks back home. This time in Paris was *his* time, after all. But he thought the world of Captain Light and would not disagree with the suggestion to his face. The two men shook hands as they said goodbye, and Jack slipped Dutko enough Francs to cover his meals while in Paris.

Jack checked in at the front desk of the Hôtel. The bellboy introduced himself as Victor. Victor showed Dot and Jack to their room. "If you want anything, Monsieur—for yourself or for Madame—please call me."

"I'll do that." Jack reached in his pockets for coins to give the youngster. "And thank you."

Outside and in, the hotel had managed to maintain its grandeur during the German Occupation. Since the liberation of Paris the previous August, the hotel had only improved its services and accommodations. Staying here was Jack's wedding present to Dot but on Uncle Sam's salary, this level of luxury was to be sustained for only one night. During their brief stay at Hôtel de Paris, the newlyweds would make the most of the lavish conveniences available to them.

A hot bath with gardenia scented bath crystals made Dot feel pampered. Jack stretched out on the feather bed like a king. After a cat nap Jack told Dot, "I suppose we should get ready for dinner." He walked over to the window and moved the curtains aside. When he peered to the right, he saw the Arc de Triomphe.

"I'm definitely hungry enough for dinner but I wonder if we can be extravagant and order room service." Dot waved a paper menu at Jack. He took the bait and agreed this was a better choice. He suggested the Coq au Vin and garlic potatoes. "Should we get a bottle of wine to go with that?"

"Absolutely. And for dessert, we'll have the wedding cake Gillie packed for us."

Dot noted in her diary the following morning: *That was very nice indeed, but we will move to Villa Stella at 16 Rue Chalgrin this afternoon.*

Villa Stella was located two streets behind the Hôtel de Paris. Jack enlisted Victor's help to move their things down the cobblestone walkway that took them to the entrance. The face of the hotel was built with white limestone blocks and it was as impressive to look at as their previous accommodations. Small window balconies clung to each of the street-side rooms breaking up the monotony of the whiteness. The lobby interior was decorated with more wood and less marble than the Hôtel but its services far exceeded their three-star rating. Jack rewarded Victor's assistance with more French coins and they said their au revoirs.

Inside the new room, Dot and Jack unpacked their suitcases before planning the daily itineraries for the rest of their Paris stay.

"Let's walk down the Champs Élysées to the Arc de Triomphe. We can find a café along the way for lunch," Jack suggested.

Dot agreed and added, "I'd like to stop by the Red Cross Services office and sign up for a tour of the city while we're out."

After lunch, Dot and Jack walked down the sidewalk along the Champs Élysées, looking at the creative displays in the windows of the boutique shops. By afternoon, they were hungry again so they found a warm patisserie serving fresh buttery croissants and dark, rich coffee. Fortified, they continued their walk which took them along the River Seine. They passed other sweethearts having romantic rendezvous. The difference was that Dot and Jack both wore the uniform of the United States of

America. This distinction earned them a smile and a hat-tip from passersby. No one presumed to breach their privacy with a conversation but Dot felt that they were welcomed visitors. Before returning to Villa Stella, Dot booked their Paris tour for the following evening.

"Make sure to see the Eiffel Tower at night," the worker advised her. She cut her eyes at Jack. She smiled at him as if she suspected they were newlyweds. "The lights are stunning. It would be a shame to miss their beauty."

Dot and Jack agreed that that would be ideal.

"If you don't have dinner plans for tonight, you mustn't miss the May Flower Club for supper. Good food, good music, and dancing 'til dawn."

The idea appealed to Mr. and Mrs. Light. They returned to the Villa to freshen up. At the club, Dot and Jack ordered the savory chicken and rice dish accompanied with the Chateau Vin Blanc. Before they finished their meal, they both were tapping their toes to the lively music played by the Glenn Miller type orchestra.

"Are you happy, Dorothy?" Jack had ushered Dot back to their table after an heroic attempt at swing dancing.

"Happier than I've ever been," she answered before a flash of pain flickered in her eyes. Jack moved closer to take Dot's hand in his own.

"It's nothing," Dot continued. "It's just that, while we're here, the world seems calm and normal but I know what we both have to go back to."

"Put that out of your mind for now. Life will be waiting for us when we get back. However, this…," he indicated the club, but also the concept of the Paris experience in general, "*this* is for us. No matter what else happens in our futures, we'll know that we made the absolute most of our time here. So block out the world, the war, all of that, and just be here with me tonight."

"Goodness. When you put it that way, how can I do otherwise?" She squeezed his hand and blinked away tears.

As the evening unfolded, the band slowed its tempo and began to play romantic ballads, an invitation to sweethearts to dance in each others' arms. Dot and Jack took the floor again, and when the band played 'Star Dust', Dot melted into a romantic puddle.

After breakfast on Thursday, Dot and Jack retraced their route past the Arc de Triomphe and continued on to the Place de la Concorde. It took them longer than the twenty minutes the doorman had estimated because they lingered over the various sights along the route. They had no strict schedule to stick to until meeting the tour at 3 p.m. Dot's picnic in the Jardin de Tuileries would have to wait until the thermometer rose above freezing. Nevertheless, they were bundled up enough to wander through the gardens a little before retracing their steps to the Red Cross Center.

The tour bus door was open. Dot and Jack climbed aboard and found two seats together on the right hand side of the aisle, giving them a clear sight of the attractions. Jack guided Dot to the window seat for the better vantage point. Cold air seeped through the window pane so Dot leaned against Jack's chest to feel his warmth. The bus had no heat, but by the time the bus was filled, the body heat from the occupants made the interior comfortable.

The first stop was Notre Dame Cathedral. It sits on the Île de la Cité, a small island situated in the middle of the River Seine. Original construction of the splendid Gothic building was started in 1163, the tour guide told them, and it took almost a hundred years to complete, although construction of some type continued for another three hundred years. Approaching the cathedral from the front, a visitor would normally see the huge 13th century stained glass 'Rose Window' located above the massive sculpted doors positioned between two magnificent stone towers.

"As you can see, the Rose Window is not in its rightful place," the guide told the tourists still sitting in their seats. "It was taken down before the Germans marched in. No one wanted to risk further damage to it so removal to an unknown location was deemed necessary. It will be returned, but I'm not sure when."

The bus swerved awkwardly and the tour guide grabbed the pole to steady himself. "Stay in your seats for a moment or two longer. We'll drive around the rear of the cathedral. From there you can view the iconic flying buttresses."

As the bus maneuvered into a U-turn at the rear of the cathedral, the guide explained the necessity of the exterior wall reinforcements.

"Looks like a Granddaddy Longlegs Spider trying to gain footing on the island," Dot commented.

Jack laughed. "If he stays too long in one place," he added, "those gargoyles up there are going to have him for dinner."

The bus drove back to the front entrance and the riders disembarked to go inside. Dot and Jack were awed by the beautiful, peaceful atmosphere within the cathedral's hallowed walls. At the altar, they lit a candle for John Holmes. Then they lit another for those who had given their lives to the war. Dot allowed the tears to flow. "Please let this war be over soon," she prayed.

The tour allowed time for coffee and pastries at a café across the street and gave them time to reflect on the wonder of Notre Dame. Back on the bus, the guide described the next cathedral they would visit. "This one is called the Sacré-Cœur Basilica. It's a much newer construction than Notre Dame. Sacré-Cœur's construction began in 1875 and was completed in 1914. There," he pointed out the front window of the bus, "you can see it rise high atop Montmartre." He explained the significance of Montmartre and that it is the highest geographical point in Paris.

"When we arrive there," he explained, "we'll be able to look across the entire city, to see its famous landmarks. Earlier in the century, because of cheap rents in this, the 18th arrondissement, many well-known 'starving' artists lived here and worked here. Renoir, Picasso, Van Gogh, Henri Matisse, among others."

The sun was setting by the time the group prepared to leave Montmartre. The tourists climbed back into the bus for the final destination of the tour. Dot looked out her window, watching lights flicker on throughout the city landscape. Approaching the Eiffel Tower, Jack took her hand and whispered, "Look, Dorothy. Look at that magnificent sight. I'll never forget this day, will you?"

Dot had no answer for this silly question. Of course she would never forget this day, or any moment of her honeymoon. She took out a handkerchief to secretly dab her eyes. This sentimentality was going to have to stop before she returned to work.

The bus returned its riders to their starting point. Dot and Jack walked slowly back to Villa Stella. They ordered dinner in the dining room, with the busy electric activity surrounding them. After their meal, they weren't ready to end the day, so they sat together on a velvet settee in the hotel lounge sipping cocktails and people-watching until late into the night.

Only one item populated Friday's itinerary—a visit to the Louvre. After breakfast, Jack ordered a taxi to take them the five kilometers to the museum. During the drive, Dot read from an

English-language brochure provided by the desk attendant at the Villa.

The museum is housed in a Palace built by Philip II. It was completed in 1202 and the 782,910 square-foot complex was used as a fortress. By the fourteenth century, the palace had become the primary Paris residence of the Kings of France.

The Louvre was designated a museum in 1793. Its objective is to conserve, preserve, and present great works of art to the people of the world. In August 1939, in an effort to protect collections of the Louvre Museum, works were taken to undisclosed locations for safe-keeping. Various paintings deemed less important than those of the Masters were safeguarded in the basement during the occupation. Paris is now liberated and has begun replacing its inventory. Please have patience as we restore our exhibits.

The museum was huge. Although the exhibits were pared down, a great deal of artwork was on display for Dot and Jack to discover. During their explorations, they saw paintings by the lesser masters and collections of ancient Egyptian and Greek sculptures. Displays of tapestries and jewels had a grandeur that took their breath away. They took time to see all that was available to them.

"I'm more tired than if we had walked the length of the Champs Élysées," Dot said after hours of standing and looking at the exhibits.

"I couldn't agree with you more. Let's go to the café we were at yesterday near Notre Dame. We can have a bite to eat and plan the rest of our day."

They ordered omelets when the server promised the eggs were fresh.

"I still have shopping I'd like to do before we leave," Dot said. "Things I need, but also gifts to take back to my pals."

"We can go to any of the Paris boutiques your heart desires, but let's go to the Army PX, too. I've heard it has a large inventory."

"I want to do that, but why don't we go back to the Villa for now, and have a rest? We can ask the Concierge for a restaurant recommendation, then have an early night."

"That's a plan," Jack agreed. "We'll hit the shops refreshed tomorrow."

"I'm sad it's our last full day," Dot admitted, "but we'll have fun shopping."

A serene stillness greeted the early morning. Dot tiptoed to the window and opened the curtains slightly. A dusting of snow had carpeted Paris overnight turning the city into a wintery wonderland. At the enchanting sight, Dot broke the silence with a hushed, *awwww...*

Jack blinked awake and asked the source of her amusement.

"Snow," she said. "Paris looks like a wedding cake with white frosting. How appropriate." She smiled. "Paris makes me poetic. Now I see why artists and writers are drawn here."

After breakfast, Dot and Jack bundled up and walked the three blocks to the Army PX. It was true that the Exchange had a larger variety of supplies than they had seen elsewhere.

"Army personnel would be fools to pass up this cornucopia of goods," Dot observed.

Wool blankets, bedroom slippers, warm gloves, woolen socks, robes, jackets, blouses, perfume, face powder, and much more were stocked on the shelves. Dot and Jack selected items they would need back in the 'real world' and they found gifts to take back for their friends as well.

On the walk back to Villa Stella, Dot stopped in a dress shop to look around. She was dazzled by the latest fashions. *And* the prices. It was a sign that the world was ready to move beyond the privations of war.

After their day of shopping, Dot and Jack returned to their room at the Villa. It was still early evening, but they ordered room service for dinner. They would drive back to Mirecourt with Dutko the following morning but they would enjoy one last cozy evening together.

Like good soldiers, Dot and Jack were awake, dressed, packed, and breakfasted by sun up. They were waiting behind Villa Stella's glass entrance doors when Dutko arrived. At this time on a Sunday morning, there was little hustle and bustle on the streets and a hush had fallen across the snow-shrouded city. The moment was magical.

Jack helped Dutko load the Jeep. The three passengers had more parcels than when they arrived six days ago. The fit was tight, but nothing was left behind on the curb.

The ride back to Mirecourt was as cold as the one to Paris, but Dot wrapped herself in her new woolen blanket. She snuggled into the corner of the back seat, sharing it with a stack of packages. She was warmer than she had expected to be.

Dutko drove at breakneck speed making conversation difficult since the speaker had to shout to be heard over the noisy current of air rushing past them. Jack watched the landscape, taking in the details of their passage. Behind him, after two hours on the road, Dot had nodded off into blissful sleep.

As they entered the outskirts of Troyes, a farm truck skidded on an icy curve in the road. It hit the Jeep and sent it into a spin. The violent impact threw Dot into the floorboard, stopped by the back of Jack's seat. Jack had braced himself and escaped meeting head-on with the windshield. Dutko, however, was catapulted out of the vehicle and landed in a ditch overgrown with thick brambles. Dot and Jack were frantic. They looked around for him, ready to come to his assistance.

"Dutko!" Dot called.

Dutko jumped to his feet and shouted *Whoa!* A reaction he might have had after a Carnival ride. Jack sputtered in relief, but Dot was frightened from the experience. Dutko checked the Jeep and found no substantial damage. The driver of the farm truck checked on the Americans and apologized in broken English. Jack shook his hand and accepted the apology.

In Troyes, Dot, Jack, and Dutko found a small café where they warmed themselves. They drank hot cocoa and ate freshly baked bread with generous hunks of farmhouse cheese. The food and warmth mended frayed nerves enough to set off again.

Road conditions didn't improve along their route to Mirecourt but knowing now how quickly a misjudgment on the ice could turn into something treacherous, Dutko drove with extra care, slowing his speed considerably. At last, they arrived in Mirecourt. It was midnight, but they were alive.

Dutko dropped Jack and Dot at their apartment and drove himself to the base. He found a vacant cot in the barracks and went straight to bed. Dot and Jack were tired but not willing to have even a brief nap. Dot would be back on duty the following morning and Jack would need to leave before dawn. They didn't waste their last few hours together sleeping.

Sixteen

Diary Entry ~ January 22, 1945
Poor Jack has gone back to his unit and I'm in a daze.

Dot was back on duty where harsh reality clashed with the magic of Paris. It left her dazed. But dazed or not, it was time to return to the real world. She would try to keep her mind on work matters but there was no guarantee that she could pull it off.

Miss Spalding walked into the ward behind Dot. Dot contrived to look alert.

"I bet it's difficult to get back into a routine, Chinnis." Miss Spalding made the casual comment as if she were reading Dot's mind. "I suppose I should address you by your new married name, although I have to admit, it seems odd to do that."

"I'll answer to both. Or either. The new name still feels odd to me too."

"Good to know I'm not alone in that," Miss Spalding's congenial nature was a comfort to her nurses. "At any rate, you won't find your first day back to work horribly busy. We have more vacant beds in the wards than when you left for your honeymoon. We're having a lull in the fighting just now which means no backlog for admitting casualties." The Chief Nurse paused briefly to look at the schedule pinned to the bulletin board. Dot shuffled through patient folders to prioritize her rounds. Miss Spalding returned her attention to Dot. "We look forward to hearing about Paris."

At the morning break, the other nurses on duty with Dot inundated her with questions.

"What did you see?"

"What did you eat?"

"Tell us about the hotel."

Dot gladly relived the sights and sounds of Paris. She gave them accounts of the tours, the food, and their luxury accommodations."

"We'll have to live through you," Elizabeth smiled at Dot. "Until we find a way to get to Paris ourselves. For myself, I can't wait to try a plate of escargots."

"Speak for yourself," Cora jumped in. "No snails for me! But I wouldn't say no to 'vin et fromage' if offered by a handsome monsieur."

Dot agreed that an R&R trip to Paris was perfect for Cora.

———

Within a day, Dot had settled back into a routine. The one event that stood out of the ordinary was the bugler signaling a Call to Quarters.

"Why are we being ordered to return to barracks?" Jane's question was for no one in particular. She hated having surprises sprung on her, but she was not alone in wanting a reasonable explanation.

Nobody knew the answer but Charlotte offered, "You know the Army has its way and we're here to obey. Although I would like to know what's going on as well."

"Possible air raid? Outbreak of the bubonic plague?" Cora joked.

"I hope it doesn't last long," Jane said. "I've got other things to do besides sit in my room."

"We've got cocoa and pimento cheese sandwiches in our room," Dot offered. "Come and join us."

"I've got a bottle of wine. I'll bring that," Elizabeth offered.

"And I have popping corn," Charlotte added.

The nurses made the impromptu gathering fun as they whiled away the time. After a couple of hours, they were allowed to return to their scheduled activities. No explanation given for the CQ.

When Jane continued to complain, Cora called her on it. "We're in this together, sunshine. Let's just make the best of it."

Jane conceded. "I know. I'm just tired and ready to be home. I hope and pray the war will end soon."

"Fair enough," Cora agreed. "That's a shared prayer. But don't hold your breath or you'll turn purple."

"Maybe that will be enough to get me on the next ship home."

"Oh-no-you-don't!" Charlotte said with fake-horror. "Nobody leaves here 'til the job is done."

———

On Dot's next day off, she went into Mirecourt with Gillie, Elizabeth, and Cora. Dot wanted to buy a sauce pan and some cocoa to have at the apartment. Cora bought freshly baked croissants from the Pain de Sucre patisserie. "We'll take these with us to the 'honeymoon suite'," she said, "and have a little party."

At the apartment, Dot heated water in her new sauce pan and made steaming cups of cocoa for them all.

"If only these walls could talk," Cora looked around the room as she stirred her hot chocolate.

Elizabeth took a bite of her pastry and said, "This is a cozy little nest. When you and Jack aren't using it you should rent it out to the rest of us! We'll have a get-away and you'll become a wealthy woman." Dot approved the notion.

When the women got back to base that evening, Dot wrote to Jack and told him about her home-making and entertaining. She posted the letter the next day and asked Gus, the postmaster, the safest way to ship her crystal pieces to the states, in one piece.

"How in the world did you find crystal?" he asked.

"Jack bought some pieces from the famous Compagnie des Cristalleries manufacturing plant when he was in Saint-Louis-lès-Bitche," she told him.

"Is Jack your beau?" he asked her.

Dot held up her left hand, showing him her diamond engagement ring and gold wedding band. "More than that," she smiled.

"Wartime romance?"

Gus was getting a little too familiar, Dot thought, but she explained. "We knew each other back home. It's a stroke of luck he's stationed here now."

"...and," the postmaster continued, "it's lucky he survived as a Son of the Bitche as well. You two have a lucky charm following you around."

"It seems so. Now about the crystal?"

The stemmed sherry and water glasses were cut crystal of red and blue and green hues and had come from a manufacturing company in France with roots dating back to 1586. The pieces were visually stunning and of such good quality that Dot wanted to insure that the set would be protected on its transatlantic journey.

Gus gave her detailed instructions on constructing a wooden crate and how to place the straw around the items.

"Follow my instructions and I guarantee they'll make it home in one piece."

Dot was confident that Hank and Fouché could build the contraption. She would make them dinner at the apartment for their efforts.

<hr/>

In February, the sun sets early in northern France. In the dimming light, loneliness and despair are magnified. Dot was on night duty again and to fend off the contagion of the gloom, Dot popped corn for the men on her ward. It took great effort to shed the cloak of battle fatigue, so tokens of defiance against the weariness were worthwhile, and popcorn made a tiny dent.

So did mail. Dot received her first letter addressed to Lt. Dorothy LIGHT. It was a mundane piece of correspondence from the Army, but seeing her married name in black and white made her see her new status as 'official'. Her spirits were further improved when Jack arrived for a visit late one afternoon. It was the first time they had seen each other since returning from Paris. They ate supper together in the dining hall and caught up on news.

"We set up headquarters in Montbronn," Jack told Dot. "The 398th is defending a new line."

The location meant nothing to Dot and it showed in her face.

"We're still near Bitche, but we're twenty miles closer to Mirecourt."

"Every mile of distance between us is agonizing," Dot admitted. "So now I have twenty fewer miles to agonize over. That's good for me. But the new HQ location, what does it mean for the war?"

"We're just one piece of the whole puzzle," Jack explained. "Well, the European puzzle, that is. Overall, things are looking good here in Europe. The Allies are finally breaking out of the German offensive in the Battle of the Bulge. The Germans threw an awful lot of weight into that fight but it weakened them as a result. That weakness means they don't have as much muscle to power up an advantage over us. And the area we're clearing now will allow us to advance into Germany. We're building strength and reserves in our manpower and firepower, and we're preparing for the drive toward Berlin. We're doing it, Dorothy. It's what we trained for and it's working. We'll crush the Germans. They started this back in '39, and here it is, five and a half years later. But we're about to win this thing once and for all."

"I want to believe you. I *do* believe you, but I'm terrified to get my hopes up, then have them dashed if we have a long road ahead of us, yet." Dot's hands had been laying flat on the table. She balled them into fists as she tried to control the frustration she felt from the endless slaughter she'd seen in this war.

"You must be so tired." Jack laid his hands over Dot's. It made her feel safe. They sat silently for a while. "Hope," he said after a while. "It's good to have hope. Hope of victory is real. That's enough for now."

"And prayers that we all survive until the end," Dot sighed

"The tide is turning in our favor. This war will end. If you're afraid your 'hopes' will be dashed because of temporary setbacks, then have *faith*. Have faith that the outcome works out, and the good guys win. Our boys *are* the best. You nurses *are* the best. That counts. We're dug in. Reinforcements are on the way. The Germans are weary and they will give up soon. We have the advantage. They can't keep going."

Dot believed Jack's assessment. As the intelligence officer, he would know. She took in a deep breath and let it out. "Good enough for me. Let's go to the apartment. I'll make hot cocoa for us. Oh, and just today I got our wedding and honeymoon photographs back. We can look at them together."

Jack had brought with him a portable oil-burning stove to warm their home. Dot made the cocoa and together in their warm little nest, they scrutinized the snapshots before calling it a night. They slept until mid morning the next day.

"This is terrific." Jack was stretched out on the bed with a feather pillow under his head. Rays of sunshine peeked in through the window. "This sun is heavenly," he told Dot, "but I'm not feeling the warmth."

"I'll light the oil stove and make coffee."

"You don't need to wait on me. I'm just being lazy."

"It's funny," Dot said, "But I feel like a kid playing house."

After coffee in bed, Dot and Jack made breakfast and sat together at the little kitchen table savoring the moment. They knew the bliss would end when Jack left to return to his unit after lunch, but in war, all you have is the moment.

Back on base Dot and Jack said their goodbyes. Dot hoped to fend off the blues by diving into her new book. Daphne du Maurier, again, diverted Dot from the constant worries she had for Jack. The relentless freezing weather made Dot want to pull the covers over her head. Gillie joined her after her shift was over.

"Hey, Chigger. I see you're doing what I had planned to do this evening. I just want to feel warm again. I'm never warm unless I'm snuggled beneath forty woolen blankets."

"Let's skip going out to the dining hall tonight and snack on peanut butter and crackers for dinner." Dot was willing to make a full-fledged 'plea' for Gillie's compliance but Gillie completely agreed with the plan. A knock on the door interrupted their conversation.

"I've got news," Elizabeth announced. "Colonel Blanchfield is making an official visit to our hospital tomorrow. She's going to the large European hospitals, making a formal announcement of some sort to us nurses."

"I wonder what she's going to tell us," Gillie said.

"I had hoped one of you two knew what was going on." Elizabeth looked from Dot to Gillie hoping for enlightenment.

"I don't know," Dot said, "But I'm curious why this icon of the Army Nurse Corps is making the rounds. I know I'm going to attend the event to find out."

By eight o'clock the next evening, the auditorium was filled to capacity. Their own Miss Spalding stepped to the center of the platform facing her nurses and asked for their attention. She made the introduction and turned the podium over to Colonel Florence Blanchfield.

Hello to you all, Blanchfield greeted her audience as they applauded her. Blanchfield was instrumental in recruiting and staffing the Army with nurses before and during the war. Her name was known to the women serving in the ANC, making her the icon Dot had referred to. Blanchfield was a giant to many, although she stood barely an inch over five feet tall. The podium would have obscured her view if she stood behind it as intended. Instead, she placed herself to its side and addressed the group without notes.

291

Good afternoon. I'm Colonel Florence Blanchfield and I'm especially happy to be here with you tonight.

I sat where you are sitting, figuratively speaking, back in 1918. I was located a hundred miles north of Paris at Hargicourt during the Great War, the war to end all wars... or so 'they' said.

She shook her head resignedly, and continued.

I helped the soldiers who came our way, to the best of my ability, as you do here. I nursed them. I let them know that their contributions and their sacrifices had undeniably been worth all they were giving. If necessary, I held their hands while the angel of death beckoned them to cross over. You've done the same thing since your deployment. Yes, you've been trained in the medical arts, but you have needed no training in the art of caring. You come by that part naturally.

Blanchfield paused. She looked directly into the faces of the nurses in the audience before continuing.

In my capacity as Superintendent of the Army Nurse Corps, it's my job to assume responsibility for your well-being at this historic moment. The job you're doing here is essential to victory. I have attempted to make sure you have whatever is necessary for you to do your job, but where I have failed, you have filled in with resourcefulness and ingenuity, as I knew you would.

Many of you have been here in Europe long enough to know the exhaustion, the weariness, and yes, the disillusionment of a war-torn world. However, you show up for duty and muster the energy you need to do your job. In recognition that this state of affairs cannot go on indefinitely, the Army Nurse Corps will soon institute a rotation plan

292

to return many of you back to the U.S. The plan is based on the point system and the rules, in theory, are simple. Those who have been here longest will go home soonest. You will earn one point for every month you've spent overseas, and additional points for various medals awarded to you from serving in battlefield conditions. Seventy-one points gets you home.

Dot's thoughts went to Maddy. She hoped Maddy's extreme sacrifices, and the sacrifices by all the frontline nurses, would see them home soon. She turned her attention back to Colonel Blanchfield.

*Are we at the end of the war? Isn't it time for us all to go home? These questions are on your mind, I know. I will say this - the war **will** end. We **will** defeat Hitler, hopefully before another winter arrives. When that day comes, others who are not yet battle-weary will transfer in to take your place as part of the post-war Transition Forces. We can then get you home as soon as humanly possible.*

Knowing your service and hard work here will soon end should serve to improve morale. Use that to help you get over this last hump before returning to civilian life. Until then, keep up the good work—you make a difference.

The nurses appreciated the pep talk, and they were pleased that they could earn points to get themselves home. Eventually.

A Tea was given in Colonel Blanchfield's honor the next afternoon where the nurses thanked her in person for coming to visit them.

Dot measured time by when she had last received a letter from Jack. Two weeks had passed since she'd had word from him. When the next letter arrived, he had bragged that he was at the Front, celebrating his one hundred days in combat.

Men are alone in thinking that is a thing to celebrate, Dot thought. Then she realized it was a wonderful thing to commemorate after all. It was late February and the normal ice-cold temperatures had warmed slightly, promising the arrival of spring. Dot believed *that* was worthy of celebration too.

Dot's letters from home showed no indication that friends and family had received word of her marriage to Jack. "They're not getting my letters," Dot told Gillie. "What must they be thinking?"

She found out what they were thinking the next day when a cablegram arrived from her sister Margie asking for news. Dot responded in kind to ease her worry. By March, Dot received letters of congratulations. One of them was from Jack's mother, Lillian Light. Mrs. Light had been widowed in 1942. Jack's father had served in the United States Army as a First Sergeant. He saw action from 1895 to 1902 in the Spanish American War in Cuba and in the subsequent Philippine Insurrection. He had also fought in the Boxer Rebellion in China. With that history in the family, Mrs. Light had personal insight into how war affected families. She sent her kind words to Dot recognizing her contributions to the war and warmly welcomed her new daughter-in-law into the family. Dot wrote back, accepting her invitation to call her 'Ma', and told her that she appreciated her understanding.

On March 8, Dot received official notice of her promotion to First Lieutenant. Fouché made a special dinner for her and her

294

friends to celebrate the occasion. Also with the arrival of March came the ability to walk outside wearing nothing heavier than a sweater. Birds tweeted a tune of hope during the longer daylight hours given to them. Although Dot felt a speck of hopefulness for herself as well, she was always worried for Jack. She knew he and his unit were moving heaven and earth to clear a path into Germany but Dot took every opportunity to listen to the stories told by the men on her ward. She hoped to pick up information about the state of affairs in Jack's area.

"We were told to pound the enemy until they surrendered. We did. And they did...," one Private told Dot.

"We're making a path to Herr Hitler's door step. We'll be ringing his doorbell soon...," another one boasted. Others made similar comments.

"We took those bastards by surprise. They didn't put up much of a fight."

"It wasn't enemy fire that got me. It was those damned mines in the fields. Rotten cowards!"

Dot absorbed the information at different levels. She was pleased for the success these men were responsible for. They helped turn the tide of war in favor of the Allies. But seeing the damage the battlefield had on these kind souls broke her heart. When she first deployed to North Africa, Dot had assumed that the men who survived their injuries were the lucky ones. Now, she wasn't so sure. Survival meant pain. It meant a lifetime of adapting to a prosthetic leg, or learning to shave left-handed. It meant nightmares, or worse, for the remainder of their lives. Dot came to the war believing deep in her heart that a life was always worth saving. Now she caught herself questioning this notion, although she knew it was not hers to question. It was not up to her to make that judgment—but the notion did cross her mind. Ultimately, all Dot could be sure of was that she was there to help. In this war, she would ease physical pain and smooth away some fears.

———————

Mid-March brought more warm days. Dot's attention was on mending mutilated limbs while Jack's attention was trained purely on the battlefront with no time to write letters to her. She accepted this as inevitable, and other than the loss of sleep, Dot was healthy, fit, and strong. Gillie, on the other hand, was suffering from fever, headaches, and vomiting.

"Those are malaria symptoms," Dot observed. "You need to see a doctor and start drinking fluids." Dot's diagnosis proved correct.

"How can I have malaria?" Gillie asked the doctor. "I haven't seen a mosquito since we moved to the frozen tundra."

"This is not new," he explained. "The malaria parasite has lain dormant in your liver. It's re-surfacing now because your immune system has been compromised. You're tired, probably somewhat malnourished. Have you had a cold or the flu lately?"

"Yes, we've been passing a head cold around."

"That'll do it. Rest, fluids, lots of food. That will get you back on your feet. You were right to come see me. I can admit you to a ward…"

"No," Dot butted in. "No need for that. I'll take on the job of private nurse for her. She'll get well faster in her own bed."

Next day, Dot brought lunch to the barracks for her and Gillie to eat together. She had stopped by mail call to pick up letters for them both. The letter from Jack was vague, but with no evidence to the contrary, Dot assumed he was safe. That evening, news of the Seventh Army crossing the Rhine reached the hospital base. Dot had joined the supper crowd at the dining

296

hall when she saw Crazy Ellis motion to her to join him at his table.

"Looks like Jack and his men have crossed an enormous hurdle in Germany," he said to Dot as she sat down.

"Looks like it." Dot frowned.

"This is good news, Lieutenant. Why the long face?"

"How can I be happy and terrified at the same time?"

"Because you're in a war zone. We're scared witless in one breath and exhilarated to be alive in the next." Ellis took a moment then asked, "Have you heard from him?"

"Yes, just today. But I know that whatever he wrote five minutes ago is old news, which is more or less like no news at all. What he wrote then is totally irrelevant now. I think of him in past tense. Like, *at least Jack was okay last week*. But I don't know how he's doing today. You know, right now." Worry lines claimed squatter's rights on Dot's forehead.

"You can't think of it like that."

"How else can I think of it? I know I'm not alone. I know I'm no different than every mother, brother, sister, wife, friend."

"Well, you *are* different because you know firsthand what war does to humans. And *that* frightens the pants off of you. Pardon my language. But that means you have to zoom out and look at things from a big-picture point of view as well as from your own personal point of view."

"Tell me just how I am to do that." Dot good naturedly invited Ellis to explain further.

"Okay, here's the big picture, logically speaking. Our boys're heading to Berlin to deal with Herr Hitler. Removing Hitler is good for the whole world. You are part of the whole world. So you've got to see it as good news too. When the war is over, we can all get back to living our own lives. That brings us to the little picture. You're in love. All you can think about is your sweetheart. It's tough for us humans to get outside our own little cocoon at times, but staying in it will drive a person crazy, and we don't want no crazy First-Lieutenant-Nurses, Chinnis..., er, I mean, Light. There's room for only one Crazy Ellis. If you go looney-bins on us we'll have to ship you home on a Section 8. Then you'll be *four thousand* miles away from Captain Light. See? Big picture, little picture. You with me?"

Dot smiled. She squeezed Ellis' hand and said, "I'm with you. But I might need a tune-up to this pep talk again tomorrow."

———

Another Easter, another Sunrise Service around a flag pole. The first had been at Camp Kilmer. The second in Italy with Vesuvius exploding in the background. This one in France arrived on April Fool's Day.

Dot and Charlotte were still standing near the flag pole when Miss Spalding told them that they, and Jane and Anne, had been tapped to go to the Nurses' Chateau in Dijon.

"Is this an April Fool's joke?" Charlotte asked.

Miss Spalding laughed. "It's no joke. You leave on Tuesday for five days. I've got another group going to the Nancy Hostel the same time as you. When you get back, I'll send out more nurses. I want to take advantage of our slow-down. I want to make sure you're rested up for the potential onslaught of casualties as U.S. forces move through Germany. We don't know what horrors the Germans have planned to protect their homeland, but we *will* be ready and rested so we can do our best. Dijon is a pretty little town, you'll enjoy your time there."

Dot and Charlotte thanked Miss Spalding and started to walk away. Miss Spalding called them back. "Oh, I meant to tell you.

298

The nurses' meeting has been moved up to tomorrow night so you won't miss anything. See you there."

Dot and Charlotte searched for Jane and Anne at the Easter breakfast Fouché provided to the church-goers. They wanted to tell them the good news. At the dining hall, the prevalent mood was generally positive. Days of sunshine contributed to this good mood, as did favorable news from the battlefront. Jane and Anne were in a similar frame of mind, welcoming the news of their R&R.

On Monday, Dot and the others picked up their leave orders and were packed for the trip before going to the nurses' meeting that night. Colonel Cady was there and he announced that Miss Spalding had received the Bronze Star. The award was well deserved as she had distinguished herself through selfless service to her nurses and the men they cared for. Her nurses were proud of her.

Tuesday morning, Dot, Charlotte, Jane, and Anne left for Dijon sardined into a Jeep. The two hour trip took them five hours. Storms ravaged the area the night before and it meant several downed trees clogged the roads. Continued steady rain made the trip miserable.

"It's just rain," Dot kidded them. "We drove to Paris in *freezing* rain and *atrocious* wind."

"Oh c'mon. Do you expect us to work up a lot of sympathy for the conditions you had to deal with, Dottie?" Charlotte was shouting over the deafening sound of the open Jeep. "You were going to *Paris* for heaven sakes. On-your-honeymoon! While the rest of us were stuck in Drab City, slogging through mud up to our ankles."

"It wasn't mud! We were skating on ice," Jane added.

"Right," Charlotte agreed. She shouted so she could be heard. "But you get my point. It's awfully hard to work up a lot of sympathy for the hardships you endured while *going on a honeymoon in Paris*. After all, you had a *husband* to snuggle with, to keep you warm."

"He sat in the front with Dutko," Dot shouted back. "I sat in the back, like a block of ice." This brought a howl from the other women. They patted Dot on the shoulder in mock sympathy.

When they arrived at the Chateau, the nurses were rewarded for having suffered. The Red Cross attendant introduced herself as Joan and welcomed the group with a brief introduction to the creature comforts available to them.

"We have twenty-seven rooms here and can accommodate forty nurses. We have a cook and two French maids. Since you're the only ones here for now, there will be plenty of individual attention to go around. Allow yourselves to be pampered. We can organize some sightseeing trips for you, or you can enjoy the peaceful countryside, as you try to forget the war." Indeed, the Nurses' Chateau sat on a lovely spot overlooking greening fields.

"Dijon is a town of a hundred thousand people and only a brief walk from here," Joan told them. "It'll probably be a little warmer here than up your way. And, we probably have more shops than you have in Mirecourt as well." She paused to see if there were any questions.

"We'll have dinner prepared for you shortly. Afterwards, if you want, you can walk into town. It's not compulsory of course, but it's safe there, even at night."

When the women returned to the Chateau after a brief tour of Dijon, Joan offered them hot chocolate to take to bed. "We also offer breakfast in bed, if you'd like to take advantage of that treat," she said.

"Has anyone ever said no to that?" Charlotte asked.

"Not yet," Joan admitted.

300

"Then we will not be the first to break the tradition," Dot answered for them all.

Wednesday was a lazy day. Breakfast was followed by reading in the lounge until lunchtime. A spring shower had stopped and the sun peeked out. Dot, Charlotte, and Anne decided to explore a hiking trail through the old forest surrounding the estate. Jane stayed behind claiming that her allergies would flair up if she was outside too long.

On Thursday, the four women agreed to go into Dijon together. In the shops they found hand lotion, women's slacks, and bedroom shoes.

"Let's go to a hat shop," Charlotte suggested. "It'll be fun to try on hats."

"What if they only have berets?" Jane asked. She was being serious.

"I bet they'll have more variety than that," Anne said. "Let's find out what's in vogue."

They tried on hats for an hour and envisioned each other as civilians.

"I wonder what the women are wearing at home," Dot said to no one in particular.

Charlotte answered, "I saw a photo of Rosie the Riveter the other day. The current fashion at home is a red bandana tied around your head." They all giggled.

In the afternoon they joined a tour to the historic town of Beaune, the wine capital of Burgundy. During the forty minute drive, the bus driver pointed out vineyards of note and other points of interest. He told them that Louis Chevrolet, a co-founder of the Chevrolet Motor Company, was from Beaune.

"Small world," Charlotte said. "I can't wait to tell my Grandpa. He's a Chevy man. He'll love it that I visited Chevrolet's home town."

The tour included a visit to a winery, and ended with a magnificent dinner at the Hôtel-Dieu.

On Friday, Dot slept past breakfast. She had a cup of coffee and a pastry in the parlor mid-morning, and then went for a long walk on her own after that. She contemplated the state of the world and her place in it. Surrounded by the glorious beauty of the area, she said a prayer, asking for the war to end soon.

Saturday arrived too quick. The four nurses reluctantly gathered their things for their return to Mirecourt. For five days they had been pampered, leaving thoughts of war behind. The break was therapeutic and no one relished returning to reality.

The Jeep arrived for the nurses to drive them back to Mirecourt. As Charlotte jumped into the back seat, she confessed, "How spoiled I am! After a few days of this extravagance, I can never eat canned ham again. But don't tell Fouché, okay?"

"If we get hungry enough, we'll eat canned ham with a smile," Dot said as she climbed into the front seat. "But we'll have it with some of this!" She held up a bottle of Burgundy.

Dot walked into her ward the following day and noticed that everyone was wearing coats. A few of her patients had scarves wrapped around their necks as well. Although the days were getting warmer, evenings and early mornings still registered in the forty-degree range. Inside the hospital, a chill filled the air.

"What's going on?" she asked. "Let's get the heat going in here."

One of the orderlies explained that there *was* no heat. "No water either," he shrugged. He was exasperated. "I reported it. I guess the engineers are working on it, but I don't know."

"We'll make do." Dot was still cheerful from the rest break in Dijon and she had worked under worse conditions. She clocked several trips to the chow hall to cart water back for hospital use before end of shift.

By Wednesday, Dot's cheerfulness had eroded. She hadn't heard anything from Jack *and* she was still dealing with the lack of water and heat at the hospital. To let off steam she went to the officer's dining hall in search of a pal to have coffee with. As she cut across the lawn, Ken Jones drove up with Jack sitting beside him. Jack jumped out before the Jeep came to a complete stop. Dot ran to him and they embraced.

Jones broke in. "Um…, I'll find Charlotte and we'll go grab a bite to eat. Meet up later?"

Jack shook Jones' hand in parting before saying to Dot. "We got a four-day pass at the last minute. Jones and I grabbed a Jeep and we didn't stop, not even to place a call to let you know we were coming. I know I should have given you advanced warning, but…"

"You're forgiven. But what in the world have you been up to? I was getting awfully scared since I hadn't heard a word from you…" Dot broke off. She was not going to let Jack see tears.

"Are you off duty? Let's get dinner. When we get to the apartment, we'll have a good long catch up."

They bought cold cuts, cheese and bread. Coffee and wine were already at the apartment. After they had eaten, Dot and Jack snuggled under a blanket on the sofa, and Jack gave Dot a brief account of the recent activities of the 398th.

"Once we crossed the Rhine, we had two more rivers to get over, the Neckar and the Kocher, which were tricky to cross. A battalion doesn't rush in and shoot'em up like a scene out of a wild west movie," Jack explained. "To protect the men and resources, the attack must be planned using information, facts, and intelligence. Where is the enemy positioned? How many men are involved? What fire power do they have? What are their vulnerabilities, strengths? When I know this, I can plan, and good plans increase the chances of achieving our objectives."

Jack's gaze had fallen on the darkened windows across the room. He thought about what else he wanted to share with Dot.

"As I said, rivers are easy to defend but difficult to cross *while* they're being defended. That's been our main focus for the last two weeks."

"I know you succeeded or you wouldn't be here." Dot was proud of Jack's work.

"The Germans were desperate to hold their ground. The place we needed to cross over had no bridges. They destroy everything before they retreat and we couldn't build a new bridge right off. It's too dangerous while the enemy holds high ground. Blake went in with his crew. They had to sneak across the river in row boats in the dead of night. On the other side, they removed the machine gun nests, and that made it possible for engineers to build the bridge. While we waited for the bridge to be built, we needed food and supplies, and the logistics of that had to be organized. When the bridge was completed, we moved the tanks and the trucks across, and we took the town. There was heavy resistance, but some of the Jerries hoofed it out of there. Others, we captured. It took us a while to get all that done. We had heavy casualties…"

Dot didn't press for more information. She understood that there must have been great effort and sacrifice for the mission to succeed. She kissed Jack's cheek to let him know he need not continue with the narrative.

Back on duty early the next morning, Dot dressed to leave the apartment while Jack slept soundly. She smiled, knowing that he would be safe for the time being. When she returned to the apartment after her shift was over, she and Jack agreed to join Charlotte and Jones for drinks at the Ravenel Bar. Afterwards they went back to the apartment where Dot made spaghetti for four.

When they had eaten their supper, the four friends played Rummy until Jack and Jones could no longer stifle their yawns. Dot rose to clear the plates, a cue for Charlotte and Jones to make their excuses and leave.

Jack was rested by morning. "I'll walk over to the hospital with you," he told Dot. "I'll get breakfast at the dining hall and see who's up and about there. I wonder if there's news from the front."

They stepped out onto the street hand-in-hand as their landlord, Monsieur Éduard, came out of his shop. He was sobbing. He hailed them to stop.

"Il est morte!" His words burst out. He extracted a giant handkerchief from his pocket and blew his nose with a great honk. "Votre Présidént, Mr. Roosevelt. Il est morte."

"Oh, no," Dot responded. The news kicked her in the gut. "How? Um… comment? Comment est il mort?" she asked him.

"Hémorrage," he said, placing his hand on his head. "Cérébrale hémorrage."

"Cerebral hemorrhage," Dot repeated. "A stroke. Oh God."

The butcher continued his public mourning. "How will we survive? How will this war now end?"

"Jack?" Dot turned to her husband. She silently pleaded with him to calm the distraught Frenchman.

"Of course we will survive." Jack had no doubt in his mind.

"He wants to know if we will pull up and go home now that Roosevelt is dead."

Jack turned to the man and put a hand on his shoulder. "Victory, my friend." He gestured to the three of them standing there, and then swept his hand as if to indicate all of France. "Victoire, mon ami. Triomphe. Nothing less than complete victory is acceptable and it's within our sights. Soon. Very soon."

Jack's words appeased the landlord for the moment. But there were millions more people across the world who felt the same devastation that Monsieur Éduard displayed in his tears for Roosevelt's death. Much hope had been placed on the American President, as well as the British Prime Minister, to stop the fascist conquests. A fear gripped the French population that Roosevelt's death would tip the balance back in favor of Hitler. Not one French citizen had forgotten that the Vichy Regime had thrown their lot in with the Nazis through appeasement. Now, the people of France wanted their country back. Nothing more. Nothing less. M. Éduard was consoled somewhat after Jack's reassurances.

———

When Dot checked in at the hospital, she saw that the tragic news of the president's death had made the rounds. Conversations were of nothing else. That afternoon, a Sergeant stood guard as the flag flew at half-mast at the base headquarters. All who were available gathered for a memorial service in honor of President Roosevelt. Later, Dot and Jack walked around town talking to everyone they passed. Dot wished she had handkerchiefs to spare for the countless tears shed for Mr. Roosevelt's passing. Jack returned to the front early Sunday morning. Dot needed another handkerchief for herself.

Back on duty that night, Dot admitted a dozen litter cases from midnight to early dawn. She organized the orderlies and together they scrambled to find beds, linens, and food for the men. None of them wanted to talk about what brought them to this moment.

News of the war came in other ways. Hank was on the radio with his contacts across Europe and in Great Britain. He relayed their messages back to the folks at the hospital. Dot wanted updates and found ways to cross paths with Hank at least once a day. He was baffled when she started calling him Tele-Hank.

"I don't quite get the new name, Chinnis," he told her. " What's that about? Let me in on the joke."

"Oh it's just that you're our third way of getting news."

"Elaborate."

"Okay. We get news from the telephone, the telegraph, and you... Tele-Hank."

"Oh, ha-ha. How long did it take you to think that one up?"

"I've been working on it for a little over a week. I'm tired, and not as quick on my feet as I used to be."

Hank gave her a hug. "I sure wish I had a sister. Will you be my adopted sister?"

"I assumed we *were* siblings separated at birth. Didn't our mother tell you?"

"Always the last to know..."

"Not from what I've noticed. You're very much in the loop. I look forward to having the latest news come from you, alone! So what else is going on?"

"Listen up to ol' Tele-Hank. The Allies have taken at least a million and a half prisoners because the soldiers in the German army can't wait to be guests of Uncle Sam. They sure don't want to surrender to Russia. Uncle Joe Stalin is not nearly as nice as we are."

At supper the next night, Dot looked for Hank. He was sitting at a table away from the others looking depressed. A huge turn-around from the day before.

"What's wrong, brother? You look like you've seen a ghost." Dot put a hand on Hank's arm.

"News is trickling in. The Nazis have been running some sort of prison camps. The camps are now being liberated by British and American forces. Do you know anything about these?"

"No. How would I know?"

"Has Jack mentioned them at all?"

"No. What are they?"

"It's horrible. Civilians. Starved and emaciated civilians. They were incarcerated for being Jews, or being political, or for being foreigners. They weren't fed. They have diseases…"

"Oh God. Why would Hitler allow such a thing?"

"He didn't *allow* it to happen, he *created* the camps. They were his idea. He used the prisoners as slave labor, or he had them killed if they were not useful. He didn't want to feed them if they couldn't work. He's a monster, the reason we're here."

They sat together for a while. Neither ate their supper. Then Hank said out of the blue, "Mussolini's dead."

"I heard. What happened?"

He was hunted down and executed by the Italians. They hung his body up in public for everyone to see."

"That's gruesome. I wonder if the Germans will do something like that to Hitler."

Hank scratched his chin in mock reflection before saying, "I kind of hope they do."

On the last Sunday of April Dot was at the end of her shift. Jack and Jones had arrived at the base and found her on the ward. Dot told Jones where to find Charlotte and he left. Jack handed Dot a big basket of azaleas.

"Beautiful," Dot said. "What's the occasion?"

"These are from Germany," he said. "We're in Stuttgart now."

"I've never had German flowers before. It's strange that something so beautiful can survive the destruction of war."

"I know. It's amazing."

"Is it far? Stuttgart?"

"Not too far. About three and a half hours from here. That's where my unit will settle, at least for the time being."

The two of them snuck away to their apartment. After an indoor picnic of cold cuts bought from M. Éduard, they slept throughout the night and most of the next day.

"How is it humanly possible to sleep for twenty hours straight?" Jack asked as he verified the actual date and time.

"I don't know, love. I guess stress builds up in the body and creates adrenal fatigue. Then we're together and we feel totally safe. We relax and the next thing we know, we have a whole day unaccounted for."

"I don't think I'll mention this to the boys."

"I don't think *I'll* mention it to the girls."

They dressed and left to go to the base. They met up with Jones and Charlotte. Together they went to see the film, 'Objective Burma' starring Errol Flynn. Eating sandwiches at the dining hall afterwards, they discussed the latest news on the bombing of Berlin.

Hank saw them and walked over to their table. "This just in," he said like a newscaster. "Hitler finally accepted that all was lost. He took his own life."

What?!? They asked in unison.

"I know!"

"It's over? The war is over?" Charlotte asked.

"May as well be…" Hank said.

Jack weighed in. "It's not official until documents are signed. Somebody else could step in to keep the war going. But I'd say, it's looking more and more like 'the end'."

"I'm not going to celebrate until we get official word," Dot said. "This is good news, but I'm afraid I'll jinx this if I celebrate now." They agreed it might be the best route to take for the moment.

———

Dot was up early the following morning. The two couples were driving to Bitche for the day and she was looking forward to the outing. When she pulled back the curtains to greet the day, a layer of snow and sleet greeted her.

"Really? Snow?!? It's the first day of May!" Dot glanced over at Jack who was still in bed. "Come look."

"I'll take your word for it. But I would suggest that *nothing* should surprise you at this point!"

"Well this cold front has sure surprised me. What about our plans for the day?"

As they discussed whether they should cancel, Jones and Charlotte knocked on the door. They were anxious for an adventure.

"We'll wear warm clothes," Charlotte said. "And I've got extra blankets to wrap around us in the Jeep. Let's do it."

Scenery along the drive to Bitche was amazing. The sun poked through the clouds several times and returned in full when they stopped to picnic near a huge Pill Box. Jack and Jones gave Dot and Charlotte a first-hand commentary about their fight there. They explained the purpose of the large concrete pyramids erupting out of the ground around them.

"We call them 'dragons teeth'," Jack explained. "They're obstacles, as you can see, that prevent tanks from advancing through the field. Ingenious really."

They took time to explore some of the sights in the region before returning to the hospital base. At supper, a rumor circulated that the war had ended. Someone announced that Berlin had surrendered.

Dot looked for Hank to get confirmation, but when she found him he said it was a rumor. Reluctantly, the base was required to return to reality.

Jack and Jones left early the next morning amid more news that was trickling down.

German forces have left Denmark and the Netherlands.
U-boats have been ordered to cease operations.

"Sure sounds like the end of war to me," Charlotte said.

"You heard what the fellows said," Dot replied. "So I'll not breathe a sigh of relief until surrender documents are signed."

<hr/>

Dot was on duty Monday, May 7. Hank tracked her down.

"The Germans have surrendered!" he assured her.

"No. I don't believe it."

"Believe it."

"Give me the details…"

"Hermann Göring, Hitler's second in command, was taken into custody by the Americans yesterday. General Eisenhower accepted the complete *unconditional* surrender of the German forces yesterday at SHAEF headquarters in Reims France. Well, this morning, at precisely 2:41."

"So, it's official," Dot pushed him.

"Um…," he stalled. "It's official, but we're still waiting for the official *announcement*."

"I'm still not celebrating," Dot said.

———

After an eternity, the official announcement of the war's end in Europe broke on May 8. Guns were fired into the air, and sirens blasted throughout Mirecourt to mark the event. Dot stood with her friends as they tried to absorb the enormity of the news. All they could do was just look at each other in bewilderment. It was hard to express what they were feeling. Miss Spalding walked up to them.

"Yes, it's good news," she agreed. "The *best* news. But I must apologize for being the party pooper here because there's still much to do. We'll continue to be here for a while, and we'll carry on with our work as usual."

Miss Spalding walked away. Their parade had been rained on. Cora broke the spell.

"I'll be back in two minutes," she said. "Don't go anywhere."

She ran to the barracks and back. She pulled a bottle of Bourbon out of a brown paper bag. "A toast," she said as she broke the seal on the bottle. "Well done, us!" She took a swig and passed the bottle.

"Well done, us!" they declared in unison.

Seventeen

Diary Entry ~ May 8, 1945
Where do we go to from here?

The war in Europe was officially over—May 8 was designated Victory in Europe Day. A formal retreat was called around the flag pole for three o'clock that afternoon and although it was a Tuesday, the day had a Sacred Sunday atmosphere about it. Individuals spoke publically to each other in reverent tones, and offered prayers of thanks in private. Miss Spalding pointed out that current patients continued to need care as the hospital continued to admit casualties.

The question, *where do we go to from here?* was a legitimate question. The war was technically over but a feeling of relief didn't come automatically to Dot or any of the other nurses as they contemplated how the peace agreement would affect them personally. Dot also wondered how the latest turn of events would affect Jack and his men.

For the moment, Dot's Army life held nothing more than the typical hurry-up-and-wait. She suspected it was true for every G.I. in Europe as well. It wasn't surprising, but it *was* irritating to have no clear idea what would happen next.

"Should we start packing?"

"They won't ship us home while we have patients to look after."

"What will happen to the points we've earned?"

"I bet we'll get home soon now."

"The process of getting home will take longer than you know." Miss Spalding had walked up to Dot's group who had more questions than answers. She was matter of fact in her explanation. "I wish there was a way to tell you definitively what the next steps are but that's not possible. I do know that we'll continue to admit casualties. Our soldiers can't automatically go home just because the Germans have surrendered. Plus, there are a million things that need to be addressed by an Occupying Force, which will be in place for years to come. The war with Japan goes on, so our troops here may be transferred to the Pacific Theater of Operations. Many of us may get transferred to the PTO too. Here in Europe, we have large areas devastated from the war. Civilians will need medical help, governments will need help building or repairing living spaces. We just don't know what's next."

Cora looked perplexed. "So, these folks started the war. They bombed and destroyed vast areas, then we bombed and destroyed their homes because of that, and now we're going to rebuild their cities for them?" Cora wasn't able to understand the logic.

"That's war," Miss Spalding said. "It's like the story of the Phoenix. A shiny new bird will now rise from the ashes."

Cora came back with, "As long as that shiny new bird doesn't try to take away everyone else's nest again, once they are rebuilt. After all, they caused the damned ashes in the first place."

"Let us pray that those in power are as smart as we are, that they have conjured a way to prevent a war like this from ever happening again." Miss Spalding looked skeptical to Cora.

Elizabeth weighed in. "I understand that we're still needed for a while longer. But do we have an idea how *much* longer we'll be here?"

"No. I'm sorry. We're entering a new phase, one that we've all been waiting for. It's the phase before the one where we get to go home."

"I have to admit that I hadn't imagined this particular part of the war," Elizabeth confessed.

"The one where the war is over but no one gets to go home?" Dot piped in.

"That's the one," Elizabeth agreed.

Before Miss Spalding left the group, she added. "I'll call a nurses' meeting to address these concerns. Tomorrow morning. I'll post the time before lights out tonight."

The nurses sat together at supper that night. Jane looked especially despondent. "I don't want to go to the Pacific." She said what everyone was thinking.

Anne agreed. "I'd rather stay here longer, even though we can earn extra points to get home quicker from there."

"We don't get a say," Dot looked down at her hands in her lap. She was contemplating how horribly far Pacific hospitals were from Jack.

A Mother's Day service was held five days after V-E Day. Dot sat quietly in the Chapel and searched for a way to calm her fears of the future. Would she be sent to the Pacific as the rumors indicated? If so, would she be up for the job? She had been away from home twenty-four months and she was drained. She had heard a variety of horror stories about women's experiences in the Pacific. Although she knew her own reality compared favorably to them, she questioned if her reserves went deep enough to draw on for a move to another hospital on the other side of the world. Dot didn't find the answers she was looking for at the service, but she knew that whatever came her way, she would do her best to endure the challenges.

Jack put a call through to Dot on Monday. His unit was still in Stuttgart, assigned to a security detail there. She didn't know what that entailed, but she knew Jack was less than four hours away. For that she was grateful.

Dot's birthday rolled around again, the third one since she'd been overseas. She didn't bother to mention it in her diary, instead she recorded that it was a slow day on her ward. She looked for things to occupy her time like tidying file folders, organizing surgical instruments, and popping corn for the men who were bedridden. Those who were ambulatory looked for ways to spend their time while waiting for news about where they would go next.

"This is exciting," Gillie told Dot. She had recovered from the malaria recurrence and was working half shifts until the doctor fully released her.

"What's exciting?" Dot replied. "Do tell. I'm all ears."

"I just got word that I'm going on leave. I'm going to Paris for a few days."

"That's great news, and just what you need. That'll be better for your full recovery than spinning your wheels here while we hunt for something to keep us busy. When do you go? Who else is going with you?"

"I leave tomorrow with a couple of gals I don't know very well."

Cora walked up. "You'll have a swell time!" she told Gillie. "I know your two traveling companions and they're stand-up gals. They won't get up to any hanky-panky. You'll be good for each other."

Gillie was happy to hear about the company she would be keeping, but she was frantic that she wouldn't be packed and ready to go before departure time.

"You'll be ready," Dot assured her. "You plan what you want to take with you. I'll iron anything you need…"

"…and I'll run to the PX for anything you don't have on hand," Cora volunteered.

Dot saw Gillie off on her Parisian adventure the next day before reporting for duty. She was assigned to the genito-urinary ward at the hospital, G.U. for short. The poor fellows assigned there had wounds to genital or urinary systems which required delicate care during their recovery. Dot's attention to detail and the knowledge she had accumulated through countless surgery assists made her the perfect nurse for the job. Also, since the job required her complete attention, she could concentrate on their care and not on her concern for Jack's safety. It was impossible to keep the other worry at bay—that she could be transferred to the Pacific Theater. But for the next several days, while Dot was on the G.U. ward, she had little time to distress over her next move.

Concerns about where the staff would wind up next were, however, at the forefront of everyone else's mind. Army Brass decided more inspections and more physical training were needed to manage the jitters setting in. By their logic, activity would keep the nurses too busy or too exhausted to complain.

"Worry is unproductive," Dot heard one of the Officers say to a Private. "Use that energy for something constructive." Dot supposed that, hypothetically, having a clean-as-a-whistle hospital floor was more useful than aimless pacing.

To prepare for the big inspection scheduled for the next day, Dot and the other nurses cleaned, neatened, and sanitized every ward in the hospital. They polished medical instruments and squared away their wards enough to pass the strictest of inspections. If they didn't pass, what was the worst that could happen to them? They had contemplated that conundrum before. If it was to be sent home, no one would squabble over the punishment.

At the end of her shift, Dot headed back to quarters to find someone to go to supper with. As she approached her building, she saw Jack sitting on the door stoop.

"Surprise," he said. With one word, Dot's worry and fatigue vanished.

"I do love surprises," she kissed him on his forehead. "Want to get some supper?"

"More than anything, but I also hoped you could put in for some leave. I've got seven days."

"I can't hope to get that much time off...," Dot broke off as she remembered the inspections and the busy work inflicted on them. "...but I'll ask. If it's a no, I can still see you when I'm not working. That's a win-win in my book."

Dot went on her own to petition Miss Spalding for leave. Jack went to the dining hall to have coffee while he waited for the verdict. Dot returned quicker than he anticipated and he assumed she had gotten an automatic 'no' from the chief nurse. Dot's expression gave nothing away until she got closer and she said, "I've got seven-days off!"

"Well what are we waiting for? Go pack your bags, Mrs. Light!"

Dot grabbed clothes and threw them into a bag. She had extra toiletries at the apartment. On the way, the couple bought groceries for a meal that Dot could make on their one-burner hotplate, a new skill she had acquired. They both fell asleep soon after they'd eaten and didn't wake up until noon the next day. Dot vowed to never admit as much to her mother.

318

Dot asked Jack, "What would you like to do today? It's bright and sunny. We should take advantage of the beautiful weather."

"I'd like to drive to Épinal, to the American cemetery there, pay our respects to John Holmes. We can make a day of it, walk around the town, have supper there."

"I'd like that, too," Dot said.

"I'll go over to the base and sign out a Jeep for us to use, then come back here for you. We can be there in under an hour by this map." Jack was looking at an area map he brought with him.

Dot prepared snacks and a thermos of coffee for their drive south. When Jack returned with the Jeep, she was ready to go.

"I want to stop at the florist to buy roses for John's gravesite," she told Jack.

A small florist shop sat on the road out of Mirecourt. The florist arranged a dozen of his finest red blooms in a vase for them.

The sunshine felt good on Dot's face. She deliberately breathed in the warmth of it, hoping to memorize the feeling of her husband by her side, a memory to be recalled whenever she and Jack were separated again. Jack was intent on following the directions to the Épinal Cemetery, located four miles outside the town of the same name. They were both content.

"Here it is," Jack said.

Dot opened her eyes after drifting into a pleasant half-sleep and looked around her. White stone crosses lined up across a green field in strict precision. Jack reached into his pocket and extracted a note with handwritten instructions. "This will get us to his grave," he said.

319

Dot and Jack walked through the field silently. They found John's resting place without difficulty. Dot set the vase of roses at the base of the marker reading:

Capt John R Holmes
398th Inf HQ 1st Bn 100 Div
January 1945

"I remember that day, Dorothy, the day he got killed. There was bitter fighting at the Maginot Line. I wasn't with him, but…," Jack took a moment to swallow his grief. "Anyway, it was a bad time. And I'm glad to be able to be with him here today."

Dot squeezed his hand. Her touch let him know she shared his sorrow. "I'm going over to the shade just there," she explained. "I want to be alone and say a prayer for John." She would do that, giving Jack time to bid his friend a final farewell.

They met back at the Jeep. As they nibbled on the bread and cheese Dot brought for the trip, she said to Jack, "I can see the wheels turning. You've got something up your sleeve."

"As a matter of fact, I do. What if we spend the night in Épinal so we can have a nice meal, with wine? We'll take our time driving back to Mirecourt tomorrow."

"I didn't pack anything."

"There will be stores. We'll buy what we need there."

"Let's do it!"

Dot and Jack returned to Mirecourt the following day and saw that a note had been tacked on the apartment door.

Maddy at 23rd General in Vittel. Let's visit.
- Eliz / Char

Dot was thrilled that Maddy was stationed nearby. She didn't need to petition Jack to get the Jeep again for them. He was game for the excursion, and began planning their route in his head. Over supper at the dining hall, Jack, Dot, Charlotte, and Elizabeth organized their trip to Vittel the next day.

They drove southwest out of Mirecourt. In thirty minutes the outline of a hospital similar to Ravenel appeared on the horizon. The 23rd General Hospital was set up to perform much the same function as the 21st and after the ceasefire of May 7, activity had slowed to a snail's pace there too. And like the 21st, many of the staff were preparing to be transferred to the Pacific. Dot hoped Maddy was not one of them.

The visitors checked in at the gate. They were told Maddy could be found at a little hut set up as a coffee shop which was located near headquarters. Dot spied Maddy first. She had put on a little weight and her hair looked fuller, shinier. Dot was pleased that Maddy's health had improved. The group hug was spontaneous and couldn't have been avoided by any force of nature.

"Sit down, sit down. I'll have coffee brought over." Maddy's social skills had not eroded over the years of wartime experience. She looked at Jack, "You're Dot's fellow. And you're a brave soul, traveling with these headstrong women."

"On the contrary. They've made me an honorary-one-of-them, although I do lack their medical skills."

"We had no choice," Elizabeth said. "He brings us French wine."

"In fact…," Jack dragged out the word *fact* as he presented a bottle of wine to Maddy.

"You are now an honorary member of the 23rd as well." Maddy graciously accepted her gift.

Fresh coffee was brought to the table, accompanied by a stack of homemade ginger snaps. "These are magical," Maddy told her friends. "Eat one and you're magically back home with Thanksgiving just around the corner."

Charlotte started the questions. "How did you get here at this hospital, and what's next for you?"

"After serving twenty-one months at the frontlines, the PTB sent me to a local clinic for a break, then they found a place for me here."

"PTB?" Dot asked.

"Powers That Be," Maddy said. "Activity at the 23rd slowed down as the war moved further east. They put me on detached service here precisely because it was slow. Victory in Europe arrived, and now we're being sorted for placement wherever we're most needed. I'll be here for a while, but I've been assured I won't be sent to the Pacific. Soon, I suppose, I'll be sent home." She looked at the others for clues as to whether they were slated to be moved to the PTO. Dot spoke first.

"We're not as sure of our future," she admitted. "We're earning points to get ourselves home but the rumor is that we're needed in the East."

"Yes," Elizabeth joined in. "We sit perpetually on pins and needles."

"Same with me," Jack added. "My outfit got to the fight late. We'll either be part of the closeout force, or we'll move over to the Pacific. Pins and needles, like Elizabeth said."

Maddy looked pained, as if her good luck were the cause of her friends' predicament.

"No, no, no." Charlotte shook her head from side to side when she saw Maddy's expression. "Don't worry about us! You've had the short straw for the entire time we were in this war. It's right for you to get to go home. We're fine."

"Absolutely fine," Dot agreed. "We've had shelter and food, and if we're transferred to the Pacific, we'll still be fine."

Maddy relaxed. The party of five spent the afternoon telling stories and sharing news. Maddy described a few of the experiences she had at the front.

"They were right to pluck me out of the group," she told them. "Jane and Anne could not have survived. They needed you three to keep them propped up. Cora needed you too, even though she would deny it. They were delicate, and as I hear you speaking of them, I can tell they've grown with your support. That's good. I compartmentalize my life. I always have. That's how I avoid dwelling on unpleasant matters. It's how I survived austere times at the front. It was a good call to pull me from the group. I did okay out there. Besides, looks like I'll beat you home."

Saying goodbye was painful. "We don't know when we'll see you again." Charlotte said. The others were concerned too.

"I'll let you know my plans when I hear something. Maybe I'll holiday at the Riviera before I go stateside. I'll send photos."

"Rub it in!" Dot kidded. They laughed. It was the best way to part.

On Jack's last two days of leave, he and Dot invited Charlotte and Jones to join them for an overnight trip to the medieval town of Strasbourg, France. It was a two-hour drive east of Mirecourt. Perched on the banks of the Rhine, Strasbourg had sweeping views of the river. Dot skimmed the Red Cross brochure and paraphrased the information.

"One notable resident of Strasbourg was Johannes Gutenberg. Born in 1400, died in 1468. Introduced movable type printing to Europe which started the Printing Revolution. The

Gutenberg Bible, his other claim to fame, was the first truly important book printed using metal type."

She continued. "Another notable resident was Louis Pasteur. Born 1822, died 1895. A biologist, microbiologist, and chemist who discovered the principles of vaccination and pasteurization which has been credited with saving many lives."

Dot had to shout over the noise of the open Jeep and stopped at this point. The others found it difficult to carry on a conversation so contented themselves with surveying the countryside. In the town, they found a park by the river and stopped to have a picnic lunch. They visited the gothic-styled Strasbourg Cathedral and lit candles. By suppertime, they were ravenous again. The manager of the hostel where they had book rooms for the night recommended the bistro around the corner. Walking to it, Dot looked up to the heavens.

"Isn't that interesting," she said. Only Jack could hear her.

"What's that?" Jack asked.

"A full moon."

"And, extra bright, too." He pulled Dot closer and wondered if it would be the last one they'd see together before they were both home.

In Mirecourt the next afternoon, Charlotte and Jones suggested a visit to the ice cream bar on base before splitting up. Jack and Jones would need to return to the front the following morning and no one wanted the day to end. They ordered two scoops each.

Days passed by but Dot didn't bother to look at the calendar. She had no prospective dates for going home and nothing to count down to. While on duty, there was only busy-work. Jack hadn't written in over two weeks, but since the fighting had officially stopped, she had relaxed her worry schedule considerably.

One afternoon, Miss Spalding came by Dot's ward to tell her that she (Dot), Anne, Elizabeth, and Cora would be going to Paris together.

"We've got little real work for you to do here. And since we can't send you home, why not see the sights? There's a Nurses' Rest House near the Sorbonne," Miss Spalding explained. "Chinnis, you know your way around Paris. See that you all have the time of your life, won't you?"

Dot was pretty sure that Cora would be the ring leader in that department, but she wasn't going to disagree with the chief nurse. Going to Paris trumped busy-work in the near-empty medical wards.

Dot went straight to quarters after work and selected the clothes she wanted to take on her trip. Gillie suggested a couple of shops she had visited when she was in Paris and thought her friends would like them too. Dot jotted them down.

Departure was Thursday night. One of the ambulance drivers drove the women to Nancy where they booked the overnight train to Paris. They tried but failed to get sleeping berths, so they spent the night dozing in upright positions for the five hour trip. They were reminded of their trek across North Africa in June two years before.

"It's not much different, is it?" Anne commented.

"Oh. Except this time we're going to *Paris!*" Cora reminded her. "That's enough of a difference to suit me."

The foursome arrived early Friday morning. An assistant at the American Nurses' Rest House who introduced herself as Beth, showed them to their rooms. "Breakfast is still available in the dining room if you want something to eat," she told them.

This was welcomed news because they were ravenous. They asked Beth for recommendations of activities for the day.

"I'd start with a spa day," she advised them. "We have an arrangement with Caron's House of Beauty, on the next block. They run specials for shampoos, perms, sets, facials, and manicures. We call it 'the works'. The salon advertises it as *tout les services*. You can drop in without an appointment and be assured accommodation within an hour."

The women looked at one another. With a friendly shrug, each indicated she would be interested in doing that.

"I'll give you brochures for other Paris attractions. While you wait to be seen, you can plan more outings for your time in Paris."

After receiving *tout les services*, none of the women were pleased with their perms and sets.

Cora struck a pose on the sidewalk outside the beauty shop. She observed her reflection in the window. "I just paid good money for an Elsa Lanchester *Bride of Frankenstein* look. I'm not going to get the 'vin et fromage' experience with a handsome Parisian monsieur that I dreamed of, am I?"

"I was a little surprised when they pulled out the electric curling machine," Dot said as she gazed, and winced, at the results of her own hairdo. "I had expected they would use the more gentle chemical solutions like the perms we have back home. Not that medieval torture contraption." She shivered in disgust.

Anne and Elizabeth were speechless.

"The electrodes might have affected my brain," Cora teased, ever the comic. "I'll never be right again."

"How would we know?" Elizabeth snorted at her own joke.

"Let's look around at the Paris women, see how we compare," Cora deflected.

326

They did that. Elizabeth was the first with her assessment. "Seems the Paris women have better sense than to have their hair done here."

"Oh well," Dot was resigned. "It won't last forever."

"Just like this war," Cora said. "They said it wouldn't last forever, but it certainly *feels* like it has."

Anne said, "We must make the best of the situation. And most importantly, we must conserve our energy for the shopping this afternoon."

"Hear, hear!" was the unanimous reply.

They found a café for lunch before visiting the boutiques in the neighborhood that Gillie had told Dot about. Dot was particularly interested in visiting Guerlain's Perfume House, the others wanted to see Paris couture. When their feet starting aching, the women agreed that supper and an early night would help them recover from the overnight train ride into Paris, and the trauma of the beauty parlor. They would start the next day with renewed energy.

During breakfast, the women made plans for the day. Anne pushed the idea of doing the *Tour de Shops* along the Champs Élysées. Elizabeth wanted to see some of the famous tourist spots. Dot was interested in taking a walk through the Tuileries Garden. It was surely more colorful than when she and Jack were there in January. Cora was game for anything, but she wanted to go night-clubbing later. She imagined the clubs would be hopping with activity on a Saturday night. Elizabeth agreed to go with Cora for the day and for the evening, too. Dot and Anne paired up to make a day at the Louvre.

"We'll do something tomorrow, all of us together?" Cora asked. There was complete agreement to the plan.

On Sunday, the four of them joined a tour to the Palace of Versailles located an hour outside of Paris. They had time to immerse themselves in the grandeur of a different era.

Returning to Paris, the women took afternoon tea at the famous Ritz Hotel. It was a luxury expense, one they would never regret. After that, they went to see Notre Dame Cathedral and then, to the Folies Bergere for cabaret music.

"What a day!" Cora slung one arm around Dot's neck and one around Anne's as they headed back to the Nurses' Rest House. Elizabeth had run ahead to open the door. They were quite pleased with themselves that they fit so much into one day.

"Anyone for a nightcap?" Cora asked. They unanimously agreed to a cocktail before turning in for the night.

Dot was awake before eight the next morning. She indulged herself with a nice long hot bath before packing her bags for their return to Mirecourt that night. The train wouldn't leave Paris until nine o'clock and the Rest House would hold their bags until then. They were apprehensive when their hostess Beth suggested they attend Maggy Rouff's Fashion Show since the salon recommendation wasn't one to write home about. But they took her advice, and loved it.

On the overnight train to Nancy, the women were able to book sleeping berths and were much more rested when they arrived the next morning than when they traveled to Paris.

Dot was back on duty the following day. Charlotte caught her afterwards as she was walking back to her room.

"I've just heard from Maddy. She's flying home tomorrow. Let's get a ride over to the 23rd and tell her goodbye."

Dot was free but wanted to see who else could go. Elizabeth had time off and eagerly agreed to accompany Dot and Charlotte.

They talked to one of the ambulance drivers, who were quickly becoming their personal chauffeurs, and off they went within the hour.

Dot, Charlotte, and Elizabeth found Maddy's room and knocked on the door.

"Come in," Maddy said. "I'm happy to see you, and glad you could come on such short notice. You can see that I'm frantically packing everything I own. The Army gives you either too long to prepare, or not long enough. Their timetable never suits me."

"Are you leaving out of Marseille?" Elizabeth asked. "I've heard that's where the ships dock that will take us home. Eventually."

"Ordinarily, that's where I would leave from. But get this. They're flying me home. I just have to get to Reims."

"That's wonderful," Dot squeezed Maddy's hand.

"Where's that?" Charlotte asked.

"I'm not sure," Maddy said. "But I'm told it's easier to get to than Paris."

"Speaking of Paris," Elizabeth said. "We'll tell you about our time in Paris while we help you pack—for home!"

"I need to let that sink in for a moment," Maddy smiled.

When every item had been stuffed into a bag or case, and when home addresses had been exchanged, it was time to say goodbye.

"You were always an inspiration to me. Your strength and your willingness to get the job done without complaining." Dot stopped to find a tissue.

"You inspired me as well." Maddy looked at the three nurses.

"If we did the same, it was because of your example." Elizabeth barely squeaked out the words between sobs.

"We'll see you back home. Write us and let us know what civilian life is like at the country club," Charlotte sniffed.

The send-off was tearful. How could it not be? But many of the tears were joyful ones. And those are the best kind.

At the nurses' meeting on the first day of summer, Miss Spalding looked miserable. "I've just been told that any of my staff who has earned fewer than 70 points will probably go to the Pacific directly from here."

Dot looked around the room. No one smiled. No one had the valid number of points to get them back to the States. And, no one listened to whatever else was said for the rest of the meeting.

Jack wrote in his next letter to Dot:

Dorothy,

A quick note ~ Looks like my outfit will be assigned to a group going to the Pacific. We will discuss this on my next visit. See you Soon, Jack

Dot didn't have the capacity to be more downhearted. She didn't want to be sent to the far ends of the earth. She wanted to wake up every morning with Jack by her side, in their own home. Was that selfish? There were millions of people who were more war weary than she was, and she knew it. But she didn't have the willpower to dig her way out of the despair she felt.

Only hours after his letter arrived, Jack surprised Dot with a 48-hour pass. Dot lost her composure and cried in front of him, breaking a promise she had made to herself. She didn't try to hide her care-worn frame of mind. Jack asked if she had done something different with her hair, and she cried again.

"Why don't we go on an overnight outing to Nancy?" Jack changed the subject and Dot was grateful for the diversion.

During the trip they discussed their future and ways to bolster their courage for whatever was next for them.

At dinner Jack excused himself briefly. He came back to the table with a bouquet of sweet peas for Dot. They were dainty and lovely. The gesture melted Dot's heart and she teared up again.

A walk through the residential area of town on the following day occupied their minds as they admired the architect of the old homes there. But nothing made either of them feel better about their prospects. Back in Mirecourt, they dressed up for supper at Club Ravenel. They wanted to make the evening special, knowing it would be their last night together for a while.

When Jack left to go back to Stuttgart, Dot had numbed herself to the potential plans for their immediate future. It was now two months since V-E Day but it was basically business as usual at the hospital. Major fighting had stopped but there were isolated incidents, and the local population continued to come in with various injuries and illnesses. Dot didn't mind. Anything to keep her busy and pass the time. But *not* knowing what was in store for her future was distressing.

Miss Spalding called another meeting and the nurses attended with trepidation. The announcement, however, was music to Dot's ears. Married nurses would not have to go to the Philippines or Southeast Asia. Her friends congratulated her graciously. She didn't know what to say to them. She found words to write to Jack, though. She knew he'd be as pleased as she was.

August arrived on a cold, dreary day. Back home, Dot would have been sipping sweet tea on a covered front porch, fanning herself. She was nostalgic for her South Carolina Ravenel. At this Ravenel, however, she was drinking a hot cup of coffee in the dining hall when Fouché saw her sitting quietly alone. He made a bee-line to her table.

"This just in, Chinnis."

"What's that?"

"War news. And it's wonderful."

"The war is over and we're all going home…," she said in a sing-song voice.

"All but the signing. We dropped a bomb, something called an *atomic bomb*, on Japan. They will surrender. It's over."

"Oh, gosh." Dot said. The notion that the war was actually at an end seemed unbelievable. She hugged Fouché's neck and kissed his cheek. As she left, she yelled over her shoulder, "You are the man of the hour!"

Dot found Charlotte and Gillie and told them what she knew. "Nobody's going to the Pacific, ladies! No-bod-ee!"

They told the next humans they saw and the whole base was informed of the new developments before lights out.

The Army wasted no time in ordering its personnel to turn in equipment belts, leggings, and other government-issued equipment.

"I will gladly return what belongs to the Army. I'm filing for a no-fault divorce! I just want 'out'," Cora announced.

Dot, on the other hand, was hesitant to let go of her government-issued gear.

"It's seen me through tough times," she admitted. "I need these things with me like a security blanket."

"We're not giving up everything," Cora tried to show concern but wasn't sure why this was a big deal. "Just stuff we will no longer need."

332

"Still…," Dot hesitated. "If no one else needs it, I'd like to keep it with me for a little longer."

The slow but sure transition back to civilian life had begun. Jack was able to visit a few days later and he had news of his own. "Since we did what we came here to do," he told Dot, "the 398th is preparing to sail to the States on September 10."

Dot reflected on these new developments. She realized that she was actually disappointed. Jack looked at her quizzically.

"What is it, love? You'll be shipping home too. This is great news."

"I'm not so sure I'll be leaving as quickly as that, but I'm happy for you. I'll miss you when you're gone."

"Let's not think about that now. Can you get away for a day? Pack a bag and come with me to Schorndorf, in Germany. I'm supposed to meet with Colonel Williams there."

Dot made the necessary arrangements and they were on their way. The meeting between Jack and the Colonel lasted hours. Whatever they talked about made Jack seem pensive in response to it. He didn't mention his future role in the war. Dot knew not to ask, but she sensed his time table had just changed.

On their way back to Mirecourt, Jack drove through Stuttgart to show Dot the area he called home for the time being. She looked around the town, quietly taking in the scene. Some of the large, commercial buildings were reduced to worthless rubble. Smoke stacks towered over the scattered remains of a brick factory. I-beams were tangled like spaghetti frozen in mid-toss. Apartments, identified by their contents, were blown off their foundations. Old women pawed through the debris, searching for something valuable enough to trade for food. In another area, a beautiful municipal park stood untouched. Jack pointed to an undamaged rooming house beyond the park where he and his men were living while stationed there.

333

"Now I can picture where you are," Dot said. "I like having an idea of what your world looks like. The good and the bad."

———————

Changes to the 21st during Dot's short time away were stark. Seven patients remained and the staff had been reduced. Dot was glad that no one from her group had left. She wouldn't have wanted to miss a goodbye party.

In late August, Miss Spalding announced in the nurses' meeting that the remaining staff would assemble and stage within two weeks in readiness for transport home.

"I'm taking bets on how accurate that information turns out to be," Cora said with a poker face as she, Dot, and Gillie walked back to quarters afterwards.

"I'll take the bet," Gillie said. "I bet five bucks the info is correct this time because there's nothing left for us to do here. But Cora, you should be a millionaire after all the bets you've wagered while we've been overseas."

Dot wouldn't bet, but she weighed in. "I'm feeling pessimistic. I'm afraid we'll be here for another Thanksgiving."

Dot, Cora, and Gillie were on duty at the hospital the next day. Dot was in better spirits and joined in the playfulness as the nurses joked around to pass the time. They imagined what goofy exercises they would require the nurses to be proficient in if they were in charge of PT.

"I'd have her lean over a rectangular object about thirty two inches off the floor for eight hours straight," Dot said.

"I'd have her walk the length and width of a room until she'd clocked forty miles," Gillie said.

Cora's contribution was to require a competition to see how many bedpans could be emptied and sanitized in one hour. "See, if you win the competition, you get to be the lead bedpan nurse on the floor."

"We get it," Gillie laughed. "But I'd poke along on purpose to let someone else win that."

"So would I," Dot admitted.

"True. No one would want to win that. I'll rethink the exercise and get back to you," Cora said.

———

Jack used his weekend pass to visit Dot. It was the last day of August, four months since V-E Day.

"Any word on your homeward-bound plans? You have just ten days left by my calendar." Dot was fishing. Jack still hadn't explained to Dot what his next mission would be.

"No official word. I have a feeling we're going to miss that deadline." The 398th would indeed be part of the closeout force in Germany but as it wasn't considered common knowledge, he didn't mention it.

"Are you upset to miss the deadline?"

"Not in the least. I'd rather stay here near you until we both can get home. I'm in no hurry."

With that information Dot relaxed. Dinner was fun that night at Club Ravenel, and their meals were more delicious than ever.

"Do you have plans for tomorrow?" Dot asked Jack. "Because I'd like to walk around Ravenel and Mirecourt and take photographs of the area, and of friends. It would be nice to have pictures of our time here."

Jack thought that was a wonderful idea, so the next day they walked through the area and visited friends wherever they found them. They chatted about post-war plans back home and Dot enjoyed hearing the ideas.

Jack had to leave after lunch on Sunday. Dot's heart broke.

"You know I'll be back ASAP."

"I know that in my *brain*," Dot said. "Now if I could get my *heart* to understand, that'd be great. I'll be fine, though. It's just the actual *au revoirs* that I hate so much."

"Fifteen girls with high points got orders to pack for home," Gillie told Dot.

"Who's on the list?"

"Elizabeth and Anne are the only ones from our group."

"That is good news!" Dot said.

"I know it is, but I'm having a hard time wishing them well. I'm turning green from envy."

"Our turn will come," Dot tried to be upbeat.

"Will it? I'm afraid the plan is to leave us here forever. Anyway, the scuttlebutt is that Elizabeth, Anne, and the others will join up with the 127th Hospital for their travels home."

"That's great news for them all. The 127th was originally being transferred to the Pacific Theater with the Transition Forces. I'm glad they can go home instead."

Three days into September and the rains had settled in. Everyone stayed inside until hunger forced them to venture out to the dining hall. At supper, Dot heard that nineteen more girls got orders to pack by the next day to leave with a convoy of other hospital personnel. She rushed back to her room to see if Gillie was there, and if she had heard the news. Dot opened the bedroom door and stopped in her tracks. Gillie was packing.

"Oh, Chigger," Gillie was sobbing. "They're sending me home without you. I don't know what to say."

Dot hugged her best friend and assured her that it would be okay in the end. "It's just a matter of days before I get tapped as well. Don't give it another thought. I'm just mad that you won't be here to help *me* pack when it's time!"

Dot and Gillie stayed up past midnight getting Gillie's gear packed.

"It was easier when we were packing Maddy's things," Gillie said.

"Well, she was flying and needed fewer things handy. Your travel situation is different. You'll need specific items for the trip to the port, and then you'll want other things handy while you're on the ship. You know the drill. The PTB didn't give you much lead time, did they?"

"Seriously, Chigger? You think they'll start being helpful now?"

"You've got a point. Okay, that's the last thing besides your toothbrush which you'll want handy first thing tomorrow morning."

"Will you see me off? We're leaving at 6 a.m."

There was no problem getting to the point of departure on time since Dot and Gillie never slept. They spent the night remembering and crying and talking about their time together overseas.

Another farewell, Dot whimpered silently. She wondered how her heart was able to bear any more goodbyes. She cried all day long. When an announcement went out that leaves and passes were cancelled for those left behind, she cried some more.

Three days after Gillie's departure, Elizabeth and fourteen other nurses were on transport trucks heading to Marseille. Dot couldn't bear seeing Elizabeth go. With her heart of gold, Elizabeth had embodied the best of them all. Elizabeth saw right through Dot's attempt at a brave send-off, and she loved her even more because Dot made such an effort.

The old group was dwindling, and there had been no mail for days. Dot was sinking into her own personal pit of gloom when Charlotte dropped by her room with orders in her hands.

"Are we heading home?" Dot asked with hope.

"No," Charlotte responded tersely. "We're going to the Nurses' Chateau in Dijon."

"What? Again? Are we going there for a 'rest'?" Dot was feeling slight resentment.

"Uh, we're not going to *rest*. We are going to be hostesses there while others are there to rest."

"You have got to be kidding me."

"Nope. It's in black-and-white right here," Charlotte gave Dot the orders.

"Oh well," Dot shook her head. "Since we're doing little more here than twiddling our thumbs, I can't conjure up a better place to do that than in Dijon. Is Cora going with us?"

"No, she's holding down the fort here."

"Oh. I may not want to hear what she has to say about that," Dot said.

"I did get to hear it. I had to wash my ears out with soap."

———

Dot and Charlotte arrived at the Chateau in time for lunch on a Saturday. Miss Louckes, the housekeeper, turned the house over to the nurses and left. Dot and Charlotte looked at each other, astonished to be left in charge with no idea what their job entailed, other than they couldn't leave it empty while wandering into town or going on any other excursions. They rattled around in the big place, but since there were no other occupants at the moment, they decided they would just please themselves.

338

Charlotte made a pot of coffee. Dot tried to call Jack, but had no luck getting through to him. When night fell, they had a bite of supper and retired early to their rooms. They both slept late into Sunday morning and continued their slow pace throughout the next day until Charlotte got a call through to Jones in the early evening. He told her that he and Jack would try to come for a visit in a few days. Dot and Charlotte felt better knowing they had a brief connection to the wider world because they were feeling quite isolated otherwise.

Monday was another lazy day. They built a fire in the evening to take the chill out of the living room. Dot wrapped herself in a blanket to drink her hot cocoa in toasty comfort.

"That's smart," Charlotte observed. "I'm going to do that too. What's that you're reading?"

"The rowdy adventures of a soldier who spent the war on the home front."

"Intriguing. Does it have a title?"

"*The Feather Merchant*. What are you reading?"

"*Mythology*, by Edith Hamilton. I'm fascinated by tales of the Greek gods. This is a fairly new book of their stories."

"We should be able to get a lot of reading done if the guest house remains guestless," Dot said. "I don't mind at all, do you?"

"No, but this rambling old place is a little bit creepy. Just us two. In case there's a…"

"Shut up!" Dot shouted before Charlotte could paint a gothic horror picture.

Charlotte giggled and went back to her book.

After an uneventful night, and after breakfast the next day, Dot had a wander around the grounds of the Chateau. She spied a bicycle propped against the garden wall. She hopped on it and tried to ride it across the lawn. It teetered and Dot fell, trapping her ankle under the spokes of the front wheel. Charlotte had been watching from the kitchen window and ran out to help.

"I might have broken my knee and ankle," Dot told Charlotte. Charlotte took a thorough look at the damage and assured her it was just a bruise.

"I'm going back to the fireside to drink my cocoa and read my book," Dot laughed at herself. "Fresh air and exercise are dangerous."

During the entire week, the Chateau was host to two guests for one night only. The Polish officer and his adjutant made few demands. They seemed happy with their short stay, and then went on their way. That afternoon a bomb squad detonated two unexploded shells in the area. Dot and Charlotte had been warned so they weren't startled, but one explosion broke the big plate glass window in the living room, so Dot arranged to have it replaced.

"What will we do for our second act?" Charlotte teased.

"I hope our second act will include a visit from our soldiers," Dot said as she crossed her fingers for luck. But Jack and Jones never showed up.

Dot called to relay a message to Jack. He called her back on Sunday morning.

"How are things?" he asked.

"Everything is fine here. Charlotte and I had hoped to see you and Jones while we're at the Chateau."

"We wanted to, but we got sent on a job. Listen, Jones wants you to tell Charlotte that he's being transferred to a Military Police battalion in Munich. We're not sure when, but this is a good job for him. He'll be responsible for the unit. But it's further away from Mirecourt. That's the bad part."

They talked a few more minutes before hanging up. Dot wasn't keen to pass the news along to Charlotte but she took it like a good sport.

"I'm going to marry that guy," Charlotte said matter-of-factly. "We'll get it worked out when we both get home. But I'll miss his mug until then."

After eleven days at the Chateau, Dot and Charlotte were directed to close up shop. Dot called HQ at Ravenel to request someone to pick them up. When they arrived back at the 21st, they found out that the hospital had merged with the 197th General Hospital. The 197th had been located in Saint-Quentin France near Normandy, and they were now moving to Mirecourt to be closer to whatever was needed by the Transition Forces there. Nurses from both hospitals introduced themselves and they attempted to create order from the confusion thrust upon them.

Jack visited in late September. The couple were at their apartment in Mirecourt for the night when Jack peered out the window where he spied a glorious harvest moon.

"Look Dorothy." He pulled her to his side and pointed up above the rooftops. "That big ol' moon is still as shiny as ever." Dot smiled, willing her tears to stay put. "Aren't we the fortunate ones?" he said. Jack's heart burst with love for his bride.

Dot smiled at Jack but silently asked herself if this would be their last time together before one of them was sent home.

On the following day, Jack prepared to return to Stuttgart. Dot walked with him to the Jeep. Jack kissed her longer than ever before. He held her tight with no plans to let her go. After a while, Dot broke away. In her heart, she knew this was a goodbye. She suspected Jack knew it too.

"Last one home's a rotten egg," she told Jack. She hoped her phony levity would mask how sad she was. Jack wasn't fooled but he loved her for trying.

Dot went to the dining hall for a cup of coffee and to see if anyone she knew was there. She didn't want to be in her lonely dormitory room. Fouché was there. He was always a calm presence for Dot, and she was glad to see him.

"What's the news of the day, friend?" she asked him.

"Rumor has it that those of us from the 21st who are still here will be moved out on October 10. At least that's what I've heard."

"That's only two weeks from now. I can hold out."

"Of course you can hold out! Holding out is the easy part. You've already done the hard part."

"Haven't we all? So how will it work? Do we board a ship home?" Dot didn't care how it worked. She just wanted to be home. She would saddle up a humpback whale and ride it across the Atlantic to get back to her beloved Ravenel, South Carolina.

"We'll probably stage in Marseille. They say we'll sail on the twentieth. But don't hold me to that."

Dot ran into Colonel Cady as she was going on duty the first day of October. He volunteered that she and the others would be home sometime in November, guaranteed. "Just get through this month, Lieutenant. You'll be home in time for Thanksgiving. It's something to look forward to."

Cady went on to tell her about the ceremony she and her group would attend the next day to receive their Meritorious Service Unit Plaques. "It's in recognition of your professional skills and tireless devotion to duty. Well deserved, too. I hate you didn't get to go home earlier, but I'm glad you're here to receive this citation in person. It's been an honor to serve with you."

"And with you, Colonel."

<hr />

After the ceremony, Miss Spalding asked to speak to Dot, Charlotte, and Cora.

"I wanted to inform you myself that I, and twenty nine other members of the 21st, have received orders to leave for Le Havre at midnight tonight."

"But not us," Cora cut to the chase.

"But not you, *yet.*" Miss Spalding knew this was a bitter pill.

"…and then there were three," Cora conceded.

Miss Spalding looked at each of them. "You're strong," she said. "You'll be okay, and you'll follow us soon."

"No one was stronger than Maddy, ma'am," Charlotte said quietly.

"Every one of you has made me proud. But I know you three will be okay until you get your marching orders. I won't say goodbye. I'll just say, see you back in the States."

Even with Spalding's encouraging words, Dot, Charlotte, and Cora were feeling blue at being left behind. They made the best of it, though, as Miss Spalding knew they would.

Dot called Jack by the relay method. Someone at HQ tracked him down through trial and error. She brought him up to date with the news as it stood.

"I'm ready to ship out, but I don't want to go so quick that I won't have a chance to see you one more time," she shouted into the handset.

Jack knew from the work he was doing, they would not see each other again. He considered telling her but decided not to.

343

On October 5, Dot asked the communications folks to track Jack down again.

"Jack," Dot yelled into the receiver. "We're heading out of here in five days."

"Say again." Jack couldn't make out Dot's words over the crackle of the portable handset he was using.

"We're leaving on Wednesday. October tenth. We'll leave here and go to the staging area in Marseille. I needed to let you know."

"That's wonderful news, Dorothy. That's wonderful. I've been told we'll sail home around the twentieth of November so we'll have Thanksgiving together, love. Together."

"Together, at home, for Thanksgiving," they promised.

As the date to leave Mirecourt inched closer, Dot was surprised that her psychological outlook was buoyed by the prospects of leaving France and going home, even though it meant a separation from Jack.

Fouché and Hank were handing their duties over to their equivalents in the 197th. They would join Dot, Charlotte, and Cora on their journey home. The packing ritual commenced on Monday in anticipation of leaving by Wednesday.

"Blast it!" Cora burst into Dot's room.

"I don't want to know." Dot said.

"We're not leaving Wednesday. We're leaving Friday instead. We have an updated departure date of October 12," Cora said. "The bet that was placed for when we would ship home? Well, everybody was wrong in the end."

"I didn't place a bet," Dot said. "If you remember, I was sure that whatever *we* estimated, the Army would find a way to prove us wrong. I suppose I'm technically the winner."

Cora smiled at Dot and agreed that she technically won but with no skin in the game the prize was zilch.

"How many more delays will we have to suffer before they finally send us home?" Cora asked.

On Wednesday afternoon, plans changed again. Fouché saw Dot and Cora having a late lunch in the dining hall. He motioned them over.

"Update, ladies. We're to have our bags packed by 5 p.m. tonight."

"You've got to be kidding me," Cora blurted out.

"We'll still leave on Friday," he said, "but our gear goes tonight."

On Friday morning, Dot tried to call Jack again to let him know this was her travel day. She was officially heading out of Mirecourt. But no luck. She would leave without one last goodbye to her Jack as she had feared.

As Dot, Charlotte, and Cora waited for transport to the train station, Jones skidded to a halt three feet away from them in his Jeep. He ran over to Charlotte first and hugged her fiercely. "Hold on to that thought," he told her. "I'll be right back with you." He turned to Dot and handed her a small parcel. "Open it," he said. She did. A full can of Brasso.

"What's this?" she asked.

"Jack says you're to take over polishing duties until he gets home to you. I don't really know what that means."

Dot couldn't speak around the lump in her throat but she dug into her pants pocket and pulled something out wrapped in a handkerchief. It was her lucky 1921 Morgan Silver Dollar.

"Do you remember this?" she asked Jones.

"Of course. I brought it to you at the train station the day you left Fort Jackson. From Jack. A good luck charm for you."

"Take it back to him for me, will you? It'll bring him good luck too. And tell him I'll have it made into a necklace when he brings it back to me in person."

Part Five

GOING HOME

Eighteen

Diary Entry ~ October 12, 1945
On the train. Left Mirecourt at 2:15. My! How crowded.

Dot boarded the train midday on Friday. She, Charlotte, and Cora found seats together, a stroke of good luck, since the number of travelers crowding into the cars seemed infinite. Men took shifts sitting in seats or leaning against the connecting doors to smoke cigarettes in the open space between the cars. After three and a half hours of travel, the train stopped at a messing center in Merrey France. Everyone exited the train to stretch their legs and eat a hot meal.

Because of the cramped conditions, sleep was fitful throughout the long night. Stopping for breakfast at another messing center on Saturday morning broke up the monotony of hours in limbo. By the second night on the train, passengers were exhausted and fell asleep wherever they were when they nodded off.

Sunday dawned, but the railway journey continued onward in fits and starts.

"Why are we stopping again?" Cora asked.

"Only God knows," Charlotte answered.

Dot said, "There must be trouble on the tracks. We don't seem to be near anything in particular, and since we're not allowed to get off, I suspect technical difficulties."

Cora laughed at the 'technical difficulties' line. "We've seen a few of those on this adventure haven't we?"

K-rations were passed around and everyone took something to eat—nothing else was available. When the train reached the outskirts of Marseille at three o'clock Sunday afternoon, passengers cheered as they departed the train.

A fleet of two and a half ton Army cargo trucks arrived at the train depot and transported personnel and gear to the staging area. Women were dropped at one end, men were taken to the other.

After the travel ordeal, Dot was pleased to have a cot with clean sheets assigned to her and access to a shower. She was weary and looked forward to a little food and the opportunity to sleep lying down. Cora and Charlotte also staked out personal space for themselves.

Going to breakfast on Monday morning, the three women paused at a bulletin board with a notice conspicuously placed for passersby to see.

INSTRUCTIONAL MEETING:
MESS TENT AT 1100 HOURS TODAY
ALL PERSONNEL WAITING FOR
TRANSPORT TO U.S.A. MUST ATTEND

"We'll be there," Cora said to the others. "Whatever they want us to do, we'll do it, as long as we're on that boat home."

A Sergeant conducted the meeting and explained the regulations to be followed by all service members waiting for transport to the U.S. Cora made notes.

350

"Since when did you care about rules?" Dot whispered to her while the Sergeant talked. She was truly interested.

"Since *not* following them will prevent me from going home!" Cora explained.

After the meeting, Charlotte looked troubled.

"Are you okay?" Dot asked. "You look pale."

"I'm not feeling very well," Charlotte said. "Something's come over me suddenly. In fact, I need to find the latrine, STAT." She took off running.

Dot and Cora caught up with her. As they walked her back to the barracks, an officer asked if he could be of assistance. Charlotte described her flu-like symptoms and he sent her directly to the 227th General Hospital where she was admitted as a patient. She was not happy.

"I won't miss my ride home because of the damned flu," Charlotte warned the nurse on duty. The nurse looked at some paperwork on her clipboard and assured Charlotte that a ship was not scheduled for her traveling group in the next day or two.

"Just relax. Enjoy being looked after," the nurse told her. "Let us get you feeling better. A troop ship is uncomfortable and crowded and you're going to want to feel as strong and well as possible."

Charlotte agreed with the nurse's reasoning and stopped advocating for a speedy discharge. If they were going to have a lengthy wait, why not spend it at the hospital, to be tended to hand-and-foot?

Dot and Cora were free to explore the area and to do as they pleased. They appreciated that they were at the Côte d'Azur, *and* since it was a surprisingly warm and sunny day, they rented bathing suits for sunbathing by the sea.

"I don't see any reason to mention this to Charlotte, do you?" Cora had ordered a chilled drink from the Red Cross hut and was savoring its fruity flavor.

"I'll let you know if I come up with a good reason, but don't hold your breath," Dot kidded.

More meetings, more instructions. Attendees learned that taking Champagne home as a souvenir was prohibited. Impromptu parties broke out. No Champagne was wasted.

Passengers were required to make a list of the items purchased while deployed in Europe and the price of them. Those lists were short. Most everyone who bought souvenirs had made previous arrangements to ship them home since there was no room in their bags for extra items.

One morning, Dot and Cora visited Charlotte at the hospital with gifts of flowers, croissants, and an Agatha Christie paperback. They could see she was feeling better but saw no reason to bring up their sunbathing.

"This is a guilt offering. I can see you've been in the sun," Charlotte called them out with a grin. "You don't have to shield me from the fun you're having because I'm having breakfast in bed every morning, so there!"

"Oh," Cora conceded. "That's true."

Five days had come and gone since the troop train arrived in Marseille. Idle hours were spent in search of anything to fill the time until a ship was available to sail them home. Every person waiting for transportation to the States would gladly have traded all that spare time for a four-foot square space to curl up in on any ship crossing the Atlantic. Instead, they attended movies and meetings. Dot and Cora met up with Hank and Fouché often. As a group, they checked in on Charlotte until their rowdiness caused the nurse to shoo them away.

Cora rushed back from an errand one cloudy afternoon to find Dot. "Rumor has it we'll sail on October 29th," she announced.

"That's ten days away," Dot calculated.

"It seems feasible." Cora was encouraged but not optimistic enough to take bets. The Army would do as it pleased, and eventually, they would be home as promised. It was futile to guess when that would be.

October weather in the South-of-France is fickle. And although Dot and Cora were blessed with sunny days, the hours ran together without distinction.

Finally, two weeks after arriving in Marseille, Dot and her group were ordered to pack *toute de suite*. They would board a ship the next day. Saturday, October 27. Bound for the United States. Two days sooner than was originally announced.

Since Charlotte's energy had returned as a result of her convalescence, she was able to board the *Hermitage* with Dot and Cora under her own steam. Hank and Fouché were a dozen people behind them and called their names.

"Meet you in the dining room. Eight tonight!" Fouché shouted.

"It's a date," the women called back to them.

<hr>

The over-crowded troop ship set sail at six o'clock that evening. Dot claimed a cot in one of the inner corridors. Charlotte and Cora followed her lead and moved their cots on either side of Dot's like bookends. They did not complain about the steerage accommodations. In the hierarchy of basic human needs, they had food, a place to lay their head, *and* they were going home. Who could complain?

At eight o'clock the three nurses found Hank and Fouché as arranged. They swapped information about where they were camping out on the ship so messages could be exchanged. Hank produced a flask filled with whiskey. Fouché requisitioned five tumblers. They drank a toast to themselves, and to the friendships forged during this incredible odyssey.

By Sunday afternoon, reasons to complain presented themselves. The *Hermitage* heaved upon the churning sea and Dot's stomach did the same.

"I don't want to belly-ache," she told the others who were propped up on their cots reading, "but I have a belly ache and I'm going to have to go topside for some fresh air or I will become a very annoying roommate."

Charlotte and Cora agreed to go with her.

"If we're going to be on deck, let's take our cameras," Charlotte suggested. "A farewell photo of Europe."

The change of scenery and fresh air was therapeutic. From the upper deck, in the cool refreshing breeze, they saw the Coast of Spain. They passed the Rock of Gibraltar—on the starboard side this time.

Dot was grateful that the war was over. A tear punctuated the thought. Dot opened the camera case she'd slung on her shoulder and snapped photos of the limestone cliff. She did the math in her head. With some rounding, she calculated seeing this same sight, but off the port side of the *Santa Rosa,* two and a half years before. She felt older than the number of birthdays celebrated overseas suggested, and was happy to say goodbye to Europe.

'Abandon Ship' drills were mandatory on this voyage as they were on the ship to North Africa. There was little chance they would be torpedoed during this cruise, but the ocean was rough and being prepared was a good idea.

Rough seas continued on Tuesday, as did more boat drills. Dot made it to the drill but stayed in her cot the rest of the afternoon. Her energy was sapped by the seasickness and remaining perfectly still until the sensations passed was helpful.

The next day was no better but Dot ventured out to the upper deck in the evening where she saw the lights of the Azores, a group of islands located a thousand miles west of Lisbon Portugal.

Thursday was the first day of November. The three women were hungry enough to eat lunch with Hank and Fouché.

"We're over halfway home now," Hank volunteered.

"It seems odd," Cora responded to the information. "I don't know why, but the time we spent overseas feels like a dream."

"An extremely *loooong* dream," Charlotte agreed, dragging out the word.

"A dream where, when we wake up, we'll be home again," Fouché added.

"Not true for everyone," Dot threw in.

"Yes," Fouché conceded. "So many lost lives. We won't forget them, but we're here, thank God. And I'm grateful."

Dot knew what he meant. Humans have the capacity to feel both gratitude and great sadness within their tiny fist-size hearts.

The promise of being home spurred Dot to endure choppy waters even though it made her feel like tossed salad. By that evening, she'd gotten her sea legs and felt better than before boarding the ship.

Sunday arrived as a warm, calm day. Sailors told her that they were now in the Gulf Stream. "That means we're getting near the end of the trip," one of them said. "When we hit cold weather again, you'll know we're close to American soil."

Monday was the cold day. Passengers cheered and danced in the corridors and on the decks.

———————

Mid-morning, on Tuesday the 6th of November, after ten days on the Atlantic, the *Hermitage* passed Lady Liberty.

"Hello, you," Dot said. "Remember me? I made it back." Dot could have sworn the 'Lady' nodded in recognition of her faithful patriot.

The ship docked at Pier 88 and the gangway was lowered. Dot, Charlotte, Cora, Hank, and Fouché left the ship together. They would be separated on the transport out to Camp Kilmer but planned to meet one last time there before heading home.

At Kilmer, the nurses were greeted with a warm welcome and shown to their barracks. After dumping their gear, everyone made a mad dash to the telephones. Dot called her mother in Ravenel.

"We've got a few administrative loose ends we need to take care of, Mama, and then we can be officially de-mobbed. We have to turn in the rest of our Army-issued equipment, then I'm sure there will be more 'waiting' for some reason or other. I'll call again the moment I know when I'll be home."

Mrs. Chinnis promised to pass the information on. Dot couldn't say a word. That damned lump in her throat was back again. But she was awfully happy to hear her mother's voice. It was one of many answered prayers.

"See you soon," they both squeaked out.

Dot hung up and joined the others as they returned the last of their gear. The bittersweet moment of not needing a mess kit or helmet at long last, competed with the longing to keep those reliable tools as treasured keepsakes.

The anticipation of seeing her family soon meant Dot didn't sleep Tuesday or Wednesday nights. On Thursday, she got word that she would leave that afternoon with the group going to Fort Bragg in North Carolina.

Dot rounded up Charlotte, Cora, Hank, and Fouché. They shared details of their homeward bound plans. They would see each other again, they were sure of it, and there was no need to get maudlin in their goodbyes. This was the story they told themselves. And it turned out to be true.

Dot selected her seat on the south-bound train at ten o'clock that night. She and the others who sat near her swapped stories of their experiences, where they'd been, and what they'd seen. The relief of going home made the nurses giddy.

"If our patients could see us now, they would never have trusted their lives to us." Laughter erupted among the nurses. They were being silly. Then, as if a switch had been thrown, they stopped for a moment of silence, remembering the torn and bloodied men they had cared for. They reflected on the bravery they had witnessed, and how the men liked to show off for them and give them gifts of candy bars.

One of Dot's traveling companions gazed out the window, a million miles away.

"Penny for your thoughts," Dot told her.

"I had a rough war," she confessed. "I was at a field hospital for my entire deployment."

"Oh." Dot said. "I see. A friend from my outfit was assigned to a field hospital too and I only know what she told me about her experiences, but it was harsh duty." Dot was sensitive to their different experiences.

"Do you think the women who stayed home were the lucky ones?" the nurse asked.

"Speaking for myself, no. Not at all. I was a nurse and my one desire was to use my skills to help out. I'm grateful I had that chance. I felt appreciated. I saved some lives. I know you did too."

"I saved some, but I lost too many. I can see every face." She turned to look out the window again, stony-faced. Tears, and the emotions they represented, would not surface for a while.

"I won't give you glib words of comfort, nor do I believe you want anything like that. They would only diminish what you've been through."

"I did my best," she said.

"Yes." Until this moment, Dot didn't believe her heart could break anymore than it had done since the start of the war. She leaned toward the woman and took her hand and squeezed it gently. "We made a difference."

"I'm not sure."

"I am. We served our country. We risked our lives to save other lives. The demands made of us, and what we were required to do to meet those challenges…, well, they changed us and shaped us. It shaped the survivors too. We don't know the far-reaching outcomes of what the men we helped will do with those lives, but it'll be good." Dot could see her words hit a note but the woman looked out the window again without responding. There is no adequate way to express some emotions.

The train rolled along throughout Thursday night. It arrived at Bragg mid-afternoon on Friday. It had been a fifteen hour trip—a price Dot willingly paid for going home.

Passengers stepped onto the platform at the station. They were instructed on the process for being released from active duty. Dot found a bank of telephones and placed calls until she reached her sister, Sadie.

"Big news!" Dot almost shouted. "I am to be out of the Army tomorrow. Five p.m."

"That is *good* news. We're all excited for you to be home."

"I'll catch a train to Ravenel tomorrow or the next day. I'll let you know when I've arrived."

"Oh no you won't," Sadie said playfully. "Tommy will drive us to Fort Bragg to pick you up. It's only four hours from here."

"Who can come with you?" Dot was afraid she was dreaming.

"Margie is coming, and Prentiss. Since he's been home from Pearl Harbor, he's talked of nothing else."

On Saturday, November 10, 1945 at five o'clock in the afternoon, Dot officially mustered out of the Army. After the Chinnis family swapped hugs, Dot wedged herself in the back seat of Sadie and Tommy's Buick. It felt like they were stuffed inside a sardine can, but Dot breathed in her freedom and finally grasped the reality that for her, the war was over.

I'm a civilian, she half-whispered to herself. *I'm home.*

Epilogue

Dot was indeed home in time for Thanksgiving Holiday as Colonel Cady had predicted. She split her time between the family farm in Ravenel, South Carolina and Margie's apartment in Charleston. Her first days as a civilian were filled reconnecting with family and friends. A great crowd gathered for the 1945 Chinnis Family Thanksgiving celebration that coincided with her mother's birthday, a tradition still observed to honor the memory of Mrs. Ernestine Chaplin Chinnis. I had the pleasure of attending Miss Ernie's most recent commemoration where the Chinnis family hospitality continues to this day.

Soon after her arrival home, Dot accepted a private duty nursing job at the home of Mr. Cox to provide end of life care for him. She remained on duty until his death.

Dot missed Jack terribly, but letters exchanged between Stuttgart Germany and Ravenel South Carolina connected them, as did gazing at the moon, now polished by Dot for Jack, and seen from two separate continents.

A train trip to Roanoke, Virginia took Dot to meet her mother-in-law, Lillian Light. Dot continued to call her 'Ma' as she was invited to do and they maintained a loving relationship throughout their lives. The conversations between Dot and Ma, recorded in Dot's diary, centered on Jack and his sweet nature.

A letter from Jack in early December 1945 estimated a homecoming in March the following year. Shortly after receiving that hopeful news, Dot and Jack celebrated their first wedding anniversary. Although they were apart, Jack arranged a special delivery of sixteen long-stemmed pink roses to Dot. Jack continued to send gifts to Dot as he had done earlier in the war before he deployed.

In late February 1946, Dot's brother Prentiss, who survived the bombing of Pearl Harbor and had met Dot at Fort Bragg on her mustering out day, married Sue Gregg. When Prentiss had sent the one-word 'SAFE' telegram to his mother, it was delivered over the telephone. Margie made arrangements with the Western Union office to send a keepsake paper-copy to her place of business. All processed mail was stamped with the company name, Hunley Drug Store. The telegram was found in the personal effects of Mrs. Chinnis at her death and has been preserved.

On March 10, 1946, Dot's sister, Margie, married Ray Brown. Margie and Ray had met before the war at a dance at the Citadel. Shortly after that, Ray deployed to England as Captain of an Army anti-aircraft unit and landed with his men on the coast of France on D-day plus four. The couple wrote each other throughout the war until he was home and they could marry. Ray remained active in the Army Reserve as a Colonel until his death in 2015.

Dot received word on March 22 that Jack would be leaving Europe on April Fools' Day. Her last diary entry was on March 26, 1946, a Tuesday. In it, she recorded: *Washed and ironed all day. No mail. Got my 2nd 100 bucks of mustering out pay* (approximately $1355 in current 2018 value). I assume there were no more entries because she was busy preparing for Jack's homecoming and there were no other events more worthy of a mention.

Dot and Jack made their home in Roanoke, Virginia. Dot worked part time at the local hospital on what she called 'floor duty' and Jack made his career as a sales manager for a trucking line. Together they raised two sons, John Randolph Light (named for the fallen John Holmes, who was to have been Jack's best man), and Richard Chinnis Light. When both sons were in college, Dot took a refresher course in nursing and returned to part-time work at the local hospital until her retirement. In addition to two sons Dot and Jack have two granddaughters, three grandsons, and three great grandchildren.

During a visit to Margie's home in late 2017, I met Dot and Jack's sons, John and Richard. They were proud of their parents' wartime contributions (Jack stayed active in the Army Reserves throughout the rest of his life). They confessed to knowing quite a bit about their father's experiences and were enthusiastic to learn more about their mother's story. Dot, who thought her contributions were 'just what anyone would do' never tooted her own horn. I'm pleased to toot it for her.

Throughout the rest of their lives, Dot and Jack enjoyed attending reunions of the 58th Station Hospital where Jack remained a lifetime, honorary member in good standing. At his death in 2001, Jack was 86 years old. He and Dot had been married for 56 years.

My last telephone conversation with Dot was at Christmas time in 2008. She told me that when her sister Margie's grandson graduated as a Medical Doctor from the Medical University of South Carolina [MUSC] a few years before, the date coincided with the 50th Anniversary of Dot's graduation from the same institution, then called Charleston Medical College. Dot was invited to attend the ceremony, and in a cap and gown, she was awarded the 50-Year Golden Medallion to a standing ovation.

On December 17, 2009, the world said a sad goodbye to Dot. She was five months shy of her 90th birthday.

Wedding of Dorothy Chinnis and Jack Light on January 15, 1945
Left to right: The Chaplain, Cornelius Hook, Chinnis, Light, Major
Spalding, and Colonel Cady

Bride and Groom in the Chapel of the 21st General Hospital

Mr and Mrs Light cutting their wedding cake

Jack and Dot Light c. 2000

Note: *Wedding photographs are courtesy of Dot Chinnis Light; photo of Jack and Dot Light is courtesy of John Light and Richard Light.*

Acknowledgements

Dot was the inspiration for this book. Our nation owes a huge debt of gratitude to her for her service to our country, and I'm personally grateful for the interest she showed in my research projects over the years. In addition to Dot, I must acknowledge other individuals for giving their time and assistance to me.

Dot's younger sister, Margie Chinnis Brown, graciously spent hours talking to me and filling in gaps about family life in Ravenel, South Carolina and sharing her own experiences from the homefront during the war. Margie read and commented on the final draft of the manuscript and I thank her for that.

Donna Chinnis, Dot's niece, read every draft of the book. She trusted me and the vision I had for telling her aunt's story. I am grateful for her love and support and for her suggestions which made the story better.

Joshua Blake, Donna's son and Dot's great nephew, is an Army combat veteran who supported and encouraged me to tell Dot's story. We had many conversations around the dining table about Army life, its traditions and the lingo specifically used by its members. He expressed to me the pride of serving our nation although, to do so, means enduring the loneliness of isolation while away from home and loved ones, and in spite of knowing the mortal risk involved. Joshua took time to read a rough draft of the manuscript while (also) moving back to Charlotte from Greensboro for a new job, *and* preparing for the birth of his first child, Jackson Charles Blake. Thank you.

Joshua's wife, Erin Stowe Blake, read and commented on the manuscript as well. She caught continuity glitches and guided me on keeping Majors and Captains straight, but more importantly, she encouraged me to dig a little deeper to understand Dot's feelings throughout her ordeal as a nurse, as a woman away from home, and away from her love. I hope I have done that.

Susan Wagoner worked with me again, as on other projects, even though she was well aware that I'm a consistently bad speller and have difficulty with compound words. If any editorial errors remain, they are mine alone.

My sister, Barbara Burris, was a great support. She asked for weekly progress reports and suggested the probable Italian language dialog that would be used by the boatman on Capri. I hope I got it correct.

One last huge thanks to my researcher, Lorraine Kensington, without whom, the historical context of Dot's story would have been bleak. Any inaccuracies herein are mine alone.

NOTES ON THE U.S. ARMY NURSE CORPS

More than 77,000 American women served in the United States military as nurses during World War II. Over two hundred died while in service, sixteen of those were killed by enemy action.

American nurses served in England, France, Germany, Holland, Belgium, Guam, The Philippines, Australia, North Africa, Italy, and at military bases and hospitals in the United States.

At the battlefront, nurses were part of the *"chain of evacuation"* established by the Army Medical Department. Nurses served under fire in field hospitals and evacuation hospitals, on hospital trains and hospital ships, and as flight nurses on medical transport planes. Their contributions reduced post-injury mortality rates among the military forces in every theater of the war. Because of their brave service, nurses were awarded the Distinguished Service Medal, the Silver Star, the Distinguished Flying Cross, the Soldier's Metal, the Bronze Star, the Air Medal, the Legion of Merit, the Army Commendation Metal, and the Purple Heart.

Additional Reading:

Bellafaire, Judith A. The Army Nurse Corps in World War II. U.S. Army Center of Military History. Web. 13 Dec. 2010.

Boston, Bernard, ed. History of the 398th Infantry Regiment in World War II. The Battery Press, 1947.

Burris, Marsha L. Paradox of Professionalism: American Nurses in World War II. The Spiral Press, 2007.

Farris, Joseph Co.M, 3rd Bn, 398th Inf Regiment, 100th Div, 7th Army. A Soldier's Sketchbook: From the Frontlines of World War II. National Geographic, 2011.

"The Army Nurse Corps." Women in the U.S. Army. U.S. Army. 11 Dec. 2010.

http://www.history.army.mil/books/wwii/72-14/72-14.HTM

https://www.americanmilitarynursesinwwii/home

http://www.army.mil/women/nurses.html

Marsha Burris brings an historian's eye to the subject of American Army nurses who served overseas during the Second World War. She is the author of *Paradox of Professionalism: American Nurses in World War II* and *Miracles All Around Me: The Unexpected Gifts of My Mother's Alzheimer's*. Marsha lives in her beloved hometown of Charlotte, North Carolina.